HANNAH and the ANGRY EYE of GOD

STEVEN JAY GRIFFEL

HANNAH and the ANGRY EYE of GOD

COVER ILLUSTRATION © by Sigalit Landau
Gone Dancing, 2024
Miniature flamenco dress coated in salt crystals
51 × 51 × 32 cm

COVER & INTERIOR LAYOUT DESIGN by Alexandru Oprescu

LIBRARY OF CONGRESS CATALOGING-IN-PUBLICATION DATA

Hannah and the Angry Eye of God
Authored by Steven Jay Griffel

ISBN: 9798988023494
LCCN: 2026936678

Dedicated to my special friend, Nataliya Z.,
who helped me imagine the character of Hannah.

PROLOGUE

Before we found the cure for cancer, before I was madly pursued by four men (a musician, a scientist, a thief, an autocrat), I had a craving for salt. I salted everything: my buttered rolls, my borscht, even my salads. Eventually, salt was my undoing—but it's not what you think.

—HANNAH BELAYA

CHAPTER 1

EUREKA!

In the very south of California there is an inland sea with no inflow or outflow. For ten thousand years a natural system of rain, evaporation and seepage kept its water level balanced. It is a very saline sea, situated in the middle of the accessible and picturesque Imperial Valley.

In the beginning (the modern beginning, the times directly relevant to this tale), Saltin's Founding Fathers looked upon this unpopulated area and saw opportunity. "Eureka!" they cried, salivating over the region's great charms and vitality.

Almost overnight Saltin City sprang up on the sea's south shore. As usual in such cases, Profit was the main motivating factor—that, and a passion for Almighty God.

Not surprisingly, Saltin developed on opposite sides of its central Commonwealth Avenue. In West Saltin, nicknamed Hedo, a dozen casinos were built, one glitzier than the next. In East Saltin, nicknamed Jeru, a dozen houses of worship were built, one more sanctified than the other. And while there were those in each camp who would not taint themselves by trafficking with their neighbor, there were just as many who maintained regular contact.

And so it was for many years: gamblers and redeemers, entertainers and evangelists, sportsmen and saviors—all venturing to Saltin.

The sick and enfeebled came too. For this needy clientele, West Saltin and East Saltin competed aggressively, each boasting that its own hot springs and waters, mud baths and salt vapors could cure and rejuvenate best.

Alas, Saltin's success was not everlasting. The mayor of West Saltin and the mayor of East Saltin collaborated on a series of great public works to ensure that the natural and delicate process that had long kept the Saltin Sea in perfect balance would continue in perpetuity. Channels were cut, rivers diverted and dams built in the shared belief that nothing on earth is so perfect that it can't be improved.

Shortly after the last ribbon-cutting ceremony, Saltin experienced the beginning of an epochal drought. Within two years the Saltin Sea lowered as if a giant plug had been pulled. Within five years most of the Saltin Sea had circled the drain, leaving behind a giant bed of dead fish and a dreadful stench. Businesses closed, houses shuttered and the once vibrant city of Saltin began to disintegrate.

The resultant economic depression was as indisputable as the large, searing sun in the cloudless sky, though the latter was interpreted variously. The citizens of West Saltin looked at the sun and blamed climate change for the loss of their sea and their subsequent woes. The citizens of East Saltin looked at the sun, saw the Angry Eye of God, and blamed the unrepentant sinners of West Saltin for their shared forsaken state.

Faced with an apparently bleak outlook, most of Saltin's citizens departed. After several decades, Saltin City was a ruined and salt-encrusted shell, its once glorious sea reduced to a mostly desiccated basin.

But this sea change was not without its positive effects. The massive and rapid water abstraction had left behind a huge salt deposit. The composition, character and concentration of this salt was unlike any other in the world. Over the years, Saltin's few remaining citizens began discovering the salt's special health benefits. Further, there remained along the southwest and southeast shores of the former sea several small lagoons that still served as therapeutic pools, providing relaxation to some and salvation to others.

ALTERNATIVE SCIENCE

According to Hannah, not all Truths are observable and testable: the most important Truths exist in realms beyond the reach of the human senses.

Not surprisingly, she'd been drawn to alternative science. Though an experienced clinician and researcher, she'd also been a member of the Cosmoenergy Federation for years, reading its alternative literature, listening to its podcasts and watching its live Skypes. One day she took the leap: she applied for a job at the Federation and was accepted. As soon as she could, she left her job as a clinician in Lviv, Ukraine, and traveled north to Moscow.

After long stretches on rails and buses, she finally arrived. With great excitement she strode through Moscow's Ostankinsky District, past the Peoples' Friendship Fountain, past the Russian Exhibition Center, past the wondrous Polytechnic Museum and then, finally, there it was: the world headquarters of the Cosmoenergy Federation. Soon she would be working side by side with the great Yevgeny Yeshevsky! What an opportunity!

She would not be disappointed. Already softened by her charming correspondence, Yeshevsky greeted her warmly and gave her a comfortable workspace. He was delighted to see that her physical charms matched her engaging personality. She was perhaps a tad shorter than he had imagined and perhaps a few plumpish pounds heavier, but her blonde hair, even at forty, was girlishly natural, and her smile and stride unselfconsciously assured. He was very happy he had hired her. In the days that followed, he showed himself to be an exemplary employer and generous colleague, describing in detail his cutting-edge work and inviting her to participate fully in his research and experimentation.

Hannah soon proved indispensable. She accepted many new responsibilities and never complained, even when long workdays extended deep into the evening and concluded with a drink in a local pub or a walk along the moonlit riverbank.

HANNAH BELAYA

I well understood the signs of Yevgeny's attentions. I just wasn't sure how to respond. I felt the need to tread carefully. Already forty and four times divorced, I'd been unlucky with men—some might say foolish. This time would be different, I told myself. I needed the job for the great opportunity it promised. Life in war-torn Ukraine had become intolerable—the economy slow, the men stupid and brutish. Painful as it was, I left behind my cozy apartment in Lviv and my nineteen-year-old son, Peter. I didn't tell Yevgeny about my son. I'm not exactly sure why. But with each passing day my omission seemed more like a calculated lie, even if I myself did not understand the calculus.

COSMOENERGY

Yevgeny Yeshevsky was well known throughout Russian scientific circles for his experimental studies of universal life energy, known generally as Cosmoenergy. According to the Cosmoenergy Federation, every live plant and animal in the cosmos is surrounded by an electrostatic field that can be measured. A heathy organism is one whose electrostatic field is normal for its species. Diseases such as cancer can be detected and quantified according to the measured imbalance of an organism's electrostatic field, also known as its biofield or aura.

For much of his career Yeshevsky used a variety of electrographic techniques to study the patterns of an organism's electric discharge to form a diagnosis of its health. Over decades he practiced and improved his diagnostic techniques in the hope that they might lead him to discover advanced treatments of disease, particularly cancer.

Ever on the lookout for new avenues of experimentation, Hannah Belaya, Yeshevsky's esteemed associate, suggested that they pursue the lead of Israeli scientists who had lately discovered the effectiveness of Dead Sea salt crystals in the diagnosis and treatment of melanomas.

Yeshevsky reworked his budget to import a large supply of the salts for study in his Moscow laboratory. Knowing that Dead Sea salt contains eighty-four chemical elements, along with many trace elements found in the human body, Yeshevsky hoped his research might be paired with his biofield diagnoses and lead him to develop new cancer treatments. Unfortunately, his experiments (in which Hannah Belaya assisted) were initially promising but ultimately inconclusive. Even so, Yevgeny and Hannah continued to believe that there might exist an even more special salt that could lead to a more general cure of cancer.

REFUSENIK

Despite a loyal staff, praising patients, a full lecture schedule and a successful blog with an international subscriber base, Yevgeny Yeshevsky felt like a failure. Denigrated by the official Russian medical community and marginalized by most European and

American associations of medicines, he did not feel like he measured up to his successful parents, both highly reputed doctors of internal medicine who had chosen to remain in Moscow rather than move to Israel or the United States when the Communist Party began allowing Jews to emigrate in the 1980s.

Unlike his conservative parents, who had a successful medical practice and no interest in relocating their relatively comfy lives, teenaged Yevgeny had been active in the Soviet Jewry movement. Like many of his contrarian friends, he had not been overly impressed with President Gorbachev's promises of *perestroika* and *glasnost*; he desperately wanted to leave the Soviet Union. Seemingly without care, he marched boldly in the Moscow protests against restrictive, anti-Jewish policies, always at the vanguard, waving flags or bearing banners. Though his parents were too busy to notice, the vigilant eyes of the Soviet authorities kept careful records.

A few years later, after obtaining his medical degree from Moscow's prestigious I.M. Sechenov, he demonstrated his long-harbored contrarian outlook by refusing to join his parents' practice, choosing instead to dedicate himself to the cause of Cosmoenergy, derided by his parents as scientific quackery. The more his parents protested, the more passionately Yevgeny worked to advance his career.

After only a decade, Yevgeny was the leading star of the Cosmoenergy movement, so mired in its research and business he no longer gave serious thought to relocating his life and work. In any case, his many applications for travel visas were always rejected. Though he never discovered the government's rationale for keeping him under loose house arrest (at least, that's how he felt), he assumed that his youthful protests had earned him the summary stamp of Refusenik. He also believed that his medical treatment of high-placed politicians and military personnel (who sought his confidential and alternative methods) had labeled him a man who knew too much.

YEVGENY YESHEVSKY

My travel restrictions were a severe limitation. After all, I had lectures to deliver, alliances to forge, conferences to attend. Social media and podcasts ameliorated the restrictions, but they were bothersome. As a workaround, I trained Hannah Belaya to be my trusted colleague. We shared work in the laboratory. We collaborated on writing lectures and papers. She even assisted me with my private patients. It was my hope that she would eventually travel in my place, as my proxy. I kept no secrets from Hannah, other than my love.

INCOGNITO

One day, a patient arrived very late in the afternoon. Only Hannah and Dr. Yeshevsky were still working.

The patient looked unnervingly familiar to Hannah, even with a beard and full head of hair. Instead of staring, she focused on the open appointment book on her desk.

"We have no patients scheduled for this time," she said, nervously.

"Tell the doctor I want to see him."

Aside from his familiar look, the patient's recognizable voice commanded her obedience.

"One second, please," she said, rising from her desk. She then walked towards Yeshevsky's office, feeling the patient's eyes on her back as he followed her.

The patient could see in Dr. Yeshevsky's eyes that he was recognized. Thickset, about five feet, seven inches, he was content, for the moment, to let his medical history speak for him. This recorded history was now on Yeshevsky's desk, an impressively thick and well-thumbed file.

Yeshevsky focused on the most recent papers in the folder. He knew not to make small talk and to keep his conversation focused.

"Are you now taking any medications?"

"No. Nothing."

"What about for a cough or a cold?"

"Tea with honey."

"That's it?"

"Yes."

Yeshevsky skimmed the rest of the file. Nowhere did he see the patient's name. He was referred to only as *P.* or *the patient.*

"Do you exercise?"

"I swim. Sometimes I practice judo."

Yeshevsky nodded, still looking at the folder.

"You have had many tests done recently."

"Yes."

"Your heart looks strong."

"Yes."

Yeshevsky reviewed a paper-clipped section of reports.

"You do not smoke?"

"No."

"You did not smoke in the past?"

"No."

"Parents smoke?"

"No."

Yeshevsky skimmed the earlier files. Some sections were heavily redacted. There were no records for certain years, suggesting that some files had been removed.

"Where have you lived throughout your life?"

"Irrelevant."

Yeshevsky drew a quick breath.

"Habit and environment can influence health."

"Irrelevant in my case."

Yeshevsky nodded, then closed the folder. He deliberated whether to stand but remained seated.

"You have lung cancer," he said from his side of the desk. "Somewhat advanced."

"Yes."

"Surgery has been described as an option?"

"I do not want surgery."

Yeshevsky nodded. "Your cancer is advancing."

"I do not want surgery."

Yeshevsky tried sounding firm and objective:

"There are no other proven medical treatments to treat your cancer."

"No surgery."

Yeshevsky paused. He needed a different tack.

"Were you referred by another patient, if you don't mind me asking?"

"You were recommended."

"By whom, may I ask?

"Your parents."

Yeshevsky froze. He and his parents had grown closer in recent years. They had finally come to accept his career in alternative medicine. Recently retired, they'd become interested in their Jewish roots and decided to make *aliyah*: to move to Israel and live their remaining days near the hills of Hebron. This idea was now their shared dream. They hoped to move before the end of the year. Having applied for a pair of visas, they were waiting to learn their fate. Yeshevsky assumed his patient knew these facts and that the government's response would be predicated on the success of his medical service.

"I need to do more research before I can treat you."

"My office will call to schedule an appointment."

P. approached Yeshevsky, who leaned back in fear. But P. had advanced only to retrieve his medical folder.

"I need those records for my research," said Yeshevsky.

"I will bring them back when I return."

After P. left, Yeshevsky stood and carefully opened one slat of the window blind that faced the front of the building on Stoleshnikov Lane. About three minutes later he watched P. exit the building and walk to the right. His vantage did not allow him to see P. make another right at the corner and then slip into the backseat of a black sedan with tinted windows.

Yeshevsky looked around the room and seemed surprised to see that Hannah had been there the whole while, standing quietly in the corner, shivering with emotion.

"Hannah, are you okay?"

He patted her shoulder. It was the first time he'd ever touched her—and she nearly flinched.

"I'm okay," she said, unconvincingly.

"Good. We have a lot of work to do."

He did not need to tell her that P. was now their greatest priority. He knew that she'd seen what he'd seen. What he didn't know was that she wanted him dead—P., that is.

HANNAH BELAYA

I would not say that I was a Ukrainian nationalist. In fact, I was barely patriotic. I regarded myself as an internationalist who loved humanity in general and in the abstract, and made few distinctions based on borders and politics. But much changed for me following Russia's invasion of Crimea. It wasn't the incursion itself, the slap at Ukrainian sovereignty that aggrieved me. It was the wounded—dazed and shredded—who were sent to my clinic in Lviv. Several of these mangled humans died in my care—there was nothing I could do to save them. In two cases I knew the mother of the dead soldier and delivered the tragic news personally—two mothers holding each other, sobbing.

During a lull in the war (one of many false calms), I was offered the job in Moscow. Peter, my son, understood the opportunity and begged me to go. "I'll be fine. Really. We can Skype in the evenings." I left for Moscow the following week, my excitement tempered with worry.

Two months later I received a text message from Peter. He'd been ordered to appear at a nearby military induction center. "Oh no!" I wailed. Peter, my one and only—Peter, who saw the Cosmos as I did, Infinite and Divine—Peter was going to war!

My taste for all things Russian turned suddenly bitter. I felt as if I were living among the enemy. I tried to reason with myself. After all, I thought, it's not as if all Russians had attacked Ukraine. There were always good people to be found. Still, I needed someone to blame—and, in this case, the target was clear: the self-infatuated, aggressive little brute whose picture I had recently seen in a magazine, riding a stallion like a shirtless Bronze Horseman. He was killing my countrymen. He had put my Peter in harm's way!

A HUNCH

Though bespectacled and slightly framed, Yeshevsky was a decisive and forward-thinking man. He immediately foresaw that commonly prescribed, nonsurgical treatments would have little effect on P.'s advancing cancer. But he was not without hope; he sincerely believed he might soon discover some new salt-based treatment.

His reasoning was not unfounded. The Israelis were not the first to advance ideas about salt-related cancer treatments. Several years before, Yeshevsky had read about American experiments in which cancerous cells were infused with a form of salt and then shined with lasers. The lasers changed the cells' chemistry, making it more acidic, which created a pH imbalance, which killed the cancerous cells. According to Yeshevsky's research, the technique was still in clinical trials. He knew there were many variables still to be tested—but it seemed to him that the nature of the salt added to the cancerous cell might prove to be the most significant variable. It was only a hunch, but many great hypotheses began with a calculated hunch.

STAGE IIIB

A few days later, an unidentified woman telephoned Yeshevsky's office and made an appointment for P. for that very evening at 6:00 P.M. It was the first of many weekly appointments, always made by the same unidentified woman from an unlisted and untraceable phone number.

As per the woman's directive, Yeshevsky dismissed his office staff before P. arrived. Only Hannah was asked to stay.

P.'s first appointment lasted nearly three hours. During that time Yeshevsky and Hannah performed a comprehensive physical examination, including blood works, X-rays, cancer screening, nutritional evaluation and several electrographs of P.'s biofield. The test results confirmed the diagnosis already recorded in P.'s file: locally advanced, non-small-cell lung cancer, stage IIIB, that had spread to the lymph nodes and both sides of the patient's chest.

"What are we going to do?" asked Hannah.

Yeshevsky loved that she said *we*. To him, it implied an association beyond their professional relationship. Though he felt closer to her with each passing day, he maintained a strictly professional tone while they were in the office, which sometimes required him to consciously will his tall, lanky, nonathletic body from intruding into her personal space.

"Until we discover a new nonsurgical treatment, let us place him on a schedule of vapor inhalations and immersive salt-water treatments. If we are lucky, we may have some short-term success while we continue our research."

For four weeks, Hannah assisted him with P.'s salt therapies, meticulously recording all the data, hoping that the alkalizing effects of the Dead Sea salts would improve the patient's unhealthy aura. At night, alone in her Moscow apartment, Hannah prayed that the salt's various minerals would add neuro-protective benefits to calm the patient's famously aggressive impulses.

YEVGENY YESHEVSKY

Even as I administered our non-invasive salt therapies, I knew that any signs of improving health would likely betoken only fleeting, short-term gains. To win this war I knew we must fight the cancer from the inside out, infiltrating each malignant cell and poisoning it to eradicate the disease. Practically speaking, I knew there was only one viable option: the experimental laser-salt technique I'd read about. That unique, aggressive treatment would give the patient (and me—and Hannah) a fighter's chance.

INQUISITION

Yevgeny and Hannah practiced how to permeate cancer cells with Dead Sea salt, how to shine the cells with lasers, and the best way to record their data. After three weeks of experimentation they felt ready.

The next time P. arrived, Yeshevsky explained to him his experimental technique, taking special care to manage P.'s expectations.

"So, you see, we are not following established protocols. We are experimenting as we forge ahead. Of course, this takes a little longer."

"Go faster."

Yeshevsky shook his head ever so slightly. "I'm afraid it's not always possible. We must study the results of each session and plan the next treatment accordingly."

"Go faster."

Before Yeshevsky could think of something else to say, P. added:

"I will increase your staff."

Yeshevsky took his time before responding: "Thank you, really, but that won't be necessary. Dr. Belaya and I are more than adequate for this case."

P. stared at Hannah. She reminded him of his whore consort, but softer, younger, and more intelligent.

"What is your name?"

"Dr. Belaya."

"What is your name?" he repeated.

"Hannah."

"Where are you from, Hannah?"

She knew there was no possible subterfuge.

"Lviv."

"Nice to meet you, Dr. Hannah Belaya of Lviv."

Hannah nodded.

"You married?"

Hannah shook her head.

"You have children?"

Hannah gasped.

"My son, Peter."

"A student? Or does he work?"

She did not mention his pending induction. "A student. He's a good boy."

RADIATIVE ATTENTIONS

Yeshevsky was surprised to learn that Hannah had a son. He couldn't imagine why she hadn't told him. (Really, he couldn't imagine. Despite being nearly fifty, he'd had little experience with women, and none with such an accomplished and intelligent woman as Hannah.) He assumed she would have confided in him very soon.

Though he lacked self-awareness in his relations with Hannah, Yeshevsky picked up immediately on P.'s interest—and how it made Hannah squirm.

Still, there was little he could do about it. Inasmuch as Hannah assisted him in almost every phase of P.'s treatments, including getting him into and out of his salt baths, he was powerless to protect her from the man's radiative attentions. Unfortunately, over the course of several weeks, these morphed from discreet staring to sly preying. One day, as Hannah helped P. into the salt bath, he leaned needlessly close to her, whispering his gratitude, his wet lips brushing her ear.

Hannah stiffened her posture to assert her no-nonsense, professional decorum. Later, alone, she kicked herself for having mentioned her unmarried state; twice she clawed her cheek for having mentioned her son. She thought about telling Yevgeny about Peter, but decided it could wait for some other occasion.

YEVGENY YESHEVSKY

The initial salt treatments were not adequately successful. The vapors and baths failed to nudge the patient's biofield needle in a discernibly positive way. The laser-salt experiments had slowed but not stalled the cancer's advance.

I remained hopeful, but I knew we needed something more effective. Each day I spent hours experimenting with varieties of salt, focusing on their various mineral compositions. At night I dreamed of salt molecules frantically bouncing inside cancerous cells while a giant laser—like God's retributive eye—shined its withering ray: blanching, starving, obliterating the diseased cells.

During rare moments of rest and relaxation, I used Facebook to interact with my international friends and associates, in many cases to practice my English. Lately, I had become fascinated with the posts and photos of a Jason Stevens from the United States, a recent connection who had glommed onto me, a friend of a friend. According to Jason's recent Facebook posts, he had recently arrived in a strange city in the very south of California called Saltin. He described it as a derelict, salt-encrusted ghost town; its former lake, now a giant salt bed with a few remaining lagoons where people came for miraculous treatments. Jason's words excited me. And while I continued to maintain a cautious distance from him, I tingled with curiosity and hope.

JASON STEVENS

For years, wandering alone, I did most of my socializing on Facebook, updating my status by posting photos of the places I was passing through: small-town bus terminals … empty midnight diners … cinderblock public bathrooms …

My old friends found these photos depressing, but they didn't understand this new me. I was actually happy now, living peacefully in the present. I didn't miss my former life. I didn't miss my former wife. But I did miss love.

I had no idea where I might go next. Sometimes a place name was enough to draw me. Once in a while I took a hint from a Facebook friend.

It was Johnny Walsh, a former bandmate turned photographer, who gave me the idea to go to Saltin. Johnny had gone to the Wildlife Refuge (just south of the former city) to photograph what had long ago been a major stopover for many species of migratory birds. The birds began skipping Saltin for points farther south when the city's surrounding freshwater pools began drying up and when the fish in the sea began to die by the millions. Consequently, the Wildlife Refuge had also become a ghost town of sorts and Johnny had gone there to record the changes for *Audubon* magazine. Johnny had posted on Facebook several photos he had not submitted to the magazine, including some shots of the salt-encrusted city, all of which had caught my eye. In South L.A. at the time, and having no other point of interest to pursue, I bussed, hiked and hitched my way to Saltin to see what I would see.

I began the trip with a bus ride to Beaumont, just south of the San Bernardino National Forest. Right outside Beaumont, on a nearly jungled stretch of disused rail line, I found three abandoned cars of the Union Pacific Railroad. In the fading twilight I made a quick inspection and assessed they would serve just fine for a night's shelter. After sweeping aside some dirt and leaves in the middle car, I laid down my waterproof ground cloth and let my mind wander. Almost immediately I thought of my old friend Johnny Walsh, who'd played so many fateful roles in my life. On this night, I focused on our early high school days, when we listened to music in Johnny's room and played basketball in the school playground. Those were good times.

Next morning, bearing the heat of the early summer sun, the heft of my rucksack, and the tug of my guitar case on my forty-five-year-old back, I resumed my hiking. And it was good. Good hiking was a combination of tolerable conditions and tolerable daydreams. Tolerable conditions were dry weather, even ground and a refreshing breeze. Tolerable daydreams were those that did not stab me with sharp regrets.

I continued my journey towards the Saltin Sea. According to the Google map on my iPhone, Cabazon was my next likely destination, about six miles away. After several hours of steady hiking, I entered Cabazon's outer precincts: lonely outposts of squat homes and a couple modest stores. At that point, I checked my phone again, this time zooming in on the map until I could see the layout of the town's streets—and that's when I noticed that one mile ahead, on the north side of the road, was a roadside attraction called *World's Biggest Dinosaurs.*

I picked up my pace. I could feel my face smiling. After passing a dozen homes with gravel lawns, three clapboard churches and two factory outlets, I came upon a giant billboard of a twenty-foot, T-Rex head, its giant jaw full of bloody teeth. I was so excited, which made my regret so painful: I had no children. Lacking a real son or daughter, I'd often taken an imaginary one to a movie or a zoo. These activities were subtle, interior dramas; nothing outwardly crazy at all. In fact, they gave me a greater sense of purposeful normality. But this day was different. I'd been journeying with everything I dearly owned weighing on my back. I hadn't showered or shaved in two days. I probably looked like a hobo. I didn't belong in this place. No one would care that I held an imaginary child's hand in mine as I looked all about in innocent wonder.

I continued on my lonely way. After hours of painful regretting, I checked my cellphone map to see what the future held in store. According to the map, a short walk south would put me on Bonita Avenue, which would lead me east to the San Gorgonio Pass. I'd never heard of the place, but I liked the sound of it.

Having reached Bonita Avenue, I came upon a sight that stopped me in my tracks. In the distance, spread over hills and valley, stood a thousand modern windmills. Like a modern Quixote, I stared at the army of tri-bladed turbines, wavering between environmental outrage and begrudging marvel. Just then a shiny sedan pulled up beside me and the driver's window electronically lowered.

"Need a lift?"

The man looked respectable: white shirt, loosened tie.

"Depends," I said.

"Where you headed?" the driver asked.

"The Saltin Sea."

"You a writer or filmmaker?"

"Photographer. Migratory birds."

The man nodded. "I'm headed in that direction. I'm going to Fantasy Springs. I can take you that far, if you like."

Fantasy Springs. The name made me smile. It sounded even better than *San Gorgonio Pass.*

With *Fantasy Springs* on my mind, I faced the passing desert scenery, the flickering dazzlement of sky, sun and sand playing on my half-closed lids.

The sedan stopped in front of a brick-and-mortar resort, fronted by manicured palms, water-spouting fountain and hustling bell boys.

"You can get the bus here for Saltin City. There's a schedule in the lobby."

I followed the man inside, where we shook hands and parted.

At the Information Desk, I learned that the last bus had just left. The next bus would arrive the following morning, 8:00 A.M. It was late. Fantasy Springs was in the middle of nowhere.

I walked about the hotel, assessing my options. The glitzy décor and posters of Vegas-style entertainment made little impression on me, but the sexy young women lounging by the pool buckled my knees. Wearied by the weight of my rucksack and guitar, I returned to the lobby, where I booked a top-floor room with a view of the pool and the mountains beyond.

That night, after a satisfying dinner, shower and shave, I sat on a king-sized bed with my laptop on my lap, reading an online article about the increasing Russian-Ukrainian tensions, which I had been following for weeks. The disturbing narrative led me to recall that my great-grandfather, Juda Tessarsky, had come to America as a teen from Kiev, worked his way from paperboy to journalist on *The Jewish Daily Forward* and then changed his name to *Joseph Stevens* in order to join the staff of the *New York Tribune.*

IMPERIAL VALLEY TRANSIT

The Imperial Valley Transit bus picked up passengers at Fantasy Springs before beginning its circuit of the Saltin Sea. Rarely did a passenger get on or off, but the stop was part of the original 1980s' route and Saltin was all about tradition.

The bus began its twice-daily trip rumbling south on Route 86 before stopping at the Saltin Civic Center on the sea's western shore.

Leaving the Civic Center, the bus continued south to Saltin City, stopping on Sea View Drive, exactly where it crossed Commonwealth Avenue, so the front of the bus was in East Saltin, while the back was in West Saltin.

Leaving Saltin City, the bus picked up Route 111, chugging northward along the sea's eastern shore, stopping outside the electrified fence of Calpurnia State Prison, a razor-wrapped, female-only facility, turreted and bulwarked against dreams of escape.

The bus then continued north on Route 111, eventually looping back into Route 86 North, which led back to Fantasy Springs.

THE SALTIN CIVIC CENTER

Jason stepped off the bus warily, a stranger in a strange land. Slowly, he approached the low, one-story Civic Center: scalloped roof and stone walls the dun color of the sea strand, its front door covered with faux starfish and slightly unhinged.

He pulled open the creaky door and entered. Inside, there was no one to greet him, but the floor was freshly swept and the walled photographs were clear, suggesting they had recently been dusted.

On the wall behind the information counter were four large posters whose corners were curled and whose colors had faded: *Saltin City, USA … Saltin: America's Riviera … Surf, Sun, Saltin … Saltin's Casinos—Bet On It!*

The centerpiece of the room was a large architectural model of Saltin City in its hey-day. On each side of Commonwealth Avenue were tiny scale models of every hotel and casino, every church and holy attraction. The detail and integrity of the scale-sized models did not reflect the decay of their contemporary counterparts.

The room's far wall was a wide window view of the empty sea bed: cracked like a desert quilt; everywhere the bones of dead fish and the glitter of salt crystals. To the right, the remains of the former great pier: now a large wooden shard, canted and half buried in the sand.

Jason walked outside and around the Civic Center to stand on the shore of the dead sea so he could better imagine how it looked when its buoyant waters stretched to the horizon. Standing among the bones of dead fish and smelling their rot, Jason felt the irony of having once been the leader of the rock band, Jason and the Argonauts: before him was a dry and empty sea; behind him, the memory of having been fleeced by his manager, who'd taken his money, his prospects and even his wife.

The worst part, as he remembered it, was that he hadn't fought back. Instead, buffeted by headwinds, thrown off course, he had drifted aimlessly for years, until washing ashore at Saltin, quite by chance, so it seemed.

Still, he wasn't entirely bereft. He had his guitar, his laptop, and the music to his unfinished rock opera. If only he could find a story to pair with the music, he thought he might restore his self-esteem and direction.

THE OLD MAN AND THE SALTIN SEA

With his brown cap, sand-colored shirt and beige pants, the old man blended so perfectly into the seascape that Jason hadn't noticed him sitting on the shard of the former pier, facing the dry sea bed. But there he was, holding a fishing pole, its dangling line listless, there being no breeze, no water, no live fish to take the baitless hook.

Jason approached and the old man nodded. Beside him was a scrawny dog—half asleep, half dead.

"How's the fishing?"

"Slow season," said the old man.

"Not biting today?"

"Not even breathing."

Jason surveyed the desolation. "D'you know if the Civic Center is open?"

"Of course," said the old man. "I'm the director and guide. Next tour begins in fifteen minutes."

Jason figured the old man was pulling his leg. He looked about, as if taking stock of the salty wasteland. "How many people live around here, if you don't mind me asking."

"Depends what you mean by *here*."

"Here, in Saltin City."

"Well, for one thing, this isn't Saltin City. It's the western beach of the Saltin Sea. To get to Saltin City, you'll have to wait for the next bus or hitch a ride."

"When's the next bus?"

"This evening, around 7:00."

Jason checked his watch. "That's a long time. Is that the only bus?"

"That's right. But you could hitch a ride, like I said."

Jason took off his hat and wiped his forehead. "A lot of drivers come by?"

"Not a lot. One, maybe two, every other day or so."

Jason was thinking.

"Come on inside," said the old man. "I'll give you the cook's tour."

The old man lay down his fishing pole. The dog remained beside it, a listless sentry.

Inside the Civic Center the old man took off his brown cap and hung it on a walled peg. Jason removed his own hat and asked sincerely, "Okay if I put my gear down?"

"Of course, right there in the corner. Thank you for asking."

Jason eased his rucksack and guitar case off his tired shoulders and carefully placed his belongings in the corner, leaving his hat—a battered old Stetson—balanced on top.

With that, the old man announced: "Okay, here we go!" But there he stopped, as if beginning and end were one and the same.

Jason was uncomfortable in the silence. After several seconds he moved towards the architectural display, which seemed to reinvigorate the old man, who approached.

"Ah, the glory that was Greece … the grandeur that was Rome … the splendor that was Saltin!" But then the old man stalled again. Rather than suffer another silence, Jason repeated his question:

"So, how many people live in Saltin City?"

"Counting the King and Pope?"

"There's a King and Pope?"

The old man smiled. "The city is divided by a wide avenue: camps of capitalism on the west, armies of God on the east. People call the mayor of West Saltin, King, and the mayor of East Saltin, Pope."

Jason thought the old man might be sun-struck crazy—or he was setting him up for the local whopper. He decided to play along.

"Yes, altogether, counting the King and Pope. How many people live in Saltin?"

"Let's see." The old man counted the fingers on his left hand. Then he counted the fingers on his right hand. Then he went back to counting the fingers on his left hand but suddenly stopped. "About twenty, pretty equally divided between the two towns."

Jason smiled and the old man continued:

"Truth is, the two towns are barely self-sustaining and they compete for visitors. West Saltin, known as Hedo by the locals, has the advantage of being on Route 86. That's where we are. Most people come to Saltin using this road, so they get to West Saltin first. East Saltin, nicknamed Jeru, has the advantage of being on the same road as Calpurnia State Prison. Occasionally, soon-to-be-released prisoners are assigned to a half-way house in East Saltin. After months or even years of correctional living, many of the ex-prisoners find the strict order to their liking and remain there."

Jason was intrigued. "That's interesting. Thank you."

"Saltin was a great place in its day, but now it's mostly dead and forgotten. What brings you here?"

"I want to see the Wildlife Refuge—or what's left of it. I hadn't really thought about the town, but now I think I'd like to see it."

"I can give you a map, though it won't do you much good."

"Why's that?"

"The town was built in the early '50s. The first and only map was based on a projection of a sizable community. But relatively few of the surveyed streets and roads were ever built."

"Why's that?"

"Well, Saltin was like one of those old Gold Rush towns. A tremendous amount of money poured in and the city was built overnight. Saltin was the next great thing. Everyone wanted a piece of it."

"Was it planned as two towns, East and West?"

"Nah. That was just people being people. The first-comers paved a central street. Those that wanted a sexy, gambling life set up stakes on one side, and those that wanted more of a spiritual thing pitched tents on the other."

"How long did that last?"

"Not long. About twelve years. But those were golden years. In West Saltin, we're talkin' oceanfront hotels, top-notch nightclubs, casino gambling, yachting—everything money could buy. At the same time—and right across the street—you could find the best evangelists, newest churches, modern spiritual retreats—all kinds of succor for the soul. It was the American Dream. But then it all went bust."

"What happened?"

The old man blew out a deep breath.

"Not exactly sure. But while things were going great, the mayor of West Saltin and the mayor of East Saltin collaborated on some expensive public works to help guarantee that the good times would roll forever."

"How'd that go?"

"Not as intended, that's for sure."

"What happened?"

"As I heard it, during the last ribbon-cutting ceremony, the heavens let loose with a rainstorm, a deluge like you wouldn't believe. All night it poured. Water ran through the streets and the sewers backed up."

"Wow. How long did that last?"

"Until sunrise. Then the rain suddenly stopped, like someone turned off a spigot. Everything was quiet. The sun rose hot and bright and stayed that way the entire day and the next, and all the days after. For years it's always been the same: a high sun with a hot glare that never blinks. I'm not sure how to explain it. Climate change? The angry eye of God? Who knows?"

"No rain?"

"Maybe twice a year. And then, only a brief drizzle."

"A few tears."

"Nice. There's a poet in you. Anyway, the sea started drying and the fish started dying and after several years there was no sea, just stench. Casinos lost their customers—churches lost their congregations—Saltin lost its citizens. Eventually, almost everyone was gone. There's not many left."

"You're still here."

"I had nowhere to go. I worked in a casino and when business fell off, I worked part-time here, at the Civic Center. The town still pays me a small stipend, which covers my groceries, and I live here rent free."

"By yourself?"

"I have my dog."

"No wife and kids?"

"I'm married, I think. But I haven't seen my wife in forty years. We never had kids."

"You think you're married? What happened, if you don't mind me asking?"

The old man gathered his thoughts.

"My wife had a good job in San Diego—financial analyst, whatever that means. I never quite understood, but it was the kind of job one could do anywhere, presumably. Since I was unemployed and struggling, and she could work anywhere, we made plans to check out Saltin City, to see if we both could be happy there. It made sense for me to go first and sort of scout out the place. If it looked like a good opportunity, she was supposed to join me. That was the plan."

"What happened?"

"Well, I liked the place and stayed. I called her, many times—even wrote to her—saying she should come as soon as she could. But I never saw her again. At least, I don't think so."

"How's that?"

"Tova—that's her name, a Jewish name. Mine's Fred, Fred Martin; but I'm not Jewish. I'm not anything. Anyway, she never showed up. I tried calling, like I said, but she never answered, never returned my messages. This was before cell-phones or emails, so I couldn't reach her. She was just gone."

"Wow. I'm so sorry. What do you think happened?"

"My honest-to-goodness thought?"

"If you don't mind."

"I think she came down here, like she said she would. From San Diego, she would have taken Route 10 to Route 86. Now, north of here there's a big sign. You must have seen it, unless you came from Mexico, which you didn't. Anyway, the sign says: *Left to Route 111, East Saltin; Right to Route 86, West Saltin.* I'm sure I told her to go right, but she probably went left, which was wrong."

"She went to East Saltin."

"That's what I think."

"But it's a small city. If she were somewhere on the other side of the main street, how is it you didn't find each other in forty years?"

"I'm not sure either of us looked real hard."

Jason didn't think the old man was being entirely honest.

"So, you think your wife made it to Saltin, but on the east side, and you were on the west side—and you never saw here again."

"Sounds crazy, I know, but that's how it is."

"Did you go looking for her?"

The old man paused. "I had a few friends in East Saltin. I casually asked about her. I described her, saying she was a friend. I never mentioned *wife*."

"Too embarrassing?"

"Something like that."

"Did she ever come looking for you?"

"I don't think so. She probably would have found me if she looked. But I'm not sure."

"And you never actually went looking for her?"

"I did, once. Maybe a year after I got here. I remember the day because it was our anniversary. Anyway, I was lonely and went looking for her."

"Did you see her or learn anything?"

"I picked up a few clues. But I never saw her again, that I'm aware of."

"What kind of clues?"

"I showed around an old picture I have of her. The only one I have—our wedding picture. One lady said the picture looked like this woman she once met at Covenant House, a women's-only residence in East Saltin. Anyway, it was my only clue, so I went there, knocked on the door, and said I was looking for a woman named Tova—but the old woman who opened the door said there was no one there by that name and slammed the door in my face. I didn't even get to show the photo."

"What did you do?"

"I left."

"You could have tried again."

"I know."

"You could have asked a woman friend to get inside and show the photo."

"I know."

"So, for all you know, your wife might still be alive and well, and living on the other side of the main street."

"That's true."

The old man seemed lost in his unhappy thoughts. "So, what brings you here?"

REGRETS, A FEW

Jason spoke openly about his past: how he and three high school friends had formed a garage band, practicing after school and on weekends—and how he'd been the unacknowledged leader because he played lead guitar with verve and was a strong, brooding singer. But he did not mention that he was Jewish. That he'd first learned about musical notation during his bar mitzvah lessons and had, during one teenage summer, given casual thought to becoming a cantor someday.

"But we were just kids. Eventually, the other guys went off to college and became adults."

"But you stuck with it. You followed your musical North Star."

"I did indeed."

Modest and self-effacing, Jason described how his passion, practice, and high principles lead him to hunger and work as a studio musician.

"Something changed. You get your big break?"

"I suppose. I was working with two L.A.-based groups, Crashing Cymbals and Sly Snakes. Both groups used the same backup singer in the studio—Renee Rivera from Austin, Texas. Oh man, her green cat's eyes and bluesy pipes enchanted everyone, including Sanford Villian, the manager of both groups."

"A good guy or a bad guy?"

"Villian was a handsome, back-slapping, bastard," Jason told Fred. "Still, he had a good eye for talent and knew how to shape bands and produce records. He thought Renee and I were the stand-out talents of the recording sessions and persuaded us to form a band of our own—though I don't think either of us needed much persuasion. Personally and musically, we just hit it off."

Fred nodded enthusiastically. He'd never known a real rock and roller.

"Anyway, through Villian's sly guidance, Renee and I formed a group, eventually agreeing on the name Jason and the Argonauts."

"Were you successful? You do albums and concerts?"

"We were quite successful," Jason said, and then paused. "But that was then. Now is now. Now I'm here."

CHAPTER 2

HANNAH AND HER HOLIES

Given the number of candles and religious icons that decorated her apartment, a casual guest might have supposed that Hannah was one of Russian Orthodoxy's fervent faithful. But she wasn't. Hannah's belief was more spiritual than scriptural, more personal than reverential. Of her many religious totems and wooden plaques, images of the Holy Mother and Child predominated. Separate from these, but just as revered, were her framed photos of herself and Peter. Just the two of them. There were no displayed photos of any of her four husbands. By fire, by scissors, by any means necessary, she had cut those men out of her life.

SHABBAT

In the past year Yevgeny had acquired the happy habit of going to his parents' apartment for Friday night dinner. Early on, his parents referred to the evening as Shabbat, even though they hadn't yet introduced any of the special traditions that marked the weekly Jewish holiday around the world.

On this Friday night Yevgeny saw the changes. On the polished sideboard there was an ancient, seven-cup brass menorah, its tall, just-lighted candles burning brightly. His mother was facing the candles, making inward-waving motions with her hands. When she appeared finished, her face peacefully composed, Yevgeny asked what ritual she had just performed. (His upbringing had been scrupulously secular: no religious training, no bar mitzvah, no prayerful celebrations of any kind.) His mother answered:

"Even though we are now retired, our days are still frantically busy. At the end of the week, on the Sabbath, we are commanded to rest. It is a time of peaceful reflection. A time to give thanks and to replenish our strength and creativity."

Yevgeny was intrigued. "Why were you waving the candleflames towards your face?"

His mother smiled in a way he almost didn't recognize. "In this way we beckon our soul energy back to its source. With our soul refreshed, we can reconnect with our friends and family—and with God." His father smiled and nodded.

What a surprise for Yeshevsky! His parents, whom he'd known all his life as a pair of rational empiricists, were now careful about their Souls! He was thrilled. He loved and admired them more than ever. His father added:

"Your mother now shops in a kosher market on Kaloshin Lane." As if to prove his point, his father pointed to the lace-covered, dining room table on which his mother had already laid a beautifully braided challah bread, three bowls of perfectly chilled borscht, and a potato beet salad. Later, they would all enjoy a main course of chicken and rice, and then two dessert treats: a syrupy compote and a cinnamon babka.

Yevgeny soon came to love these Shabbat meals and looked forward to them with acute yearning. At the same time, he was saddened by a poignant realization: if his parents' fervent wishes were answered and they were allowed to move to Israel—he might never see them again.

KNOWLEDGE AS POWER

Yevgeny saw Hannah as a beautiful, sensual, alluring woman, who was also the perfect adjunct and confidante, so close his equal she might someday serve as an extension of himself: his proxy to the outside world. He redoubled her training, intent on teaching her everything he knew.

Hannah's mind was quick, capacious, supple. She was, as the saying goes, a motivated learner. For her part, she surmised that the more work she did, the less Yevgeny would bother her with his romantic notions. She also understood that knowledge was power: the more she learned, the more likely she'd be able to help her son Peter.

Meanwhile, P. was becoming increasingly infatuated with her. As yet, he hadn't taken any untoward liberties, beyond snuffling her ear with wetly whispered gratitudes. As always, Hannah's response was a strong shiver, which P. misconstrued as animal excitement, which encouraged him to pursue her with increased desire.

GUT FEELING

Knowing that their salt-based therapies and laser treatments had not yet proved effective, Yevgeny and Hannah each wondered: *How much time do we have? What can we try next? What will happen if we fail?*

Yeshevsky had a gut feeling about the salts from the former Saltin Sea. One day, after work, during a stroll by the river, he told Hannah all he knew about Jason Stevens.

"He found me on Facebook, a friend of a friend. From his page, he seems an interesting man. Damaged but hopeful."

"How so?" Hannah was intrigued that Jason would admit that he was damaged. None of her four husbands had ever expressed weakness, or even vulnerability. Jason suddenly interested her.

"We have exchanged messages several times. In this way, we get along quite well. From what I gather, his life was damaged by a failed music career, the betrayal of his manager, and the infidelity of his wife. It seems that his unfinished opera and his soulful wanderings give him hope."

Hannah listened with growing curiosity.

"How old is he?"

"Mid-forties, I think."

"Divorced?"

"I would think so. He didn't say."

"Any children?" She immediately regretted the question. She wasn't ready to talk to Yevgeny about her own son.

"I don't know. He never mentioned any."

"What does he look like? Have you seen photos?"

"Yes. He posts photos on Facebook. He appears tall, maybe a little over six foot. Slender. Rangy. Rather darkly handsome. A hale, outdoorsy tan."

She was interested. "Does he work?" Her husbands were lazy connivers; the last, her fourth, would rather steal than work.

"I was curious about that too. Of course, I didn't want to pry, but I gather he'd made a fair amount of money early in his career, and even with some personal reversals, he can now live off it—provided he lives frugally."

"Did you tell him about our experiments with Dead Sea salts?"

"Not exactly. I told him I am a physician and scientist and alluded to our general interest in salt therapies."

"You didn't mention P., did you?"

"Oh god, no. I think we want to be very careful what we say to Mr. Jason Stevens."

"What *we* say?"

"Yes, *we*. He asked about my staff and I told him about you."

"Nothing too personal, I hope," Hannah joked.

"Our secret is safe," Yeshevsky said, smiling.

Hannah winced. She liked and respected Yevgeny but did not think she could ever love him. She wanted to tell him soon, just to clear the air. But the occasion never presented itself. The time never seemed right. Besides, she knew how sensitive men could be at times—and how brutishly obdurate they could be at other times. She hoped one day to tell Yevgeny how much she respected him and how much she enjoyed working with him, but that another marriage wasn't for her. *It's not you* (she imagined herself saying to him), *it's me. I have been married four times. It is enough. I want to concentrate on myself—my work, my son, my feelings.*

"I'd like you to friend him on Facebook," Yeshevsky told her. "Don't use your own name. Make up a name, a new account—don't tell anyone, not even me. Find out all you can about Saltin, especially its dead sea and its salts."

ASTRAL LOVE

Hannah created a new Facebook account, using the name *Astral Love*. Fearing *Astral Love* might be a silly name, she made sure her profile sounded serious: "Cosmologist. Scientist. Internationalist. Humanitarian. Music lover." Her profile photo was a joyous starburst set against a background of cosmic darkness. She noted her residence as "Here, There, and Everywhere."

After studying Jason Stevens' Facebook page, she spent several days filling out her own page with details designed to attract Jason's attention. She seeded her timeline with stories of her personal journeys through the Carpathian Mountains. She wrote of her experiences on the streets of Lviv, Kiev and Odessa. She posted videos about Nino Katamadze, her favorite Georgian jazz singer. She posted articles about Bob Dylan's Nobel Prize and Leonard Cohen's passing. She posted a video about the over-commercialization of the Dead Sea's muds and minerals.

Along with her Friend Request, she sent Jason a message: *You are friend of my Facebook friend. I love your pictures cold bathrooms, empty lunch place and wonderful, salt-covered city Saltin. I also liked that you placed a video of himself playing the guitar. You write music? It is very beautiful. I would like to hear more.*

FACEBOOK MESSAGE FROM JASON TO ASTRAL

Nice to meet you, Astral. It seems we have much in common: two people searching for harmonies—spiritual, celestial, musical—perhaps we'll find that they are all related.

As you have seen from my posted photos, Saltin is a Death-blasted landscape. It reminds me of a post-apocalyptic city, like Chernobyl, but covered with salt. The salt is everywhere, a carapace, a disease. And yet, there is extraordinary beauty here and even examples of struggling life. And where there is life, there can be love, so I am hopeful.

I arrived here only a few weeks ago, so I am still learning about this strange place. For all its death—you can smell the stench of rotted fish for miles—there is something life-affirming about the salts. I haven't yet heard any personal testimonials, but the word on the street is that the salts here can relieve pain and restore vigor. Who knows, maybe they can bring eyesight to the blind and cure cancer! You'd know better than I would—you're the scientist.

By the way, I can tell from some odd constructions that you use Google Translate. But don't worry, even those phrasings are charming and poetic in their way.

One more thing. I don't suppose that "Astral" is your real name. I'm not asking you to reveal it. I like "Astral." It seems to fit what I know about you. But I'd like you to call me Simcha. It's my Hebrew name and means Happiness. That's what I'm looking for.

MEANWHILE, BACK AT THE FEDERATION

Yeshevsky explained to P. that the salt vapors and baths were not yielding positive results.

"I suggest we dispense with those treatments," Yeshevsky said. "Meanwhile, I'll continue researching new combinations of lasers and salts."

"Stop the vapors but continue the baths."

"But the baths haven't proved effective."

"Continue the baths."

Yeshevsky's dark suspicion was confirmed: P. enjoyed the baths even though they weren't demonstrably helpful. He also understood that the baths placed Hannah in an indelicate situation: alone with a nearly naked P. in a heated room, infused with soft music, and behind a closed door. But what could he do? Only one person was needed to prepare the salt bath, and P. had made it very clear that he preferred Hannah's company.

HOME AND AWAY

In modern times, the autocratic rule of a world power is a time-consuming position that usually involves extensive travel. In all the previous years of his virtually self-appointed and self-assured rule, P. had many meetings in many foreign cities. In the past year his travels included:

Belarus (Union State meeting)

Greece (official visit)

Kazakhstan (Supreme Eurasian Economic Council meeting)

Uzbekistan (Shanghai cooperation organization meeting)

Azerbaijan (trilateral meeting with Azerbaijani and Iranian presidents)

Hangzhou, China (G-20 Leaders' Meeting)

Kyrgyzstan (CIS Summit)

Turkey (global energy summit)

Armenia (CSTO summit)

Goa, India (8th BRIC summit)

Berlin, Germany (peace talks on Ukraine and Syrian civil war)

P.'s meetings away from home used to weigh him with a heavy heart and a high degree of angst. Though he could count on his secret police to keep his family safe, he worried that his absence would pique his wife's temptation and increase his children's vulnerability. Though his fears were factually unfounded—projections of his own insecurity and illicit desires—his wife grew tired of her husband always being away, and his daughters became sadly accustomed to having an absentee father.

P.'S JOURNAL ENTRY

Alexander the Great had a thousand mistresses. I had but a few, and still it caused so much stupid calamity. Simple fact: As Maria became generally tiresome and boring in bed, I turned to Helga, my whore-consort. Helga was not boring. Helga was wildly skilled. Like Scheherazade, she worked desperately to spin new sexploits to justify her employment. I liked her, but—bottom line—she was a whore, nothing more, and eventually, her warranty expired.

All such things run their course. Even with Maria. When I met her, she'd been a linguist—French, German, Spanish—and had worked as a stewardess, very good job in Soviet Russia. After we married and I had gained power, she wanted to be involved in public life. But I shut that down. It simply couldn't be. She could not have a life of her own in the public eye. Too dangerous. Too much potential for complication and embarrassment.

With me gone so often, Maria grew frustrated and bored. I'm sure she knew about Helga, but she did not interfere. Perhaps she understood that Helga was a simple whore.

But one day a Moscow newspaper reported rumors about my affair with Nadia Gumilyov, a former gold medal Olympic gymnast—a woman of extraordinary flexibility. I immediately closed down the newspaper—and made sure it never printed again—but the damage was done. How Maria howled when she found out, and kept raving, even though I passionately denied any involvement.

Moving forward, I tried to maintain my marriage and my secret love, but Nadia was also upset by the newspaper article. She said she felt dirty and diminished. "How can you say diminished?" I said to her. "I am the richest and most powerful man in the world." Still, she sulked and pouted and would not let up. Finally, I said, "Enough already. What do you want?"

This was the year of the Sochi Olympics. I took control of that event like it was my pet project. And why not—all eyes would be on Russia. It had to be perfect. But first I had to deal with Nadia. I knew she would not ask for more money, as I had already given her plenty. And I knew she was smart enough not to mention marriage. "I want to be the torch bearer," she said. "When our team marches into the stadium for the Sochi Games, I want to carry the flame. I want that honor." It sounded good to me. In fact, I thought

I was getting off easy. Nadia was a two-time gold medalist and had also won a bronze medal. She was worthy of that honor. "Okay," I said, and gave her my word, whatever that meant.

I thought I'd made a good deal. For the most part, the Games were a great success and shined much golden light on Russia and on my leadership. But there was an unfortunate incident that I had not foreseen. As Nadia proudly carried the torch into the stadium, some foreign broadcasters and journalists speculated about our relationship on live television. Maria was in the stadium with me during the opening ceremonies and learned of this later. She was humiliated, inconsolable, screaming that the entire world now knew her shame. It was over between us. I accepted this without too much fuss. But I had to privately laugh when she publicly asked for a divorce, claiming she did not like public life and was afraid of flying. A stewardess afraid of flying! But okay, I did not argue. In fact, I was glad it was over. I breathed a great sigh of relief.

Ironically, the whole thing soured me on Nadia. She no longer interested me. More trouble than she was worth. Besides, she was getting older and her extraordinary flexibility wasn't what it was.

For several years I did not need any woman other than Helga. But then, as fate would have it, I met the beautiful Hannah Belaya, who looked like Helga, but was brilliant, younger, and could cure what ailed me.

FACEBOOK MESSAGING

It soon came to pass that Astral and Jason messaged each other twice a day: when Jason awakened and before Astral went to sleep. Rather than curse Fate for putting nine time zones between Saltin City and Moscow, they marveled at their planet's rotational axis and the blessing of Facebook that united all the peoples of Earth.

PACKAGING

Hannah and Yevgeny were alone in the office, late in the day.

"How's our dear friend Jason?" he asked.

Hannah did not like when Yevgeny referred to Jason as his "dear friend." In her mind, Jason was already more hers than his.

"Have you learned anything new about the Saltin salts or their use in treatments?"

"Not really," said Hannah. "I'm going slowly. I need to build his trust. I just can't blare out an ulterior motive."

Yevgeny shook his head. "All well and good. But P. isn't getting better, which is to say, he's getting worse—though slowly, thank God."

Hannah dropped her gaze.

"Look," said Yeshevsky. "Time isn't on our side. We have to move ahead. Press Jason. Tell him you're a scientist. Tell him you've studied Dead Sea salts and you're eager to compare the Saltin salts."

"I was thinking along those very lines. But I wanted to go slowly."

Yevgeny looked at her incredulously. Hannah got the message.

"Should I ask him to send samples?" she asked.

"No. At least, not in the usual way. We need to be clever about this. We need to protect ourselves."

Hannah nodded uncertainly. "What should we do?"

Yevgeny paused. Hannah had the impression that he was about to describe a plan he had already developed. She was right.

"I don't want any record that connects us to Saltin or to Jason Stevens. This morning I deleted my personal Facebook account. From now on, I will only use the Cosmoenergy website for messaging."

"Should I delete my Facebook page?"

"You used a fake name and new email address for your second account?"

"Yes."

"Does Jason know your real name?"

"No."

"Then we should be okay—for now. Tell Jason I'm having some computer problems and that I'll be in touch when I can. Don't refer to me by name."

"What about the salts? You don't want him to send a package of sample salts?"

"I do. But a large package—like the kind we got from Israel—might draw attention."

"Then what can we do?"

Yevgeny smiled. He was about to demonstrate his brilliance.

"Tell Jason you are competing with other teams of Moscow scientists who are all working on new, salt-based therapies. Say nothing more about that. Then say that some of the scientists you know are unscrupulous and would try to discover—by any means in their power—what salts you are using in your experiments."

"I like it. A good cover. But then what?"

"Ask Jason to buy a bunch of generic t-shirts. Typical American shirts are good—but they must be one hundred percent cotton and say nothing that refers to Saltin. In fact, Jason should go to some other town or city to buy the shirts. Tell him to buy no more than two shirts at a time in any one store. Hopefully he will not have to drive too far."

"What does this have to do with salts?"

"Be patient. I haven't finished."

"But we're asking a lot of Jason."

"We are. But a lot is riding on him. Besides, I have the feeling that he's big-hearted and quixotic."

"What does that mean?"

"He's a Romantic. He's impulsive. He's looking for the meaning of life. He's eager to help others who are trying to do good."

Hannah smiled. She liked the description. "Okay, but he barely knows me," she said with a nervous laugh.

Yevgeny nodded. "You can offer to repay his expenses, but he won't accept. Anyway, I haven't yet described the hard part of his task."

"I figured that much. What else does he have to do?"

"He has to wash the shirts in cold water and dry them in the sun. Remind him to use medical gloves when handling the shirts."

"He'll think I'm crazy!"

"It's important. You'll see. Now, where was I?"

"He's using gloves to handle the shirts."

"Yes, thank you. So, after the shirts are washed and dried, he'll be ready to prepare the salt samples. He should begin by identifying various water sources from the remains of the Saltin Sea—puddles, lagoons, runoff, whatever. For each source, he should take a shirt and immerse it in the water and then let it air-dry."

"Okay, go on," said Hannah, noncommittally.

"Next, he should identify sources of dried salt—the former sea bed, caves, wherever. In each of these cases, he should spread the salt on the inside of a shirt and then put the shirt in a warm, moist place where some of the salt is likely to dissolve."

"How many shirts are we talking about?"

"As many shirts are there are sources of salt."

"What if he identifies a great many sources?"

Yeshevsky paused to think. "Good point. Let's not leave it to chance. Let's limit the number of sources and t-shirts to twelve. More might look suspicious."

Hannah smiled nervously. "The whole plan sounds suspicious. He'll think I'm nuts."

"He'll probably appreciate the edgy secrecy of it all. Let him think that we are crazy Russians—that's okay."

"I'm Ukrainian. Remember?"

"Of course. I was making a joke. But don't mention to him that you are Ukrainian. The less he knows, the better."

Hannah let this pass without comment. Some of Yevgeny's directions were overbearing. She understood the importance of the mission, but she felt entitled to exchange with Jason as she pleased. Something about him intrigued her.

"A few more instructions. He should label each shirt with a tiny and discreet number, 1 to 12, and then make a list that correlates each number to its source of salt, noting the location as specifically as he can."

"Down to the meter?"

"More exact, if possible."

"Down to the centimeter?" said Hannah, slightly sarcastic.

"Yes, of course! Hannah, this is not a game. We are scientists. Exact records will be of great use to us."

"Okay," said Hannah, thinking the plan would be too annoyingly complex and cumbersome. She was afraid Jason would decline to help. Worse, she was afraid she might lose him.

"I see your look. You think this is too much for Jason. I assure you it's not complicated at all. When we review it, you will see how simple it really is."

Hannah nodded, annoyed that Yevgeny sometimes seemed able to read her mind but was so clueless at other times. Yevgeny continued:

"So, when all the shirts are ready—all dried with salt—he should fold them as neatly as he can to make them look new. Tell him to put each shirt in a separate plastic bag and then to put all the bags in a box, pressed together, so the package doesn't look conspicuously large."

"Got it."

"Then he should drive to any other local town or city—the farther away the better—and send the package to an address I will provide."

"Got it."

"Also, remind him—emphatically—that when he sends the package, he should send *only* the shirts—no handwritten cover letter, no receipts, no store tags—nothing to indicate where the shirts were purchased. At a later time, he will send us his list of source locations."

"Got it."

"Finally, but this is also of great importance: Jason should use cash—*not* credit card—when he buys the shirts and sends the package. Also, he should use a fake name and phone number on the sender label of the package. No one checks these unless the package is lost, which is very uncommon. That's it."

Hannah sat in silence, imagining how she would explain the lengthy process to Jason—and what his reaction might be.

"Okay," she said. "I understand everything."

Yevgeny touched her shoulder. Hannah winced. She did not like when men touched her uninvited. "I saved the best part for last," he said.

Even with her mind roiled with thoughts and emotions, she was clear-headed enough to pre-empt:

"Salt residue on a bunch of shirts won't be enough for us to use as test samples."

Yevgeny smiled. Hannah's comment was savvy and perfectly introduced his triumphant moment.

"You are correct, Dr. Belaya. But we can analyze each salt sample in the laboratory. Whatever its unique molecular composition, we ought to be able to replicate it ourselves."

He half expected Hannah to leap up and kiss him for all his brilliance—but she remained seated—impressed, but silent. Yevgeny continued:

"We will re-create the Saltin salts in our own laboratory. We can create as much as we need. If my hypothesis is right and the salt alters P.'s malignant cells as we hope and the chemically altered cells are destroyed by the laser—we just might discover a cure for cancer!"

"Perhaps a Nobel Prize!" said Hannah.

"Our names will be linked forever!"

Hannah darkened. She'd already taken that vow four times.

COMPLICIT

Despite its cumbersome details, Hannah liked the idea of hatching a secret plan with Jason. A complicit partnership would bring them closer, open the door to other secrets and interests. Her husbands had never discussed their interests with her. She suspected they hadn't any (or any worth discussing) and had not seemed to care about hers. *But what about Jason? What kind of man is he? He says he is a wanderer. But what does that really mean? Is he running away or seeking something? Does he walk aimlessly, or is he drawn to certain places? . . . Other than music, what are his interests? Does he like to read? What kind of books? ... He posts sensitive, shameless, introspective photographs—how has he learned so much about himself?*

Recalling that Jason had asked her to call him by his Hebrew name, *Simcha,* she wondered: *Is he Jewish? He must be.* She hoped he was. To her, it was a strange and exotic thing, yet another way in which Jason appealed to her.

Hannah looked forward to this mission of the Saltin salts. Its secrecy and edginess made it more appealing. Complicity can be a good thing.

"OPEN YOUR EYES"

Though his discussion with Hannah had gone well, Yeshevsky was worried. When planning an experiment, he did not like to leave to chance any factor that could be controlled, which was why he was concerned that something might get lost or distorted in Hannah's communication with Jason. After hours of reconsidering the various possibilities of failure, he decided it would be better if he communicated with Jason directly. Of course, it had already been decided that Hannah would communicate with Jason, not him, which put Yeshevsky in an awkward position. He did not want to usurp Hannah's newly entrusted responsibility. He knew she would feel slighted—personally and professionally—and this was the last thing he wanted to do to his proxy-in-training. Still, he was nervous. There was so much riding on the success of this experiment—possibly their lives.

Yeshevsky imagined telling Hannah that he was changing the plan: the look in her teary eyes told him he was making a mistake. Still, he couldn't shake his doubts. He couldn't sleep. Finally, he thought of a ruse by which he could get his written directions into Jason's hands without his own direct involvement. It was a somewhat complicated scheme (involving the integration of coded directions into a translation of a Russian folktale) that Hannah would share with Jason. He explained the plan in detail to Hannah, uncertain whether she'd be impressed with his inventive brilliance or aghast at his meddlesome madness.

Hannah asked that she be allowed to think it over.

The next day she met with Yeshevsky before their co-workers had arrived.

"Your plan is brilliant," she whispered (ostensibly, so no listening device might overhear). "But don't you often say, that all things being equal, the simpler solution is the better one?"

Yeshevsky nodded.

"Isn't that right?" she added, moving closer.

Yeshevsky drew a quick breath.

"And doesn't it follow that extraneous steps, however brilliant, must be avoided?"

Yeshevsky nodded again.

"You see," said Hannah, smiling, "I learned from the best. And now, I want to share something with you. Please close your eyes."

Yeshevsky closed his eyes, vacating all thought.

"Now, listen closely," she said, her moist breath heating Yeshevsky's ear.

Slowly and carefully, Hannah recited Yeshevsky's original plan, exactly as she intended to convey it to Jason. When she finished, she squeezed his hand once and said, "Open your eyes, Dr. Yeshevsky."

Yeshevsky saw her smile and knew she understood the plan perfectly. Their conversation ended, Hannah turned and sashayed back to her office. Yeshevsky stared at her receding figure, thinking: *What a woman!*

The next day, Hannah (as Astral) wrote to Jason, explaining in ordered detail exactly what she wanted him to do. Jason was anxious to please her.

CANTILLATION

Simcha and Astral began exchanging Facebook messages about their respective pasts. One day, Simcha explained how his bar mitzvah had opened his eyes to spiritual and musical directions.

My teacher, Rabbi Gershon, taught me a lot about the destruction of the Second Temple and the forced exile of our people. I learned the word "lamentation" and to this day it gives me chills.

For my bar mitzvah, the rabbi trained me to recite my haftarah, my allotted portion of the Prophets that would follow his reading from the Torah. I had already learned how to read Hebrew, but the rabbi taught me how to chant it—to make the words come alive. I had no idea the Bible was musical—that the Torah was chanted mostly in a major key, and the haftarah in a minor key. I was just learning to read music and play guitar and I hung on Rabbi Gershon's every word. Sad to report, I never became very adept at reading music, but I always remembered what the rabbi told me about the cantillation marks—the special signs in printed Hebrew texts that indicate accents and how words should be musically phrased. Secret: in my untitled and, so far, wordless opera, I wrote the music as best I could—with the help of a personal code based on the cantillation symbols.

ASTRAL'S RESPONSE

I did not know musical qualities of the Bible, but it makes sense that the Creator would like his words to be like music—the universal. I would like to hear your recording opera—if possible. My heart will deliver a speech.

FOUR LIVES

Astral sent a second response to Jason's message:

Something like your bar mitzvah, I had my confirmation in Lviv, the city of my birth. Sad thing about Lviv: for hundreds of years, conquering nation changed its name and sometimes his personality too. According to Austro-Hungarian government, the city was called Lemberg. Later, after First World War, the city became part of Poland and was called Lwów but returned to Lemberg when the Nazis were. When the Russian arrived, they called the city Lvov. When the Soviet Union collapsed and Ukraine became independent state, the town was renamed Lviv. Four names: Lemberg, Lwów, Lvov, Lviv. Four different personalities imposed. I think I told you, I had four husbands. I used to be ashamed, but no more. My shame is not married four times. I was always looking for happiness—you, Simcha, would understand that. My shame, that I allowed myself to be changed by four men, whom I married. I allowed myself to be who they wanted me to. That was my shame. When I see the various names of my beloved city, I think of my four husbands as four-conquering peoples. But no one stood the test of time. No one had enduring spirit.

This returns me to my confirmation. I had privilege of appearance in St. Nicholas Orthodox Church, the oldest architecture in my city—thirteenth century! In a sense, my church reminds me of destruction of your temple—and also your enduring Jewish spirit. Many times, my strong church—large stone white blocks—suffered fire, flood, unbelieving invaders and local thieves—but its dome still stands and its shining lights still can be seen at great distance.

For my confirmation I sang "The Prayer of St. Michael the Archangel." I am not a musical, but I love to listen to music. I love all musics. My favorite classical is Dvořák's "New World Symphony." It is always a thrill, like soaring over plains and continents. When I listen to this music, I think to myself romantic stories.

I know you will find words to your opera when right time comes. When you do, you will find full voice and be whole. I think, maybe, you will one day hear my voice, something chipmunk! Nevertheless, I hope you like it.

A COPING MECHANISM

One day, Yevgeny invited Hannah to a local pub for an after-work drink. He'd been there once or twice before and knew that the place was friendly and casual—the ambience he thought best. A half hour after their arrival, the pub became crowded, blaring and distractive. Hannah seemed to like it. The noise made it easier for her to retreat behind her placid expression to a place of private thoughts. The next time Yevgeny invited her for an after-work drink, Hannah suggested they return to the same place. Twice more they returned before Yevgeny decided he'd had enough. He craved a place that was quieter, more conducive to intimate conversation.

One evening he asked Hannah if she would like to get a bite to eat instead of a drink. Hannah deliberated a full ten seconds and then agreed, somewhat reluctantly.

Yevgeny led her to the Matreshka Hotel, where the food was fine and the setting decorous. Four times in four weeks they dined together, with no change in their routine or its outcome—a handshake and a wave goodbye.

For Hannah, accompanying Yevgeny for drinks and dinners was part duty, part penance—the price she must pay for being a woman in a man's world. Throughout each conversation she smiled and answered politely, occasionally pausing to give the impression that a particular point or question was meaningful to her.

In his way, Yevgeny also felt the falseness of these polite conversations. He yearned to rip off his mask and reveal his passionate thoughts. Unable to rip and reveal, he obsessed. Many a night he lay awake, recalling Hannah's every mood and manner, assessing whether anything she'd said or done belied even a heartbeat of romantic feeling for him.

With no evidence to support his romantic hope, Yevgeny began to think that Hannah might have a great talent for emotional subterfuge. Like himself, he knew she'd been raised in the Soviet Union under Big Brother's ever-watchful eye. Like himself, he knew she'd had overbearing parents. Considering these factors and more, he convinced himself that poor Hannah had suffered decades of emotional subjugation and was now using a thick veneer of emotional distance as a coping mechanism. He would have to look deeper to discover how she really felt about him.

JASON'S FACEBOOK MESSAGE TO ASTRAL

Thank you for entrusting me to collect your samples. I followed your directions very carefully. It was actually fun. I imagined I was part of some stealth team collecting forensic evidence that could save the world. Even if you don't save the world, I'm sure your scientific research is very important. I'm happy to help! You should receive my package in three days. By the way, I would love to visit Lviv someday. Meanwhile, I would love to hear your voice. When you have the time, please send me a brief audio message on Facebook, even if it's only "Hi, Simcha. This is Astral. Nice to meet you."

ASTRAL'S FACEBOOK MESSAGE TO SIMCHA

Dear Simcha, the package arrived this morning. It looks perfect. You did a good job. Thank you! If my team wins Nobel Prize (just joking), I can fly to U.S. to meet you (if I can get a visa), or I can send you plane ticket to come to Lviv (if they will let you in). Things are very difficult in Ukraine because of war with Russia. [At this point, Hannah thought of Peter and began to cry]. *Anyway, shirts in laboratory and we analyze different samples salt. Wish us luck!* [As soon as she sent the message, she remembered Simcha's request. She took a few seconds to compose herself and then recorded and sent the following audio message:] *Hi, Simcha. This Astral. Nice to meet you. Forgive me if I sound like chipmunk.*

ELEMENTAL IDEAS

The analysis completed, Yevgeny and Hannah learned that the composition of the Saltin salts was similar to that of the salts from the Dead Sea. There were, however, two notable distinctions: the Saltin samples had much larger concentrations of lithium and iodine. The news excited both scientists, especially Yeshevsky, who was more familiar with the many references to lithium and iodine in recent cancer treatment literature.

Lithium (a silver-white, alkali metal, best known for its use in batteries and treatment of bipolar disorders) had already proved helpful to patients with small-cell lung cancer. Though there was evidence to suggest that patients treated with chemo or radiation had high risk of sudden death when treated with lithium, Yeshevsky was intrigued with the idea of testing this highly reactive and flammable substance in his laser-blasting experiments.

He was also intrigued with the Saltin salts' high concentration of iodine, an element that occurs naturally in every human cell and which has been used for generations as an antiseptic.

Because a deficiency of the lustrous, purple-black metal can lead to many cancers (including thyroid, stomach, colorectal and lung), it was long believed that iodine-enhanced table salt could help prevent deficiency-related diseases. However, because iodized salt is bleached and processed, its efficacy as a health supplement has proved negligible. Yeshevsky hoped the Saltin salts' high concentration of naturally occurring iodine might prove more effective in his battle against lung cancer. He and Dr. Belaya prepared for their next round of laser experiments.

"I'm ready when you are," said Hannah.

"Locked and loaded," said Yevgeny, patting the laser. "Let's see what this big boy can do."

DARK SHADES OF MEANING

Hannah regarded Yevgeny as a gentle soul who would not hurt a fly, which is why she found it so disturbing that he used so many violent words to describe his laser experiments: *target* and *kill, battle* and *obliterate, poison* and *annihilate.*

Had she been more self-aware, she might have realized it wasn't his violent words she resented, but the fact that they reminded her of her son's dangerous situation. Six months after Russia invaded Crimea, Peter was drafted into the Ukrainian army and sent east for training. Since then, his only contact with his mother was by occasional email, always redacted by the Army Communications Center: *I am fine, Mother, and in good spirits. We train in small groups with* ██████ *instructors. I am learning how to shoot guns and related tactical exercises. In a few weeks my training will become more specific. I volunteered for medical training, citing my work as your occasional assistant. I will write more when I can.*

Two weeks passed before Hannah heard from him again. The silence was agony. *Hello, Mother. I hope you are well and not worrying too much. I got my wish—I am receiving medical training. I thought this would be a good idea—better than looking for ██████ or close-assault tactics—but it did not occur to stupid me that I would be sent to the front lines near █████ to treat the badly wounded.*

For several weeks Hannah did not hear from him again. Every time Yevgeny referred to his laser as a weapon of destruction, she looked away so he would not see her tears.

P.'S JOURNAL ENTRY

Even though I wore a wig and fake beard and presented a redacted medical file, the medical team at Cosmoenergy recognized me almost immediately. That's okay. In fact, it's preferable. Better they know who I am. It makes it easier.

Yevgeny Yeshevsky is very smart and inventive. So is his very able-bodied assistant, Hannah Belaya. Some of the new techniques they are using to halt my cancer have been her idea. She is beautiful and smart and brave, and I like the way she trembles when I am alone with her. If I want the truth from her, it is good that she fears me. The fright takes over and chases away her guile. But I do not want her to be too afraid. I'm not a barbarian. She is a special woman and I want her to want me. Also, I can't help thinking that with my daughters married and Maria remarried, I need a wife, of sorts—maybe even an actual wife—a beautiful woman who can help manage my health would be perfect.

JASON'S FACEBOOK MESSAGE TO ASTRAL

I hope your lab experiments are going well. I provided you with salt samples from every source I could think of, except one—the caves. The salt in the caves is embedded with other rocks and I did not know how to extract it. I considered sending you a bottle of salt vapors—but that is easier said than done! I think it would be easier for you to come here one day and test the vapors yourself. ☺

I think you would find Saltin interesting. It is a strange, almost otherworldly place. For every object that is salt-corroded, there is a tiny plant in the crack of a road struggling for life. When I first arrived, I saw these extremes as a metaphor for Saltin, a binary sort of place: life or death. Later, when I became familiar with the divided city, I understood that it could also be seen in terms of sin or salvation.

But now I'm beginning to see the city's subtleties and complexities. After all, the two opposed sections, West Saltin and East Saltin, aren't formally separated. They are divided by a shared street that is easily crossed. Some people cross it every day, back and forth—and some never do, as a matter of personal principle. The two towns are like two different scenes in the same snow globe. When things are quiet and settled, you can see the differences distinctly. But when things get shaken, it's almost impossible to tell where you are.

I hope the same wind that blew me here will one day be at your back. Perhaps we can figure this place out together.

JASON'S FACEBOOK MESSAGE TO ASTRAL

One more thing, dear Astral. As I think you know, I am something of a lonely wayfarer. I largely keep to myself. I play guitar. I work on my opera. I read books and newspapers—but I do not do much socializing. If it were not for Facebook, I would have very little human interaction. Perhaps it's sad to say, but Facebook is largely my window on the world. This is how I learn about people. This is how I share.

You have been very open with me about your past and your work, but you share so little about your current life. When I look at your Facebook page, I see charts of our solar system, paintings of winged angels, health and science articles, but not a personal word about you—and not a single photo.

I assume you have your reasons, but the truth is, I want to know more about you. And I want to know what you look like. I want to picture you when I think of you, which is often. I hope you can send me a photo or two. I would treasure it greatly and promise that no one will see it but me.

HANNAH'S SELF-REFLECTIONS

Hannah thought she might tell Jason of her difficult childhood: her beautiful mother made haggard before her time by the impoverishments of Soviet rule and her father's stinting love and violent outbursts.

She thought she might explain how her past impacted her present relations by making her emotionally tentative and noncommittal.

She thought she might tell Jason how she found solace in solitary walks; how she'd found God and Science in nature and discovered they were one and the same.

She thought she might tell Jason about Ruthella, her best friend, a never-married yoga instructor and photographer who had a cottage in the Carpathians near Lake Synevyr; how they sojourned there when they could, walking on tangled paths of immemorial origin, keeping an eye out for forest marten and ermine (which they both thought would make great pets), napping side by side on beds of sun-warmed spruce needles.

She thought she might tell him a great secret: how once—and only once—she and Ruthella disrobed completely on a strand of hidden shore and then swam naked together, except for the nibbling fish and iridescent dragon flies. She did not think she could tell Jason how she and Ruthella shared pots of coffee late into the night, generally avoiding any discussion of men, more likely to argue whether Carpathian vampires inhabited the spirit or astral realms.

SELFIES

Hannah had a bright, multi-mirrored mystical side, but she was not without vanity. The same woman who saw herself as stardust, who yearned to meld with the Oneness, could sometimes stare at her reflection for hours with a fetishist's delight.

This was no contradiction for Hannah. She was Nothing. She was Everything. She was a mass of energized atoms. She was a woman on a crowded bus. She was Hannah Belaya, physician and scientist. She was Astral Love, hopeful heart shining in the dark Cosmos.

At the moment, she was Astral, staring into her bedroom mirror, considering which mood was best for the photo she planned to send Jason. She had decided to send only one photo, but that posed a problem. What single image would show her as womanly, but not conspicuously sensual? Serious but also spontaneous? What single image would convey her desire—after four marriages and four tumultuous unmoorings—for a stable, loving union?

JASON'S FACEBOOK MESSAGE TO ASTRAL

Thank you so much for the photo—I love it! I hoped for two—and you were brilliant enough to send two images in the same photo! It's amazing—almost magical, like some kind of optical wizardry. When I look at the image straight on, I see a strong but sensitive woman. When I look at it from a sharply left angle, I see your strength accentuated, almost to the point of militant aggression. But as I move to the right, your image softens, until, at the far right, your image is one of beaming grace. The photo really is quite extraordinary—very Sphinx-like—not that you are inscrutable, but that you are comprised of such a wide range of highly developed feelings and attributes. That is what I call the whole package!

~Simcha

A SABBATH GUEST

Like many people besotted with unrequited love, Yevgeny bent reality to fit his fantasy. Very soon he was ascribing to Hannah feelings even more passionate and wanton than his own. From his point of view, Hannah's ability to maintain her professional decorum was a miracle of restraint, worthy of his ever-increasing respect and ardor. Still, he hoped to move the relationship along:

Perhaps I should take her someplace more romantic. Not that stupid, noisy pub or that fussy hotel, but a quiet, romantic place—perhaps that elegant French café, just off the avenue? And then it occurred to him: *Perhaps I should invite her to my apartment for dinner.*

And then a monumental idea occurred to Yevgeny. So monumental, he had to sit down to think it through: *Perhaps Hannah might be more to me than the perfect proxy and lover. Perhaps she could be my life partner. Perhaps she could be my wife.*

The idea staggered him. Never before had his romantic mind projected so boldly. *Instead of cooking for her, perhaps I should invite her to a Sabbath meal in my parents' home. I think she would enjoy meeting them. After all, my parents are both doctors, partners in love and science. Hannah would love their new spirituality. The candleflames would seduce her.*

HILLS OF HEBRON

Yevgeny's parents, Boris and Riva Yeshevsky, had lived to a ripe old age and fulfilled most of their shared goals. Together, they reckoned they had only two items remaining on their bucket list: to see their son married and to live their remaining days in Eretz Israel.

Like many recent converts, they were particularly fervent: having read that Hebron was more Jewish than Jerusalem, they wished to live near its ancient hills and to be buried there, as close as possible to the Cave of Machpelah, where Abraham, Isaac, Jacob, Sarah, Rebecca, Leah—Jewish patriarchs and matriarchs—lay for thirty centuries.

But first things first: they were still awaiting approval of their visa applications.

RED-FLAGGED

"When will we know?" Riva asked her husband.

"I don't know," Boris said, throwing up his hands in exasperation.

Thirty-two weeks earlier, husband and wife had gone to the Main Directorate of Migration Affairs to personally submit their applications for a pair of visas to Israel. As both were upstanding citizens, they'd had reasonable expectations of success. But months passed without any official response from the government. Bureaucratic inefficiency might account for a couple months' delay, but thirty-two weeks? That was excessive, even by Russian standards.

Boris and Riva began worrying that something was wrong. They thought their applications might have been red-flagged because of their son's record as a 1980s Refusenik. Privately, they argued that Yevgeny's record should have been expunged long ago; that his misdemeanor was a youthful indiscretion;

that he was now a noted scientist and doctor—and no threat to national security.

"Who do we know who can help?" Boris asked.

Husband and wife had been A-list doctors in Moscow with many government officials among their patients. One Tuesday afternoon they discussed their situation with Riva's cousin, Mikhail Friedmann, an Assistant in the Ministry of Transport, who knew his way around government circles.

"I might be able to help," said Friedmann. "My wife went to school with Olga Borodin, a police colonel, who recently was appointed Director of Migration Affairs. She essentially controls immigration and passports. I'll do what I can and let you know."

Boris and Riva thanked him but knew they should not get their hopes too high. As a married couple they had lived restricted lives behind the Iron Curtain in the 1970s ... tasted hope during the *glasnost* and *perestroika* of the 1980s ... been giddy during the dissolution of the Soviet Union ... but were disheartened, again, during the darkening days of the 1990s when the new Russia seemed to be readying itself for its next Stalin. With P.'s eventual accession to power, followed by his continual self-perpetuation as president, they lost all hope of seeing a free and democratic Russia. This was the backdrop behind their spiritual awakening. After several years of study and preparation, they were keen to make *aliyah*—to move to the Land of Israel, their rediscovered spiritual homeland, where they hoped to spend their remaining years in peace and freedom.

P.'S JOURNAL ENTRY

The trouble with being top dog is that I'm expected to solve every major issue and dilemma. It's ceaseless. Every day brings new problems. One day I have a Pussy Riot. Next day I have falling oil prices. Then Crimea, the Baltics, Aleppo. Every day another headache. And then there's my health. My cancer is still progressing, although it has been slowed. Yeshevsky said he received samples of various citrate salts from China and had begun using them—along with my own cancerous cells—in laser experiments.

All this shit is so wearying. I miss Maria. She knew how to take care of me. Oh well, thing of the past, live and learn.

I have a salt bath scheduled with Dr. Belaya on Thursday. At least that is something I can look forward to.

DARK REVERIES

One late rainy evening, before going to sleep, Hannah stared at Jason's Facebook photos of public cinderblock bathrooms, the kind found in national parks and campgrounds. She imagined him in the shower, lonely and shivering, and yearned to comfort him.

Her heart full of nurturing love, her thoughts turned to her son Peter, somewhere in eastern Ukraine. Dreamily, she imagined an army field hospital, a network of camouflaged tents, Peter in one of the smaller tents, reading. Suddenly, following a clap of thunder, she heard an explosion and a scream, and she imagined Peter splayed on the muddy ground, screaming, his chest torn, a soldier kneeling beside him, fumbling with bandages, Peter's blood spilling into the mud.

Hannah screamed, which startled her cat, which screeched, which shocked her into a shivering consciousness.

KEEPING ABREAST

"There is no such thing as a former KGB man," P. once famously said. Not surprisingly, he'd proudly energized and expanded the old spy department when he became president in 2000, reinventing the KGB into an even more efficiently formidable bureau, transforming its mission from authoritarian oversight to totalitarian control. With his new Federal Security Service (ФСБ), P. could oversee domestic surveillance, border security, foreign intelligence, counter-intelligence, electronic intelligence and state-controlled businesses from a single office: the ultimate in one-stop autocratic management.

Surveilling the offices of the Cosmoenergy Federation and the private communications of its personnel was child's play for a man of his means and meanness.

IN LIFE, AS IN VITRO

Test results using the Saltin salts were promising. Whether Yeshevsky's laser *blasted, obliterated* or *annihilated* P.'s sample cells, the cancer appeared to be shrinking. Still, as with all experiments, the sample size was small. It remained to be seen whether the laser, when trained directly on the affected areas of P.'s lungs, could kill the cancer without killing the patient.

LASER LIGHT

Despite their scientific training, Yevgeny and Hannah regarded laser light with almost holy awe, referring to it as the Wonder Wave, the Living Light, and the Glare of God.

Aside from grand metaphor, they regarded laser light as a great medical tool whose heat could cut tissue and membranes more precisely than surgical blades; sterilize the edge of its target, reducing the risk of infection; and seal blood vessels, reducing bleeding, swelling and pain.

With P. anesthetized on their surgical table, the two doctors injected a solution of Saltin salts into a small mass of cancerous cells in his left lung. After waiting for the salt to alter the cells' pH level, they donned their protective eyewear and focused the laser beam directly on the diseased target.

The salt baths might help, but this was their best shot.

SALT BATHS

The use of saltwater, or even salted water, is not a new-fangled, New Age medical treatment. Way back in the day, Hippocrates, Father of Medicine, noted the healing effects of seawater on the injured hands of fishermen. Ever since, hydrotherapies involving salt have been used to alleviate joint and muscle pain; painful skin conditions, such as psoriasis and eczema; and, more recently, the side effects of cancer radiation treatment.

Safe and relatively inexpensive, saltwater therapies are commonly practiced in spas, holistic centers, health clinics and do-it-yourself home treatments. The *Journal of the American Medical Association* describes salt baths as safe and innocuous but has not published a single empirical study to support its tepid endorsement. Anecdotally, most people who take salt baths claim the experience makes their skin feel pleasantly detoxed and debrided; overall, they say they feel happily relaxed after a treatment. (There is no record of anyone incurring serious harm as a result of a salt bath, other than Melvin Coolidge of Waco, Texas, who—while relaxing unattended and inebriated in his own, private, Deluxe Turbo Spa—succumbed obliviously to the seductive pulse of its jetted salt waters and drowned.)

UNDENIABLE BENEFITS

Although the salt baths provided P. with no calculable benefit (other than a slight uptick on his electrostat), the doctors believed the warm saline waters and attendant vapors provided some soothing relief to his sick lungs. Even so, when Dr. Yeshevsky saw that Hannah was becoming increasingly uncomfortable in her role as chief bath attendant, he told P. that the baths were unnecessary and should be ceased. P. had other ideas.

"I value the baths, doctor. They bring me great relaxation and relief. We will continue them."

A WORTHY COMPLEMENT

With each weekly visit to the Cosmoenergy Federation, P. noted that Hannah was taking on additional responsibilities, quickly progressing from assistant to co-equal. At the beginning of the fourth salt-laser treatment, Yeshevsky turned to her, as if she were his co-pilot, and signaled that she should take control of the machine. P. noted how Hannah beamed with authority and empowerment. *Here's a special woman!* he thought. *Here is a woman who might be useful to me.*

BEST PROTOCOL

Because P.'s cancer was being slowed, the doctors decided that alternating weekly laser and salt bath treatments would be the best protocol to follow. Such a plan would allow them sufficient time to analyze data and adjust their therapies between treatments to maximize effectiveness. P. agreed, reluctantly. He now had to wait two weeks between salt baths.

NAKED AGGRESSION

Leading up to the day of his next salt bath, P. made sure his secretaries booked no conflicting appointments. He needn't have worried. His team knew the time-slot was sacrosanct but could only guess why the President set aside two hours every week to visit the Cosmoenergy Federation. Only his two most-trusted agents, Akhmerov and Zubilin (who always waited for him around the corner, in a black sedan with tinted windows), knew it was a health-related issue that involved a forty-year-old Ukrainian doctor (blonde and divorced), who had a son named Peter in the Ukrainian army, serving in a front-line army hospital. They knew all this (and much more) because they had followed their boss's orders to monitor Hannah Belaya's electronic communications and to tail her each night after she left the office.

As usual, P.'s appointment began with a private meeting with Dr. Yeshevsky to discuss his condition and prognosis. Meanwhile, in a small back room, Dr. Belaya prepared his salt bath. While Yeshevsky blathered on about cell walls, pH balance and metastasis, P. anxiously fingered a CD jewel case in his pocket (recordings of his favorite Russian love songs, along with two versions of "Blueberry Hill," one by Fats Domino, the other featuring himself as pianist and singer, recorded at a charity event).

He looked at his watch and stood. "My bath should be ready now."

Yeshevsky remained seated, feeling craven and useless.

P. stood outside the backroom door, which was slightly ajar. He smiled and rapped twice.

"Please, come in," called Hannah.

She sounds very glad to see me.

"The bath is ready," she said, avoiding eye contact.

Very coy—treats me like any other patient.

He placed the CD jewel case on a small round table beside the bath, where he knew she would see it. She then handed him a large bath towel and stepped outside the room, closing the door behind her. She waited a full two minutes (plenty time for him to take off his clothes, put on his bathing suit and settle into the bath) before she knocked twice, lightly but firmly.

"Come in," he said buoyantly.

As per the previous treatments, she expected him to be in the bath; head propped, legs extended, as if relaxed on a water-chaise in a swimming pool. But he stood before her, starkly naked, even in the dimly lighted room. Her instinct was to avert her eyes but the act felt demeaning, unprofessional, weak, and so she forced herself to make a cursory glance in his direction, as if nothing was special or amiss.

For several seconds he just stood there, proudly wearing nothing but a wig, fake beard and an impressive erection—a thick-chested, grinning satyr.

"Please," she said. "The bath is ready."

Oh, she is a tough cookie, this one!

As soon as P. moved towards the bath, Hannah picked up the CD and turned to insert the disc in the small stereo. She did not turn back to P. until she sensed he was in the bath and mostly submerged.

"Are you ready?" she asked.

"I am ready for you, Dr. Belaya."

Ignoring his suggestive response, she pressed the stereo button to start the music.

"Or, should I call you *Hannah*?" he said over the first few notes.

Pretending she didn't hear him, she said, "The bath lasts ten minutes. I will be back in fifteen. Plenty time for you to get dressed. If you need assistance, please press that red call button on the table." With that, she switched on the bath's whirlpool jets and turned towards the door.

"Hannah, if you don't mind, can you stay a few minutes and listen to the music with me?"

AN IMPERIAL PERK

P. reclined in the hydro-spa like a Turkish sultan, Hannah kneeling behind him on a red silk pillow, reluctantly massaging his shoulders, pulling away her hand whenever P. attempted to lead it further down his chest.

Eventually, P. lay peacefully, luxuriating in the warm, pulsing waters, listening to stereophonic love songs—the unquestioned ruler of the largest country on earth, enjoying an imperial perk.

As soon as the waterjets stopped, Hannah pulled back and P.'s head slipped from its cozy, breast-supported perch.

Without the agitating jets, the salted water became still and nearly transparent. P., lying naked and relaxed, felt suddenly vulnerable. He was glad when Hannah excused herself so he could exit the bath in private.

UNSETTLED

P. took his sweet time drying and dressing. Still, he felt clammy and chafed when he walked his wool suit out of the office.

"See you next week," he called to Yeshevsky, who was standing outside his private office like a hapless sentry.

Yeshevsky nodded, but as soon as the office door closed behind P., he hurried to the back room where he found Hannah inside, fully dressed, though her clothes looked unsettled and damp, as if she had been wrestled and splashed.

"You okay?"

She was on her knees, scrubbing the salty scum from the emptying tub. She did not look up.

Yevgeny picked up the wet towel and tossed it into a bin. He then gave the room a once-over. Seeing that the stereo was still on, he pressed a button that ejected P.'s CD, which he put in his pocket.

When he left the room, Hannah was on her knees, still scouring the tub.

THAT NIGHT

That night, Hannah failed to cry herself to sleep. Every time sleep approached, four thundering horsemen appeared on the horizon of her dreamscape (their pounding hooves synced to her pounding heart), shocking her into wakefulness. Sitting upright in bed—profoundly conscious—she understood the dream's message: she must never allow another man to take from her what she didn't want to give.

That night, Yeshevsky understood he must do everything in his power to help Hannah. It was his responsibility—his profound obligation—to protect her, to save her.

That night, P. realized that he'd become quite smitten with Hannah Belaya. Before sleep overtook him, he outlined a plan to capture her heart.

That night, unnerved by a premonition that Hannah was in danger, Jason turned on his laptop and wrote Astral Love a Facebook message: *Please be careful in these strange times. I hope Fate brings us together. Perhaps, together, we can help save each other.*

~Love, Simcha

OBLIGATIONS

Hannah would not speak to Yevgeny when she left the office after scouring the bath. The next day, she was generally sullen, though even more efficient in her duties.

Yevgeny didn't know what to do. To whom could he appeal? There was no higher authority in his world than P., which led him to think of his parents and their new Jewish god. On that point he remained skeptical: *How can a pair of elderly doctors and life-long empiricists suddenly embrace God without forsaking what they believed all their lives? Was it possible?*

It occurred to Yevgeny that his parents' sudden religious fervor might be an elaborate ruse, something to do with their avowed yearning to move to Israel. He wondered: *Did they need to seem genuine in their passion to convince the Russian authorities to let them go—and to convince the Israeli authorities to let them in?* He wasn't sure. But he was certain they wanted out of Russia and, being Jewish, Israel made sense.

Now middle-aged himself, Yevgeny could see his parents more clearly for what they were: two caring, retired physicians who'd married early and had one child—a precocious son—upon whom they'd heaped all their hopes and dreams. Thinking back through the many years, he recalled their thousand kindnesses and wondered how he could have loved them so little for so long. True, they hadn't supported his Refusenik stance. And true, they hadn't supported his choice to practice alternative medicine. But hadn't they always been generous and protective? Hadn't they played their parental roles as naturally as he had played his role of rebellious son? He wondered: *Shouldn't I reevaluate my feelings now that our roles are reversing, now that they are old and increasingly reliant upon me?*

It suddenly occurred to Yevgeny: *I must do something to repay my parents—before it's too late.*

Thankfully, he knew the two things that mattered most to them: moving to Israel and seeing him married. *How wonderful if I could make both their wishes come true*—a double *mitzvah,* he thought, a word he had only recently learned.

STRATEGIC THINKING

Yeshevsky had his emotional blind spots, but he could also be impressively insightful. Having long lived away from his parents so he could not be controlled—and just beyond the government's reach so he could not be censured—he had become an independent and strategic thinker.

For example, believing that he'd become a person of interest to the highest power in Russia, and that his personal and professional communications were being monitored, Yeshevsky thought he could turn these facts to his advantage. And so:

The evening following P.'s recent salt-bath treatment (after all the staff had left, except Hannah and himself), Yeshevsky handed Hannah a handwritten note and stood beside her while she read it: *I'm going to send you an email tonight from my home computer to yours. Do not take it literally. It is part of a plan I have to help protect you. After you read the email, please write back, thanking me and saying that you look forward to hearing from me again. Trust me.*

Hannah looked at Yevgeny with a mixture of amazement and incomprehension. Yevgeny saw trust in her eyes. He believed they now had a special understanding that boded well for their shared future.

Delicately, he withdrew the note from her hand and placed it on a nearby ceramic plate. He then drew from his pocket a matchbook, struck a match with a recently rehearsed savoir-faire, and put its flame to one corner of the note, which immediately blackened and curled.

Together, Hannah and Yevgeny watched the wisp of upward-trailing smoke.

YEVGENY'S EMAIL TO HANNAH

Dear Hannah,

I never seem to get the chance to tell you how proud and grateful I am for all your extraordinary contributions. Since you joined our staff, you have become indispensable to our success. In fact, I have come to rely on you as an extension of myself. Speaking frankly, I am hard pressed to think of any work-related responsibility that you do not handle perfectly well. Already, you are as proficient as I am in the treatment of our best-known patient. And I recognize that it was your idea to use those citrus salts from China in our laser process. That seems to be the key to our success so far.

I plan to be out of the office on several occasions in the near future. My parents have been waiting a long time for approval of their travel visas to Israel. They are old and may not be the most effective advocates for their case. As soon as I can make an appointment, I plan to visit the Ministry of Transport—and, if possible, speak with the Director of Migration Affairs—to see if I can help get their visas approved.

My parents are well-regarded citizens and deserve this accommodation. Further, they have pledged to work as medical consultants at a new hospital in Hebron, which treats both Israeli and Palestinian patients. It would be a public relations win-win for the Russian government if they could make this small event happen. Ideally, if I can help clear the paperwork for their visas, I would like to travel to Israel with my parents and help install them in their new home.

If I am away for a few days, or a week or so, I am entirely confident in your ability to manage the office and our patients' treatment. I know I am asking a lot, and I know you have gone a long time without a vacation. Perhaps, if the work is slow, you can take a few days between treatments of P. to visit Lviv for a few days. We can stay in touch by email. I will see you when I return.

Gratefully yours—
Yevgeny

HANNAH'S EMAIL TO YEVGENY

Yevgeny,

I am proud that you are confident in my abilities and I thank you for your acknowledgment. If called upon, I will do my very best to carry on in your absence. I await further word from you.

Hannah

P.'S JOURNAL ENTRY

Every day I deal with so much noisy crap: that American Snowden (more trouble than he's worth) the fallout from that downed jet . . . the Americans crying about our interference in their holy elections . . . and now, worst of all, that fool of a new president.

I always knew he'd be trouble. Years ago, he ran a beauty contest in Moscow and got caught with young girls, but I took care of it and kept a record. And then he wanted to build fancy condos in Moscow, so I let him borrow from our bank in Germany. The man's an idiot! But now that he's president, he's a useful idiot. So I'll remind him about the young girls and the money he owes—and then I'll ask him about lifting sanctions, weakening America's alliance with NATO, and pulling out of Syria.

Oh, so much on my mind and still my thoughts fly back to Hannah! Oh, what joy listening to love songs in a warm bath with you beside me! A shame the bath ended before you could hear me sing my favorite song, but I will see you soon for my laser treatment, and a week after that we will have another bath—completely alone this time, if I can get that fool Yeshevsky out of the way.

ACTION AND REACTION

Yeshevsky was right: P. considered him a person of interest and was monitoring his emails and phone calls.

Knowing this, Yeshevsky had correctly predicted that P. would investigate the status of his parents' visas, approve them, and expedite them. He also had correctly predicted that P. would (at long last) approve a visa for him. He was, however, pleasantly surprised that P. had ordered the government to purchase *three,* one-way tickets to Israel, in the names of Boris, Riva, and Yevgeny Yeshevsky. He was even more surprised to learn that the tickets were already at Domodedovo Airport and that the flight to Jerusalem was scheduled to depart in just two days!

Yeshevsky was still reeling from these revelations when he learned that the government had already sent a moving van to his parents' apartment. The four-man team had orders to pack the Yeshevskys' belongings and to see that these were properly transported to the airport and loaded onto Tuesday's Aeroflot Flight 506, departing Moscow at 7:10 A.M.

Yeshevsky had underestimated P.'s pressing desire to establish a clear path to Hannah's heart. And while he'd correctly intuited the amazing reach of the unbridled and unprincipled autocrat, he hadn't reckoned how swift and simple P.'s plan might be. He certainly did not foresee its ultimate consequences. But then, no one could.

Still, it could not be said that Yeshevsky had been out-maneuvered. As part of his own prepared plan, he arranged two more office meetings with Hannah, during which he conveyed (through whispered conversations and handwritten notes—subsequently burnt and flushed down the toilet) his strategy for saving the woman he hoped one day to marry.

YESHEVSKY'S SECOND HANDWRITTEN NOTE TO HANNAH

The next day, Yeshevsky handed Hannah another handwritten note. Once again, he stood beside her while she read it silently.

I am leaving Tuesday morning to accompany my parents to Israel. All the arrangements were made by P. without my knowledge. I don't know his full intentions, but I think it's clear to us both that he wants you—and wants me out of the picture. I'm not by nature an alarmist, but I fear for your well-being. Here's my plan:

Continue coming to work every morning as you always do. Do not change any detail in your habits or schedule. On Monday, I will be out of the office, preparing for my Tuesday departure. I will write you an office email to explain—in official terms—why I'm away and how I hope to continue directing the Cosmoenergy Federation from Israel. I will also email the other staff members to explain my absence.

On Tuesday and Wednesday, you will work as usual—except for my absence. Now, here's the big part: on Thursday you will attend to P.'s laser treatment by yourself. I'm sure he will not distract you—at least not much—he takes these treatments seriously, as he should. After the treatment, remind the other staff that you are going away for three days, visiting friends in Lviv. I will write the staff something similar and designate Dimitri as manager in your absence.

When you go home that night, pack a light travel bag—something you might use for a three-day vacation. The next morning, proceed to Lviv by whatever means or route you usually take. Spend two days with your friends or on your own, whatever pleases you. On the morning of the third day, destroy your cellphone and go to the Lviv International Airport. (Don't worry, before I leave, I will give you a new cellphone, all paid for.) Take a bus or taxi to the airport, pay cash, no receipt. Go to the Lufthansa terminal, where you will pick up a ticket in your name and board your flight to Kennedy Airport, New York City. When you arrive, just relax awhile. Busy yourself in the airport for several hours. Buy a magazine or newspaper to practice your English.

That evening, around six, go to the American Airlines terminal, where you will pick up a ticket in your name to Tucson, Arizona. A friend of mine will meet you at the airport in Tucson. She is a tall, slender black woman named Bethany Church. She's living at the Tucson Yoga and Ayurveda center. You'll stay with her for a few days. She will drive you to California, to Saltin City, where you will meet our mutual friend Jason.

Take this note home with you. Memorize it. Then burn it and flush the ashes down the toilet.

Yeshevsky took the liberty of pressing her hand and then saying aloud (for the benefit of unseen listeners), "Hannah, it's late. Enough work for one day. Go home and rest. I'll lock up."

YESHEVSKY'S THIRD HANDWRITTEN NOTE TO HANNAH

The following evening, Yeshevsky met with Hannah in the office for a third time to continue their planning.

"Do you have any questions?" he whispered softly, his lips close to her ear.

Hannah shivered and shook her head no.

Yeshevsky then handed her another note, and once again stood uncomfortably close to her while she read it. This note described what he thought Hannah should expect to find in Saltin.

I am sure Jason will be helpful, even attentive, but you can decide for yourself in which part of Saltin you want to live: east or west. I understand the choice is changeable.

Wherever you live, I expect you will continue your research. Again, Jason should be helpful in showing you all around the Saltin Sea and what remains of its city.

Through Bethany, I will send all the basic tools and supplies you will need. From Israel, I will buy a laser machine and have it sent to you, when you are ready. As soon as possible, I'll devise a means of getting your salary to you.

Of course, it is my greatest hope to join you when I can.

CHAPTER 3

DIRECTIONS

Driving southeast to Saltin City, the smell of rotten fish is faint, unless the wind is blowing northward and your windows are open, in which case a fishy tang will snag your gill before you get within ten miles of the Saltin Sea's north shore.

At that point, you have a choice: go right on Route 86 (a surprisingly major, four-lane highway that skirts the sea's western shore) or left on Route 111 (a poorly paved, two-lane road that skirts the sea's eastern shore). Midway along the western shore you will pass what remains of the Saltin Civic Center. Midway along the eastern shore you will pass Calpurnia State Prison. Farther south, having encircled the sea, both routes become a single, two-lane road, known as Commonwealth Avenue, which leads into Saltin City. This same road exits Saltin City and leads through what's left of the Saltin National Wildlife Refuge. The road then continues to the Mexican border, where there is a U.S. Border Patrol checkpoint monitoring both northbound and southbound traffic.

THE PALACE

Most of West Saltin's former casino hotels, like the Riviera, La Playa, and Belmonde, had been left to rot and ruin, their windows shattered, their façades and foundations crumbling.

Surprisingly, some of the hotels' original furniture and accoutrements (curtains, dinnerware, mattresses) remained in place, though these were largely degraded from forty years' exposure to sun, salt and mouse shit.

The Palace was the lone exception. The leading citizens of West Saltin made modest exertions to maintain this single citadel of grandeur in order to remember their past and to help pretend they had a future. The most prominent among them inhabited the first floor, the second being reserved for the mayor, ironically referred to as King.

ROOM WITH NO VIEW

Jason chose not to stay at The Palace. Instead, heeding Fred's suggestion, he found a habitable space in one of the nearby derelict hotels, a former supply room, whose thick windowless walls had adequately protected it through the years. In this free haven, across the street from The Palace, Jason laid down his rucksack and guitar case.

Most days, Jason was okay with his situation. He didn't waste a lot of time with regrets and second-guessing. But there were times, usually late in the day, around sunset, when he thought wistfully of the fine house he'd shared with Renee for many years. Ironically, it wasn't the space and amenities he missed, but the company of a woman with whom he could share his hopes and dreams.

MESSAGES FROM THE PALM LUXE

Jason's windowless room on the second floor of the Palm Luxe included a mattress (courtesy of a previous occupant) but no electricity or plumbing. For these amenities he had to cross the street and enter the lobby of The Palace. Once a week he rented a modest room there so he could shower, shave and sleep on a real bed with a fresh sheet. Six days a week he slept in his windowless cell, like a soul-searching penitent.

It was from this room (and from the lobby of The Palace, where the wi-fi was more reliable) that Jason continued his Facebook correspondence with Yevgeny Yeshevsky. Initially, he'd been excited by the idea of connecting with a Russian scientist, but Yevgeny's messages were reserved and, truth be told, a little boring. Jason was beginning to regret this correspondence when he'd been contacted by Astral Love, one of Yevgeny's associates.

He and Astral had hit it off immediately. Of course, he didn't know that she'd been asked by Yevgeny to contact him and to establish a relationship. He didn't know that she'd studied his Facebook page and had seeded her own with details calculated to attract him.

Despite her obvious pseudonym, Jason was impressed by Astral's bio:

"Cosmologist. Scientist. Internationalist. Humanitarian. Music lover." He was also taken by her residence, described as "Here, There, and Everywhere." Almost immediately, he regarded her as a kindred spirit.

Hannah felt the same way about Jason. Although contacting him had been part of a necessary deceit, she was honestly engaged by his portrayal of his life, and she hoped—even more than she realized—that he would respond to her personally, which is exactly what happened.

Jason wrote to her with considerable interest. He was profoundly moved by her revelations of her four failed marriages and how she compared them to the four times her beloved city of Lviv had been conquered and renamed. He loved Astral's soulful descriptions of the Carpathian Mountains and her explanations of her scientific work. Most of all, he loved the way her Google-translated messages were a kind of weird poetry, their odd constructions communicating more honesty (he thought) than conscious artifice ever could.

In turn, Jason shared with Astral the rudiments of his own story. He wrote how his bar mitzvah rabbi was the first to teach him about musical notation. He wrote about his rock-and-roll marriage: the seven prosperous years and the seven lean and childless ones. He wrote how his manager had betrayed him and run off with his wife. He wrote about his years of lonely wandering.

After only a few weeks of messaging each other twice a day (when he awakened and before she went to sleep), both bemoaned the nine time zones that separated them.

Still, it wasn't until Jason received the miracle photo from Astral (the selfie portrait that expressed her entire range of personality, from militant aggression to beaming grace) that he began to fall in love with her. Staring at the photograph, Jason saw no contradiction in the polarities of her character. He saw a complicated, sensitive soul—betrayed, damaged—but still bending to the light.

SHE RECALLED

Hannah recalled (with painful clarity) the previous week's salt bath: how P. had posed nude like a glowering satyr … compelled her to knead his shoulders like a harem girl … used his penis, like a bobbing baton, to keep time to the music … how he'd risen, meek and small when the agitated waters had cleared … how she'd scrubbed the tub like a demon to eradicate every stinking trace of him.

MISSED OPPORTUNITY

(In preparation for P.'s first laser treatment, Dr. Yeshevsky had made three small ports below P.'s sternum to accommodate three invasive surgical tools: a thoracoscope's miniature camera; a device for removing diseased lung tissue; and the laser itself. After each treatment, the ports were temporarily sealed and bandaged.)

P. was all business when he arrived for his next laser treatment, greeting Hannah wryly: "Nice to see you again, Hannah."

Minutes later, he lay on the surgical table, mildly sedated; his heart monitored; his pumping lungs on video display.

Hannah stood over him, staring at the three cables (white, black, silver) that snaked into his three thoracic ports.

It wasn't the Hippocratic Oath or fear for herself that stopped her from frying the bastard's lungs. It was her belief that her sweet son Peter, somewhere in eastern Ukraine, would pay for her moment of weakness; that, and the fact that she would soon be traveling to the United States to meet Jason, her Simcha.

GOODBYE, DEAR PLANTS

Hannah reminded the staff that she would be taking three vacation days to visit friends in Lviv and that Dimitri would serve as manager while she and Dr. Yeshevsky were gone.

That night she packed a light travel bag and the following morning took a train all the way from Moscow to Lviv. The trip took almost twenty-four hours but was inexpensive and gave her time to think. The following day she spent visiting friends at her former clinic and in the early evening met her friend Ruthella at the Coffee Mining & Manufacture café, one of her favorite haunts. On the morning of the third day, she destroyed her cellphone, smashing its memory card with special violence. Before leaving for the airport, she said goodbye to each of her many plants (to be cared for by a neighbor), her tears falling almost as freely as the water from her long-stemmed jug. Given the unpredictable and often violent vagaries of life, she thought she might never see her beloved Lviv again.

IN CHARGE

Hannah and Yevgeny were confident in Dimitri's ability to manage the office in their absence. Though they regarded him as a rock of reliability, neither of them had the slightest idea what he was really like, having never asked him anything about his personal life, beyond its surface facts. To be fair, Dimitri (sweet faced and prematurely bald) did not invite easy conversation; and despite his outward efficiency, seemed always inwardly focused, a living, breathing engine of internal combustion.

Dimitri read Hannah's email with enthusiasm, regarding it as an invitation to demonstrate his leadership qualities. With Hannah in Lviv and dear Yevgeny in Israel, he was in charge. He ruled the roost!

Dimitri was determined to prove to Yevgeny that he deserved to be his right-hand man, not that superfluous bitch with her ensnaring charms—such was his opinion of Hannah since the day she arrived.

KOSHER BREAKFAST

Aeroflot Flight 506, departing Moscow for Hebron, departed promptly at 7:10 A.M. Yevgeny and his parents were happily surprised to find themselves seated together, but they didn't talk much. Their long-anticipated trip had been so suddenly approved that each felt the need to catch their breath after a week of whirlwind preparation. Riva was thinking of their unfurnished apartment in the new settlement. Boris was thinking of the new children's hospital. Yevgeny was thinking about Hannah. Each kept their own counsel until breakfast was served. All three ordered tea and orange juice. Before Yevgeny could complete his breakfast order, his mother put her hand on his and shook her head.

"Just tea and orange juice for the three of us," she said to the pretty stewardess. And then, to Yevgeny, "We were going to order kosher, but our friends said the airline makes it awful, so we brought our own food. We have for you too."

HANNAH EN ROUTE

Hannah walked six blocks to the bus station, where she paid cash for a ticket to the airport. (Other than her light travel bag, she'd left everything behind, including her photo albums, spiritual plaques and tokens, and keepsakes of Peter's childhood.) At the airport, she walked directly (but unhurriedly) to the Lufthansa terminal, where she picked up a ticket in her name. Two hours later she boarded her flight to Kennedy Airport, New York City. Despite the wide seat, personal entertainment controls and caring stewards, she never felt comfortable, suspecting everyone on the plane of being a Russian agent.

She breathed a bit easier after landing on American soil and proceeding through Customs. After walking down a long concourse of brightly lighted shops, she entered one to try on a pair of expensive shoes and another to sample a new perfume. Her goal was to appear like any other forty-year-old American woman, and she would have, had she not used a pocket mirror every five minutes to check her makeup, turning it left and right to see if she were being followed.

After an hour she needed to use a bathroom. Thinking the women's restroom would be a safe haven, she sat awhile without fear of being spied on, turning the pages of an American magazine about famous people, most of whom she did not recognize. Eventually (her back aching, her bottom chafing, her stomach empty) she went looking for a more comfortable place to rest and soon found an American diner. Using her most careful English (and trying very hard not to sound like a chipmunk), she ordered a Bavarian ham sandwich, a salad with Russian dressing, and a large cup of French vanilla coffee—foods that sounded European. Based on the meal's appearance, she had ordered well. But the ham was artificially sweetened; the "Russian dressing" was a sweet goop; and the coffee tasted like a candy drink that had been boiled, not brewed. All in all, she thought the fault was hers; in time she would be more knowledgeable and discerning.

For a couple hours she sat in the diner, practicing her Americanization by studying several other weekly magazines, occasionally looking up words on her laptop's online dictionary. (She understood spoken and written English surprisingly well but knew she would occasionally struggle to make herself understood.)

That evening, around six, she walked to the American Airlines terminal, where she picked up a ticket in her name to Tucson, Arizona.

BETHANY CHURCH

Flying over the United States, Hannah saw rolling meadows, quilted farmlands, soft brown mountains and quiet rivers. Even the clouds seemed light and welcoming. Near the end of the flight, as the plane approached the airport, she continued staring out the window, admiring large houses with well-tended lawns, tennis courts, blue swimming pools and green golf links. For the moment, it was easy to forget her recent memories of Lviv: wounded soldiers; long lines at the market; barbarous men calling to her.

Hannah closed her eyes and thought of Bethany Church. Yevgeny had said very little about her, other than she was tall, slender and black. Hannah imagined how Bethany would stand out in Lviv, or even Moscow, but wondered if she would be easy to spot in a crowd of Americans.

A half hour later, Hannah emerged from the exit tunnel into the crowded terminal, dazed by the sudden brightness and din of foreign voices. Bethany Church was waiting for her with an outstretched hand. She was unmistakable.

"Hello, dear Hannah. I am Bethany. Let me help you."

MANY LIVES

Just over six-feet tall, wearing plain hemp sandals and a simple white dashiki, Bethany led Hannah out of the terminal toward her car, parked in a distant lot. As they walked, Bethany asked Hannah no questions but talked only of herself. Also fortysomething, Bethany told Hannah that she was a fashion model; designer; dancer; photographer; women's rights activist; supporter of indigenous, women-made products; and Ayurvedic healer.

"So many lives you lived!"

"And still live," said Bethany. "They are all part of me."

Hannah nodded knowingly. "And man?" she asked.

Bethany's laugh was loud and resonant, as of battles survived and memories preserved.

"At present, only in my mind—not in my bed."

They gave each other winks and linked arms, like sisters.

ON THE ROAD

Belying her simple attire, Bethany's car was a luxury sedan with leather seating, burled wood dashboard, yellow Bakelite knobs, and all the latest electronics. Bethany showed Hannah how to customize her bucket seat and temperature controls, then pushed a round black button that started the engine with a silky purr.

Sitting in a magical car with a giant black woman and Ayurvedic healer, flying through the American southwest of sand and buttes and flowering cacti, Hannah forgot all about Russian agents, at least for a while.

YEVGENY IN HEBRON

Upon arrival at Jerusalem International Airport, Boris, Riva and Yevgeny were brought to a special room and processed by special Israeli agents who then handed them off to a pair of Israeli soldiers who drove them to a new settlement in the Jewish sector of Hebron (a Palestinian city in the West Bank), navigating through several security checkpoints along the way.

The new settlement (only seventy-two units) was on a hillside, within sight of the Cave of Machpelah (where the holy Jewish Patriarchs and Matriarchs lie interred for thousands of years). Yevgeny was grateful that the authorities had jumped the waiting list to get his parents housed in a choice two-bedroom apartment. Still, he had not foreseen that he would be living with them, sharing their apartment, as he had when he was a boy. At the moment he was alone in his room, the smaller of the two bedrooms (the one without its own bathroom), trying hard to accept his new circumstances: a fifty-year-old man in a little boy's room.

He worked hard to get acclimated. Yevgeny cared little for his personal furnishings (he let his mother see to them) but made a point of quickly setting up a modem for reliable phone reception and internet access. That accomplished, he was able to maintain operations of his Cosmoenergy Federation (very important, given his thirty-thousand worldwide subscribers) while also managing his Moscow office (helped hugely by the fact that Israel and Moscow shared the same time zone, which he only just realized).

It was Monday. On Thursday morning he knew Hannah would write an inter-office email to explain that a sudden illness had delayed her return and that Dimitri would perform the laser treatment when the patient arrived that evening. By that time, he knew Hannah would be in Bethany's care, somewhere in the American Southwest.

Yevgeny was satisfied with his plans. He had protected Hannah from an immediate threat while also providing for her ongoing professional needs. Further, he had protected himself (ethically and legally) by having prepared his staff to continue P.'s laser treatments and salt baths.

Though he had done what he could, he had no idea how far P. would go to get what he wanted.

ON THE ROAD

On the northwest trip from Tucson Airport to the Yoga and Ayurveda center, the weather was perfect and the two women continued chatting warmly. Though Bethany did most of the talking, Hannah shared a few facts about her career and her beloved Lviv, but did not mention her four husbands or a word about her son. Hannah liked Bethany but did not want to be loose-lipped. She did not know what—if anything—Yevgeny had told her about the laser-salt treatments or whether he had mentioned P. Hannah did not think Yevgeny would have mentioned P., but she couldn't be sure. Clearly, he had told Bethany about Jason Stevens, but Hannah did not know how much he had shared. Did he tell Bethany that she and Jason had already established a deep, personal connection through Facebook? *No,* she thought. Yevgeny might guess at that, but he couldn't possibly know.

SAGUARO

Though Bethany knew Hannah would be staying with her for a few days, she wanted to extend their present trip for the sheer delight of its novelty. Driving slowly through Tucson National Park, she pulled off the highway several times to follow some byroad into the Sonoran Desert.

"Oh my God," said Hannah. "The plants! You say *cactus*?"

"Yes, but a special kind. We call these suh-wah-ro. What do you think?"

"Beautiful, but so many." Hannah had seen pictures of saguaro before, usually one or two at a time, but she had not expected to see a thousand of them together.

"They can weigh five hundred pounds and live two hundred years."

Hannah looked at the great expanse of saguaro and started to cry, as she usually did when she happily imagined herself a small part of the magnificently great universe.

NEVER TOO OLD

A few days after their arrival, Yevgeny went with his parents to visit the Cave of Machpelah, hiring an English-speaking docent to guide them. (In the past couple months, Hannah,

Yevgeny and his parents had all worked hard to improve their English skills. Hannah wanted to communicate with Jason without the crutch of Google Translate; Yevgeny wanted to master English, the most common language of his Federation's international membership; Boris and Riva believed they were too old to master Hebrew but might manage with English, with which they already had some facility.) As they approached, Yevgeny was immediately struck by two gigantic facts: the Cave of Machpelah isn't a cave at all but a huge, above-ground, multi-level sanctuary with two blue-domed minarets, all surrounded by high crenellated walls.

"One, two, three," said his father, counting the stone steps that led a long way up to the burial site. He stopped on the seventh step and turned to face his wife and son. "Seven hundred years ago, the Muslims took control of Hebron. They declared this holy place a mosque and would not let Jews enter. In fact, Jews were not allowed past this seventh step." With that, he continued climbing and counting: "eight, nine, ten—" Yevgeny followed him, and with each step felt a deepening of his own Jewish rootedness.

Later, during their guided tour, there was much talk of the great souls buried within. After the riveting account of how God had miracled Sarah's ancient barrenness into Isaac's birth, Yevgeny's mother turned to him, "You see, Yevgeny, it's never too late. By Abraham's standards, you are still a boy. Plenty time to marry and have children—if you hurry."

Not surprising, Yevgeny's thoughts turned to Hannah. He knew she had a son (she had admitted as much to P. when he'd assailed her with questions) but she had never told him, which pained him, deeply. Perhaps (he thought) she could bear another child. She wasn't too old. Not even half as old as Sarah.

YOGA AND AYURVEDA CENTER

Everything about the place bespoke balance and wellness: hot desert sunlight and cool stone floors; exercise and meditation; swept gravel and tended patches of green; brass chimes and polished woods; fiery spices and healing herbs; guided nutrition and informed abstinence; inhaling and purging.

"You will stay three days," said Bethany. "I will help you relax and strengthen. You know massage?"

Hannah did not understand her meaning.

"You know *abhyanga*?"

Hannah smiled. She was familiar with oil massage therapy.

"You know steam therapy?"

Again, Hannah shook her head.

"Ah, you know *svedana*?"

Hannah smiled, and then frowned. She had used steam therapy to treat P.

"Yes, I know."

Bethany nodded. "For three days we shall teach each other. And then I will take you to Saltin City, where you will meet Jason."

Hannah brightened at the news.

AKHMEROV AND ZUBILIN

P.'s pair of personal security agents waited several hours (while their boss was being briefed by representatives of Syrian President Assad and Turkish President Erdogan) before telling him that Dr. Belaya was still on vacation in Lviv and would not be present that evening to supervise his laser treatment. Hearing the news, P. remained impassive. Akhmerov and Zubilin, sensing his disappointment, trembled while awaiting his eventual response: "Find her."

AN INWARD GLANCE

P. had not been surprised when Maria told him he was a terrible husband and she was filing for divorce. In fact, he'd expected it. Believing that his KGB training and autocratic responsibilities had made it impossible for him to be faithful and considerate, he was able to let her go with a clear conscience. Still, as he watched his once-beloved Maria pack her things, he thought he might be a bit more sensitive and understanding in the future—if he ever found another woman he cared about.

These thoughts had been on his mind since his last salt bath with Hannah. Passing her on his way out the door, he thought she'd seemed upset. He said nothing at the time because he'd been so surprised. He thought he'd impressed her with his generous effort to make a CD mix of his favorite Russian songs and with his brave ardor. But now, learning that she would not be present to supervise his upcoming laser treatment (and already suspecting that she might be thinking—or have already acted—on more radical ways to avoid contact with him), he gave serious thought to how he could make things right with her. He could not bear to think that Hannah might also have packed her bags and walked out of his life.

BETHANY'S ADVICE

After three days of wellness sessions, long walks and endless conversations over tea, it was time for Bethany to transport Hannah to Saltin City. She herself had never been there but had Googled the place and learned many things about its curious history and a few things about its current situation. For the past three days she had also been exchanging emails with Dr. Yeshevsky, who was writing from Israel on what he believed was a secure line. She explained all this to Hannah.

"I know about the salts. I know Jason sent you samples. I know you intend to continue your research. I know about P."

Hannah looked surprised.

"You are wondering why Dr. Yeshevsky told me so much?"

"Yes. I am thinking."

Bethany nodded. "Dr. Yeshevsky wants to make sure you remain safe and productive in Saltin. I'm only five hours away, and I have friends in San Diego and in Mexico. That's one reason why he asked me to help you."

"One reason?"

Bethany smiled. It seemed Hannah understood more than her limited verbal skills suggested. Assuming (correctly) that Hannah wanted to hear more, she continued:

"Years ago, I had terrible asthma."

Bethany mimed a fit of labored breathing. Hannah nodded to show she understood.

"It got so bad, I couldn't dance. I couldn't even work a long day as a photographer."

Hannah nodded sympathetically.

"I didn't know what to do. The injections weren't working. The inhalants weren't working. My doctors didn't know what else to prescribe. So I started exploring alternative treatments and that's when I learned about the Cosmoenergy Federation. I was very impressed by what I'd read and so I wrote to Dr. Yeshevsky to learn more. He was very polite and caring, and his emails were charming because his English wasn't very good at that time. But he was so earnest, he tried so hard, you understand?"

Hannah nodded. She understood well enough.

"Eventually, we set up a long-distance, doctor-patient relationship. He's very good with technology, as I'm sure you know."

Again, Hannah nodded.

"He's very warm and friendly, and with live video-conferencing I felt like I was with him in his office."

Hannah recalled the days when she was first getting to know the Great Yeshevsky (as she'd thought of him then). He was indeed very charming and very brilliant.

"He was very interested in my asthma. He told me he had a new method of treatment and asked if I'd be willing to try it. I was desperate and told him so. He said we should get started right away and when I agreed, he asked me to take a blood test and send him the results. I told him I would and later that same day he sent me an email with a list of additional data markers he wanted measured—things not usually associated with asthma. Also, he asked me to send him a complete list of everything I ate for two weeks—every snack, every piece of gum, anything that went into my mouth."

Despite the fact that she herself was a doctor and scientist, Hannah felt the conversation was too personal; she did not need so many details.

"Well, bottom line, he designed a personal course of treatment for me—and it worked! My asthma is so much better now, I am barely aware of it. I don't feel hampered in any way. I can dance" (she twirled about) "and I think I could make love all day, if I wanted." She gave Hannah a wink.

Hannah stared at Bethany, who was tall, black and exotically beautiful. She saw herself as a fading blonde and a tad stocky.

"And get this: Dr. Yeshevsky wouldn't accept any payment from me. Not a penny. He said he had tried some new ideas as part of my treatment and was gratified that they had worked. I was thrilled, of course, and wished I could thank him in person. But for some reason he could not leave Russia and I never got the chance. We've stayed in touch through email, Facebook and his Cosmoenergy website."

Hannah listened, refraining from further comment.

"I feel so grateful to Yevgeny. What I learned about Cosmoenergy inspired me to explore other wellness methods. Over the years I discovered Ayurveda, which has brought me so much health and happiness. I thank Yevgeny for healing my body and soul."

Hannah nodded uneasily. Twice Bethany had referred to Dr. Yeshevsky as *Yevgeny,* causing Hannah to wonder if there was anything romantic between them.

"I owe him a lot. I know he is now in Israel. When he asked for my help—and when I learned that it meant helping a sister in trouble—I told him I'd do everything I could."

"Thank you, my Bethany friend."

"You're welcome," Bethany said, wrapping Hannah in a long-armed hug.

Hannah was uncomfortable with the embrace but grateful for the break in the conversation. So much English at one time was difficult and tiring, and this conversation had been strangely unsettling.

AKHMEROV AND ZUBILIN

P.'s pair of personal security agents had grown close to each other over the years. Like their boss, they'd had their initial training and service in the KGB and had refined their skills in the FSB. (Both were masters of disguise, martial arts, surveillance, computer hacking and a wide range of weaponry.) When P. was first elected president, he chose them for the Presidential Security Service (SPB) that oversaw his own safety and that of his family. Over the years they had become his most trusted personal agents, priding themselves in their willingness to take a bullet for their leader. P. knew of his agents' willingness to take a bullet for him and applauded their dedication.

Having exhausted all available rationales, Akhmerov and Zubilin finally told P. that Hannah would not return to Moscow from Lviv in time for that evening's laser-salt treatment.

"We think she is *in the wind,"* said Akhmerov, using his favorite American spy jargon. "She's *off the grid,"* said Zubilin, backing up his partner.

"Find her," P. repeated.

CHAPTER 4

GOODBYE AND HELLO

Bethany drove through the desert shrub of southern Arizona into southernmost California. The traversed desert was a limited spectrum of sere browns and yellows, but there were occasional patches of colorful wildflower bloom and bright ferric striations in the hills. Some veteran travelers find the landscape monotonous but Hannah saw the passing panorama as endlessly fascinating, even if she didn't know a mesquite from a mesa.

During the last leg of the journey (Route 78 North) the women passed through the Saltin National Wildlife Refuge before entering Saltin City. GPS put them on Commonwealth Avenue and they drove its full length north until they reached the southern shore of the Saltin Sea. The scene took their breath away. Aside from the apparent schizoid urban planning (corroded casino hotels on the left, corroded churches on the right), the sea itself was a salt-encrusted wasteland.

Bethany parked on Commonwealth Avenue, near the remains of the boardwalk. Below the boardwalk were remnant waters of the Saltin Sea: small lagoons where visitors might enjoy mud baths and therapeutic springs. The smell of putrefied fish was not so pungent here, as the wind tended to blow north.

"I shouldn't stay long," said Bethany.

"I understand," said Hannah. "I be okay. Jason knows I am coming."

"He found you a place to stay?"

"Yes. He knows an old man, a fisherman, who works like local guide. The old man told him a good place."

Hannah reached into her pocket and withdrew a small piece of folded paper.

"I don't know how to say it," Hannah said, unfolding the paper and handing it to Bethany.

Bethany pronounced the words on the paper: "Covenant House."

"Covenant House," Hannah repeated.

"Okay," said Bethany. "Give me your cellphone." Hannah handed Bethany her phone, which she had received from Dr. Yeshevsky only a week before. Bethany reached into her stylish shoulder bag, withdrew another cellphone, and gave it to Hannah.

"Here is a new phone. Do not call me. Do not call anyone you know in Russia or Ukraine or Israel. The call could be traced back to you. This is what Yevgeny told me to tell you."

"What is the phone use to me?"

"You can use it to make local calls and send messages. Avoid using your old laptop. Yevgeny will buy you a new one. Download Facebook and set up a brand-new account and use it to send messages to me. If you and Yevgeny need to speak with each other, use the private feature of the Cosmoenergy message board. Avoid naming people and places, if possible."

Before them the almost empty Saltin Sea stretched to the horizon: no water, no boats, no birds. It was a quiet place, but uncalming. The stillness made them both uneasy.

"I must go now," said Bethany. "I will return in a week to bring you most of the equipment and supplies you will need for your continuing research."

"You are very good to me—and to Yevgeny."

Bethany smiled, turned and walked to her car. Hannah watched as she made a U-turn and headed south on Commonwealth Avenue.

TWO EXCEPTIONS

Most of East Saltin's sanctuaries and houses of worship, like The Nazarene, The Grove and House of Galilee, had been left to rot and ruin, their tolling bells rusted, their buttresses sagged, their bemas and baptisteries dusty and cracked. Surprisingly, much of their original furniture and accoutrements (pews, candelabra, religious texts) remained in place, though these were largely degraded from forty years' exposure to sun, salt and mouse shit.

Covenant House and The Mount were the lone exceptions. A small group of determined women had continually maintained Covenant House as a women's-only residence. The Mount was the other exception. The leading male citizens of East Saltin made modest exertions to maintain this single bulwark of godliness in order to remember their sins and the proper pathway to salvation. Most of these citizens inhabited the first floor, the second floor being reserved for the mayor, sometimes referred to as the Pope, or His Holiness.

COVENANT HOUSE

From the look of their belted white tunics, the staff appeared to be an order of Catholic nuns. In fact, none of the women had taken vows or even had religious training.

Their mission was moralistic, not theistic. Their motto, memorialized in a large, plainly stitched needlepoint, hung conspicuously in the front parlor:

COVENANT HOUSE
Where men cannot deceive our daughters

All temporary female residents were referred to as *daughters*. Permanent residents were referred to as *sisters*. The head of the establishment was called *Mother*. Any female who requested shelter was admitted, although anyone seeking long-term residence was expected to contribute to the upkeep of the House. The original behest provided Covenant House with an endowment meant to last "until the end of days" (provided the invested principal continually earned an effective yield of three percent and expenditures were budgeted).

The building was elegantly yesteryear, modeled after a well-known, nineteen-century Parisian home for "fallen" French girls. In its heyday, as many as a dozen daughters resided there, not counting staff. On this day, while Hannah sat in the front parlor filling out a brief application, there was only one daughter in residence, along with two elderly Sisters and a Mother, who was referred to in reverent tones.

In addition to the application, Hannah was given a document that listed the rules, which were few but inflexible:

No music, games, etc., on Sunday

Curfew—11:00 P.M.

No man past the parlor

After asserting that she understood the terms and rules, Hannah was given a tour of the community room, exercise room, library and chapel, before being shown to her room, which was small and spare but included a single, unbarred window and a private sink. There was no closet or mirror. The bathroom was communal and down the hall.

Hannah sat on her bed (one pillow, threadbare sheet, thin yellow blanket) for two minutes. Finally, she sighed, stood, and began removing her possessions from her travel case and arranging them into a small, three-drawer bureau. She placed her health and hygiene items on the single shelf by the sink.

After all her personal effects had been arranged, she sat again on her bed, thinking of all that happened since she had left Lviv.

Several minutes later she powered on her new phone, accessed the internet (thank God there was a connection—she had forgot to ask), downloaded the Facebook app and checked for messages. There were three.

FACEBOOK MESSAGE FROM JASON

Hello, Astral! Have you arrived yet? I am sitting in my room like a nervous little boy. I cannot wait to meet you, but I think we should wait. It might not look so good if we are seen together right away. No one should know how we met online. No one should know you are here to study the special salts. I like your story: you have weak lungs and your doctor prescribed salt vapors and baths. No one will suspect that story. Other people come here for that same reason. Anyway, send me a message when you are settled into Covenant House. I will have my friend Fred meet you and show you around. As you know, Fred manages the Civic Center—which, like almost everything else in Saltin, sounds more impressive than it is—but he knows Saltin well and will give you a tour. That's it. I'm looking forward to meeting you! Oh, one more thing. What name will you be using publicly? I think "Astral Love" would stand out more than you might like, though I do like the sound of it.

TEXT MESSAGE FROM BETHANY

I hope all went well with Covenant House. No hurry to respond. Write only when you must. Also, I suggest you delete all messages after you read them.

PRIVATE MESSAGE FROM YEVGENY (VIA COSMOENERGY MESSAGE BOARD)

My dear, I hope this message finds you well. I am temporarily sharing an apartment with my parents. We live in the Jewish section of Hebron, a Palestinian city in the West Bank, not so far from Jerusalem. The other day we visited the place where the great Jewish Patriarchs and Matriarchs lie buried. I was especially moved by the story of Sarah. Did you know she was ninety years old when she gave birth to Isaac? You see, age is but a number!

By the way, I heard it did not go so well when P. came for his laser-salt treatment. He was not happy that Dimitri was the presiding doctor—and not you. He made threats. Dimitri made two things clear to him: He had no idea where you are (the truth) and he was the only other person (besides me and you) who knows how to prepare the cells and use the laser (also the truth). I worry about Dimitri. I regret involving him, but he is a doctor and P. is our patient.

I hope all will go well with your research. I have heard strange things about Saltin and I'm interested in what you think. I'm interested in everything about you.

Yevgeny

P.'S JOURNAL ENTRY

Even though I knew it was a laser treatment and not another salt bath, I was very disappointed to hear that Hannah would not keep our appointment. With Yeshevsky banished to Israel (reports say he lives in Hebron with his parents), I had expected Hannah to greet me. I had expected to be alone with her. In fact, I had been bursting with excitement before I was told she would not be there and was likely gone. Shocked and angry, I insisted on going to the Cosmoenergy office as if I suspected nothing. My agents pleaded with me not to go. Something could happen, they said. It is dangerous, they said. I must not take such a risk, they said. But I needed to see for myself. If it is true—that my Hannah has fled or was abducted or something else—I want to know all who are accountable.

AKHMEROV AND ZUBILIN

The two agents understood their orders: find Hannah or find another job. They were grateful for the second-chance. (In the old KGB days, their apparent slip-up would have left them *Permanently Reassigned.*)

P. gave them the time and tools to succeed. He gave them leave from his personal security team ("Agents Bely and Belkin will take your place") and upgraded their security clearance ("The Bureau will assist you any way it can").

Finding Hannah was their one and only mission.

They began with standard avenues of investigation: They examined Hannah's phone records. They interviewed everyone who worked at the main office of the Cosmoenergy Federation, along with her landlord and all known associates. They searched her Moscow apartment. They looked everywhere for her computer—but it was gone. They surmised she used a laptop or tablet—or both—and had taken it with her. In any case, the missing hardware was only a minor impediment. Enlisting the assistance of supremely gifted Bureau hackers, they soon had access to all her contacts, downloads and internet browsing history. They learned nothing relevant but were not surprised. Moscow was not Hannah's comfort zone. They would have to go to Lviv to explore her natural habitat. Besides, that was the last place they had her located.

The two agents decided to visit Lviv, compiling a list of people and places to investigate. They were most interested in examining her apartment. When they arrived (with lock-pick tools and false police papers), they examined every closet, every drawer, every shelf—everything that could be turned inside-out or upside-down. They photographed extensively. They checked almost every object and surface for fingerprints. They bagged all papers for further scrutiny, even coupons and receipts. Three pieces of evidence seemed particularly promising: (1) a photo album of her life, including pictures of her confirmation at St. Nicholas Orthodox Church, four sets of wedding photos (though none showing a husband), snapshots of a baby/boy/young man, presumably her son; (2) an army induction notice for a Peter Belaya, presumably her son; (3) postcards from friends in Greece and Poland.

To help determine where Hannah might have gone, the two agents wanted to check recent security video from car rental agencies, rail and bus terminals, border crossings and the airport. But they faced three significant problems: (1) Ukraine was a sovereign nation and most of Lviv's civil employees would not willingly cooperate with a request for assistance from Russian operatives; (2) Even if they had access to the videos, it would take a long time to review them all; (3) Wherever Hannah wanted to go, she was probably already there.

MOTHER MARY

Standing behind the top-floor window of her apartment, Mother Mary watched Fred knock on the front door of Covenant House.

The woman formerly known as Tova recognized Fred immediately. (Through the years she had managed to occasionally spy on him from a distance, which gave her the sense of having grown old with him.) On seeing Fred right in front of the House, within easy reach of his voice, her feelings were oddly mixed. He looked handsome, as she remembered him, but (unlike forty years ago) his knocking and inquiry were not meant for her but for the fading blonde who only yesterday had sat in the parlor, smiling sweetly as she filled out her application for residence. The woman formerly known as Tova felt a prick of jealousy, though she would not have recognized the feeling as such. *Something doesn't smell right,* is what she thought. She would keep an eye on that woman. As Mother Mary, she had her responsibilities.

FORK IN THE ROAD

Thirty years earlier, Tova had left her job as a financial analyst to follow Fred to Saltin, as per their agreement. Fred had hoped the booming casino economy would suit him better than the cutthroat corporate world where she worked and where he had tried but failed to succeed. Ironically, while Tova recognized that her well-remunerated corporate career had been grueling and bruising (and had left her overworked and emotionally unrewarded), she disrespected Fred for not having what it takes to succeed in such a pernicious environment. That was her surface thinking. But there was more that was deeper. What really irked Tova was that Fred's failure to succeed had prevented her from leaving her well-paying corporate position years earlier when she might have been able to have a baby: for it was motherhood, not money-making, that promised Tova the greatest reward. She never explained any of this to her husband. Instead, and for many years, she nursed the private regret that Fred had ruined her best chance at happiness and fulfillment. It was angry futility that spurred her to quit her job and to follow Fred to Saltin.

She'd been driving south on Route 86 when she came to a fork in the road, just as Fred had described. She could bear right, remaining on Route 86, or she could bear left and take Route 111. Both roads led around the Saltin Sea to Saltin City. At that moment she could not remember which road Fred had told her to take. Or maybe she did. Maybe this was the moment—that led to the choice—that would separate them for forty years. Whatever her reasoning, or confusion, she turned left onto Route 111, a poorly paved, two-lane road that skirted the sea's eastern shore.

About ten miles down the road, Tova saw a sign for Calpurnia State Prison. In a sense, the sign was unnecessary, for the prison's hulking presence announced itself: a large, bunker-like facility with high walls; menacing towers fitted with searchlights; and a wide perimeter of razor-topped fencing. Driving by, she imagined what horrors might compel a person to attempt escape. Continuing alone towards her uncertain future, she had the oddest feeling that she herself was an escaping prisoner.

CALPURNIA STATE PRISON

Calpurnia State Prison was the first female-only prison in California, an experimental departure from those facilities where male and female inmates were segregated by gender in separate cell blocks but housed under a single roof.

The idea of a female-only prison was progressive for its time but had not fully accounted for the atavistic and ungovernable hunger of male guards who constituted the majority of correction officers and who raped and tormented the female inmates at will. Despite these horrors, Calpurnia's male warden and all-male board of directors boasted of the institution's advanced educational and correctional programs, especially those for unwed mothers and inmates convicted of nonviolent first offenses. One of these programs was an early-release system that allowed vetted inmates to leave Calpurnia for Covenant House in nearby East Saltin to complete their sentence under the vigilant supervision of the Covenant staff and a female probation officer who visited once a week.

Thirty years ago, one such prisoner, Caitlin Connor (convicted of selling her boyfriend's bowling trophies and beer bottle collection to pay for her drug habit), had been a halfway resident of Covenant House for all of two months when a woman on the street approached her, just as she was leaving the House to begin her daily two hours of unsupervised freedom.

"I think I'm lost," said Tova. (Having just arrived in East Saltin and not seeing anything like the ritzy casinos Fred had described, Tova had parked outside beautiful Covenant House to ask for directions.) "I'm looking for a man in West Saltin."

"Yeah," said Caitlin, smiling. "You sound lost."

CAITLIN AND TOVA

Caitlin told Tova that she'd never been to West Saltin, even though it was only a few blocks away, just the other side of Commonwealth Avenue.

"Why's that?" Tova asked.

Caitlin explained how she had arrived at Covenant House by way of Calpurnia State Prison. She then explained how West Saltin's gambling and ungodly ways made it off limits to her; in fact, visiting there would violate her special probation status and could send her back to prison. (She shuddered at the thought.)

During those two hours of outdoor freedom, Caitlin told Tova the story of her life and told it truthfully, which made Caitlin feel good for the telling and made Tova feel good for the listening.

The two women related to each other. Despite the differences in their ages and backgrounds, they saw themselves as two souls on the same spectrum: wily and willful, wounded and wanting. They also recognized that it was the bond of their femaleness, more than any other attracting similarity, that drew them together.

LIFE SAVER

While Caitlin talked, she led Tova on a perfunctory tour of East Saltin, describing each landmark dismissively, for she had come to despise these bastions and totems of paternalistic power.

"Look around," Caitlin had said. "What a nightmare! Everywhere you look is a tribute to a male god, a male prophet, a male saint. Only men could have built this horror show. It's just another kind of prison."

Caitlin shook her head sadly. "There's only two attractions here that feature women: an exhibit of Miriam launching baby Moses into the Nile, and a statue of Mary looking up at Jesus and weeping rigged tears."

"How do you stand it?" Tova asked.

"Covenant House. It saved my life."

A RESPECTABLE POSITION

Tova arrived at Covenant House in an emotional quandary. She loved Fred, she supposed, but their marriage hadn't been working. She was willing to concede that neither of them was wrong; they just weren't right for each other, or had failed to make it right.

She'd had these thoughts for a long time. She'd had them all the years she'd been triumphing while Fred stayed home, swilling beer after beer, depressed by his failure to land a job worthy of his intelligence and skills.

EXISTENTIAL CRISIS

When Tova entered Covenant House (already older than most of the other women) she'd made it clear that her stay would likely be short. She still planned to go to West Saltin to meet her husband.

But thirty years would pass before Tova felt sufficiently motivated to cross Commonwealth Avenue. Meanwhile, with each day she remained in East Saltin, she knew Fred's worry must be increasing. She knew she was being cruel, but she could not stop herself from punishing him (and for punishing herself) for her childless fate.

Days turned to weeks, weeks to months.

Over time, Tova adapted to her new surroundings. She took long walks throughout East Saltin until she had a docent's knowledge of every sanctuary, statue and exhibit. She also began taking an interest in Covenant's other residents. It didn't matter if they were transient or long-term; she wanted to know their stories and was willing to listen to them patiently and without judgment.

Tova soon became Covenant's go-to person for all sorts of practical advice. She was especially helpful when sharing her expertise on banking, checking, loans or taxes. She also seemed to know quite a bit about men and marriage, though she never shared a word about her own status or personal history.

Meanwhile, Mother Ruth (the head of Covenant House at the time) watched closely as Tova's status among the women ascended. At first, Mother was quite jealous of this upstart who'd only recently arrived. But Mother Ruth was a highly principled woman with no higher regard for anything in this world than the success of Covenant House. As such, she quickly came to appreciate how well Tova related to the other women and how well she was able to advise them in ways that bettered their lives, which was, after all, the secondary purpose of Covenant House, right after the protection of its daughters from the designs of dangerous men.

When Tova had lived there six months she received a note from Mother Ruth, requesting her presence that evening, at seven, in Mother's top-floor, private apartment. Tova was terrified. Knowing that Covenant House was fully occupied, she thought Mother was going to ask her to leave (to accommodate some new girl whose situation was more immediately imperiled) or to commit to a long-term residency (for which she still wasn't ready). For Tova, the note represented an existential crisis. As she saw it, she had three options: (1) apply for a long-term residency; (2) catch the next bus out of East Saltin; (3) cross Commonwealth Avenue to West Saltin to find her husband Fred.

MOTHER MARY

Mother Ruth was a busy woman who did not like to beat around the bush. At seventy-six and in failing health, it was her sworn responsibility to find a worthy successor: someone with financial experience, leadership skills, and the special wisdom necessary to help women of all ages and wounds.

"I've been watching you for months," Mother Ruth told Tova. "You are competent, sensitive and mature. Best of all, from my point of view, you really seem to care about all the women here, irrespective of their circumstances." Mother spoke for ten minutes about Tova's competencies and the requirements of the job. Three times she mentioned the needs of Covenant House's *daughters*. They needed protection. They needed guidance. They needed love.

Though spoken softly, Mother's words sounded like a clarion call to Tova, reverberating in that part of her heart where her unexercised maternal instincts lie.

Tova might have resisted the temptation of the crowning apartment in this fairy tale chateaux. She might have resisted the surprisingly robust compensation. But she could not resist the opportunity to nurture daughters (even if they numbered twelve, some old as herself). Fred would have to wait. He would eventually get over her and move on with his life. In fact (she'd reasoned), he would be better off without her. She was too different, too demanding for Fred. He should be free to live his own life as he pleased.

And so, six months later, almost a year to the day of her arrival, Tova became Mother Mary, replacing Mother Ruth as head of Covenant House. She wouldn't see Fred again until a year later, when he finally found the gumption to come looking for her. Another thirty years would pass before he returned, this time asking about the newest of her daughters, a forty-year-old woman named Hannah.

WHAT'S IN A NAME?

Hannah had messaged Jason that she had settled into Covenant House and was looking forward to meeting Fred and getting a tour of the city. For her own protection—and for Jason's—she'd decided not to use *Astral*, her Facebook name, as it would call unwanted attention to herself and likely lead to confusion. Inasmuch as she'd already used *Hannah Belaya* when filling out Covenant's application for residence, she decided she would take the path of least resistance and use her real name. *Any why not?* she thought. *This is America!*

EAST SALTIN TOUR

"Nice to meet you, Fred. My name is Hanna Belaya."

"Hanna, the pleasure is mine."

Fred led Hannah away from Covenant House, unaware that Tova's intensely focused gaze would track them until they were out of sight.

Hannah was happy to meet Fred and to have a tour of the city. (Though deeply grateful for the free room and board in Covenant House, her room was small and the atmosphere constraining. Further, she was anxious to see more of the *crazy salty city,* as she thought of it. Finally, she knew that meeting Fred was prelude to meeting Jason, and she was most anxious for that.)

Fred was happy to meet Hannah. Though the situation was eerily reminiscent of the time, nearly forty years before, when he'd come to Covenant House in the hope of finding his wife, he was glad to know Hannah—and Jason too. They were nice people, still with life ahead of them, and meeting them buoyed his hopes for Saltin's resurgence.

"There used to be a lot to see in Saltin," he said.

"Jason told me. He said the sea emptied and all the business ruined."

Fred gave a pained smile. "That's it, in a nutshell."

Hannah shook her head. "I do not understand."

Fred remembered that she was from Europe. "I meant, you said it correctly and simply: *The sea emptied and all the business ruined.*"

Fred was quiet. Hannah thought her question might have put him in a bad mood.

"Why people come here in beginning?" she asked.

Fred paused.

Hannah regretted her words, thinking she was being too pushy.

"Sorry if I ask bad question."

"No, not at all. It's a perfect question."

Hannah was grateful for his calm way. She thought he might be wise. Jason had said he was a fisherman who relaxed by fishing a dry, empty sea.

Fred explained, as simply as he could, that the people who had founded (and funded) East Saltin were evangelists who wanted to spread the Word of God. To accomplish their mission, they'd designed East Saltin as an ecumenical expo, replete with houses of worship, statuary and exhibits meant to plant or revivify seeds of faith.

Hannah indicated that she understood well enough.

"Sadly, almost all of it has been lost to neglect and erosion," said Fred.

"You say *sadly*. Are you believer?"

Fred shook his head. "No, I'm not. Perhaps if I believed in something—anything—my life might have been different."

"You are not happy?"

Fred looked at Hannah wonderingly. Had she been an English-speaking American, he would have been annoyed by her directness. But her foreign boldness was refreshing. He thought he liked her and could trust her. Even so, he shrugged off her question and continued with his tour.

"Over time, the elements—sun, wind, sand, salt—destroyed almost everything in Saltin. In this part of town, only Covenant House, where you are staying, and The Mount, where the mayor lives, are in good shape. But there are some other places that are worthwhile to see."

He led her to a small church with an outsized front façade that featured a 1:2-scale simulation of the great North Rose window of Chartres' Notre-Dame Cathedral. Much of the circular stained-glass window was missing. Recently dislodged pieces were strewn about like gem stones. Hannah chose two that were small and smooth and could be handled safely: a piece of blue (likely from Mary's robe, or the sky) and a piece of red (likely from a rose, or a spill of blood).

Fred then led her to another small church with an outsized front façade that featured a full-scale simulation of the great door of Wittenberg Castle Church, upon which Martin Luther had nailed his revolutionary Ninety-Five Theses. These famous protests (here written in English and etched on metal plates) were now mostly eroded. Hannah ran her hand over the worn lettering but understood only sadness, as if a Holy Spirit, once present, had long departed.

Fred then led her to a small, inconspicuous building that had once been a synagogue. Inside, only the pews, bema and ark remained, though the latter had been emptied of its velvet-covered, silver-breastplated Torah. Nothing else of value could be seen. Not a single prayer shawl or skullcap; certainly, no siddur or any other Holy Book had been left to rot. But on every right-side doorjamb there remained a mezuzah, meant to safeguard good-hearted Jewish visitors. The sight of these totems reminded Hannah that Yevgeny was living in the holy city of Hebron and would likely contact her very soon.

Leaving the synagogue and continuing on their tour, Fred and Hannah walked along a path that recreated the Via Dolorosa. Later, they inspected the abandoned Holy Land

Amusement Park. Fred pointed out Salvation Mountain in the near distance, but it was too far to walk.

"One day I'll take you there. We'll use a golf cart to get there."

Just then they saw two golf carts puttering along the streets.

"Why little cars?"

Fred smiled. "We used to have a lovely golf course, but not a blade of grass remains. The entire course is covered in sand and salt and looks like the Sahara Desert. Anyway, people use the old golf carts to get around. We have a gas station—but only one of its pumps works. Twice a year a truck from San Bernardino comes to replenish its underground tank."

Hannah did not understand all of Fred's words, so she just smiled, thinking that whatever she needed to know would become clear to her in time.

With a nod of his head, Fred indicated the direction of their next destination. "C'mon. I'll take you to the boardwalk and show you The Mount, where the mayor of East Saltin lives. Sometimes he's called the Pope, or His Holiness."

"He is very holy?"

"Uhh, not particularly."

Fred and Hannah walked north along Commonwealth Avenue until they came to the boardwalk and the mostly empty sea.

"The beach on this side of the avenue is called Bethlehem. Right there, on the other side, it's called Bombay. Here's The Mount."

Hannah looked to the right. With her first glance it was hard to tell if the place was holy or secular. Its architecture was an odd fusion of austere and ornate styles, something for everyone. The main effect was redbrick Baptist, but there were also Romanesque and Gothic elements, including an arcaded portico and dome. All six of East Saltin's leading citizens lived on the first floor. The mayor resided on the second floor, which also had some rooms to rent. The main floor contained the lobby, restaurants and meeting rooms. Only one restaurant was still functional. Only one meeting room was ever used. Altogether, eight people currently inhabited The Mount. In its heyday, the place was packed and reservations were a must. Now, there were no crowds. There was no busy season.

"We do get tourists," said Fred. "Maybe a hundred a year come to treat their rheumatism or respiratory problems."

"They come for the salts?"

"Yes. Our baths and vapors are special because of our salts."

"It works?"

"People say it works amazingly well."

"Why not more people come?" asked Hannah.

Fred made a sweeping gesture with his right arm. "Look around, my dear. The city is ruined. No taxis. No streetlights. Limited electricity. We struggle to pick up our garbage. We'd love to return Saltin to its former glory, but right now it's broken and stinks of dead fish."

"Still, some people come."

"For the salts. Some for the apocalypse."

"What means that?"

"*Apocalypse*—like the End of Days."

Hannah nodded. "People believe?"

"Not exactly. But we get photographers and filmmakers who see Saltin as a good setting for a post-nuclear disaster. Like Chernobyl. You know Chernobyl?"

Hannah nodded, sadly. [Chernobyl was once a thriving city in eastern Ukraine. In 1986, a nuclear reactor there suffered a massive malfunction, spewing toxic plumes in every direction for a thousand miles.] She knew people who knew people who had died of the poisonous radioactivity. She had seen many pictures of the abandoned city, now an overgrown wasteland.

"Yes," she said. "Saltin is like Chernobyl—except with salt. It reminds me also of Pompeii."

"How so?" said Fred, thinking of a spewing volcano.

"In Pompeii, the people and city are covered with ash. Here, salt covers all."

Thirty years in Saltin, Fred had never thought of Pompeii. He liked Hannah. She was smart and had a fresh eye.

WEST SALTIN TOUR

At the north end of Commonwealth Avenue, a narrow stretch of boardwalk remained partially intact, wide enough for two people to walk abreast in either direction for about fifty yards. Fred and Hannah had walked to the left and now stood in West Saltin, right above Bombay Beach. Despite its surrounding desolation (perhaps because of it), Hannah felt a sense of mystery, even romanticism. Suddenly, she yearned for Jason. She wished it were Jason who was with her, filling her ears—and her heart. She imagined wandering the salty city beside him, searching together for a story to pair with his opera music. *I could play the heroine!* she thought. *Our story would have a happy ending!*

"From here you can see the lagoons and shallows."

Fred's words interrupted her reverie. Jason went *poof* and Hannah's attention refocused on Fred.

"The original leaders in East Saltin wanted to rename this sea *Galilee*, but the name *Saltin* was fixed in California's geography. In any case, the leaders in West Saltin fiercely opposed the idea. *Galilee* would have sent the wrong message to their constituents."

Hannah guessed at his meaning. "West Saltin does not want to be holy and good?"

"The people in West Saltin have other priorities."

"What is more important than holy and good?"

"Making money. Lots of it."

Hannah winced.

"I'm joking. Sort of. It's just that, for the people who came to West Saltin—myself included—God wasn't our number one priority."

Hannah was digesting this and did not respond.

"You have to understand," Fred continued. "This town was built for gamblers. High rollers, not holy rollers."

Hannah gave him a blank look.

"Never mind. Bad joke."

Hannah nodded uncertainly.

Fred sought to change the mood.

"Here's The Palace," he said, pointing to his left.

Even Hannah (who had never owned a television set and who generally avoided current events) recognized The Palace as a scaled-down version of London's Buckingham Palace. Only one-third the size, the building to her left was still impressive. And while a discerning eye could tell that its stone was white granite and not Carrara marble, most visitors were impressed by its regal look.

"Jason lives here?"

Fred knew that Jason lived in a windowless cell in a nearby decrepit building but occasionally rented a modest room at The Palace so he could shower, shave and look presentable.

"He lives nearby. But he is here now, waiting to meet you. Are you ready to meet him?"

FATED AND MIRACULOUS

Jason believed that his marriage, his separation, his unfinished opera and his years of lonely wandering had led him to this crazy salty city.

Hannah believed that the bane of her four marriages and the blessing of her son … her work with Cosmoenergy and laser light … her relations with Yevgeny and P. … had all led her from her home in Lviv to this crazy salty city.

The two of them, Jason and Hannah, regarded their imminent meeting as fated, like the fixed stars in the night sky, and just as miraculous.

A GOOD START

Fred texted Jason that he and Hannah were on their way. Concerned with the couple's privacy, Fred had planned the meeting to appear serendipitous, but this was quite unnecessary, as no one else was in the lobby at the time.

Leading up to this fated moment, Jason and Hannah had spent considerable time wondering how they might greet each other. Independently, they'd come to think that a friendly hug and a chaste kiss would be a good start. But the thought of Fred's presence and the public place (even if empty) inclined them both to conclude that a warm, slightly prolonged handshake would be better. Moments after introducing them, Fred said goodbye and left them alone.

Jason and Hannah smiled at each other nervously.

"You will please call me *Hannah*?"

"Hannah," Jason repeated, as if committing it to memory. "It's a beautiful name. Simple. Elegant. It's a palindrome."

"What means that?"

"Backwards or forwards, the name is the same."

Hannah pictured her name in English and realized Jason was right. She smiled, believing this odd fact must portend something special. *Nothing is coincidence,* she thought. *All is connected.*

"And what I call you? Are you *Jason* or *Simcha*?"

Jason paused to think. "Please call me *Jason*. In your heart, if you like, you can think of me as *Simcha*."

Hannah liked the idea.

"So, you are *Jason,* like the ancient story?"

Jason laughed, a little uneasily.

"Well, yes, we have the same name."

"The sailor who found the Golden Fleece."

"Yes."

"You will find your Golden Fleece?"

Jason paused. "I hope so."

"You not sure?"

Jason shrugged. "Honestly, I'm not sure what I'm looking for."

Hannah nodded. "Tell me."

Jason paused. "Well, the thing is, I don't have a clear goal. It's not like I'm searching for something solid and valuable."

"Maybe something you create."

"Perhaps. Yes."

"Maybe you looking for something inside, not outside."

Jason smiled. "You are very perceptive. I've always thought my Golden Fleece was inside me."

"Inside is more wild and dangerous than the sea."

Jason was moved by this. "Yes. I feel that way too."

"You have idea what it is?"

Jason paused to think. "I've always felt that my goal should be some special musical achievement."

"Like your opera?"

"Yes. I think that's it. I can't seem to work on anything else."

"The music part is done?"

"I believe so. It feels complete. It has a beginning, a middle and an end. When I play it—usually on the piano, though I am a better guitar player—it sounds right to me. Like nothing could be changed."

"When you hear the music, what you think about?"

"Ah, perfect question. But not so easy to answer. When I listen, I feel like I am hearing a story. I imagine an unseen voice, like a narrator. Sometimes I imagine people talking."

"What they say?"

"I don't know. I hear them, but I can't tell what they're saying. I feel like I should know. How could I not know? It's very frustrating."

Hannah took a step closer. She touched his hand but did not hold it.

"You are very brave. To achieve great thing is a big struggle. If it come easy, it would not be great success."

Jason was silent for several seconds. "I'm talking too much about myself. I want to know about you. You've had your own hard struggles. I want to know all about them—when you are ready."

Hannah was silent for several seconds. "I will tell you. You will tell me."

"Yes."

"You will help me with my science—with my salts?"

"Yes. Gladly. You will listen to my music—and tell me what you think?"

"Yes. With pleasure."

Jason released a deep breath. "I am very happy to finally meet you, Hannah. It feels right."

"I feel same way. We shall see how life travels."

"Yes. By the way, how do you like Covenant House?"

"It is strange, like old English novel."

"I am a fan of the Brontë sisters and Jane Austen."

"Stop—you are stealing my heart!"

They both laughed.

"I think Covenant House is more Brontë than Austen," said Hannah. "I feel a lot of dark secrets."

"Is there a crazy lady in the attic?"

Hannah laughed; she was well read and understood the reference. "I think maybe yes. There is an old woman named Mother Mary who is boss and lives upstairs. I don't think she trust me."

"Are you okay living there?"

"Yes, I am fine. It has good things. I feel safe, like in convent. It is nice to live away from the men—though I mean no insult to you."

"I'm not insulted. I like that you feel protected."

Hannah paused to think how she should phrase her next thought.

"I do scientific study. The special salts here could maybe help cure some disease."

"I understand. You are doing important work."

"Yes. Scientists want to find cures. But it is good to make discovery first."

"You mean fame and fortune?"

"Yes, but not for me. I do not need such things, but for people I know."

Hannah felt the pressure of many complications (P., Yevgeny, Peter). Not quite ready to share these feelings with Jason, she remained thoughtfully silent.

"I understand," said Jason. "But I sense there is something else you want to say."

Hannah smiled, as if to acknowledge that Jason had read her mind. When he answered her smile with one of his own, her expression changed. In that moment, she was grateful for his friendship. That would be enough, for now.

"Yes," she said. "How it is: some people want to discover cures before me—or stop me from discovering—or take from me what I discover." It wasn't the whole truth. But it would suffice, for now.

Jason took a step towards her. "What are you saying? Are you in danger?"

"No, I do not think so. I am silly. I just wanted you to know." Hannah regretted this weaker sex ploy, but she knew she'd need his help, sooner or later.

Jason addressed her with his most serious tone: "Look, Hannah. I know you are smart and strong, but everyone needs help sometimes. I just want you to know that I am ready to help you."

Hannah's heart was glowing.

"I live nearby," said Jason. "I can come to you very quickly."

"You do not live in Palace?" Hannah knew the answer but wanted to hear Jason's words.

"No. I live in a broken building. I live like a prisoner in a jail cell."

Hannah looked at him admiringly. "You live like a musician in a monk's cell."

Jason shrugged. "My choices are my choices. I have my reasons." He reached into his pocket. "Here, take this paper, it's my cellphone number. We can stay in contact through Facebook. But if you need me, call me. Please."

Hannah took the number. "Thank you. But I will not call—unless it very needed."

"Thank you. I like knowing that you have it."

They looked at each other nervously.

"I think I made a bad mood," said Hannah.

Jason drew a calming breath to reset the conversation. "We were talking about life goals."

"Yes. I have my science and I'm looking for cures."

"I have my music and I'm looking for my story."

Hannah nodded. She wanted to ask a question that had weighed on her mind for a long time.

"I have question. I hope you don't mind."

"Please ask. Anything you like."

"Okay. I thank you."

Hannah removed a water bottle from her carryall, unscrewed the cap, took a long sip, then returned the bottle to the bag.

"Okay. I ask: On Facebook you say *It's complicated.* What is truth? Are you married?"

Jason breathed a sigh of relief. He'd thought she was going to ask if he intended to work again. He didn't know the answer and was worried his uncertainty would disappoint her. Being asked about his romantic status was, comparatively speaking, a walk in the park. Though he hadn't felt comfortable discussing his marriage while they were correspondents, he was ready to share his heart now.

"I met a beautiful singer from Texas named Renee Rivera. She had a voice as smooth as honey, powerful as a church organ. We were the stars of a musical group called Jason and the Argonauts."

"You were success?"

Jason described their long career in terms of its biblical quality: seven years of plenty, in which they both filled their bank accounts like overflowing granaries, followed by seven lean years, in which they both lost much, especially in terms of their equity in love.

"Bad business made bad marriage?"

"Not quite so simple. Before the seventh year of plenty had passed, I asked her to marry me and she joyously accepted. All our bandmates and friends and family were at the wedding. Everyone was thrilled for us, except our manager, a guy named Sanford Villian, who believed that wedding bells would toll the beginning of the end of our success, which is basically what happened.

"What was bad in marriage?"

"Well, bottom line, as we say, after years of concert touring, I wanted to put down roots to settle down. You understand?"

Hannah nodded.

"But Renee still loved to perform live. She loved going on long concert tours. Also, I wanted children *soon*; she wanted them *someday*. Neither of us could say what *soon* or *someday* exactly meant, so we argued—a lot. And then the economy was bad, which affected our business, which further affected our love life."

"She lost her love?"

"For me, yes. But she fell in love with our manager. At least, she fell in love with whatever promises he made to her. He stole her away from me."

"You have not heard from her?"

"No. Not for ten years. A couple months ago I heard from an old friend who'd been the drummer in my first band, when we were still in high school. He no longer plays music, but he knows Renee and did not mention her. He's a photographer now. He photographed a wildlife area just south of Saltin where migratory birds used to rest."

"What means that?"

"Migratory?"

"Yes."

"Birds that fly to different homes for different seasons."

"Like you, they wandering."

"Yes, I suppose I am."

Hannah had another burning question.

"You have children?"

Jason shook his head sadly. "No. It's my biggest regret."

Hannah offered a compassionate frown but inside she smiled. She was sorry for his void but glad there were no other claims on his heart. She quickly calculated how old she would be in nine months. *Not impossibly old,* she thought.

"I am glad you are here," he said. He wanted to hold her hand, but they were in a public place. "You have a special kind of wisdom. I think you have a special heart."

Hannah's heart quickened.

Jason continued: "I know you are here to do your scientific work. Perhaps you would like Fred to show you the lagoons and the salt caves. There are also many areas of the empty sea you can explore. If you like, I can help you." He touched her hand for a few tingling seconds and then withdrew it, embarrassed.

Jason's sincerity moved Hannah. She was past her pouty moment when she'd learned that he'd been married and hadn't told her. *So what?* she thought. *We are not young. We both have led adult lives. Haven't I a suitcase of personal complications I haven't yet shared?*

SEPARATION ANXIETY

For all their honesty and positive momentum, Jason and Hannah were uneasy when they separated. So much had gone unsaid. So much pain still needed to be shared. Unfortunately, the broken, desiccated city was an inhospitable place for the emotionally wounded.

Thousands of miles away, in Moscow and Hebron, two other pained souls rued their separation from Hannah.

P.'S JOURNAL ENTRY

Where has my Hannah gone? How could she disappear into thin air? My agents are studying every lead, every shred of evidence. My gut tells me Dr. Yeshevsky is responsible. He is the only one who could have orchestrated her disappearance. He understands the larger world. He has the means—and the motive:

He took her on evening walks along the Moskva River. He took her, several times, to the same pub for drinks (where, I'm told, he did all the talking and she did the listening—or pretended to).

He took her, on several occasions, to the Matreshka Hotel, where they dined but did not get a room.

His motives are clear. He likes her. He's smitten by her. Perhaps he even loves her. But he is too weak for her. She needs a real man.

But what are her feelings? Much more difficult to know. But she did not hold his hand on their moonlighted walks. She did not get a room with him at the Matreshka Hotel. She did not share her feelings—whatever they are—with anyone by email or phone text (we would have known if she had).

So, what does she feel for Yeshevsky? We do not know. All we know for sure is that for all her intelligence and capability, she is his assistant, his employee. How does she really feel about that? Of course, she would be nice to him, tactful and respectful. He pays her well. She seems to enjoy the work. She needs the paycheck. Without her job, she would be sent back to Ukraine—not a pleasant prospect, given the situation.

So, what do we know? We know Yeshevsky cares for her and might go to great lengths to protect her. We know she respects him and cannot afford to go against his wishes. So, where does that leave us?

If Yeshevsky saw me as competition for Hannah's heart and wanted to take action, his only practical course would have been to send her somewhere beyond my reach. But where? Israel? Unlikely. Neither of them speaks Hebrew. They would stand out in the crowd. Europe? We have assets everywhere. Difficult to evade our scrutiny. Yeshevsky is smart, but he is not a professional in this arena. Where then? Where would he send Hannah? Canada? Possibly. The United States? Likely.

Tomorrow, when I meet with Akhmerov and Zubilin, I will review their progress.

WELL PLAYED

After reviewing the evidence provided by his trusted personal agents, P. was convinced that Hannah must have traveled to the United States by way of a plan masterminded and funded by Dr. Yeshevsky. Furious, he slammed his fist on his desk, spewing all four curses he had banned from the arts and media.

The two agents were used to his violent outbursts. What they didn't hear (and what might have unnerved them) was P.'s silent, scathing, self-indictment: *Goddamn sonofabitch! He played me! That Jew bastard played me! He knew I would approve his parents' visas to Israel. He knew I'd also banish him there to give myself a free shot at Hannah. Once in Israel, he knew he could play puppeteer and remain beyond my reach. Sonofabitch! Okay, he's good, better than I thought. But this match is not over. He is betting that I cannot find Hannah. But I will find her. And I will have her.*

RUNNING DOWN LEADS

P. had already ordered his staff in China to check out the source of the citrine salts that had been sent to Yeshevsky's Cosmoenergy office; similarly, he'd ordered his assets in Israel to check out the manufacturers, distributors and all those involved in medical research relating to Dead Sea salts. The investigation confirmed that a variety of Chinese and Israeli salts had been shipped to Yeshevsky's Moscow office about six months earlier, but there was nothing to tie the shipments to Hannah's disappearance.

P. ordered agents Akhmerov and Zubilin to go to the United States to find Hannah, choosing New York City as the starting point of their mission. They had twenty-four hours to prepare. Akhmerov said they needed only six. Zubilin thought they could do it in four.

Twice before the two agents had served in the United States as an undercover team, traveling as Anderson and Zimmer. They knew the language; in fact, they had mastered the accent and idiom of nine different regions, so they could blend in almost anywhere, as necessary.

They already had the deepest cover possible: expertly forged birth certificates, charts of vaccinations, dental records, school transcripts, deeds, rental agreements, driver's licenses, U.S. passports, tax records, social security numbers and credit cards. It would take only a couple days to make sure all the documents were fully updated.

"Boss, as Anderson and Zimmer, we're more American than most Americans," joked Akhmerov.

"Our cover is so deep we could get elected president," joked Zubilin.

"Hell, anyone can get elected president—with our help!"

The men continued joking about the way they had influenced the American election and the clown they had helped elect president. P. let it go. Usually, he would not allow such disrespect, as it demeaned his efforts to outshine and outclass his adversary. But the American president's recent antics, especially his idiotic Twitter statements, were becoming increasingly bothersome.

While the two agents, now as Anderson and Zimmer, made their final preparations before flying to New York, P. watched with great interest as the American investigation into Russian interference intensified, knowing the American president would be under increasing pressure to distance himself from all things Russian. The irony of the situation weighed heavily on him. He had counted on the new American president to reduce (or remove altogether) the onerous sanctions that had been leveled against his country in recent years. In fact, it was this very hope that had motivated him to martial so many special resources into getting this particular candidate elected. If the new American president now refused to remove the sanctions (or worse, ordered more to give the appearance of distancing himself from Moscow in order to legitimize his purloined presidency), then he—the mighty P.—would look like a meddling fool who had been outplayed.

With so many pressures (including the formidable threat from an oppositional candidate in his own upcoming election), his only respite was to think about Hannah. There were times he desperately wanted to hold her—and times he wanted to beat her senseless.

He assumed it would all work out. That's the way people think when they are unaccountable to any other person and do not believe in a Higher Authority.

YEVGENY'S JOURNAL ENTRY

Oh, how I miss my Hannah! I have only myself to blame, but what could I do? I had to send her away for her own good. There was no other choice. She had to be protected from that evil bastard. Of course, I feared we might lose our own special connection, but I had to make the sacrifice.

But now my immediate fears are vanished. She is safe and she loves me, I know it. She follows all my suggestions to the letter. Though it must pain her, she has not sent me a single message of any kind. Clearly, she does not want to endanger our plans. She trusts me. She trusts that I know what's best for us both.

Hannah's brave commitment encourages me to reconsider what I want out of life. It has led me to rethink my goals. I think I shall always be dedicated to my Cosmoenergy research and to medical healing, but I've begun to see that my life's purpose must also be self-nurturing. Just as my aura is uniquely mine, my life's goals should include my most personal desires—which is to wed my darling Hannah and to raise our child together.

ONGOING TREATMENT

In addition to his normal busy schedule, P. was now on a whistle-stop election campaign that made it very difficult for him to be in Moscow on a specific day, much less a specific time. As a result, he missed consecutive laser-salt treatments. On both occasions, Dr. Dimitri Grushina, surrogate for doctors Yeshevsky and Belaya, told the unnamed person who set up the bi-weekly appointment that he and his staff should not be held not responsible for the efficacy of their treatment if the patient failed to attend. This message was tactfully communicated to P.

P. knew he should take his health more seriously. He understood that the cancer (which had been slowing) could make a ferocious comeback if its treatment were continually interrupted.

For convenience's sake, P. wondered if Dr. Grushina and his equipment might be added to his campaign retinue, but after considering all the necessary preparations and precautions, he realized that the idea's reality would likely compromise the secrecy of his treatment, which could not be risked, especially during an election campaign that was being monitored honestly and vigilantly for the first time. With so much at stake, it made little sense to risk damaging his political mystique with revelations of dire illness.

MESSAGE FROM YEVGENY TO HANNAH

Dear Hannah, I hope you are well. The knowledge that you are safely ensconced, beyond the reach of the Evil One, gives me comfort, as does the idea that you will soon be back to work. As to your work, I leave it to you to find an appropriate place for your research. I will bear all expenses, of course.

Here, on the other side of the world, my parents have settled in well. Our apartment is sunny and comfortable and very close to the new hospital—and to the Cave of Machpelah, where they sojourn daily, like a pair of ancient pilgrims. For me, life in Hebron is less satisfying. The political tension is fascinating but I have done no research, which is maddening. However, I have been able to orchestrate a pair of fundraising and membership drives, which has raised considerable money for our Federation.

Eventually, my plan is to leave Hebron to visit you, work alongside you, and then decide together what our next steps should be.

Yours—

HANNAH, ALONE WITH HER THOUGHTS

"Next steps" makes me very nervous. I know he's thinking of our relations, professional and personal. This is so tricky and frustrating! I dealt with his amorous pursuit in Moscow, but what can I do when he arrives in Saltin? There are twenty people in the entire city and almost all of them live in one of three buildings. And Jason lives here. Where can I go for privacy? I can't always run to my room.

If only Yevgeny weren't so pushy. I mean, he's not bad looking. And we do share so many interests. I think the best thing for me is to keep my mind and options open. And that includes remaining single. If I ever do marry again, I have to get it right.

MESSAGE FROM YEVGENY TO BETHANY

Dear Bethany,

Yesterday I sent you a package which should arrive in about ten days (sorry I can't be more exact; it is being sent in a very circuitous way ☺). Please deliver it at your earliest convenience—it is slightly large, but not very heavy. I'm sure you'll be able to manage it, perhaps with another person's assistance.

I thank you again for your help. I am exceedingly grateful. I know you volunteered, but I insist on compensating you. You are an extraordinary woman.

Namaste.

MESSAGE FROM YEVGENY TO HANNAH

Silly me, I almost forgot, in about two weeks our mutual friend will bring you the first of several packages of supplies you will need for your research. Eventually, I will also send you a Wonder Wave, but that will not be so easy—it is conspicuously large and heavy and there are only two manufacturers and I do not wish for us to be discovered.

Also, I have set up an American bank account for you. At the end of each week I will wire you your salary, along with a stipend for living expenses. I think you will find it a generous arrangement. You should be able to save for a rainy day—though I hope our future is sunny.

OFFICE OPTIONS

For the time being, Hannah blocked thoughts of Yevgeny to concentrate on where she might set up her office. The place must be large enough to accommodate a sink, desk, two chairs, an examining table (which could double as a patient bed) and a laser machine. It should also be clean, quiet, secure and have a reliable source of electricity.

She hadn't many options. Newly arrived at Covenant House, she could not request a larger room (much less, a large second room) to serve as her office. She considered The Palace (where the King lived) and The Mount (where the Pope lived), but as far as she knew, those places were inhabited only by men (gamblers in one, evangelists in the other), and the thought of working among so many male strangers made her feel queasy and vulnerable. She considered asking Jason for his assistance, but she did not want to risk being invited to work in the same derelict hulk in which he lived, even if the elements could be kept out and electricity be brought in. Having dismissed all her own ideas, she spoke to Fred, explaining that (in addition to needing the lagoon spa treatments for herself) she was a scientist looking for office space to do important salt-cancer research. As a calculated throwaway, she added, "If my theory is right, I could make Saltin great again."

FRED'S CIVIC DUTY

Fred was anxious to help Hannah. She was sweet, pretty and looking for a cure for her illness. And he had so few friends. Really, he was very lonely. And he had the space, the perfect space: an unused room at the back of the Civic Center, opposite his own room, and while it didn't have a sink, there was a bathroom next door with a large sink. And he could let her have it for free; after all, he was the manager. Besides, if her research were successful—it would give Saltin hope!

TRAVELING LIGHT

Anderson and Zimmer planned to spend three days in New York—or three hours—or they might receive new orders at any time. In any case, they had no return ticket and thus no idea how long they would be abroad.

They traveled light, each with a single piece of carry-on luggage, just under the airline's legal size and weight limit. They carried no guns, knives, wire garrotes, etc. After all, they weren't assassins—or were no longer assassins—at least, they were not expecting to assassinate anyone on this mission.

CONTACTS AND HAUNTS

Because it is not possible to conduct an exhaustive search of New York (the city is too vast and complex), Anderson and Zimmer quickly settled on a plan to visit those destinations most likely (in their shared opinion) to attract Hannah. Taking into account location and accessibility, they agreed to focus their efforts on the boroughs of Manhattan, Queens, and Brooklyn, ignoring (for the time being) the Bronx and Staten Island. They knew what they were doing. "Hey, it's not our first rodeo," they joked, laughing at another of their favorite Americanisms.

As to their home base, they had a choice of a dozen or so Russian safe houses scattered about the city. Some had full-time occupants but most remained vacant until an agent or asset or contact was assigned temporary residence, which might last a single night or twenty years (as in the case of Vasilis Shapovalov, real-estate agent by day, secret agent by night, who was finally allowed to retire and return to Russia, where he now lives with his family in a comfortable house in a suburb of St. Petersburg).

Anderson and Zimmer chose a vacant two-bedroom apartment in a West Side Manhattan neighborhood called Hell's Kitchen, which used to be worthy of its fearsome moniker but had over many years become tastefully gentrified. After quickly settling in (flipping an American quarter to choose bedrooms), they opened the secret safe (whose combination could be remotely changed), availing themselves of a choice of weaponry, American cash currency and additional passports, should they be necessary.

The next day, after a hearty American breakfast, they began their investigation by visiting geographically prioritized destinations in Manhattan, including the Ukrainian Academy of Arts and Sciences and St. Volodymyr Orthodox Church. All these visits proved fruitless: they made some new contacts but learned nothing germane to their mission.

On their second day, they traveled between Manhattan and Queens, visiting the Ukrainian National Home, St. George Ukrainian Catholic Church, and Korchma Taras Bulba, where they shared cured herring, pickled vegetables and an order of potato and mushroom dumplings. Again, these visits proved fruitless.

On their third day, they traveled by subway to Brooklyn, where they visited the Polish American Congress (Hannah had many Polish friends) and the Holy Ghost Rectory, before taking an Uber south to Brighton Beach, a community famous for its Ukrainian and Russian populations. There they visited stores, shops, restaurants, asking questions (direct, angled, inveigling) that were more personal in nature, often focusing on Hannah's four ex-husbands, especially husband number four, Anatoly Bychkov (a recently released felon and father of Hannah's beloved son Peter), who had emigrated to the United States.

At the Ukrainian National Home, they met an unshaved and seedy fellow who recognized Bychkov's photo and said he thought he lived on Brighton 4th Street, near Ocean View Avenue. He didn't know the address but remembered it was next door to a Starbucks.

Outside, Anderson made a call on his cellphone. He spoke the daily code phrase, requested a car, then abruptly hung up. Without further discussion, the two men headed to a local coffee shop they had passed earlier. A half hour later, while having their mid-day coffee and sandwiches, Anderson's phone rang. Instead of saying *Hello,* he repeated the code phrase of the day and ended the call. Two minutes later he received a text message: *Coney Island Aquarium—main parking lot—back fence—gray Honda Accord—doors open—keys & registration in glove compartment. Delete.*

HUSBAND #4

For two days, Anderson and Zimmer staked out the Starbucks and the old apartment building next door. Alone in the car for long stretches of time, they brushed up on their colloquial English, pretending they were a pair of New York buddy cops. Every couple hours, they took turns stretching their legs and bringing back food: almost always hot dogs, burgers or pizza from Nathan's Famous, the landmark eatery on the ocean boardwalk, about a mile away.

On the second day, a few minutes past seven P.M., they were both in the car when someone matching Bychkov's description approached the apartment building. The two agents exited their car, approached Bychkov casually (one in front, one from behind), and (speaking in English) invited him to get into their car for a little chat. "We just have a few questions" was how they put it.

The scene must have looked odd: three sizable men in the backseat of a Honda Accord, parked on Brighton 4th Street. But there they were: Bychkov in the middle, turning his head left and right to answer their alternating questions.

Very soon (and to his great relief), Bychkov understood that he wasn't being accused of having a forged passport. Hannah was their chief interest. These men (Russian? Ukrainian? American?) wanted to know what he knew of her current situation. Pleadingly (and truthfully), he told them he had no current information. He explained that Hannah had divorced him in the third year of his seven-year prison term and he had proof because she'd sent the divorce certificate to his warden, who'd had it delivered to his cell. All he knew about Hannah—and he made it clear that he'd heard this from friends, and friends of friends—was that she had become some kind of doctor or scientist and that their son, Peter, whom he had not seen in more than twelve years, was a good boy, a smart boy, and was in the army. "I say prayers for him every night," he said, his eyes welling with tears. The agents did not respond. "That's it," Bychkov said. "That's all I know."

The two agents looked at Bychkov as if he hadn't said anything at all. Half a minute of silence passed. Bychkov thought the interrogation was over. But the two agents suddenly renewed their questioning (forcing Bychkov to continue turning his head, left and right), repeating some questions they'd already asked. Bychkov always gave the same answer, or no answer at all. After a while, the agents knew this lead was a dead end, for now.

"I think we're through."

"If you hear anything about Hannah Belaya, call us."

"Take this card."

The card was plain: no wording, no names, no insignia. Just a black phone number on a white background. Bychkov took the card and promised he'd call if he heard anything.

With that, each agent swung open a door and got out. Bychkov exited silently, then walked directly towards the Starbucks without turning around. He didn't look back until he was inside. By that time the car was gone.

He took his vanilla latte to the back and sat alone, thinking.

He thought it was telling that the two spooks had come out of nowhere—like in a dream—to talk to him on this day. He saw it as a sign. Hadn't he been thinking of Hannah and Peter? Hadn't he been wondering how he could contact his ex-wife? (Ever since coming to America—via Poland, on a forged visa—he'd stopped drinking and gambling and his life had continually improved. With each improvement, he'd imagined contacting Hannah to tell her how he was changed and how he deserved another chance. He still loved her, though he still blamed her for not having asked her brother to loan him money to pay a gambling debt, which had led him to rob two stores, which had landed him in jail, which had separated him from Hannah and Peter, his beautiful little boy, now all grown up. *And was this fair?* he thought. *Was it right to keep me away from my own flesh and blood? A young man should not be deprived of a loving father's influence. I have every right to see him! Yes, I am a felon, there is no argument there. But I am contrite and rehabilitated—and I deserve another chance!)*

Bychkov remembered the card. He lifted it from his shirt pocket and stared at the phone number, then turned the card over and stared at its blank side. For a while he lost himself in that whiteness, thinking of his wife (his Hannah *Belaya*) and marveling on the aptness of her translated surname: *White.*

And then he had one of his clever ideas, perhaps his best one yet, certainly one that would alter his life forever: he would follow the agents. It made perfect sense. After all, if the agents were in such hot pursuit of Hannah, she was likely in the United States; and if that were true, the agents would eventually lead him to her. Bychkov smiled, thinking that when he and Hannah finally reconnected, they could renew their love—and having found Hannah, he would surely find his son.

PETER WRITES TO HIS MOTHER

Mother, I am writing this letter by hand and hope to send it to you soon, but I don't know if you will receive it. I regret terribly that I have not communicated with you in quite a while but I am surely not to blame. When my group was moved towards the front, meaning towards the most active fighting, our commanding officer collected all our cellphones and all our tablets, for those who had. We were told these electronics could pose a security risk, "should they fall into the wrong hands." I do not like to speculate what that phrase was intended to convey, but I think we both understand. But let me say right now that I am fine and in good health. Our medical group is paired with an advance unit and even though there has been no fighting for weeks, we have not been allowed to communicate outside our military precinct and I doubt I will ever see my phone again. In fact, knowing how corrupt our government is (aren't they all?), I'm sure my phone has already been sold on the black market or been resold on Amazon or eBay. Perhaps when I am out of the army I'll find my phone for sale online—for twice its original cost! What a world!

I hope this letter brings you some peace, and I hope you write back, though I have no way of reading messages or email, and actual letters are not being delivered here.

Your loving son, Peter

HANNAH AND THE TEETER-TOTTER

Hannah was by nature a positive person. Though she believed the universe was amoral (operating beyond the ken of human thought and judgment), she liked to think that a generous human action might still influence the teeter-totter of a person's fate.

Regarding her son's fate: in her serene state of mind, she accepted that whatever will be will be. But in her dark moods, when she imagined Peter's life imperiled, she saw herself as a potent agent of revenge: an assassin, aiming her laser bullet at the heart of the shirtless Bronze Horseman as he cantered by with haughty indifference.

HANNAH AND YEVGENY

Hannah spent much of her time walking around East Saltin (which she preferred to think of as *Jeru*), visiting shrines and houses of prayer. Her itinerary often reminded her of holy Hebron, which reminded her of Yevgeny.

When thinking of Yevgeny, she invariably thought what a good man he is: what a wonderful scientist and how their work might yet lead to great discoveries that could save many lives. She also thought he would make a good husband and father; and while she did not love him, she spent hours imagining her life as his wife. It was an option.

HANNAH TELLS JASON OF HER PAST

Hannah spent much of her time with Jason. She loved listening to his stories about growing up in southern California and loved telling him—as best she could—what it had been like growing up in Lviv. She was not a confident storyteller. English was her fourth or fifth language and she'd been raised in a Soviet culture of suspicion, where people survived by keeping their thoughts to themselves. Even so, she was ready, perhaps for the first time, to describe her life, as she remembered it. And so, she presented Jason with her life story, her facts scattered and disordered. Over the course of many days, her narrative went wider and deeper, as she kept circling back to her childhood for reasons to explain her present self.

I was born 8 August, 1975, in city of Lvov, then Soviet Union but now Ukraine. I was very lucky girl, born in intellectual family. My dad, a retired officer, lecturer of criminology. My mom, a programming engineer—rare profession for the time. The two grandmothers and one grandfather all took part in the Great Patriotic War; grandfather lost an arm at the battle of Stalingrad. I have a brother, younger by three years.

My family was standard Soviet family. Our life was standard Soviet life. Small wages, queues in shops. There was shortage of absolutely all normal food. Delivery of goods in the shops was early in the morning and I had to stand in long queue. There were three types of bread—white, black, gray. Two kinds of sausage. For the holidays, work people given a celebratory grocery list. War veterans had a special grocery list. For all, minimum clothing, minimum shoes, etc. I never worried about the deficit. I was a child and did not know better. In way, it was good preparation. I do not need so much things to make me happy.

My parents were always at work; I dealt with the younger brother. My father was strict and sometimes cruel. He cried a lot and sometimes beat me. Mom always humiliated. When he retired and was already ill, he ceased to be aggressive. We talked a lot. We were able to find common ground in last years of his life. He told me of knowledges that have been banned. After his brother's death, he learned from the archives that the pope changed several times documents that gave us different surnames. He feared persecution by the authorities. I saw his cruelty was out of fear.

Unfortunately, Mama. It's weird, but she did not do anything for me. Before father's death, she said, "I never loved you." Now I understand all reasons, but as a child I suffered greatly.

My consolation was a library. In addition to works of Karl Marx, Friedrich Engels and Lenin collection (my father was member of the Communist Party), were many books by other authors. I have gift of speed reading. I devoured many books. Dostoevsky, Balzac, Strugatskie brothers, Bulgakov, Arthur Conan Doyle—the list is endless. Books and life in books was the only way to escape from reality. In school we studied foreign and domestic literature. I read clandestinely reprinted banned books—Bulgakov and Nabokov and others—and everything changed for me and I read more. Books formed my inner world, my view of the world.

The position of my parents was tough. All my symptoms and talents suppressed. My father was very afraid of the opinions of others. And so, my childhood was different from all the children. I have some happy memories. For example, when I went on summer vacation to mother grandmother in the village, I walked in the cemetery of rural children, telling them horror stories. I drew strange figures, brought home sick animals, once brought home a lost boy, etc. Another summer I went vacation in a camp in the Carpathian Mountains. We did sports, music, dancing.

Religion, God was not in my family. Soviet Union—a country without faith. A terrible country. Terrible manners. But there were very intelligent, educated people. The only place where I could realize itself was a school. I am happy, and was a good student. I went to the music school in the drawing studio. I sang in the school choir. I was a pioneer leader!!!

In the house were constant scandals. I have always defended the younger brother. With eleven years old, I started to leave the house. I distinctly remember it. When the cries of the parents was impossible to listen to, I just left the apartment, quietly opened the door and went nowhere. I wandered the streets and when it became dark and scary, I went back and slept in the stairwell between the floors, on the stairs.

My parents were fearful people, had no spiritual education. In the end they did not like each other, and the children did not know the parental love. I suffered a lot. Sometimes the psychological pain was unbearable. Several times I tried to slit my wrists. Because of this experience, I always feel the suffering of the people, especially children. In adulthood, I experienced a "touch of God" and I was on the "other world" (world of the dead). I saw hell and wanted to kill myself. It was a very deep mystical spiritual experience.

The divorce of my parents beginning of a new nightmare. I was looking for a family in my husbands. I frantically tried to do the right family.

HANNAH AND THE GLASS STONES

Hannah spent much of her time in her new office at the Civic Center but liked it best when Fred was away. He was a nice man but seemed to think she required his friendship—perhaps even his protection—and tended to foist upon her his smiling, incessant chatter.

Alone, she had plenty time to think and to not think, to be quiet and still, at one with her heartbeat and the heave of her lungs.

One afternoon, after an unsatisfying meditation, she sat alone in her office, thinking of her son Peter, whom she hadn't heard from in more than a month. It was then she noticed the plastic bag on her desk that she'd filled with pieces of colored glass (collected during her many visits to the derelict church modeled on Notre Dame, outside which lay pieces of the replica Rose window). She took hold of the heavy bag—shards and chunks of various shapes and colors—and brought it outside to the back of the building, which faced the desiccated basin of the Saltin Sea.

About twenty feet away there was a four-step stone staircase that led down to the dry seabed. (Unlike the nearby pier, which had been constructed mainly of wood, the staircase was in good shape.) Holding tightly to the heavy bag, she descended slowly, one step at a time. Finally, standing on the dry seabed, she looked upon the strange wasteland that stretched to the horizon and thought: *Hannah's one small step for mankind.* She looked at the sun to get her bearings and then began walking due east, across the empty sea towards its opposite shore, a thin layer of salty sand crackling under her feet.

Every fifty yards or so she looked back to make sure the Civic Center was exactly behind her. Each time she checked, the Civic Center appeared smaller and smaller. When she could no longer see the Center, she decided she'd walked far enough. At that point, she opened the bag of colored glass pieces and spilled them freely onto the sandy seabed. When the bag was empty, she took a few steps backward and appraised her work. She was not pleased. She'd thought the pieces would have assumed a more artful design, but they hadn't. They were nothing more than a chaotic spread of broken glass.

Hannah considered what to do. She wanted to do something that honored Peter. She felt his presence in the sky, watching her.

Akin to free writing, she began organizing the pieces on the dry seabed, working intuitively, removing some stones, shifting others, until she thought she saw the likeness of Peter's face. With that thought in mind, she began refining her design, using blue pieces for Peter's light eyes, dark pieces for his hair, and lighter-colored ones for his skin. She refined her mosaic until she thought it could not be improved, given the pieces at hand.

It was then she realized she hadn't used any of the blood-red stones. At first, she wasn't sure what to do with them, but then she gathered them all in her two fists, walked a dozen strides away and tossed them as far as she could, hoping they would eventually bleach in the deathless sun. She then put the empty bag in her pocket and proceeded westerly, until she had the Civic Center in sight.

BETHANY SETS HER COURSE

Bethany spent Wednesday easing through the steps of a gentle detox. On Thursday morning she meditated. Her afternoon was a light lunch, a yoga class and a solitary walk around the rim of a nearby canyon. When she returned, Yevgeny's supply package was waiting outside her door.

Early the next day (just after sunrise, so as to avoid attention), she packed the supplies into the trunk of her luxury sedan, pushed the round black button to ignite its engine and set her course for Saltin.

Had she not been so preoccupied with memories of Dr. Yeshevsky she would have paid more attention to the glowing sunrise (infused with reds and oranges from the ferric dust stirred high by the strong morning breeze). As it was, she mused on Yevgeny (as she recently had begun to think of him). *Were it not for him, I might not be alive. Surely, I would not be living life so fully.*

For many years she'd harbored a keen desire to meet him, but travel to Russia had never been practical and he'd never been able to travel abroad. Atop her bucket list was her fervent hope that they would one day meet.

As she drove, happily, exultantly, Bethany recalled how she'd suffered acute pangs of buyer's regret in the days immediately following her purchase of her luxury sedan and how it was only with the help of her therapist and life coach that she'd been able to accept her extravagance as part of accepting her complex self: an introspective, sensually indulgent, middle-aged ascetic who still craved occasional reminders of her glamorous past.

It was nearly 11:00 A.M. when Bethany pulled in front of Covenant House. Having already texted Hannah of her imminent arrival, she lowered her windows and cut her silky engine. (She'd considered getting out of the car to embrace Hannah, but decided it was wiser to avoid attention.)

Having heard Bethany's car, Hannah made her way downstairs, excited to see her new friend and to get her supplies, which would allow her to kick-start her onsite research.

Standing to the side of her upstairs, front-facing double window, Mother Mary wondered with growing anger at the audacity of the driver of the slick black sedan parked in front of her precious daughters' home: *It's gotta be a drug dealer or a pimp*. And then: *That hussy, that blonde bitch, it must be her.*

And then she remembered her own dear Fred, knocking at her door the other day, looking for Hannah, and she thought: *Maybe he needs money, poor thing. How much can this broken city pay him to live in the Civic Center all by himself, sitting all day on that broken pier, fishing that empty sea, thinking god knows what. And why doesn't he have enough sense to get out of the sun?*

Her eyes filled with tears because she knew she'd broken his heart (and maybe his mind) by abandoning him and then hiding from him when he'd sought her. *But he'd never buy or sell drugs. He never even smoked. It must be the blonde bitch's fault.* And sure enough, as if confirming her worst suspicions, Hannah skipped out the front door, approached the black sedan as if it were her chauffeured ride, opened the passenger-side door and slid in shamelessly, right next to the dealer, leaving Mother Mary to speculate: *She came to this country to be a criminal! Oh, I'm going to look into this. If I never do anything else for Fred, I'll save him from Hannah, that bitch on wheels. I owe him that much.*

TIRED, NOSTALGIC, JADED

P. and his team were occupying the mansion of a billionaire friend in a suburb of St. Petersburg. Three of the first-floor rooms were filled with campaign activity. In one room, junior staff were gathered around a large television, watching unruly crowds protest the government's recent arrest of the opposition party leader. In a second room, P.'s campaign managers were frantically phoning mayors and district leaders across the nation, reminding them to do all they could to ensure that only properly registered voters cast a ballot. In a third room, a much smaller cadre of managers (all handpicked by P.) watched BBC broadcasters discuss suspected Russian meddling in the recent American presidential election.

Having already visited each of the three busy rooms, P. wandered alone through the upper-story rooms of the mansion. He was tired from long days of smiling and specious rhetoric. He was nostalgic for the days when his wife and children adored him. He was jaded from his long tenure as national leader. (He was seeking an unprecedented fourth term; he had been in power since New Year's Eve, 1999. The Russian people had known no other leader in the twenty-first century.)

Physically and emotionally spent, he collapsed onto a leather chair in an empty den, elbows on his knees, hands covering his self-pitying eyes. He sensed a hard knot in his chest (like a wad of dirty gum) and the unnaturalness of the feeling (especially for a man who took such pride in his clean living and judo-toned body) was met by a wave of self-disgust.

Though not in the habit of second-guessing himself, on this rare occasion he whipped himself for his laxness that was responsible for the foreign body that had infiltrated his defenses. Having been cavalier with his health, he knew he must immediately address his disease or face irremediable consequences. *I must return to Moscow for my treatments as soon as possible. I have learned my lesson. Never again will I forsake my health!*

STILL WATERS

The Russian counterpart of *Still waters run deep* is somewhat more sinister, suggesting the devil behind a calm exterior. It was the phrase people most often used to describe Dr. Dimitri Grushina, the man currently in charge of the Cosmoenergy office in Moscow.

Suffice to say, Dimitri was not an open book. Still, he was not morose or mean, simply quiet and reserved; which was why (sadly) he was thought antisocial.

After thirty-six years of embattled self-discovery, he had finally grown comfortable enough in his own plumpishly soft body to know that he wanted to share it with other men. Sadly, he had few friends and no social network to speak of. Before joining the Cosmoenergy staff at age thirty-four, he'd had only three sexual encounters. They'd all been casual and physically satisfying but had left him wanting more, especially in the way of affection.

Sweet Dimitri yearned to be half of a committed loving couple. He hoped, with all his heart, that his better half would be his boss, Dr. Yevgeny Yeshevsky, who was unmarried, quiet, sensitive, intelligent and easily mistaken for gay.

A SQUEAKY THIRD WHEEL

Yevgeny respected Dimitri's intellect and talents as a scientist and was almost positive that he was a closeted gay—and that's where Yevgeny wanted to keep him, as far as their personal relationship was concerned.

Yevgeny meant no disrespect. He was an ardent supporter of LGBTQ rights. But he had no love (or lust) for Dimitri and, further, did not want to sanction, even tacitly, any such a relationship in his office, lest one of his government clients find out and object. (For Yevgeny, it was enough that the government had finally approved Cosmoenergy as an alternative science and as a provider of alternative medical treatment; he did not want to complicate matters by having the Federation associated with alternative lifestyles, which were opposed by P.'s government.) And so, when Dimitri had angled to get closer to him (by pressing his case to become his official right-hand man, which would have made them nearly inseparable during work hours), Yevgeny decided to look outside the office for another doctor who might be a more comfortable fit for his growing business.

It made perfect sense that Yevgeny would seek candidates within the larger Cosmoenergy community. As it turned out, after only several weeks of corresponding with Dr. Hannah Belaya, a clinician from Lviv, Ukraine, he was convinced that she was the right doctor for the job. Hannah seemed every bit as brilliant as Dimitri—perhaps more so—and had the advantage of being a woman: not only would it help his business to have a female doctor, but hiring her as his main assistant would send Dimitri a message (the wording of which Yevgeny had not bothered to spell out, even for himself).

And so it was: Dr. Yeshevsky offered Dr. Hannah Belaya the job as his main assistant and she accepted. Dr. Dimitri Grushina quietly seethed. He felt professionally usurped and romantically betrayed. He wanted to scream his disappointment—but didn't, at least not for a while. He was a dedicated scientist and doctor and kept his sanity (and his silence) by repeating to himself several mantras, which he wanted very much to believe: *Personal matters have no place in the office. Science is all. The patient is paramount.*

CLENCHED AND ROILED

After Hannah's arrival, Dimitri pledged (to himself) to be a good soldier, to do his best as the *third*-highest ranking member of the Cosmoenergy staff. But that was before Dr. Yeshevsky began lapping after Hannah with puppyish infatuation.

To Dimitri's horror, everyone in the office knew (because he believed everyone saw) Yevgeny's pathetic attempts at discretion. And while he thought everyone smirked, Dimitri smoldered, because he knew how cheaply Yevgeny had sold himself.

The situation grew worse. As a good son, Yevgeny had accompanied his parents to Israel but some snafu had marooned him there—and while he was gone, Hannah was left in charge. What humiliation for Dimitri! With Yevgeny in the office, he might pretend he hadn't been leap-frogged by Hannah, but there was no masking the obvious when Yevgeny was away. The boss had left clear instructions that Hannah was his proxy and that she would direct P.'s laser-salt treatment—with Dimitri's assistance.

As humiliating as it all was, Dimitri appreciated having been entrusted and trained with the new, secret, cutting-edge technology. He even fantasized about some research he might do to improve its techniques. But then Hannah went away for a long weekend and did not return. At first, Dimitri worried (as did all the staff) that something terrible might have happened to her. But Dimitri received a phone call (on his private cell) from Yevgeny in Israel, who offered vague assurance that Hannah was okay (something about a sick aunt in Poland). Yevgeny told Dimitri that he was in charge of the Moscow office for the foreseeable future.

Dimitri privately crowed about his sudden ascendancy. He felt admired and validated. But his sense of achievement faded after two days when he sensed something lacking. It took two more days for him to realize that the missing factor was Yevgeny's live presence; that without Yevgeny's warm smile and shoulder-to-shoulder support, his ascension meant little.

The situation grew worse. The more Dimitri thought about it, the more likely it seemed to him that Yevgeny and Hannah were somewhere together, tangled in each other's naked limbs. Dimitri thought he saw the situation for what it really was: an elaborate scheme hatched by two lying lechers to forsake all professional responsibilities for the pleasures of the flesh—patients be damned! At that point, Dimitri screamed, though privately and behind heavy doors.

For nearly a week, Dimitri dispatched his office responsibilities in a near somnambulate state (though the staff hardly noticed, such was his usual stony reserve). His depression might have lasted a long while had Yevgeny not called him after a week had passed. On hearing Yevgeny's voice, Dimitri's spirit rebounded: he still hoped their relationship might yet spark into reciprocated love. But Yevgeny had something else in mind.

"Dimitri, I've been thinking: Our patient has not had a laser-salt treatment for nearly a month. I attribute this to his busy campaign schedule. But I think he will soon return to Moscow and then I think his office will call you to schedule an appointment."

There was something else Yevgeny wanted to tell Dimitri, but he was uncomfortable saying it, so he just blurted it out: "Dimitri, you will have to perform the treatment yourself, without assistance from anyone. I know it is asking a lot, but it is certainly doable. I do not want anyone else—other than the three of us—to know anything of the technique and protocols. If our treatment proves as successful as I hope, you will be amply rewarded."

Before Dimitri could respond, Yevgeny inquired about his health and then asked about his mother's. Yevgeny's warm solicitous tone went a long way to softening Dimitri's heart.

"I appreciate your caring and confidence," said Dimitri, a catch in his voice and a tear in his eye.

"I am grateful for your dedicated service, Dimitri. I will call again next week."

For several days Dimitri felt better about the situation. And then one afternoon, lunching in a coffee shop across the street from the office, reading a free copy of *The Moscow Times* that he'd picked up on the way in, he came upon an article by an opposition party supporter that detailed P.'s long history of opposing LGBTQ rights. With increasing agitation, Dimitri read of the current government's classification of homosexuality as a mental illness; its continued resistance to gay pride parades; its proposal to fine and arrest citizens who promulgated the idea of homosexuality to minors; the recent revelations of gay concentration camps in Chechnya. This last detail was more than he could stomach: his guts clenched and roiled at the thought of his tortured brothers and sisters. As soon as the spasm eased, he felt the pressing need to use the bathroom. He stood up gingerly and quickstepped to the men's room but it was locked. Minutes from a potential colonic catastrophe, he left the coffee shop in a hurry, mincing his way across the street towards his building's lobby. Mercifully, an empty elevator cab awaited him. He rode it to the same floor as his office, exited before the doors fully opened, hurried to the right towards the public bathroom, accessed a private stall, locked it, pulled down his pants and underwear and evacuated a hot, foul rush before his buttocks touched the seat.

WITHOUT A TRACE

Later that same day after all his co-workers had left, the receptionist's phone rang. Dimitri stared at the ringing machine as if he knew who the caller was, which he intuitively did. Lifting the handset he asked warily, "Hello?"

The caller's words were toneless. "Please prepare for the patient's arrival on Monday at 6:30 P.M." The caller immediately disconnected, negating the possibility of further discussion.

Dimitri checked his watch and the wall calendar. It was 6:15 P.M., Friday evening. The patient, P., would not arrive for three entire days.

Dimitri stared blankly ahead for ten minutes, recollecting all the scenes he'd conjured while reading the article in the coffee shop. The concentration camp scenes, so unspeakably sordid, forced him to look away.

In that moment he made a decision that would alter his life forever. A part of him wanted to act quickly (so he would not change his mind), but Dimitri (ever the diligent scientist) knew he must work carefully and thoroughly for his best chance of success.

With paper and pencil, he listed every place in the office where Yevgeny stored information related to their laser-salt work. After his list was completed and carefully reviewed, he hunted down every handwritten note, receipt, notebook; every sample of salt he could find; every digital file, electrostat, electrograph; even the external hard drives on which all digital and digitized information were backed up, and then he deleted, shred, burnt, flushed—did whatever was necessary to eradicate all laser-salt information from Cosmoenergy's records. He did the same with his personal information. Every reference, every piece of data related to his personal or professional life was similarly eradicated. When he walked out the door it was as if Dimitri Grushina and laser-salt research had never been there.

IMPULSES

All his life, Dimitri felt like an outsider. Only two people ever encouraged him to feel differently: his mother and Yevgeny, each in their different ways. His mother could nurture, but her attempts at validation humiliated him. Yevgeny could validate, but his nurturing was only professional.

Dimitri had his *reasons* for destroying Cosmoenergy's evidence and for leaving P. medically forsaken, but his *impulses* are what really fueled his drastic actions. He needed to break his binding cords. He needed to reset the rules he lived by.

TO AND FROM

To and *from* are the defining characteristics of all travel. In the case of Dimitri Grushina, he had a pretty clear idea what he was leaving: Moscow on the macro level; his mother on the personal level; P. on the professional level. Moscow was the city of his birth and he would miss it. His mother was his emotional lifeline and he would miss her terribly. He would not miss P. In fact, he feared P. (or one of his henchmen) would come after him.

As to where he might go, Dimitri first considered Israel (hoping to reconnect with Yevgeny) but decided against it. For now he needed his space. But he also needed his work: the salary and salvation that science provided. If he could not remain in Moscow or assist Yevgeny in Israel, he thought he should go to the United States, to that place in southern California where their salt samples came from. There he thought he might work safely and successfully. He hoped Yevgeny would agree.

TAKING LEAVE

Dimitri was surprised how easy it was for him to leave Moscow. It helped that he had such a small apartment (only two colorless and droopy plants, no cat or parakeet); no car to be towed away; no close friends; only a mother who was in good health and self-supporting. Further, with debtless credit cards and an impressively robust bank account, he was easily able to afford the airfare to New York City. It also helped that he had a current passport and an inviting window of opportunity: there still were two days before he was expected back at work; two days before P. would arrive at the office for his expected treatment.

Dimitri did not tell anyone of his departure, not his mother, not Yevgeny. He wanted to place the greatest distance between himself and P. before he was discovered missing.

WORRIED

When Dimitri arrived in New York he shaved his sparse beard in an airport bathroom and bought a cowboy hat at a Southwest Airlines kiosk he happened to pass. Knowing he would not get an attractive exchange rate at the airport, he used his credit card for an advance of only five hundred dollars, which he assumed would get him through the next couple days. Paying cash (and thus avoiding Uber), he took a taxi to Manhattan, got out at the Port Authority (the city's major bus terminal) and from there paid cash for a bus to Philadelphia, where he knew he could get a Frontier Airlines flight to San Diego, and from there a bus to Saltin City. That's as far as he'd planned.

En route to Saltin, Dimitri had many hours to consider the fast action of the past couple days. He wasn't troubled by his destruction of the laser-salt records (he knew Yevgeny must have at least one offsite backup, likely a cloud-based server only he could access), but he was haunted by the fact that by leaving his patient in the lurch (without recourse to comparable treatment), he had violated his medical ethics oath. He worried about professional censure. He worried even more about his gay brothers and sisters. He worried most that Yevgeny might not forgive him.

MONDAY, 6:30 P.M.

"I am here to see Dr. Grushina."

The receptionist's hand flew to her mouth. She hadn't been expecting him. He wasn't on the patient schedule. She was alone and had been planning to close the office in the next few minutes.

"Was he expecting you?" she asked.

"Certainly."

The poor woman was unnerved. She didn't know what to do or say.

"One moment please."

As if to buy herself some time to think, she walked to Dr. Grushina's office, stood there in a panic for several seconds, and then returned, trembling.

"He's not able to see you now."

P. sensed he was alone with a doddering fool. Without word, he walked past her, directly towards Dr. Grushina's office, which was near the rear treatment room. With a glance he saw that Grushina's office was empty. With two steps and another glance, he saw that the treatment room was likewise empty. He strode back to Grushina's office and entered. Everything was exceedingly tidy; the desk had recently been swept clean, save for a wooden inbox that contained a single sheet of paper, which he lifted to examine. Centered on the paper was a single paragraph printed in an old-fashioned font that suggested a special law or covenant:

I WILL NOT PERMIT considerations of age, disease or disability, creed, ethnic origin, gender, nationality, political affiliation, race, sexual orientation, social standing, or any other factor to intervene between my duty and my patient.

These words were perfectly legible, despite the large red crisscross that x'd them out.

A GRUDGING SMILE

Staring at the empty chair, P. thought: *Grushina, Yeshevsky, Hannah—all gone. Who will treat me?*

As a former KGB agent and now de facto head of FSB, P. knew a conspiracy when he smelled one. And this one was pungent. He pictured Yeshevsky in Israel (effectively beyond his reach) and a grudging smile crossed his face. He thought (with a degree of competitive admiration): *Refusenik. Scientist. Spymaster.*

P. left the office without looking at the trembling receptionist. He took the elevator downstairs, exited the lobby, made a right at the street, walked to the corner, made another right, then looked for the large black sedan with the tinted windows and new pair of bodyguards.

CONSPIRACY THEORY

With his reelection virtually assured, P. was less concerned about news leaks regarding his impaired health. Having hastily convened a meeting with key FSB officials, he gave the order to track down Dr. Hannah Belaya and Dr. Dimitri Grushina, both suspected of collaborating against the state, directed by their employer, Dr. Yevgeny Yeshevsky, President of the Cosmoenergy Federation, currently residing in Hebron. (P. did not tell anyone of Akhmerov and Zubilin's mission; he wanted the two initiatives to compete on independent tracks.)

The FSB officials saw the mission as relatively simple and expected a quick resolution. This should not be surprising: these were the same high-ranking officers and technocrats who had directed the successful hacking of the German, French and American national elections. Finding two absconded doctors, whose evasions were being directed by an uprooted, crackpot scientist (which is how they regarded Yeshevsky) was not considered by them a very great challenge.

But P. was beginning to think that the situation might be more complicated. He thought Yeshevsky might be receiving intelligence—and possibly material support—from the Israelis, or even the Americans. He'd also begun to wonder if Yeshevsky's clever maneuvers had less to do with protecting his staff and more to do with protecting the secret recipe of Cosmoenergy's life-saving, cancer-fighting regimen.

P. had always been motivated by dual, turbo-charged desires: to drive Russia to a position of world prominence and to procure for himself as much personal wealth as possible. The latter desire drove him to consider that the first-to-market potential of Cosmoenergy's proprietary information might be worth tens of billions. With that much additional money, he could shake the world until his dying breath.

P. did not share these thoughts with his FSB officers. He wanted to keep them focused on a single goal: find one of the three doctors who could save his life. (He knew apprehending Yeshevsky was improbable, as he was likely protected by Shin Bet. Hannah or Dr. Grushina were more viable targets. Either would do. Understandably, P. preferred that Hannah be found. Hannah had added value. He still saw romance and love in their shared future. He imagined the two of them as Russia's new royal couple, standing on a grand stage, waving to an adoring crowd; she, holding their baby son—a male heir—Russia's future!

Feeling a surge of excitement, P. rubbed his breast instinctively, but instead of feeling his excited heart, his fingers found the hard knot in his left lung. *No time to waste,* he thought. *I must find one of the doctors. My life depends on it. Russia's future depends on it!*

CHAPTER 5

PERSONAL QUESTIONS

Bethany parked her black sedan behind the Civic Center, where it could not be seen from the highway. Once parked, the women moved the supplies from the car into Hannah's new office, which had been readied with new lighting, a new stainless-steel sink and a used but serviceable desk (courtesy of Fred).

Inside, Hannah accepted Bethany's offer to help set up the shelves and the specimen cabinets but insisted on handling all the delicate and sensitive instruments herself, especially the multiphoton microscope, capable of showing living tissue at the cellular and even molecular level.

While they worked and chatted, both women wondered about each other's relationship with Yevgeny.

Bethany wondered: *How close were they? Did they work together? Late at night? … Were they friends outside the office? Were they lovers? Did he stay over? Did she? … Did they have stirring conversations about science? Did they discuss God? … Does she have children? How old is she? … Is she in love with him? Would she marry him?*

Hannah wondered: *How long did her treatment last? Is it true, they never met? How often did they communicate? Did they send emails? Did they Skype? Did she dress sexy when they Skyped? Did they talk dirty? … Did she ever marry? Ever have children? . . . How often does she communicate with Yevgeny now? Does she love him? Does he love her? Does she want to marry him?*

INTRODUCTIONS

The women heard the puttering noise of a small vehicle turn off the highway and park on the gravel lot in front of the Center.

Hannah correctly assumed it was Fred (whose perks included the use of one of the town's municipal golf carts) and while she would have preferred that he not meet Bethany, she had prepared herself for the possibility.

"Hello," she called with false brightness—but then stopped cold at the sight of Jason. (Despite lately meeting each other every other day, even for only an hour, he had never visited her at the Center, and so this meeting, with Fred by his side, seemed an unnatural surprise, an unexpected advancement in their relations, which, to that point, had consisted only of public meetings by the lagoons or in the hotel lobby where they occasionally held hands—if they were alone.)

"Nice to see you both," she said, regaining her composure. And then, pointing to the statuesque black beauty trailing behind her, "This my friend, Bethany. She bring supplies for my research."

Hannah had told Bethany about Fred, the director of the Civic Center, the gatekeeper to Saltin.

"Nice to meet you, Fred."

"Pleasure is mine," he said, happy to have yet another attractive person visiting Saltin.

Bethany's attention shifted from Fred to Jason. She liked the younger man's rugged style and wide shoulders; she felt drawn by his blue eyes and strong gaze. *No wonder Hannah never mentioned him,* she thought.

Jason (struck by Bethany's ebony beauty and graceful carriage) moved forward to shake her hand. Fred watched their interplay closely, as did Hannah.

"Nice to meet you, Bethany. I'm Jason."

His extended hand was tan, hairless, strong, with long, tapered fingers. His handsome face was weathered but welcoming, a soulful expression in his eyes, she thought.

"Nice to meet you, Jason."

He smiled, his hand holding hers.

She smiled too. "I'm curious," she said, slowly releasing his hand. "What do you do?"

He smiled again. "I'm a musician."

"A musician," said Bethany.

"Yes. Though these days I'm more of a wandering minstrel."

Hannah did not understand all his words. When he spoke with her, he used simpler words. She resented that he spoke to Bethany with words she did not know.

"You sing for your supper?" asked Bethany.

"No need. I have enough coin to keep me going—at least for a while."

Bethany nodded. "Where *are* you going, if you don't mind me asking."

Jason shrugged. The simple gesture touched both women, but as neither responded, Jason continued:

"I've written the music to a modern opera. Still looking for the right words."

"You have the basic story?"

"A work in progress," he said. Again, no one responded, so he added:

"Somehow, I wound up here, in Saltin. Maybe it was Fate. I don't know."

Fred smiled because he was standing in a circle of new friends. He was happy that Jason had come to Saltin; happy that Jason had brought Hannah, and Bethany too. *Perhaps,* he thought, *this is the start of Saltin's renaissance: the arrival of new, talented people.*

Bethany was happy because the day had turned out so pleasantly. She hadn't been looking forward to her long return trip to Tucson, but now she knew she'd spend the hours thinking about Jason, who'd come out of nowhere—just dropped from the sky—which was, in her experience, the way Fate usually worked.

Hannah was happy because her office was well supplied (lacking only the laser machine, which she expected to arrive soon) and she now could begin her important research in earnest. She was also happy that Jason had made a surprise appearance and hoped it would advance their relationship. With all that, she worried that Bethany (her only female friend in that part of the world), whom she suspected of being her competitor for Yevgeny's affection, might also come between herself and Jason.

ELEGIAC

Hannah left with Bethany (who offered to drive her back to Covenant House, before heading back to Tucson), leaving Jason and Fred alone, exactly where they had met, several weeks earlier.

"So, you're still here," said Fred. "Most visitors take some pictures and get back in their cars. Don't even stay the night."

"Like I said, something led me here. And now that I'm here, the place intrigues me."

Fred assumed it was Hannah who intrigued him, maybe Bethany too. "What do you mean? What intrigues you? I'd like to know." He was curious, and a little salacious; he wouldn't mind some saucy details from his younger friend.

But Jason's mind was elsewhere:

"Saltin's like two different moods. Of course, there's East and West, which is really strange, but even stranger—and more remarkable—the city is dead and alive at the same time, like a cemetery."

"A cemetery?"

Jason heard ire in Fred's voice. "I meant no disrespect."

"Saltin is no cemetery!"

"Sorry, let me explain." Jason gathered his thoughts. "First, I happen to like cemeteries. They're generally nice places: trees, grass, flowers—and very quiet. Easy to hear my own thoughts. When I'm in a cemetery, surrounded by the dead, I'm intensely aware of my beating heart and my living consciousness. It's a beautiful feeling. Puts me in a special mood."

"What kind of mood?"

Long pause.

"*Elegiac.* I think that's the word. When I'm in a cemetery, I tend to think well of all the nearby dead and that helps me think about my own future, in a more hopeful way."

"And Saltin makes you feel this way?"

"Yes, it fills me with hope."

"Really?" said Fred, intrigued by the line of Jason's reasoning. "That's unusual. I think most people see the devastation and regard Saltin as a dream gone bad. Like the Fall of the Roman Empire."

"I get that. But, for me, I see the remains of Saltin's former glory as signs of encouragement: like a high standard or a goal. And when I see survivors, like you, persisting amidst all the devastation, it gives me courage. Saltin intrigues me. It gives me hope."

"Hmmm. A subject worthy of your opera?"

"You read my mind. Yeah, that's what I've been thinking. But so far, all I have is the background, the setting. I need characters. I need their stories."

"Conflict? Love? Villains?"

"Yes. Of course!"

Both men laughed.

"You planning to draw from real life or use your imagination?"

"Both," said Jason. "I need all the help I can get."

The two men (who'd moved inside when the women had left) chatted a few minutes more. During an interlude, Fred stood up creakily and stretched.

"Like to take a walk?"

Jason assumed he meant along the dead shore but Fred had another idea.

"I'm in the mood for my Jesus walk. Join me?"

"Jesus walk? I don't think so. Doesn't sound kosher."

Fred laughed. "You Jewish? My wife was Jewish."

"I'm a devoutly lapsed Jew."

"Perfect! You're hired. C'mon."

Jason followed Fred out the back entrance which faced the dry sea. From there he could see four cement steps and (twenty feet to the right) a cement ramp, both of which led down to the sea bed. They took the stairs.

"I'm no expert, but didn't Jesus walk on water?"

Fred didn't respond. Instead, he began a slow and steady pace across the dead sea, Jason following. It was broiling hot.

After a minute, and already sweating, Jason asked, "Fred, what are you thinking?"

Fred stopped and turned to face Jason.

"Usually, when I first start this walk, all I see is a dry, empty basin. But as I continue walking, headed northeast, toward the opposite shore, I close my eyes and begin dreaming that the sea is filling with water. At first, it's just some puddling, but then the water gets deeper and deeper and soon covers my ankles and before long, reaches my knees. Then the water continues rising, but so does my body, and before I know it, I'm walking on water.

"That's when the dream intensifies. And it's always the same: I'm dressed in a flowing white robe, walking purposefully towards the far shore—and I see her, also wearing a flowing white robe, walking towards me. My hands are spread wide, as are hers. We're crossing the sea to save each other. Both of us need saving."

Fred's eyes were wet.

"The woman—is that your wife?" asked Jason.

"Yes."

"What happens?"

"I don't know. The dream always ends before we meet."

Jason held his tongue.

Fred remained silent for several more seconds and then redirected the conversation.

"You said you were married."

"I was. I don't think we're married now."

"You don't know?"

"She left suddenly. We spoke only a few times after—and never again in person. I don't know if she ever filed divorce papers. If she did, I never got them."

"If she sent them, you probably would have received them."

"I didn't stay put. I went away soon after she left me and I've been on the road ever since. If she sent papers, they never caught up to me."

"You were never notified by email?"

"Don't think so."

"You never signed any documents?"

"That's right."

"So, technically, you're not divorced."

"I don't know. I don't know how the law works in such cases. But in my heart,

we're divorced. It took a while, but I've moved on."

Fred mulled the details for several seconds.

"What's her name?"

"Renee."

"As in 'Walk Away Renee'?"

"More like 'Runaway Renee.'"

"She left you?"

"Yes. I said that."

"How long since you've seen her?"

"About ten years."

"I haven't seen my wife in forty years."

"I know, you told me."

"You miss her?" Fred asked, thinking about his own wife, Tova.

"Occasionally. But I think I've done a pretty good job of moving on."

"You live out of a rucksack and sleep in a windowless hole."

Jason took the comment as a joke and laughed. "I'm happy enough. Are you?"

Fred thought about Tova. He still missed her.

"Happy? I wouldn't say happy. Content. That sounds about right."

"But you still miss her?"

"Yeah," Fred said, pawing the sand with the toe of his shoe. "I still miss her, when I'm reminded of her."

"That happen often?"

Fred looked down. The question had nicked a nerve.

"Yeah, lately," said Fred.

"Really? What reminds you of her?"

Fred paused. "Happy couples."

Jason gave him a quizzical look. "That's surprising. There aren't a lot of couples in Saltin, much less happy ones."

"I'm thinking about the ones who visit. Met a nice young couple the other day. They came from San Diego to check out our spa waters. They looked happy."

Jason nodded. Fred continued, changing direction again: "About two weeks ago some people came by in a truck to scout the area as a possible movie setting."

"Another post-apocalyptic thing?"

"At this point, that's all we're good for, aside from our salts. But you never know. Just between us, we were recently visited by a large group—and they weren't here for our salts or our apocalyptic landscape."

"They come for our boardwalk dining?"

"Nope."

"They come for the Saltin Film Festival?"

"Nope. But I like the way you think."

"Oh, I know. They came to see the world's biggest empty sea."

"You're getting warmer, wiseass. But you'll never guess."

"Give me a clue. One clue."

"Lithium."

A GRIZZLED SCHEHERAZADE

During Saltin's glory years, the city's two mayors met each month to review their shared municipal responsibilities. These included the collection, treatment and disposal of sewage; fire protection; police protection; emergency medical services;

construction and maintenance of recreational facilities; improvement and maintenance of street lighting, landscaping, etc.

In more recent years (after the emptying of the sea, the departure of the businesses and the disintegration of the infrastructure), the two mayors and their unofficial associates (including Fred) met twice a year to discuss how to attract tourism and business investment, despite the city's seemingly hopeless outlook. These meetings were largely perfunctory. Nothing new was ever said, nothing new was ever thought. But their most recent meeting had been an exception.

Two months earlier, a team of chemists from University of California-San Diego, joined by a team of geologists from Stanford University, had been soil-testing a dry, prehistoric lake about sixteen miles southwest of the Saltin Sea. Test results revealed that the dry unnamed lake, only one-twentieth the size of the Saltin Sea, contained an amazingly rich concentration of lithium. Team leader, Professor Edwina Lazar Orosco, at University of California-San Diego, suggested that she and her colleagues reconvene at a later date to explore the much larger Saltin Sea. If the latter contained anything like the same proportion of concentrated lithium, it would be the largest known deposit in the world.

Without mentioning her team's findings at the smaller lake, Professor Orosco contacted the two mayors of Saltin, requesting permission to do some soil testing of their dry sea, promising that her team's work would leave behind almost no discernable trace.

The two mayors gave their consent as part of an agreement they sent to Professor Orosco, which she countersigned and returned. Upon receiving her signed document, the two mayors invited the professor to contact Fred Heinz, Director of the Saltin Civic Center, if she needed any onsite advice or assistance.

About six weeks later, Professor Orosco stopped by the Civic Center to inform Mr. Heinz that her group would soon commence its work.

Fred was immediately taken with the silver-haired professor, who moved like a sylph but dressed like Indiana Jones. She seemed to like him too and invited him to call her Edwina. "Thank you," he said, smiling. "Please, call me Fred."

Fred told Edwina that he knew Saltin's three hundred forty-square miles better than anyone and offered his services, however he might be useful. "Thank you," she said, thinking Fred very kind and gallant. He gave her his cellphone number and told her that wherever she was on the sea, she had only to text him her GPS coordinates and he would come, bringing anything she might need.

"Oh my god, do you walk on water, too?"

"That's another story," he said, smiling.

The next day, Edwina and her group began their research. As leader, she was all business, all the time, except when the group rested or broke for lunch, and then her thoughts flew to Fred. She was taken with the old man and his dead sea and hoped to see him again. But, try as she might, she could think of no ruse to compel him to visit her camp that wasn't brazen and unprofessional. With no opportunity for distraction, she concentrated on her work.

After two weeks of acquiring soil samples, the group's field mission was nearly complete—the next day would be its last. Edwina's desperation caused her heart to race. (She was not young. At seventy-one, she was the oldest person on the faculty. Her retirement was imminent; in fact, this field trip was her professional swan song—the university's gift to her before she called it a career. Soon, she'd be all alone. Her husband, an esteemed biochemist, was dead ten years. They'd been a good match, though their decision not to have children haunted her more than ever when she imagined her unemployed senior years: no husband, no family, no faculty friends. But all this did not explain her sudden attraction to Fred. She barely knew him. Why was she so intrigued? She pictured him fishing a dead sea—directing a civic center no one visited—and saw a colorfully eccentric soul, imbued with his own wisdom, hard won through many lean years. His resolve impressed her. He seemed to have found answers to the questions that were unsettling her. Also, he seemed to like her.)

The end of the field work provided Edwina with the stratagem she sought. Having scheduled a special luncheon for the next day, she invited Fred to join her team, hoping he would regale them with tales of Saltin's former glory—and, perhaps, exchange some nice personal words with her.

The team had picked a spot in the northwest corner of the desert sea, where the smell of putrefied fish was carried off on the Baja wind. Just in case the winds were contrary, Edwina brought flowers and lemons; along with all the salad and fruits to complement the wraps and desserts, the group had before them a flavorful and fragrant repast.

It was high noon, the appointed lunch hour, and there'd been no word from Fred. Edwina stared worriedly into the distance, its sere emptiness a metaphor of her imagined future. And then, on the yellow horizon, she espied a small approaching sandstorm. She tensed immediately but the sandstorm soon diffused, revealing a dune buggy, hard charging across the desert sea. A half minute later, on closer view, she saw it was a battered golf cart, Fred at the wheel. To Edwina, he looked like Rommel standing tall in the turret of a Panzer.

Dusty as hell, Fred joined the welcoming group, gathered like a Bedouin tribe under a striped canopy. Edwina gave him two towels—one damp, one dry. After he'd cleaned his hands and face, she insisted he eat. When he hesitated, she filled a plate for him. "Thank you," he said, smiling. "You're welcome," she said, smiling. And then: "If you wouldn't mind, I think everyone would like to hear the story of Saltin."

Fred was happy to play the part of a grizzled Scheherazade. As soon as the team gathered round, he commenced entertaining them, telling one story after another of Saltin's golden boom. He described Madonna singing at the star-studded grand opening of The Palace. He told how the real Pope had sent the Archbishop of Siena to bless the fountain waters outside The Mount. He explained, with special relish, why Saltin was called California's French Riviera and how the Saltin Regatta drew thousands of spectators to watch souped-up motorboats set world speed records. With extraordinary detail he described how fifty Old-World craftsmen had recreated the magnificent North Rose window of Notre Dame. He shared (almost under his breath, as if he were confiding an insider's secret) how private planes had circled the area at three thousand feet so land developers could have passengers bid on unsold parcels—so valuable and desirable, the contract ink was always dry before landing.

Although Fred was wise enough to look into the eyes of each of his enrapt listeners, he always lingered on Edwina's, which glittered with pride. Later, when they had a moment alone, he asked if he might write to her and she smiled. "Yes."

After the long luncheon, the geologists and chemists packed their equipment and returned to their respective universities to analyze their collected samples. During this time,

Edwina and Fred kept in touch by text message and email, sharing information about themselves, but no intimacies, as yet.

Two months later, when the integrated report was complete, Professor Orosco wrote to the two mayors, thanking them again for granting her and her team access to the Saltin Sea. She said she'd happily send each of them a copy of the report but preferred to see them in person to explain what her team had discovered.

The two mayors excitedly invited her to their upcoming, semi-annual meeting. Regarding her as an important dignitary, they emptied their entertainment budget in her honor, providing a variety of sandwiches and wraps, salads, fruit platters and dessert that nearly rivaled the desert luncheon Fred had attended.

During the beginning of the luncheon, while everyone was making chit-chat, Edwina announced that the publication of her group's report had been her last professional responsibility. "As of this moment, I am retired—a free woman!" Everyone congratulated her heartily, though Fred checked his enthusiasm, unsure how the news would affect him personally. Edwina marveled at his impressive tact, seeing it as yet another example of his wisdom and composure.

Edwina held off on her real news until dessert was served. When she was ready, she asked for everyone's attention. As soon as it was quiet, she cut to the chase:

"Essentially, our research concluded that a substantial amount of lithium is scattered throughout much of the dry Saltin Sea. However," she said, breaking into a wide smile, "near the sea's northeastern corner, in an area equivalent to sixty-seven square miles, we found an incredibly rich deposit. This deposit is as large as any deposit in Chile, owner of the world's largest lithium reserves. In fact, the Saltin Sea may prove to be the single largest lithium deposit in the world."

If she expected hoopla, she was disappointed. The room was quiet. No one knew much about lithium.

"I see," Edwina said, misreading the audience. "You're aware of the lithium but concerned about the extraction process."

Some of the attendees nodded vaguely, which encouraged Edwina to think that she was reading the room correctly.

Stanley Rankin, who'd been ruined by Saltin's collapse but had remained in West Saltin for decades—hanging on, ever hopeful—asked directly: "Just how valuable is this deposit, based on your best professional estimate?"

Edwina was ready for this moment. In fact, she had rehearsed it. "Well," she said, "I have great news and not-so-great news. The great news is the market timing." With that, Edwina turned to her notes.

"Let me begin by saying that lithium is an extraordinary mineral. Under normal conditions it is the lightest known metal and the lightest solid element. It never occurs freely in nature but only in compounds. However, because of its solubility, it is commonly present in ocean water and is usually obtained from brines."

Edwina looked up and smiled. As there were no comments or questions, she returned to her notes.

"For many years, lithium has been used to manufacture certain mood-stabilizing drugs and batteries for small appliances. Today, lithium batteries power millions of smartphones and laptops around the world. But even that's small potatoes. The demand for lithium is exploding."

Edwina looked up and smiled again. Her audience had barely stirred.

"If you'll excuse the pun, the driving factor behind the great demand for lithium is electric vehicles. Many of the giant companies—Apple, Amazon, Google—are now competing with major auto companies to develop electric vehicles, which are powered by—you guessed it—lithium batteries. Now, these are not your grandfather's batteries. Some of these batteries use more than ten thousand times more lithium than a smartphone. That may be hard to grasp but consider this: The production of just one million electric cars would use about the same amount of lithium as *every smartphone ever sold*. And—make no mistake—*millions* of electric vehicles are expected to be sold in the next few years. Tesla's Model 3, the one designed for the mass market, had about five hundred thousand pre-orders last time I checked. And that's just one manufacturer. I happen to know that Chinese auto battery makers are aiming to produce one hundred twenty gigawatt-hours per year. How big is that? Well, it's nearly three hundred fifty percent larger than Tesla's Gigafactory output, enough to power one and a half million electric vehicles *per year*. And that's just the Chinese. Also consider: several of the automobile manufacturers say that by 2023 all their new cars will be hybrids or fully electric vehicles. At the same time, there is worldwide interest in phasing out the sale of gasoline- and diesel-powered vehicles. What will take their place? Electric vehicles. And how will these vehicles be powered? Lithium batteries."

Edwina looked up. Now she had their attention. There was quite a buzz.

"How much is our deposit worth?" they all wanted to know.

"It's beyond my ability to calculate."

Almost everyone erupted with excitement. Only Stanley Rankin, the old curmudgeon, remained sedate. "What's the not-so-great news?"

Edwina had been expecting this too.

"Remember what I said about lithium?"

"Yes! It's found in ocean water. We have an entire sea of dried-up ocean water!" Hoots and cheers!

Edwina shook her head and the room grew still.

"I'm afraid the empty sea is a problem. You do have a great deal of concentrated lithium—sixty-seven square miles of it. But dry mining is expensive. The process is most cost-effective when lithium is extracted from brine."

The disappointment was palpable.

"So, what do we do?" It wasn't so much a question as a whine, a plaint, an existential cry for help.

"I don't know," said Edwina, shrugging her shoulders sympathetically. "With the great need for lithium, more effective dry-mining processes might be discovered in the future."

"But that could take years," said the King.

"We don't have years," said the Pope.

"I don't have an answer," said Edwina. "Other than refilling the Saltin Sea."

CHAPTER 6

CLEVER RUSE

During her early weeks in Saltin, Hannah had established herself as a patient suffering from respiratory disease and rheumatoid arthritis. It was a clever ruse, for when she visited every mud bath and spa lagoon (ostensibly to see which worked best for her body and biology), she easily obtained salt samples for later study in her office.

Of course, she also needed to do a wider search, but the dry Saltin Sea was nearly three hundred forty square miles. To acquire salt samples from its extensive shoreline and vast interior she needed help.

SETTING SAIL, TOGETHER

"Of course, I will help you."

Jason took her hand, discreetly. They were standing on the remnant boardwalk in the late afternoon. They were alone. Someone looking at the empty sea from an upper-story window of The Mount or The Palace might have seen them, but it's unlikely he or she could have discerned their clasped hands, much less their entwined fingers. Their risk was small but their thrill was great.

"It will be hard work," she said.

"It's important work," he said. "You're a scientist, looking to cure cancer. You came to this country by yourself.

You are very brave. I want to help you." He gave her hand a little squeeze.

"Besides," he said, pointing toward the desert sea, "going out there alone is dangerous. Look how it stretches to the horizon in all directions. That's dangerous for anyone. I'll go with you. You'll teach me how to use your tools and I'll help you."

Hannah moved closer to Jason, laying her head on his chest. His shirt was warm from the sun. She felt his heartbeat on her cheek. She felt safe.

THE WAITING GAME

Relations between Jason and Hannah had barely evolved since their first meeting. Both Jason and Hannah were okay with the slow advance. Both knew their correspondence had been daring because distance had made it safe. Both knew that physical proximity was a commitment of sorts. Both had their reasons to be wary. Wordlessly, both knew that the other was hungry for love but hurting in many ways. Both knew the way forward must be taken slowly.

PAINT JOB

"Fred, could I borrow your golf cart from time to time? I'll gladly pay for its use."

Fred was considering the request when Jason added, "Hannah wants to collect salt samples from all over the sea, but I don't think she should go alone." And then, "Of course, no one knows the sea better than you, but you've been busy. Besides, she wants to discuss some ideas she has for my opera."

Fred had mixed feelings. He'd really enjoyed showing Hannah around the city and would have liked guiding her around the sea.

"My cart needs to be charged—and it badly needs a paint job. I was planning to take care of it this week." His words were petty, and he knew it.

"I'll do it," said Jason. "I'll charge the cart. I'll even repaint it for you."

The cart really did need a paint job. Besides, Fred knew he could use any of the city's other carts.

"Okay. We can do that."

THE ARGO

Jason told Hannah about his plan. He said he would be ready in a few days. The following Tuesday morning, when he knew Hannah would be alone at the Civic Center, he knocked on her door.

"Your ship awaits you."

"My ship?"

"Yes, come see."

Hannah left her office, stepping out the back door that faced the sea. Indeed, her ship awaited her.

"It's beautiful. Who painted this, you?"

Jason made an extravagant bow.

"I named her *Argo*, the ship the Argonauts sailed."

"You are genius!"

Fred's golf cart looked like a mini, ancient galley—on wheels. A rooftop fringe fluttered in the breeze like a topsail. Each side panel was a curved ram horn. The hood was emblazoned with the profile of a forward-looking eye.

"Who is this eye?"

"The goddess Athena. She will watch over us."

Hannah's eyes watered with happy tears. "No one ever do for me anything like this."

"This ship will carry us across the Saltin Sea."

"We find your Golden Fleece?"

"We sail in search of our dreams. I am Jason, your captain. And you are Hannah, my first mate."

"Maybe I be captain," said Hannah, flashing her competitive spirit.

Jason drew her close. "Let's be fair. You are scientist, I am your assistant. We are sailing, I am your captain."

Hannah smiled, her heart full of love. "Yes, my captain!"

MAPPING

Using a digital map of the Saltin Sea, Hannah divided the region into fifty numbered sectors (each approximately 6.8 square miles) and determined the coordinates of each sector's boundaries. This information would help her record the exact location of each salt sample she found. For example, having established each sector's exact center, the location of one early salt sample was recorded as: *sector 36; northwest 58°; 81.5 meters; 13 cm deep.*

CHECKLIST

Hannah used a checklist to prepare for every excursion: wide-brimmed hat, long-sleeved shirt, long pants, hiking shoes; specimen-collecting tools and containers; fully-charged laptop, extra battery, charging cord; fully-charged cellphone, portable cellphone signal booster (on loan, courtesy of Fred); bottled water; knife; blanket; granola bars; multipurpose binding/towing cords; emergency medical kit, etc.

EVERY PICTURE TELLS A STORY

Jason assisted Hannah on almost all her excursions. After two weeks he was able to anticipate which tools she'd need to extract a particular salt sample, depending on its location and depth.

Typically, they worked 7:00 A.M. until noon, at which point the overhead sun was too oppressive to endure. At noon, they'd load their tools and salt samples onto the cart's flatbed extension, which Jason had expertly jerry-rigged.

Most days they drove directly back to the Civic Center, where they ate lunch in the shade of the building's rear wall, seated at a small table for two that Jason had found abandoned in the derelict hotel he called home. On these days, Jason often played guitar for Hannah. Sometimes he happily played the wordless music of his opera; sometimes he played fiercely tightlipped, struggling to find the lyrics to pair with the visions in his brain.

Hannah saw his struggle and wanted to help. She wanted to be his partner in music as he was her partner in science.

One day, instead of returning to the Civic Center after their morning labor, Hannah directed him to a spot about a mile due east of the Civic Center. When they were about fifty yards away, Hannah asked him to stop the cart.

"Come," she said. "I want to show you."

They walked together holding hands.

After twenty yards, Jason saw a line of shimmering color in the near distance. As they approached, the line increased in width and depth until it looked like a small oasis of colored crystals. They stopped about five yards away.

"What is this? It's beautiful," said Jason.

He walked a wide circle around the colored stones but could not discern any pattern or meaning. It was beautiful but inscrutable, like the mysterious handiwork of some vacated civilization.

"It is my son, Peter. The two piles of blue stones—those are his eyes."

Once described, Jason clearly saw Peter's face.

"I didn't know you had a son."

"I *have* a son."

"Sorry."

Jason wondered if Peter was flesh and blood, or a figment, like his own imaginary children.

Hannah approached him and took his hand. "I want to tell you my story. I want to know your story. Our stories meet here, in the middle of the Saltin Sea."

Jason's mind flashed back to his early exchanges with Astral Love, which had felt so profound and fated. Now, standing in the middle of a desert sea with his flesh-and-blood Hannah, he felt certain that his life story and hers would form the two twining threads of his opera.

CHAPTER 7

TRACKING THE TRACKERS

Believing that Anatoly Bychkov was still their best play, the two Russian agents spent six more days observing his movements. During this period Bychkov left his apartment each morning at 6:30, walked six blocks to the Coney Island Cab company, emerged twenty minutes later in a yellow medallion taxi, which he drove (on average) ten hours before returning it to the garage. Each evening he walked directly back to his apartment, often stopping by the Starbucks next door for a coffee and a sandwich.

Although the agents continually changed their parking spot, Bychkov knew they were watching him. He assumed they didn't believe his story about not knowing Hannah's whereabouts. He understood she was very important to them but could not imagine why. He also understood that when they stopped watching him it would mean that she was no longer important to them—or they had a better way of finding her.

One day, after taking a fare to Kennedy Airport (and sensing that he had not been followed), he drove to an internet café in Howard Beach and paid cash for a half-hour session, during which time he sent a half-dozen emails to friends and associates to learn what he could about Hannah and his son Peter. Two days later he went to another internet café to check his email, once again paying cash. He had three responses to his earlier emails but learned nothing relevant.

That night he found himself staring again at the agents' business card. He still believed this connection would be fortuitous, but being an active, self-reliant fellow (who had run with a clever crowd of sharks and shysters), he felt the need to help ensure Fate's success.

Two days later was Sunday, his day of rest. He'd been sipping a cup of instant coffee while watching the street from his window. When he heard the unmistakable sound of a basketball bouncing in the hallway, he grabbed his wallet, opened his apartment door, and spoke to his twelve-year-old neighbor before the boy went downstairs.

"Mikey, how you like to make twenty bucks for two minutes' work?" He opened his wallet and pulled out a legit bill.

"What's the play?" Mikey sounded like a streetwise kid, which he was.

Bychkov led Mikey downstairs to the building's dark vestibule. They stood in the shadow, looking out a large glass door with a wide view.

"You see that gray car on the left, four cars down?"

"I see it."

"Good. Now listen carefully."

All Mikey had to do was dribble his ball up and down the block, waiting for his friend to come by, like he always did. At some point, he had to lose control of the ball behind the gray car. When he went to retrieve the ball, he would stick a magnet under the car where it couldn't be seen. Bychkov took the flat, tiny metal tracker out of his wallet and gave it to Mikey.

"A bomb?" the boy asked.

"Look at it," said Bychkov, as if talking to a fellow pro. "It's the size of a quarter. That look like a bomb to you? No bomb."

"What is it?"

Bychkov lowered his voice to suggest confidentiality. "The men in the gray car robbed my friend. I want to track their car, so I can tell the police where they live."

Mikey nodded. Bychkov gave him the twenty-dollar bill and the tiny metal tracker.

"Put the magnet in your pocket. Bounce your ball for at least five minutes so they don't notice you anymore. Then do what I said. You understand?"

"Got it. No problemo."

Bychkov patted the boy's shoulder and went back upstairs. He returned to the same window, which had an acute view of the gray Honda. For about ten minutes he watched Mikey practice his dribbling up and down the block. Sometimes Mikey dribbled high, sometimes low, sometimes between his legs. Sometimes he used a stutter-step to fake an imaginary opponent. When the ball finally kicked off his knee and rolled behind the gray car, Mikey hustled after it, as any kid would, and with impressive nonchalance placed the magnet, grabbed his ball, and jogged back to the sidewalk to continue his dribbling. Five minutes later his friend came by and the two boys walked off in the direction of the school playground. About ten minutes later, Bychkov left his apartment for his Sunday morning stroll on the boardwalk.

WILLFUL COMPLICITY

Meanwhile, P. was becoming more obviously sick. In recent days his hand flew to his chest so often, his staff thought he had developed a tic. His situation was becoming dire.

Mostly, P. blamed Yeshevsky, the traitorous Jew, for forcing Drs. Belaya and Grushina into hiding, where they would not be able to treat him, but he suspected all three of willful complicity.

Knowing his life was at stake, P. had to find at least one of the traitorous doctors as soon as possible. In his heart, he hoped it would be Hannah. He prayed it would be Hannah. He needed her special attentions. He needed her love and affection. If she apologized and seemed contrite, he would let her live.

A SECOND SWEEP

Following his aborted appointment with Dr. Grushina, P. ordered FSB agents to sweep Cosmoenergy's offices looking for information related to salt research and cancer treatment. Unfortunately, they found nothing—testimony to Dr. Grushina's scrupulous eradication of samples, data and correspondence. P. was furious and ordered another sweep. It was during this second sweep that an agent found an unlabeled specimen slide still clipped to the stage of a microscope that had been placed in a cluttered box and left in a cluttered closet. The slide was carefully removed, bagged, and sent to a laboratory for examination. Lab scientists immediately saw that the specimen was a salt compound. But what kind of compound—and from where? After performing various tests and spectra analyses—and then comparing the resultant data with international databases—it was determined that the sample originated in southern California, very likely in a large, dry, inland basin called the Saltin Sea.

ANDERSON AND ZIMMER HEAD WEST

The agents received a coded text message directing them to a secret safehouse in San Diego, where they would lay low until they received further instruction.

They were glad to leave Brighton. The stakeout had been awfully boring. Bychkov never broke with his daily routine and they'd learned nothing new about Hannah Belaya. Still, they'd enjoyed several homecooked-style Russian meals and did not expect to enjoy such a perk in San Diego.

Anderson entered the safehouse's address into their car's dashboard GPS and off they went on their westward journey, driving steadily and conservatively to avoid attracting attention.

Anderson did most of the driving by day, Zimmer by night. They talked about politics, soccer, their wives and kids—but always in English.

Anderson had told his wife he was going to Chechnya. He'd said it was a delicate matter and wasn't sure when he would be home. Zimmer had told his wife he was going to Ukraine. He'd said it was a complicated situation and wasn't sure when he would return. The two agents had worked together for twenty-five years but their wives had never met.

BYCHKOV HEADS WEST

When Bychkov left for work on Wednesday morning the gray Honda was gone. He smiled because he was prepared. Still, he was anxious that the gray sedan might reappear before he returned home that evening. Despite his anxiety, he returned via his usual route, even stopping to pick up a large coffee and sandwich at Starbucks. Before entering his building, he cast a few darting glances up and down both sides of the block to make sure the car was gone. It was. *If the car is still gone in the morning, I will follow them,* he thought.

That night he slept very well, deep dreaming of Hannah and Peter. In his dreams they were together again, a happy family.

Next morning, as soon as he awakened, he peered out his street-facing window. As he hoped, the car was gone. Wasting no time, he showered and shaved, thinking: *This is the first day of my new life.* (He'd felt that way only five times before: on his wedding day; the day his son was born; on entering prison; on leaving prison; the day he arrived in America.)

As soon as he finished his coffee, he pulled out from underneath his bed a pair of black leather valises—one large, one small—a gift from his dear mother, now deceased. The valises were already packed.

He had no plants or pets. He had no unopened mail or other papers. He left his bed unmade and dishes in the sink. He was ready to go. He might be gone several days. He might never return.

He left the apartment quickly—without the valises—calmly walking downstairs and out the building.

His car was parked around the corner, to the right. It was a dark-blue, two-door Ford he'd bought for five hundred dollars. It had needed transmission work, but he'd done most of it himself and it now ran surprisingly well. He hadn't used it while being watched. He didn't want the agents to know he had a car. The car had license plates and was properly registered.

He started the car, drove it around the block, then pulled into the empty hydrant space near the front of his building. Returning to his apartment, he grabbed his two valises, carried them into the hallway, put them down, then locked his door without any sentimental leave-taking. He then carried the valises out the building and to his car, carefully arranging them in the trunk so as not to scratch their fine leather.

His car had a full tank of gas. His secondhand smartphone was fully charged. (The same Russian friends who'd sold him the car had also sold him the tracker and cellphone. For guys who worked in a local lumberyard, they had an impressive inventory of new and used electronics for sale: cash only; no receipt, no warranty, no return.) He took his time getting his GPS tracking app online. The first info he received was very clear: the gray Honda Accord was in motion, traveling west on I-76 at fifty-four miles per hour, approaching Harrisburg, Pennsylvania.

GRUSHINA HEADS WEST

Dimitri Grushina found the bus trip to Philadelphia interesting because he was in a foreign land and the most banal details—like signage and fencing—seemed exotic to him. He was surprised how surprising America could be. In fact, he'd been startled by his reflection in the bus window, his beardless visage and American cowboy hat combining for a high-voltage existential jolt.

Later, in Philadelphia's airport, waiting to board a Frontier Airlines flight to San Diego, his mind alternated between two imagined images. The first was P.'s rage on discovering that his own doctor had forsaken him, leaving behind an ironic, x'd-out letter by way of explanation. The second was of Yevgeny in Hebron, visiting ancient places of sanctity, feeling vitalized by their holy positivity—his bioenergy increasing, his aura glowing brightly.

FINAL ARRANGEMENTS

Having learned that Hannah had set up her office and was busy collecting salt samples, Yevgeny spent many deliriously happy hours imagining the two of them together, exploring the desert sea, searching for the miracle salt that would make them both famous.

Yevgeny was very proud of Hannah and very proud of himself for hiring and training her as he had. She was brave, strong, self-reliant, a wonderful scientist—and would be a wonderful mother too.

His thoughts turned to his parents, happier now than they had ever been. For many years they'd known shared love and respect, but in making *aliyah* they'd found a special peace and grace. Their lives now seemed to glow with a kind of completeness, which made Yevgeny think of his own life and Hannah's. She had done everything he had asked of her. She needed only the laser machine and samples of cancer-diseased cells to continue their important work. But getting her a laser machine to match the model they'd used at Cosmoenergy was a tricky business: the machines were manufactured in Europe and could be traced. Even so, despite having to work through back channels to preserve anonymity, he was able to purchase a comparable laser and send it to the Yoga and Ayurveda center in Tucson, Arizona.

Only one more thing needed to be done before Yevgeny could join his love in Saltin. He needed to finish his preparations for Hannah's wedding dress.

TRANSFORMATION

Months earlier, while studying sample salts from the Dead Sea and first falling in love with Hannah, Yevgeny read several online articles about an Israeli artist who had submerged a black wedding dress into the Dead Sea for two months. (The wedding dress had been a replica of the one worn by the Hasidic heroine in a 1920s' production of S. Ansky's classic play, *The Dybbuk,* in which a young bride is possessed by the evil spirit of her dead lover who died before they could marry.) Yevgeny visited the artist's website and saw a slideshow of the wedding dress's amazing transformation from black silk brocade—to salt-flecked, salt-covered, salt-crystallized white gown. For Yevgeny, the gown's metamorphosis was a metaphor of his growing affection for Hannah, from professional respect, to carnal yearning, to enlightened passion.

Certain now of his devotion for Hannah (and convinced of her deep and abiding love for him), he contacted the artist to see if she would be willing to sell him the salt-sequined wedding gown. But the artist had already signed agreements for a series of international exhibitions that featured the gown and was unwilling to part with her unique creation.

Undeterred, Yeshevsky contacted two members of her production crew (who'd been named in one of the online articles) and offered them twenty-five hundred dollars each if they would repeat the artist's experiment with a dress of his choosing. The two young men agreed.

From the start, Yeshevsky had a very special dress in mind: the heavily brocaded black gown his mother had worn to his thirteenth birthday party (in lieu of a bar mitzvah, which was banned by the Soviet authorities). The somewhat extravagant affair remained fixed in Yevgeny's memory as the height of his mother's grace and beauty (her comely shape and stature, even at forty, very much like his own dear Hannah's). He knew his mother still had the dress (he'd helped her pack it during their hurried move to Israel) and when he told her that he would like to remake it for a special friend of his, his mother did not hesitate to hand it to him, thinking and praying that her son had finally found love and was planning to marry.

With his mother's dress in hand, he arranged with the Dead Sea artist's two assistants to reprise their celebrated experiment. All went nearly as expected. Two months later,

Yevgeny had a beautiful wedding gown for his Hannah—only, he had not counted on it being quite so heavy. At fifty pounds, it weighed nearly a third as much as his bride to be. Further, the gown had lost its flexibility—it would be very difficult for Hannah to wear. Still, Yevgeny loved it. It was a piece of art, created from his mother's own gown and transformed by the amazing salts of the Dead Sea. He would present it to Hannah on the day he proposed, a mystical token of his profound love.

When he packed for his trip to California, the white, salt-crystalized wedding dress required its own large container.

NEW ARRIVAL

After landing in San Diego and reacquiring his luggage, Dimitri took a bus to Saltin City. The trip was expensive (one hundred fifty dollars) and took six hours. On hearing the bus driver finally announce the word *Saltin,* Dimitri hurriedly exited via the rear door. As soon as his feet touched ground, he was confused. Expecting to see Saltin City, he saw only a single building: a lonely outpost beside a desert sea, its roof ridged like a giant scallop shell, its front door slightly unhinged and covered with faux starfish. He was struggling to understand American reality when Fred emerged.

"Welcome to the Saltin Civic Center. I'm Fred Heinz, director, caretaker and guide. How can I help you?"

"Saltin City? Is this here?"

"No, no, no," Fred said, shooing away Dimitri's faux pas with his gnarly hands. "Saltin City isn't what it used to be, but it can't be confused with this place."

"How can I get there?"

Fred was about to explain when the door behind him opened. Having heard an accent she thought she recognized,

Hannah had come to the front door and remained there in the shadow, her right hand visored over her eyes.

"Dimitri, is that you?"

Dimitri took two steps closer, and squinted.

"Анна?"

Fred turned to Hannah and said, "He just missed the last bus to Saltin."

"It is okay," said Hannah. "He can stay in my office tonight."

Fred's mind reeled in at least three different directions. He waved goodbye to them both and walked towards the remnant pier to have himself a good think.

HANNAH AND DIMITRI REUNITE

When on foreign soil, there's nothing like seeing a familiar face and hearing one's native tongue to propel two slightly acquainted people into each other's arms, which is exactly what happened to Hannah and Dimitri as soon as Fred had left them alone.

When the shock abated, Hannah led the way inside to show Dimitri their new office.

"I love what you've done with the place," Dimitri said in English, which cracked them both up—two people who had never even joked in all the months they'd worked together in Moscow.

"When you become cowboy?" she said, pointing at his new hat.

"I am home on the range," he said, making a joke that Hannah did not understand but laughed at anyway.

The mood remained light until Hannah made tea and set two cups before them. At that point, facing the prospect of sober conversation, disturbing questions occurred to them both.

"Hannah, I thought you were tending a sick aunt in Poland—or went to meet Yevgeny."

Hannah was embarrassed, not because Dimitri had imagined her in the arms of Yevgeny, but because she and Yevgeny had concocted plans without letting him in on their secrets.

"I'm so sorry, Dimitri. We had to do it. Yevgeny was so worried about my safety—and then he went to Israel. I'm sure you know who was behind that. Yevgeny had no choice. He had to work quickly to get me far away, where P. would not find me."

"Someone could have told me," Dimitri said softly.

"There wasn't time. Besides, Yevgeny trusted you—and only you—to take charge of the whole office. And because he had so much faith in you, he had the foresight to train you in the laser-salt therapy. Beyond that, he couldn't tell you more, without putting you in danger—and Yevgeny cares for you too much to ever do that."

Dimitri appeared quite emotional.

"But what are doing you here?" Hannah suddenly asked. "Who is running the office? Did you treat P. on Monday?"

Dimitri stared into his teacup. "Oh, Hannah. I couldn't. I just couldn't. I couldn't bear it."

"What happened?"

"I'm sorry. I had a sort of breakdown. I couldn't treat P. I had to leave."

"Just like that? You left?"

"No, not just like that. I covered our tracks. I carefully destroyed or erased everything we had ever done with salt research."

"What? Yevgeny will kill you!"

Tears pooled in Dimitri's eyes and ran freely down his cheeks.

"I'm so sorry. But it's not as crazy as you think. Before you arrived, I believe Yevgeny set up a daily backup of our entire computer system. I'm quite sure of it."

Hannah softened her tone. Still, she was angry and frightened. "But, Dimitri, what do you think P. will do? How do you think he will react?"

"I don't know. I'm sorry."

Hannah did not want to frighten him, but she felt she had to state the obvious:

"For sure, he will have his agents hunt for us. And they will find us."

RELATIONS

After they finished their tea and calmed their nerves, Hannah led Dimitri inside the Civic Center and gave him a quick tour. Referring to the posters and various artifacts, she explained Saltin's history as best she could. Using the architectural model of the city, she pointed out the lagoons, the boardwalk and how Commonwealth Avenue divided Saltin into East and West. She then indicated Covenant House, briefly describing what it was like to live there with nun-like sisters. Finally, she pointed out The Mount and The Palace, explaining that he would likely find lodging in one place or the other. (She did not mention the possibility of finding a free, squatter's residence. The idea of squalor depressed her, though she made an exception for Jason, romanticizing his artistic, wayfarer's existence.) She then mentioned Jason, explaining how he had fortuitously become Yevgeny's friend on Facebook and that it was Jason's revelations of Saltin's special salts that were responsible for them both being in this strange place together. She said nothing about her personal relations with Jason. Nor did she say anything about her relations with Yevgeny, other than he had financed the office and was planning to arrive in Saltin very soon.

"Oh! Do you know when?"

FRED AT THE PIER

Years ago, Fred saw a spotted dog in the shade of the broken pier near the Civic Center. Longing for company, he approached, but the dog retreated, walking backwards, his eyes focused on Fred. The scene repeated two days. On day four, Fred set a bowl of water and some food in the slatted shade and walked away. The next day, the dog reappeared, but the food and water were gone. Fred refilled the bowl, left some more scraps, and then walked away, his back to the dog. Eventually, the dog allowed Fred to sit nearby while it lapped and devoured.

Fred felt bad for the mutt, until he realized they made such a good pair. That's when Fred took up dry fishing the empty sea, the sporting life of dreamers, so he and the mutt would have company.

Lately, Fred was starting to believe that he was living the dream: that people with money and skills and new ideas were returning to Saltin. It seemed to him that more were arriving every day. He planned to talk to the two mayors about getting more rooms readied at The Palace and The Mount. He knew there would be investment costs (electricity, lamps, bedding, plumbing), but he thought these would quickly pay for themselves and turn to profit when news of Saltin's rebirth traveled far and wide.

Staring at the empty sea, Fred imagined new airplanes flying low, assessing land parcels and properties for redevelopment. He thought of the new fellow who'd just stepped off the bus and of Hannah, Jason and Bethany. He imagined a long queue of new visitors waiting to enter the Civic Center, some already seated out back in his new seaside café.

P. AWAITS WORD

Some weeks following his reelection to yet another six-year term as president, P. breathed a sigh of relief that brought a sharp pain to his chest. Though he'd been aware of the growing knot in his lung for months, his impacted breathing was a shocking intimation of mortality. Now, he felt desperately pressed to act.

With all three of his doctors out of contact and beyond his reach, it was a major coup of his agents to have discovered a connection between Cosmoenergy and the Saltin Sea. P.'s instincts (which rarely failed him) suggested that Hannah or Dr. Grushina would likely show up there, if they hadn't already. However, if his agents (who were on their way) could not locate and return one of the doctors to Moscow, he would have no choice but to aggressively seek out one of the doctors for treatment, wherever he or she was, even if it meant traveling incognito to Hebron or all the way to that godforsaken, empty sea in the very south of California.

To help ensure his success, P. ordered that Dr. Grushina's mother and Hannah's son be located and surveilled. If necessary, they could quickly be taken into custody. All leverage was good leverage.

LOW CONCENTRATION

While updating the deep cover of Anderson and Zimmer, FSB research analysts discovered a scholarly article (recently printed in a pair of American university journals), describing what was believed to be the largest dry lithium deposit in the world. The deposit was in the northeast corner of California's empty Saltin Sea, very close to the southern terminus of the San Andreas Fault. The analysts noted that Russia's own lithium deposits are widespread in hard-rock pegmatites of low concentration, where extraction is too difficult and costly to be viable. The analysts emphasized that this situation had forced Russia into costly lease arrangements with nations with access to more highly concentrated deposits of dry lithium or to rich, brine-based lithium sources. The analysts further noted that the Russian government recently opened the world's largest lithium-ion battery plant in Novosibirsk. The facility, referred to as Lithotech, was expected to produce a wide range of lithium batteries, energy storage applications, and emergency-power supplies, though its profit margins were expected to be small because its business plan was predicated on the use of hard-mining techniques of low-concentrated lithium. The analysis concluded that Lithotech's profitability would increase exponentially if Russia had direct, proprietary access to rich, brine-based lithium sources, or even to dry resources of greater concentration.

COVER STORY

Five days after arriving at their safehouse in San Diego, Anderson and Zimmer received a courier package containing their updated deep-cover documents, fancy laminate business cards, and a pair of personalized scripts that described them both as representatives of American Lithium, a Detroit-based, auto battery manufacturer that owned more than twenty, cutting-edge, dry-mining patents, several of which were described in some detail.

According to the script, the two reps were sent to Saltin to examine the lithium site themselves. If the property was as advertised, and free of all liens and encumbrances, and the owners motivated to sell, they were empowered to make an offer to purchase seventy square miles of the dry seabed for the building of mining and extraction facilities.

The package also contained bio notes on the mayors of West and East Saltin, along with the address of the Saltin Civic Center and notes on its director, Fred Heinz.

SIDE BY SIDE

According to Anatoly Bychkov's tracker, the agents' car had remained parked at the same San Diego address from ten in the evening to seven the next morning during the past five days. Bychkov noted the days, times and address on a slip of paper.

Bychkov did not think suburban San Diego was the agents' final destination, but he couldn't be sure. For all he knew, they already had Hannah under surveillance, observing her every move from their house directly across the street. He imagined the agents, side-by-side in the darkness, spying into her open bedroom window with their zoom binoculars, whispering shameless encouragements as she began to undress and he thought: *These are just like the bastards who sent me to prison, dragging me from my wife and son.*

SALTIN BOUND

Having received their updated documents and internalized their scripts, Anderson and Zimmer (reps of American Lithium, experts on the soft mineral's extraction and manufacturing) had the perfect cover to venture to Saltin to track down Dr. Hannah Belaya while also assessing the lithium situation.

Using their new professional personae, they wrote a letter to Fred Heinz, Director of the Saltin Civic Center, asking for a meeting. According to their notes, Fred was more than just a gatekeeper; he had the ear of the two mayors. Mr. Heinz responded immediately and enthusiastically, scheduling the meeting when he knew Hannah would be away. He didn't want the lady with the bad lungs and Russian accent to sour Saltin's best business prospect in years.

WORDLESS PRAYER

After sweeping the sand and salt from the exhibition hall's floor, Fred dusted the posters and architectural model that had been the vision of Saltin's Founding Fathers.

At precisely noon a car pulled up and parked in front of the Center. Fred closed his eyes and prayed that his expected visitors were Heaven-sent: that they'd come to reward his long-suffering soul with the promise that he would live to see Saltin reborn. He was in a joyous mood—until he heard scuffling shoes and a tentative knock, and then his mood plummeted into a pit of doubt. During this brief but intense crucible he swore he would do anything he could for these men if it meant new life for Saltin.

MEETING OF MINDS

Fred thought the meeting was going well. Each of the reps had accepted a cup of coffee and seemed perfectly content to chat, mostly about life in Saltin today.

"It's remarkable that you stayed here all these years, Mr. Heinz."

"Please, call me Fred."

"Well, Fred, you have a survivor's persistence."

"And a pioneer's vision. Good for you!"

"Aw, you know, if you believe in something, you give it your all. I believe in Saltin. I believe it has a rosy future. I guess you do too."

"The scientific report was very impressive."

"But we do have concerns."

"Because it's dry lithium?" asked Fred.

"Precisely. You know your lithium!"

Fred smiled proudly.

"Now, as we said in our letter," began Anderson, "our company owns a number of high-tech patents for mining dry lithium. But even with our efficient means, it would be impossible for us to turn a profit if our initial costs were too high."

"What does that mean, practically speaking?" Fred asked.

"To be frank," began Zimmer, "there's no infrastructure in place at the site. There are no roads, no source of potable water, no nearby energy grid to tap into."

"Without the assistance of state or federal government, we would have to create the necessary infrastructure ourselves."

"But let's be clear. We're not suggesting the government get involved. As an experienced man like you knows, government oversight and paperwork would delay the project for many years."

"What we'd like to do," said Anderson, "is to assess the area ourselves, and if it proves as promising as we hope, we'd like to share with you—and the mayors of your city—our proposal to create the required infrastructure, along with the building of the mining and extraction systems."

"Which brings us to the subject of the cost of the land," said Zimmer. "If our assessment proves positive, we'd like to buy seventy square miles of the area that includes the lithium deposit identified in the scientific report."

"Couldn't you just lease the land?" Fred asked.

Both men shook their heads.

"Quite frankly, we're not thinking about a quick strike and pulling up stakes."

"We're looking at a long-term play here."

"We're not looking for a landlord."

"We're looking for a partner."

"We're talking commitment."

"We're talking about making our stockholders rich."

"We're talking about the rebirth of Saltin City."

They paused to let this comment sink in.

"And let's be very clear, we wouldn't be here talking to you if we didn't think we had a solid plan and a fair offer."

"But we do need to purchase the seventy square miles."

"Hey," said Zimmer with a big smile and open arms. "We're prepared to pay a very fair price—millions of dollars. We just can't afford to pay a crazy sum, not with all the infrastructure and development costs involved."

Fred's vague dream of New Saltin was coalescing into a clearer, more vibrant vision. "I'm sure your plan is fair," he said, his heart racing. "I'll share the news with our two mayors and set up a meeting as soon as possible."

Fred smiled, feeling triumphant. He saw himself as a wheeler-dealer, playing point on a major financial deal that could change the fate of Saltin. He thought of Edwina and how she would see him in a new light. He thought of Tova, his corporate wife who'd left him because he'd disappointed her. *Oh, if she could see me now!*

CHAPTER 8

BYCHKOV IN SALTIN

Bychkov's tracking data indicated that the agents were now parked in Saltin City. According to his GPS map, he was near the north shore of the Saltin Sea, though he couldn't see a drop of water anywhere. He noted that the highway was about to split: Route 86 to the right, Route 111 to the left. As far as he could tell, the routes were nearly the same length, but Route 111 seemed like the road less traveled, so he took it—and soon regretted his decision.

Route 111 closely paralleled the blighted desert sea: miles of blondish sand and salt mixed with gray swatches of lithium. There were no islands, no swells, no trees; just a flat salty basin, an invisible miasma of decayed fish and an unremitting white sun hovering above.

As Bychkov passed through the wide shadow cast by the looming walls of Calpurnia State Prison, he flashbacked to his ten years inside a rank and gloomy cell, recalling how his fierce determination to reunite with Hannah and his son Peter had helped him survive.

Eventually, Route 111 fed into East Saltin, a forlorn, salt-diseased Podunk, almost as destitute as the empty sea he had passed. There were very few people on the street; one of them suggested he go to The Mount if he wanted a room with electricity and running water.

On the way to The Mount, Bychkov wondered: *Are the agents still tracking Hannah? Did they find her here? What could have brought her to this godforsaken place?*

At The Mount, the clerk at the registration desk greeted him warmly.

"Good afternoon. How can I help you?"

"I'd like a room. Single bed. I'm alone." Bychkov was confident in his English, developed during his years in Brooklyn.

"Excellent. Let me check what's available." (As of that morning, only three other rooms were habitable; Dr. Dimitri Grushina had taken one of them.)

"Okay. I see we have an available room. How long will you be staying?"

Bychkov wasn't sure. He wasn't sure of anything.

"Can I pay by the day?"

"Of course. But I can give you a better rate if you book three days or more."

"Just one day, for now."

"Okay. That's great."

The clerk was finishing the registration when Bychkov asked, "Do you have a map of the city?"

"A map? No, not a current map. We used to sell old maps as souvenirs. But I don't have any left."

"Oh. Too bad."

"Well, if you really want one, you might get one at the Civic Center. In any case, it's a good place to visit. The director, my friend Fred, knows everything about Saltin. Tell him Buddy sent you!"

Bychkov carried his two pieces of fine leather luggage to his room on the second floor. Not knowing how long he would be there, he did not unpack. Instead, he lay on the old bedspread and duvet, staring at the ceiling, thinking mostly about what he would say to Hannah when he finally saw her again. He also thought about the two agents. They would not be happy to see him.

He sat up and reached for his shoulder bag. He checked it about six times a day. He checked it once more to make sure his sunglasses and gun were just as he had left them.

THOUGHTFUL ACTION

Bychkov very much wanted a map. In prison, he'd had no plan of escape. Without a plan, he'd had no real hope. Without hope, his incarceration had been a living death. Once free, Bychkov determined to live a life of thoughtful action. He'd left Ukraine with a well-considered plan; in Brooklyn, he'd cleverly turned the tables on his trackers to pursue his wife. A map could help him systematically explore Saltin. If his Hannah were there, he would find her.

A PAINED SMILE

It was easy enough to find the Civic Center. It was right off Route 86, the only standing building on the west shore of the dead Saltin Sea.

Bychkov parked his blue Ford out front and cut the engine. Standing beside the car, he was stunned by the bleak surround of desert nothingness (save for the derelict pier and what looked to be a dog sleeping in its shadow). With his shoulder bag positioned for easy access, he knocked warily on the slightly unhinged door, thinking the two agents might be inside. When no one answered, he entered with a light step.

Inside the main exhibition room, he noted the posters and artifacts but avoided inspecting anything too closely, lest he relax his hair-trigger readiness.

From the near distance his attentive ears picked up a musical strain that was vaguely familiar, like a favorite song from his childhood. It appeared to be coming from outside, so he stepped slowly back into the bright sunlight, walking carefully around the building, hugging its walls, following the sound.

And then he saw her, his darling Hannah. Standing in the shade of the building's back wall, she was watering potted plants and singing. She looked good. A little older, a little heavier, but with more high color than he remembered. Sensing his stare, she looked up, gasped, and dropped the water pitcher, which crashed and dribbled itself dry.

"Hannah."

She could not say his name. She could not say anything. (Such is the shock of colliding worlds.) She felt trapped, her back to the dead sea. Then she remembered her darling Peter, out there in the desert, all alone.

"Anatoly!" she said, turning him about. "Come, let us go inside, out of this heat."

Much of Hannah's fear was based on her feelings of guilt. In their early years (before Anatoly's arrest) she'd accepted his sullen quiet and occasional ferocity as the price she must pay for male companionship. But over time she realized that she'd made yet another bad deal. And then he was taken away. As the prison years passed, her memory of him became increasingly distant. She did not write to him or send him photos of their son except once a year, on Christmas. Eventually, she filed divorce papers and had them sent to his warden. She did not expect to see him again in this life. But there he was, standing in front of her, his chest a little thicker, his hair a little thinner, an ominous bag slung over her shoulder.

"You are looking well, Hannah."

"Thank you."

"How are you doing these days?"

"Very good. Thank you."

She did not know what else to say.

Anatoly looked about casually before asking, "So, how is our Peter?"

Hannah gasped. Bychkov smiled at her distress. But it also upset him.

"You okay, Hannah? The heat bothering you?"

Hannah breathed deeply to steady herself (but did not dare close her eyes, as she normally would).

Anatoly let go the Peter question, for the moment.

"Hannah. Hannah. Hannah. I am so happy to see you. I have dreamed of this day for many years."

"You look well, Anatoly," she said, trembling.

"Thank you. You look very well. Beautiful, in fact."

Hannah did not want the conversation to proceed in a romantic direction. To change the tone, she opened the door to her laboratory and led him inside.

"Come. This is where I work. My office."

Anatoly looked about with only cursory interest. As the minutes passed, he grew increasingly angry that she had dismissed his earlier question so easily. *Who does she think she's talking to? I'm her husband! I'm the boy's father!*

"So, how is our Peter?" he repeated, a little curtly.

Hannah heard the rough insistence in his voice. She knew she must answer him.

"He is well. He has a job back home. He is a good boy."

So, this is how it's going to be, he thought, knowing that Peter was in the army.

"That is good to hear. One day I would like to learn more about him. You know, fill in the gaps."

"Of course. I understand."

Each second passed slowly, painfully.

"It is amazing," he said, "that we should meet in this god-forsaken place, on the other side of the world."

Hannah was tempted to say something about God being everywhere, but it was not the right time—not while she was alone with him—in the middle of nowhere, with that ominous bag on his shoulder.

"So, what brought you here, Hannah?"

She decided her best course was to tell an approximate truth:

"I was working in Russia, doing medical research. We were studying special salts to use in cancer treatments. We studied salts from the Dead Sea in Israel and from China and elsewhere. We learned about the unusual salts here and came to study them. One of my fellow scientists is also here. Another one is expected any day."

Hannah's words rang true but Anatoly suspected she was hiding other truths. He wanted all her secrets.

"Are you planning to be here long?" he asked.

"I do not know. It depends on the research."

Anatoly did not wait for another silence.

"I assume you are living in Saltin."

"Yes, I live alone in a women's home. I am here to work."

Anatoly was disappointed that she asked no questions about him. He hoped to convey his disappointment by abruptly ending the conversation. "Okay then. I assume at some point you can find some time for us to have a nicer conversation. It would mean a lot to me."

"Yes, of course. I am very busy just now, but we will have a nice talk."

"Wonderful. Thank you, Hannah. I am very proud of your work as a doctor and scientist. It is very wonderful. I hope our

Peter takes after you." He noted Hannah's pained expression. "I hope to see you soon. I am very happy that Fate has brought us back together."

He smiled, waved goodbye, and returned to his car.

On the way back to East Saltin he remembered the map and smiled, assuming Saltin would have only one women's residence.

HANNAH PONDERS GOD AND LOVE

Why does God challenge me so? I was not the best daughter, no I wasn't, but why does God send me so many brutish men? Four times I decided enough is enough. Four times I chose a man I thought would be good and caring and protective. Four times I was wrong. What's wrong with them? What's wrong with me?

But I learned from Peter that men are good if they are loved early. I think Jason and Yevgeny must have been loved early, but certainly not Anatoly. I know his rough story and I am not surprised how he is. As for P., for sure, he is another who went unloved.

JASON AND HIS OPERA

Every morning but Sunday, Jason pulled up in front of Covenant House in his self-styled chariot and waited while Hannah skipped blithely down the stairs and out the building. Unknown to them both, Mother Mary watched grimly from her upstairs window.

They never spoke until they reached the Civic Center. Even then, they walked in silence to the back of the building until they were sure they were alone. And then they embraced.

Most days they sailed their motorized Argo far into the desert sea, Hannah using the GPS coordinates on her phone to direct her captain. When they arrived (or "laid anchor," as Jason liked to say), Hannah disembarked to hunt for salt samples while Jason remained on board to write the story of his opera, using the history of Saltin and his ongoing experiences with Hannah and their Saltin acquaintances as context.

Jason remembered very well the day Bethany brought Hannah and her supplies to the Civic Center. It was the first day he saw Hannah at her place of work and the first time he laid eyes on Bethany. Lately, whenever he thought of his fated connection with Hannah, Bethany's ebony beauty glowed in the back of his mind like a persistent afterimage.

TOVA AT THE WINDOW

Tova winced at the idea that she could set her watch by the daily arrival of the slut cart. *Bad enough the black drug dealer parked right out front, but this brazen cowboy parks his pimp-mobile there every morning at 7:00! I'm sure he's in cahoots with Hannah. He's probably selling the crystal meth she makes in her laboratory. Why doesn't Fred stop her? Does he even know? He's a gullible man—and not the quickest fellow. Maybe he doesn't know. I wonder if they've threatened him. I'm going to tell Marge what's going on. I know it's not her job as probation officer—but the welfare of our girls certainly is. These drug bastards belong in Calpurnia State Prison, not on the streets of Saltin.*

BETHANY HEADS WEST

In the late morning, Bethany took a hot yoga class (105°F), which opened her pores, warmed her muscles, and quickened her blood, leaving her feeling clean, supple and detoxed. Instead of breaking for a light lunch (as she usually did), she went immediately to a meditation class, where she wordlessly reconnected with her energy flow and chakra systems, relaxing her body and emptying her mind until she really did feel renewed and receptive. Afterwards (but while the golden effects still lingered), she was notified that a large package had arrived for her. Imagining she'd been sent a rare and exotic gift, she hurried to the concierge and signed for the package with an indulgent flourish. Only then did she notice the industrial-style logo on the return label (a narrowing beam of concentrated light) and realized that the package was not a gift but a weighty request; so weighty, she needed someone to haul it by luggage trolley to her parked car and help hoist it into her trunk. That accomplished, she emailed Yevgeny to tell him that the eagle had landed and she was ready to head back to sea.

CHANGE IN PLANS

Yevgeny had planned to meet Bethany in Tucson and travel with her to Saltin (to help her transport the weighty laser machine), but his own luggage (which included medical and scientific tools, his laptop, and the large container filled with Hannah's crystal wedding gown) was challenge enough. And so, as soon as Bethany confirmed receipt of his package, he arranged to fly from Israel to New York, and then to Palm Springs, California, where he planned to rent a car and drive to Saltin City. There he expected to meet Bethany for the first time—and to reconnect with his darling Hannah.

BETHANY'S ROMANTIC HARMONY

Over many years Yevgeny had been her doctor, healer, confessor and confidant. Each phase of their long-distance relationship had brought them closer and she now found herself half-hoping that their long-awaited meeting might be fateful in some permanently enjoining way. Disappointed to be traveling alone, she consoled herself by nursing her outlier hope that something magical would happen when they embraced for the first time. Though he was older, and not very physically attractive, she hoped her chakra training had raised her to a spiritual plane where such mundane standards were irrelevant—and if it turned out that she was not yet sufficiently elevated, she could take solace in the fact that there were still men like Jason around: handsome, soulful musicians, searching for their own romantic harmony.

SUSPICION

Driving through the Sunday morning desert (ignoring its awakening contours and changing colors), Bethany decided she'd stay awhile in Saltin to see if she couldn't kickstart an exciting new chapter in her life.

It was mid-afternoon when she finally parked her fancy black sedan in front of Covenant House and shut the motor. There she sat, completely still, collecting her thoughts. When she was ready, she drew down her vanity mirror, adjusted her lipstick and tidied her hair. She then opened the door and swung out her long ebony legs. Stretching them to her full runway height, she strode buoyantly towards the white lacquered door of Covenant House, carrying a casually elegant French market bag, a gift from an old admirer.

Inside, she did not immediately see a concierge or a bellhop but then remembered (vaguely) that the establishment was a social relic with amber-preserved ideas of protecting innocent waifs, divorcés and older women—all preciously referred to as *daughters.*

As Fate would have it, Mother Mary (Tova) had been watching from her upstairs window when the black sedan arrived, inciting her memory of Hannah hurrying downstairs and into the same waiting car, its motor running like a heist vehicle. Glaring down, Tova recalled everything she'd recently heard about Hannah: buying salts at the lagoon, motoring about the empty sea with some vagrant musician, cooking up crystals in her lab, all of which confirmed her worst suspicions: *She's no good.*

"Hello? Anyone here?"

Tova heard the querulous tone coming from the downstairs parlor.

Short on staff, Mother Mary answered the call herself. Wearing a long-sleeved white surplice over dark slacks, she left her room and walked to the head of the stairs, pausing there to stare down on the brazen black drug lord. After several seconds she descended dramatically, vaguely hoping her noble attitude would encourage the drug lord to reconsider her cheapened life.

Bethany watched her slow descent impatiently. When Tova reached the last step, Bethany simply said, "Hello. I'd like a room."

Tova was caught off guard. "What do you mean?"

"I mean, I'd like a room."

"Here?"

"Of course, here. I'm standing here."

"Have you tried elsewhere?"

When required, Bethany could prevaricate as easily as she breathed.

"I certainly did. I looked everywhere. But there is nothing available that suits me."

While Tova thought, Bethany cast her eyes upon the framed needlepoint that hung conspicuously on the wall. "You cannot put me on the street. I am my mother's daughter."

Before Tova could respond, Bethany said, "Please. I need a place to stay where I can feel safe."

Tova wavered.

"I can pay you," Bethany added. "Five hundred dollars a week. Please give me a room. The best you have. I'll abide all your rules. I promise."

IN SELF-DEFENSE

Tova would not have said that she'd caved or even capitulated. She'd done only what she'd had to. In fact, imagining herself before a judgmental Board of Directors, she grew strident in her self-defense: *I took an oath to protect the daughters of our community. And that's what I've done for forty years. Without bias or prejudice, I offer a haven to all those who seek safety here. I feed our daughters. I guide them to be better, stronger women. I encourage their spiritual growth, self-reliance and self-improvement. I teach them how to protect themselves. I teach them how to survive!*

One more thing—the fiduciary thing—all this, everything we do here, stops when we stop paying our bills. When our funds are insufficient to keep our doors open, they will close and—very possibly—remain closed forever. And so, if you're wondering why I've been accepting more paying customers lately, it's in order to keep this place open. If it closes, it's no use to anyone.

Besides (Tova thought, only to herself), *I need to keep close tabs on this Bethany person. And on Hannah too.*

UNANIMOUSLY APPROVED

Anderson and Zimmer told the mayors and their associates what they had already told Fred, but now that they were wearing suits and sitting around an old conference table, their words carried more weight.

"We thank all of you for inviting us here. We hope you accept our proposal. We'd love to play a role in Saltin's renaissance."

The champagne was popped.

"Here's to Saltin's renaissance!" said the mayor of West Saltin, *aka* the King.

"Here's to our partnership!" said the mayor of East Saltin, *aka* the Pope.

The Saltin team drank heartily. The Lithium reps sipped happily.

"Here's to Saltin City: Let it be rebuilt!" the tipsy King toasted.

"Here's to Saltin City: Let its glory be great!" clinked the red-eyed Pope.

Contracts, riders, title searches and deeds passed round and round. When the final document was signed, there was a unison call for a final toast:

"To Saltin's success!"

OBSERVE, DO NOT ENGAGE

After the meeting, Anderson and Zimmer rented the last two habitable rooms at The Palace. Then they began their work. The first thing they did was install a system to record all electronic communications sent and received from the hotel. Next (and for the following three days), they explored most of West and East Saltin on foot, looking very much like a pair of backpacking tourists who took an excitable and hands-on delight in exploring points of interest around the derelict city. (In fact, they were casually installing dozens of spy-cams that doubled as common objects: thermometers, rocks, even leaves.) During the two days that followed, they drove about the larger Saltin area, performing an initial reconnaissance of Calpurnia State Prison's perimeter, the Saltin Wildlife Refuge and the two federal checkpoints that monitored border crossings.

That evening, from Zimmer's room, the two agents sent a heavily encrypted file to a dark web account that went directly to P. Like good journalists, they were careful not to bury the lead:

Hannah B. and Dimitri G. are here. Yevgeny Y. expected to arrive in a week. Preliminary analysis of Saltin City and immediate environs follow below, along with copies of signed contracts regarding American Lithium.

The two agents went to bed thinking they'd receive no response until the following morning. They were wrong. An hour later they received a message:

Observe. Do not engage.

One action: Procure one entire floor in The Palace, preferably the top. Details below.

NECESSARY PRECAUTIONS

The next morning, Anderson and Zimmer greeted the mayor of West Saltin while he ate breakfast in The Palace's best—and only—working restaurant.

"Good morning, gentlemen. Please join me," said the mayor.

The two agents sat down and ordered black coffees. After an exchange of pleasantries they got down to business:

"Our rooms are fine, thank you. But we need another floor."

"Another floor?"

"Yes, an entire floor."

The mayor was thrilled but flabbergasted. "Well, that's not possible at the moment. We have an empty floor, but it's not exactly move-in ready."

"We understand," said Anderson. "But we are anxious to begin our work and need the space for additional personnel who will be arriving soon."

The mayor was too excited to speak. Lucky for him, he was rescued by Zimmer.

"We've taken the liberty of drawing up a proposal," said Zimmer, handing the mayor a one-page document.

"It's really quite simple," said Anderson. "We agree to develop the entire floor— preferably the top—according to our own design and specifications. We will assume all costs involved in its creation and outfitting."

"All costs?"

"Everything. Construction to carpeting. In return, you will give us a five-year lease agreement at one dollar per year. At the end of five years, we can renegotiate the terms. Even if we decide to vacate, which is extremely unlikely, your hotel will have a new floor that can be rented or leased, as you please."

The mayor pictured the existing floor and shuddered: it was broken, filthy and badly eroded. It needed to be gutted before it could be rebuilt.

The mayor sipped his coffee slowly to settle his nerves. When he was ready, he put the cup down carefully and read the proposal, word for word. When he finished, he read it again. It was concise and comprehensive and appeared to be a win-win for both sides. Once again, he pictured the upstairs floor, but this time he smiled. Its renewal would be a huge step towards reclaiming the once grand Palace.

"However, we do have one other stipulation," said Anderson, "and it's nonnegotiable."

"What's that?" said the mayor, suddenly worried.

"We will need complete privacy," said Anderson.

"Absolute, lockdown security," said Zimmer.

"The floor must be off limits to everyone."

"And we mean *everyone*."

"No one will have access but us—and other members of our staff."

"No hotel maintenance."

"No window washers."

"No fire or police inspectors. We can't take any risks."

"Why so drastic?" asked the mayor.

"We can't let our business secrets fall into the hands of our competitors."

The mayor nodded but looked uncertain.

"These are necessary precautions," said Anderson.

"They're not at all unusual," said Zimmer.

"All top companies are cautious nowadays."

"Take your time. Think it over."

"But we need your decision as soon as possible."

"We'll check with you tomorrow."

"It's a great offer."

"Let's make Saltin great again!"

YEVGENY'S HEAVY LOAD

Yevgeny carried a heavy load of emotions up the steps to the Cave of Machpelah. Having lived in its shadow for several months, he felt a keen compulsion to visit the tombs of the great Patriarchs and Matriarchs one last time before he journeyed to the other side of the world, where he hoped to marry Hannah under a traditional wedding canopy—set near the shore of the Saltin Sea.

FISH IN A BARREL

P. was almost giddy with delight when he learned that the three Cosmoenergy doctors would soon convene in Saltin City. It was almost too good to be true. *Like shooting fish in a barrel,* he thought (recalling his favorite Americanism).

He began to plan. *Who should treat me? They all are excellent doctors. They all are experienced with my case. They all are familiar with the special technique of destroying salt-injected cancer cells with a trained laser.*

And then he wondered: *Who should I punish? They all betrayed me. But only one is beautiful. Only one haunts my dreams. Only one might stand beside me—in place of Maria—when I wave to adoring crowds.*

COURTESY OF AKHMEROV AND ZUBILIN

P. was very pleased with the work of Akhmerov and Zubilin. Just when he'd begun to despair that his untreated cancer would cut him down in his prime, they'd located Hannah Belaya in Saltin City, USA, where she lived in a women's residence, had a separate office to study her collected salts and had already been joined by Dr. Grushina.

And there was more (courtesy of Akhmerov and Zubilin): there was Jason Stevens (itinerant musician, close companion of Hannah's); Fred Heinz (Director of the Saltin Civic Center); Tova Moskowitz Heinz (*aka* Mother Mary, manager of Covenant House—Saltin's women's residence—separated from husband, Fred Heinz); Edwina Lazar Orosco (friend/consort of Fred Heinz, retired professor, whose expedition discovered the large tract of concentrated lithium in the Saltin Sea); Lyndon Cartwright (mayor of West Saltin, *aka* King); Francis Fordham (mayor of East Saltin, *aka* Pope).

Having eyes on all these people (along with the continuing surveillance of Dr. Grushina's mother and Hannah's son) gave P. a sense of security.

P. appreciated the investigative talents of his agents. They were KGB before they were FSB and knew what they were doing.

TRUMP CARD

P. was anxious to get to Saltin to resume his cancer therapy. He was also anxious to see Hannah. *This time it will be different,* he told himself. *I'm sorry I made such a bad first impression* (he imagined saying to her). *I hope you understand. It was a crazy time. I was very anxious about my health and the election. But that's the past. Today is a new day. I want to know you better. I mean that, sincerely.* (He actually did.) *And I want you to know me. Not what the newspapers say, but the real me.* (To a certain degree, this was true.) He imagined looking into her eyes, waiting for her response, all the while knowing he had a special trump card in the back pocket of his brain: the knowledge that her son was alive and well in a detainment camp, outside of Sevastopol, in Russian-controlled Crimea.

THIRD FLOOR OF THE PALACE

In Anderson and Zimmer, P. had two, English-speaking colleagues to explain his cover story: He was a Russian manufacturer of lithium batteries—a business partner of American Lithium—who'd come to Saltin, hoping its highly reputed salts would help cure his lung disease. The story was solid and held out for P. a troika of promises: health, romance, prosperity. But there was work to do. Before P. could advance his ideas and agendas, the entire top floor of The Palace must be readied for his occupancy.

A Russian-owned, American-fronted construction company arrived from Los Angeles to guide the project. As per P.'s precise instructions, the company would create six standard hotel rooms with every expected convenience; one deluxe master-bedroom suite with radiant heated floors, mirrored ceiling, steam-shower stall, jetted tub, and his-her, gold-accented porcelain toilets and sinks; one replete exercise training center, including a regulation, tatami-padded judo mat; one large conference room, outfitted with interchangeable curtains, flags, lecterns, desks, department seals and insignia.

For twenty consecutive days (sixteen hours a day), a caravan of trucks brought dozens of workers and tons of materials to The Palace. At the end of the twentieth day, Zubilin sent an encrypted email to P.'s private, dark web account: *Open for business.*

The next day, P. landed in New York City in a private jet, an American-made Gulfstream G550, which could accommodate fifteen but carried only three (in addition to P. and the two pilots): a pair of black-suited FSB agents and his personal masseuse and consort, blue-eyed Katya (whose mother had held the same position for twenty years, before being aged out of her usefulness). P. and his small contingent remained aboard the plane while it was checked and refueled for its flight to Palm Springs, California.

Seven hours later, the jet landed and its four passengers transferred to a waiting black Buick Regal with tinted windows, which immediately began its journey to Saltin City. Already disguised in his wig and beard, P. stared at the passing scenery, fantasizing about Hannah and his fiefdom of lithium-rich America.

PURIFICATION

One week to the day earlier, Dr. Yeshevsky had arrived at the airport in San Diego. Unlike P. (who would be driven directly to The Palace and ensconced in his gilded, third-floor digs), Yeshevsky leased a car and drove himself to The Mount.

Though Bethany's reports and his own research had done much to prepare him, Yevgeny was stunned to see Saltin's devastation, the blasted scenes reminding him of the wasted Cities of the Plain and Lot's wife, a pillar of salt.

Though anxious to see Hannah, Yevgeny felt the need to purify himself before meeting her again. (He'd been impressed by his parents' descriptions of their mikvah baths but had no interest in making that ritual immersion part of his own routine. Ever the passionate contrarian, he had his own idea how best to cleanse his body and soul.) Soon after checking into The Mount, he walked towards the broken boardwalk in search of the spa lagoons. There was one surrounded by tall potted plants that curtained the lagoon with a degree of privacy. He spoke to the manager and negotiated a fee for the next three mornings, during which time no one but himself would be admitted. The manager agreed but insisted on being paid in advance and Yevgeny happily complied.

After carefully considering his options, Yevgeny decided he would recite a different prayer during each of his morning cleansings. On the first day he would recite: *Therefore shall a man leave his father and his mother, and cling to his wife* (GENESIS 2:24). On the second day: *Houses and riches are the inheritance of fathers, while a wise wife is from the Lord* (PROVERBS 19:14). And on the third day: *Your wife shall be as a fruitful vine within your house, your children like olive clusters around your table* (PSALMS 128:3). He hoped the three mornings of bathing and prayer would prepare him well for his reunion with Hannah.

FOUR SUITORS

Jason believed he was falling in love with Hannah. She was a wonderfully wise and beautiful companion and each day they explored the desert sea was a thrilling experience for him. One day, when they were done with their salt-collecting and had returned to the relative comfort of her office, he confessed his long regret of having never been a father. Baring his soul, he described how he'd sometimes bring an imaginary young son or daughter into a park or movie theater just to share the experience though their innocent eyes. Hannah held his hand and cried—not only for the poignancy of Jason's pain but for the uncertain fate of her own real son, Peter, whom she had left behind. Despite such honest moments shared with Jason, and despite all his emotiveness and creativity, Hannah was beginning to see that Jason was passive about their relationship and wondered if his needs and hers were indeed a good match.

~

Anatoly carefully planned his renewed relationship with Hannah. He thought of good questions he might ask about her work. He practiced telling her about his own accomplishments (as though they were a résumé of white-collar bona fides). He rehearsed a speech about the importance of a father's positive role in his son's life. As a potential trump card, he honed a false story of his contacts in the Ukrainian army and how he might learn where Peter was stationed and when he would return home. Anatoly hoped all these strategies would incline Hannah to trust him again: a good first step towards forgiveness which, if nurtured properly, might flower into renewed love.

~

Yevgeny was cleansed but still unclear how he should approach Hannah. Should he reestablish their professional relationship and wait for a private moment to declare his undying love? Should he meet her for a casual drink, catch up on their lives, and wait for the right moment to share his vision of their married future? Either way, he worried he would bumble through, blunting his chances for success.

~

P. thought his approach towards Hannah could use some tinkering. He thought it might be better if he acted more like a regular person than an overlord:

Of course, she must see my humanity, see what a big heart I have. I'll take her to visit my old apartment in St. Petersburg, where I was raised. Perhaps she'd like to see an old photo of myself with my young daughters—hmmm, maybe not.

I could tell her how much I love the Beatles, maybe sing a few songs for her. Oh, I know, I'll share a video of my beloved doggies: Tuffy, my baby Bulgarian Shepherd, and Vadek my Akita. Oh, most important, I must tell her how I love the Church. Tell her how devoted I am. This she must understand.

COSMOENERGY WEST

The three doctors were together for the first time since their days in Moscow. Yevgeny was looking over the shelves and cabinets, the sink, the examining table, the power outlet for the laser.

"Hannah, given what you had to work with, the office looks very impressive."

Hannah nodded courteously. "Thank you. It took a month to get the place ready. Since then, I've been collecting salt samples from all around the area."

"What is your labeling system for identifying each source?" Dimitri pointedly asked.

Hannah described her scrupulously developed system: "With software I found online, I created a map of the sea and divided it into fifty sectors, like America—one for each state. I made sure it is accurate to the centimeter."

Yevgeny applauded. "Well done, Hannah!"

Dimitri nodded and then asked: "I suppose it wasn't difficult to access the local lagoons, but how did you navigate the desert sea?"

Hannah had anticipated the question. Even so, it made her uncomfortable.

"Jason," she said, turning to Yevgeny, "has been kind enough to drive me about to help me collect samples."

"Drive you?" asked Dimitri.

"Yes, in a little golf cart. He designed it to look like the mythical ship of the Argonauts."

"Like Jason and the Argonauts?"

"Yes," she said. "Those who searched for the Golden Fleece."

Yevgeny and Dimitri were perplexed but Hannah continued:

"Using GPS and digging tools, I collected more than two hundred salt samples."

"So many, Hannah!"

"Jason's help was essential."

"I will compensate him."

"Oh, he wasn't working all the time. Mostly he play his guitar and sang."

Yevgeny felt a pang of jealousy but ignored it.

"Your process and effort are first rate," he said, moving on. "But I have good news and bad news. The good news: Soon we will have real diseased cells to test with our new salts. The bad news: the cells are inside the lungs of a living patient. I think you know who it is."

"He is here?" said Hannah, fear in her voice.

"Are you sure?" Dimitri asked, frightened for his life.

"He will arrive soon. They are working night and day in The Palace, getting ready an entire floor."

"Oh God," said Hannah. "It's him."

"Sounds like him," said Dimitri.

"It's him," said Yevgeny, his words like hammered nails. "He has found us. But let's not forget: He needs us. We may be the only three people on earth who can save him."

"But he doesn't need all three of us," Dimitri noted, shaking his head.

SURVIVOR

Yevgeny asked Hannah and Dimitri if they were familiar with the American TV reality show *Survivor*. Dimitri lied when he said he'd never watched the popular show (with the hunky, nearly naked men) but admitted knowing its premise: two teams of fit men and women compete in physical and mental contests in a tropical or jungle setting; ultimately, there can be only one winner—one *survivor.*

"During the early weeks of each TV season," explained Yevgeny, "the group that relies more on teamwork is usually leading. But once the two large teams are reduced to a half-dozen or fewer individual contestants, it's—"

"Every man for himself!"

"No," said Yevgeny, shaking his head. "That's a recipe for disaster."

Dimitri looked down.

Hannah was about to say *friendship* but changed her mind and said in Russian what she really meant: *"Soyuz."*

"Yes!" Yevgeny said. *"Soyuz:* alliance."

"Alliance," Hannah repeated, practicing her English.

Yevgeny smiled at her. "Alliance is a vital strategy for people with a shared need or goal."

Dimitri wasn't sure where this was going and it made him uncomfortable.

"Where are you going with all this, Yevgeny? You are usually so direct."

Yevgeny winked at Hannah as if the two of them shared a secret. Hannah gave no sign of understanding.

"There are all kinds of alliances," said Yevgeny. "Business, marriage, political. I think the three of us need more alliances to ensure our safety and success here."

"Okay, alliances are good," said Dimitri. "Whom do you have in mind?"

ALLIANCE

"First of all," said Yeshevsky, "it is no one's fault that P. found us. We each did what we could to leave without detection. Perhaps I was a little naïve on this point. After all, P. has the greatest, worldwide intelligence network at his disposal. He was bound to find us. But it is good, I think, that we are all in this place together, where we are supposed to be.

"Second, I do not mean to alarm you, but you have to understand, P. would not come here alone, even if his life depended on it."

"Who is he with? His agents?"

"Think broader, Dimitri. Not just in terms of agents. Think of alliances. Who owes him a favor? Who has he influenced?"

"Who has he bought?" said Hannah.

"Exactly!"

Yevgeny took a step back in order to face both doctors equally.

"Let me be clear: To protect ourselves, we should regard every person in Saltin as possibly working with P."

"Everyone?" said Dimitri.

"No!" said Hannah, stamping her foot. "Not Jason. Not Bethany. About others, I cannot say. About them, I am sure."

Yevgeny mulled this for a few seconds. "Okay. I agree. They are both potential allies. But let us be clear: alliances are not without risk."

"But what is meant by alliance?" asked Dimitri. "I mean, how far do we go? Do we take people into our full confidence? Do we tell them everything—or is that needlessly dangerous?"

Yevgeny was overcome with emotion. He took several deep breaths to regain his poise. "I've made mistakes," he said. "We all have. But I made no mistake when I chose the two of you as my managers and surrogates. I love you both. If anything should happen to me, I know Cosmoenergy is in good hands."

Hannah and Dimitri flashed to his side.

"Please, don't talk that way," said Hannah. "Everything will be well."

"It is my pleasure to serve," said Dimitri, likewise struck with emotion.

"Thank you," said Yevgeny, shaking free of them both in order to face them again.

"I have given this much thought," he said in a calmed voice. "Normally, I would not compromise our medical ethics, but P. does not abide by ethics. He is off the ethical spectrum, capable of the absolute worst—even with you, Hannah. And so, I think we must bring Jason and Bethany into our circle for own protection—and for theirs. I shall let them know the full situation—and, yes, that includes revealing P.'s real identity."

"Really, Yevgeny?" said Dimitri. "That is risking much."

"After their shock, I think it will work in our favor. They will understand what is at stake and not second-guess our decisions, especially those made in the heat of the moment."

Dimitri wanted Yevgeny to elaborate, but the longtime head of the Cosmoenergy Federation said no more.

YEVGENY AND JASON

Yevgeny arranged to meet Jason in his windowless room on the second floor of the Palm Luxe, the dilapidated, largely open-air hovel he called home. When he arrived (in the early morning, before the spa lagoons opened for business), Jason was sitting on his threadbare mattress, writing in his notebook. As soon as Yevgeny entered, Jason stood and gave him a warm greeting, unconcerned about his hobo appearance.

"Hello, Yevgeny! It's good to finally meet you!"

Yevgeny knew Jason had once been a successful musician, that his wife had left him, and that he'd essentially been a wanderer ever since. He needed to know more. Before he took Jason into his confidence, he had to know how he felt about Hannah.

"It is nice to meet you, Jason. Since we first spoke online, I have worked hard on my English."

Jason smiled. "You have an accent, but you speak very well."

"Thank you. And I thank you for reaching out to me. Forgive me if I seemed distant at first. I have clients who work for the government. You understand?"

"Of course. Hannah explained the situation to me."

"Well, I am glad you two have become friends. I understand you help her a great deal when she is collecting salt samples. I would like to pay you. You shouldn't work for free."

"No no no. No money, please. I am happy to help her."

Yevgeny looked him in the eye and smiled knowingly. "You care for her, don't you?"

Jason took the jolt but held his ground. He remembered Hannah saying that she and Yevgeny were close—something about drinks and long walks.

"We've become good friends, if that's what you mean."

Yevgeny felt a pang of remorse; he believed Jason was a good man.

"I am glad you are good friends. I hope the same for you and me."

Yevgeny then launched into a surprisingly fulsome account of his history with Hannah. (It was a strategic telling. By setting the record straight, Yevgeny wanted to lay claim to Hannah's hand, such was his old-fashioned turn of mind.) He told Jason about their early correspondence and how he eventually offered Hannah a job in Moscow.

"Must have been a very good job offer for her to leave Peter."

Yevgeny knew Hannah had a son because she had said so when P. had questioned her in his office. But Hannah had never mentioned her son to him. He'd assumed it must be a very painful subject for her, and that she would share her feelings freely when she felt the time was right. But she had apparently shared her feelings on the subject with Jason. What was he supposed to make of that? For the time being, he buried those thoughts and continued with the lengthy story of how he and Hannah came to be in Saltin, along with Dimitri and Bethany.

Jason listened with one ear to Yevgeny's long story of cancer cells, salts and lasers. His attention spiked when Yevgeny described a brute patient who'd molested Hannah while she'd been administering his salt bath. Jason's interest grew more intense when he learned that the brute was the same patient whose diseased lung had been the target of Hannah's laser treatments.

"There is more," Yevgeny said, somewhat ominously. "The patient in question is P."

Jason was stunned. "Wait. Are you saying that the president of Russia molested Hannah?"

"Yes. And I had the very real fear that he would do so again—and worse. And that is why I helped Hannah leave the country."

"Good. But why come here?"

"We needed a place far away, where it would be difficult for P. and his agents to find Hannah. It made sense to come here. You are here. The salts are here."

"What about Dr. Grushina?"

"I did not know Dimitri would also come here. He made that decision on his own, for reasons he has not yet fully shared with me."

Jason raised his hand, beseeching Yevgeny to halt his story while he absorbed its astounding facts. Yevgeny looked about the room. He saw a laptop and an open notebook filled with handwritten notes. With nothing else of interest to look at, he resumed his story.

"The three of us—Hannah, Dimitri and myself—broke our sworn medical oaths when we decided to do what we did."

"But you were protecting Hannah."

"Yes, but we were also imperiling the life of our patient—and the leader of our nation. The repercussions will likely be profound."

"What's that mean? What's going to happen?"

Yevgeny explained that P. had recently discovered that all three doctors were gathered in Saltin. He was expected to arrive any day.

"P. is going to come here. To this place? Impossible!"

"He needs our treatment. Without it, he would surely die."

"But he doesn't need all three of you."

"Exactly right. And I will do all I can to keep Hannah safe."

Jason gave Yevgeny his strong hand. "I'll do anything you want. Just tell me what to do."

ANCILLARY

Bethany knew her role had been ancillary. Yevgeny had called in a favor and she'd happily obliged and he'd paid her well. But now she wanted more. When she'd been young and ill, she'd loved his healing words. Now healthy and in her full maturity, she wanted his endearments and warm embrace. At least, she thought so. She wanted something. She knew she was still beautiful and alluring, but she also knew that in a few years she would be fifty. She wanted her life to matter.

YEVGENY AND BETHANY

Yevgeny sent Bethany a message that he wanted to see her. Though they both resided in East Saltin (Yevgeny at The Mount, Bethany at Covenant House), she asked that he not come to her door, suggesting instead that they meet at The Palace, in West Saltin, where they could get a drink. Yevgeny was glad for the suggestion. The prospect of visiting Covenant House made him nervous. Hannah lived there; she might be very jealous if she saw him with Bethany.

Lingering over their drinks, Yevgeny and Bethany chatted warmly, referring many times to their long-standing relationship. As they talked, Yevgeny sensed that Bethany's feelings were becoming heated and more personal. The vibe was exciting and he wasn't sure that he wanted it to stop. (Tall and beautiful, black and lithe, the idea of Bethany had always thrilled him. In the past, when they were separated by five thousand miles, it had been easy for him to maintain his professional comportment. But her ebony flesh was now within easy reach, and she was exuding not-so-subtle signals that she was attracted to him.) He wasn't sure what to say. He wasn't sure what he felt or how to act. He thought he should mention Hannah. Perhaps Bethany didn't know how he really felt about Hannah. Perhaps she knew and didn't care.

"It's very warm in here," he said, suddenly dizzy. "Let's get some fresh air." He stood awkwardly, then hurried to the nearest exit that led to the boardwalk, Bethany following.

When they reached the boardwalk, he turned to face her. With the bright sun behind her, her white dashiki was nearly see-through: her white panties and small breasts enticingly visible. To avoid a full swoon, he turned to face the dry sea, steadying himself by double gripping the splintered railing. Bethany joined him, staring silently at her own empty sea, thinking: *Perhaps it's silly to think he could be my man. Even in these strange circumstances, he is an odd one. Still, he means a great deal to me. His methods cure; his words console. But I don't think he is strong enough to hold me—the way Jason might. Still, I should give him more of a chance. I owe him my life.*

Looking past the lagoons at the desert sea, Yevgeny considered the possibility of Bethany as his life partner: *After all, I have no commitment from Hannah. I cannot say with certainty that she will explode with happy tears when I ask for her hand in marriage. Of course, I expect to her to be thrilled. I pray she will be thrilled. But just in case she isn't, for whatever reason, it makes sense to have Bethany as my backup plan, especially as she now seems so romantically interested in me. It would be a pity to lose out on them both. I mean, at my age, how many options do I have? If I am ever to marry and have children, will I ever have such a pair of choices again?*

"What are you thinking, Yevgeny? You look perplexed."

Yevgeny knew he'd been thinking dreamily but was not disposed to share his thoughts. But he was ready to segue into his most pressing matter:

"I'm sure I told you, back in Moscow, an important Russian official and patient of ours had forced his attentions upon Hannah and when I protested—things got complicated."

"You told me that much. But I always assumed there was more."

"I couldn't tell you more, my dear, without involving you and risking your safety."

Bethany took hold of his sweet, gentlemanly hand.

Yevgeny gasped, thrilled at her touch but mortified that Hannah might see. He leaned closer to speak even more confidentially, but also to block Hannah (or anyone else) from seeing Bethany's hand on his.

"Without getting into too much detail—"

Yevgeny told her the entire story (more or less). He expressed his warm feelings for Hannah but did not mention the word *love* and left out the part about the crystal wedding gown. He told her about patient P., including his condition, his treatments and, finally, his real identity. He described how P. had become obsessed with Hannah and how he had treated her roughly. He explained how he'd had to choose between saving P.'s life and allowing Hannah's to be jeopardized. He told (in quick summary) how Hannah and Dimitri had arrived in Saltin and how they all hoped to continue their scientific research.

"Here's the problem," he said. "P. knows that Hannah and Dimitri are here. By now, he must know that I'm here too. I'm sure he's on his way."

Bethany's eyes opened wide.

"He's coming here? Why?"

"To get his treatment—to have his way with Hannah—to take vengeance on us all. Who can say?"

Bethany shivered with fear.

"How could he come here?" she asked. "The world watches his every move."

"He will not come as himself. He will be perfectly disguised."

"Still, everyone in Russia will be wondering where he is."

"Trust me, he has thought of that."

"Okay. But where will he live?"

"He will live in The Palace. That is why I think so much construction work continues there. He needs a home away from home."

"Oh my god. You live there too. Aren't you frightened?"

"He is not the ideal neighbor," Yevgeny said with a wry smile. Then, regaining his serious tone: "Truthfully, I'm too busy to be frightened. I must concentrate on what we need to do to prepare and protect ourselves."

"Who is *we*?" she asked.

"Me, Hannah, Dimitri—and Jason."

A moment of silence.

"What about me?"

Yevgeny risked much in taking both her hands in his.

"My dear, the situation is very uncertain—and potentially dangerous. I have no idea how it will turn out. It is best if you leave right away and tell no one, including me, where you are going."

There was a pause. Bethany had been waiting for Yevgeny to say more.

"That's it?" she said, a teary catch in her voice. "You can say goodbye so easily? After all these years?"

Yevgeny drew a deep breath.

"Easily? It tears my heart. But if it means your safety, I must do it. Someday, life permitting, I will try to find you."

Bethany burst into tears. She'd known so many inconsequential men. Twice Yevgeny had tried to save her life.

"I'm staying," she said with fierce determination. "Nothing can make me leave. I am not afraid. I will help you any way I can."

Yevgeny regretted being so manipulative. But now he had what he wanted: another ally—and another romantic option.

CHAPTER 9

TOVA

For many years Tova had rarely traveled more than a few streets from Covenant House and usually avoided Commonwealth Avenue altogether. *But these are trying times,* she told herself, *and trying times demand new rules of engagement.* In thinking this way, Tova was being true to her truest self: She'd been a corporate analyst, a risk-assessor. When her corporate life no longer satisfied, and when her married life no longer inspired, she'd left her job and husband and answered the call of Covenant House.

At the moment, she felt the draw of a Higher Calling: All her core principles—everything she had accomplished over the past thirty years—was being threatened by outsiders of suspect backgrounds and motives. She had decided to make a stand. But she was alone. She needed a friend, a confidante, an ally. She thought of Sister Sharon and Sister Carmel, but both were arthritic and sickly and neither would be worth a damn in a fight. She thought of Caitlin, but she was too flighty to be entrusted.

She thought of Fred. (So close, yet so far away!) *Poor, stupid Fred, always chasing success beyond his natural pay grade. Still, he was sweet and faithful. If only I had approached him two months ago, before that professor lady had swindled his heart.*

(She pressed an old linen handkerchief to her eyes, soaking it with sorrowful tears.) *Oh, Fred, I needed my space. I needed my life. But I shouldn't have left you as I did. That was terribly cruel. Perhaps we will have one last chance to help each other.*

A car pulled up in front and a bitter gorge rose in her throat. She strode to the window and parted the curtain to confirm her worst suspicion. But it wasn't the drug dealer's black sedan. It was the unmarked patrol car that belonged to her dear friend Officer Marge Schenk, who'd come from Calpurnia State Prison to check on the excitable and independently minded Caitlin Connor, now in her fifties, who'd continually infracted minor house rules over the past thirty years that were insufficient to return her to prison but which continually extended her term as a halfway parolee of Covenant House. (Long ago, as Mother Mary, Tova had accepted the fact that Caitlin was a special case who would never be completely rehabilitated inside Covenant House but was allowed to remain because Mother Mary liked her—as did all the sisters and daughters through the years—because Caitlin was so emotionally honest and gave every appearance of wanting to stay where she was.)

On this day, Tova was so preoccupied with all the strange and suspicious events lately occurring in Saltin that she decided to table any discussion of Caitlin in order to enlist Marge's immediate advice and potential help. As soon as Marge entered her upstairs apartment, Tova made her pitch.

"Listen to this," she said, presenting a tray of tea and sandwiches. "A couple months ago, this lady professor from a local college led a team of scientists in an excavation of our dearly beloved dead sea. Guess what they found?"

"Salt?"

"Yes, plenty of salt, of course. Guess what else. No idea?"

"No idea."

"Lithium."

"Lithium?"

"It's a mineral; a kind of metal, I believe. They've used it for years to make batteries and drugs. Thing is, lithium has become quite valuable. There's actually a booming worldwide market for it. Anyway, this lady professor and her group published a paper claiming that our dead sea has a fabulous concentration of lithium and this paper was noticed by a company in Detroit, called American Lithium, Inc. As I heard it, the company contacted the professor, asking if she would set up a meeting with the two mayors of Saltin, who she had acknowledged in the report. Now, this professor, I forget her name—Natasha? Tatiana?—whatever, she didn't know the mayors personally, but she'd already established a warm relationship with Fred Heinz, who'd helped her obtain the mayors' written permission for the excavation."

"Who's Fred Heinz?"

"You don't know Fred? He runs the Civic Center, knows everyone in Saltin and has the ears of both mayors. Anyway, it seems to me that she must have sweet-talked Fred into asking the mayors if they would meet with her and the two men from American Lithium. Well, long story short, on Fred's strong recommendation, our genius mayors granted an audience to the professor and the two reps."

"How'd it go?"

"Actually, I heard they put on quite a good dog-and-pony show."

"How good?"

"Well, they convinced our feckless leaders to part with seventy square miles for just a few million bucks."

"Million?"

"Yeah, *million*. But seventy square miles! For that much property, they're getting it for a song. As soon as I heard about it, I was sure the deal was a rip-off and it made me angry."

"What are you thinking?"

"I'm thinking the lady professor was offered a kickback. Happens all the time. She'd probably taught all her life, saved nothing, was close to retirement and scared shitless she wouldn't be able to support herself. She was the perfect target—needy and vulnerable.

"So they used her."

"Yup, clear as day: those American Lithium boys used her. They got her to snuggle up to Fred so he would go to the mayors and vouch for them."

"But the mayors had to agree."

"Of course, they agreed. They're poor bastards and they trust Fred. That's why they didn't do any vetting—they just signed the damn contracts."

"At least they'll have some money in their pockets, more than they ever dreamed of."

"Still, it's a relative pittance. Not nearly enough to rebuild Saltin—and wasn't that their dream? Saltin will remain dry as a bone, so what did the mayors really get for selling a valuable chunk of our empty sea? Thirty pieces of silver?"

"But as is, it's not valuable. If not for the lithium, it's just a piece of desert crap and they were lucky to get anything for it."

Tova shook her head. "Personally, I think there's more here than meets the eye. I don't trust those men from American Lithium."

"What are you thinking?"

"Okay, get this: As soon as the contracts were signed, those American Lithium fellas announced plans to bring over a Russian mining partner. Not an American Russian—a Russian Russian—a Roosky! And listen to this: Those reps also made a deal with the mayors to renovate the penthouse of The Palace and this Russian guy has already moved in—all by himself, like some all-powerful czar."

"It does seem suspicious."

"Suspicious as hell. And here's the final kicker: I think this Russian czar guy has been meeting with Hannah—another Russian, or something like that—who lives here but cooks dope in her lab in the back of the Civic Center—without Fred's knowledge, I'm sure—and sells it to the black drug dealer in her pimp mobile."

"How do you know all this?"

"I have eyes and ears, that's how I know!"

"It's unbelievably brazen."

"But no surprise, right? We have no police here."

"Uh, hello?"

"Yeah, I know, but you're a women's parole officer. We have no actual police in Saltin."

"You have the federal Border Patrol, just south of here."

"You see criminals coming here from Mexico? No. They're coming from Russia!"

Tova took a few calming breaths before she continued.

"It's not like I'm imagining all this stuff. And it's all happening at the same time, so it can't be a coincidence."

"Are the folks here concerned?"

"Are you kidding? They're tickled pink. They're dancing in the streets. The fools in West Saltin think their witnessing a renaissance; the fools in East Saltin think their witnessing a resurrection. They're all fools! They all believe they're making Saltin great again. But you know what I think? I think they're selling their souls to scum criminals, mobsters and devil Russians. We're doubly corrupted here: we are losing God and Country."

"I'm getting the picture."

"I had to tell someone and you're the only person I know around here who has a brain, a badge and a gun."

OFFICER MARGE SCHENK

Christ, I make less money than my moron husband and that's ridiculous since I'm like seven times smarter. That I'm actually a cop and he's just a corrections officer makes it worse.

Life is fucking unfair. The moron never went to college. He started as a security guard! I graduated college, went to the Academy and passed every test with honors. But I'm a woman, so they made me a parole officer.

It wouldn't be so bad if Norman wasn't such a filthy brute, poking every hot new piece that books into Calpurnia. I should have dumped his stupid ass long ago. And do what? Live on my own? Can't afford it. Unless, of course, I do something really special. Something the bosses would have to acknowledge with a big raise—and a promotion. Maybe all the way to detective! Oh man, if I had that, I could blow off my asshole husband and have a real life!

FIRST THINGS FIRST

With only one parolee residing at Covenant House, Marge was required to visit Saltin only once a month, twice at the most. If she were going to crack the case (which was how she saw the situation), she knew she had to be there every day. She quickly realized: *If there were more parolees at Covenant House, I could visit nearly every day without raising an eyebrow of suspicion.*

It took her two days to review the files of all Calpurnia prisoners who had fewer than six months left on their sentence.

When she finished, she had identified six inmates who might easily qualify as halfway parolees at Covenant House.

The next day, during the warden's lunch hour, she handed him six applications. He signed each one without pausing to wipe his hands on a napkin. Within a week, all six women were living in Covenant House and Marge had her excuse for spending more time in Saltin.

HANNAH AND ANATOLY

Anatoly visited Hannah the following Thursday (again, late in the day). Again, she was standing alone in the shade of the Civic Center's back wall, watering her plants. Not wanting to startle her, he rapped lightly on the wall. Not wanting to frighten her, he'd left behind his ominous sack (though his gun was tucked in his pants, under his shirt). Despite these considerations, Hannah recoiled as soon as she saw him.

"Hannah, you okay?" he asked, speaking in English.

She retreated another step.

"You surprised to see me?"

"No," she said, collecting herself. "I expected you come again."

"That's good," he said, keeping his distance. "You know, I came a long way to find you."

"Why?" she said, with open-eyed honesty.

"Why?" he said, his voicing rising. "You don't know why?"

Hannah was silent.

"Really, Hannah? You cannot imagine?"

Noting the change in his tone, she spoke carefully.

"I'm not sure. You were gone many years. I moved on with my life. I hope you moved on with yours."

"I wasn't *gone*. I didn't leave you. I was in prison."

"I know."

Silence.

"We are still tied together, Hannah."

"No. I sent you divorce papers. You did not argue. You said nothing."

"I was in prison!"

"Yes, I know."

"Do you know why I was in prison?"

"You broke the law," she whispered.

Anatoly drew a deep breath.

"I broke a small, stupid law."

"Still, you broke the law," she said, with more conviction.

He drew another deep breath.

"Do you know why I did it, Hannah?"

She shook her head, but remained silent.

"I did it to give you and Peter a better life."

Hannah let several seconds pass before saying, "You might have tried working better job."

Anatoly exploded. "Stop it, Hannah. Stop it right now. These are old arguments."

Tense silence.

Hannah let the silence run its course. When the time was right, she smiled and approached him slowly.

"Tolya," she said warmly. "We are older now, and different."

Hearing his nickname soothed his heart.

"Hannah. Hannah. I still love you."

Hannah nodded, accepting his words.

"Tolya, here is truth, so help me God: We were right for each other, until we were wrong for each other. Life is change. There is no fault. Not yours, not mine. This is life."

Anatoly shook his head but spoke in a calm voice. "No, Hannah. What made me wrong for you is fixed. That's what

I came to tell you. You say you fell in love with me, and then you fell out of love with me. I am saying, I have changed. I am now like the man you first met, only better."

"Oh, Toly," she said, placing her hand gently on his shoulder. "Now it is my turn. Please listen: I see you have changed. It is a good change—and I appreciate how far you have traveled to see me and to tell me about your change. But I am changed too. I am a full doctor now—and research scientist. I am new person, with a new life."

Anatoly nodded to show he understood.

"I am very proud of you, Hannah. You have done very well. I want to be part of your new life."

Hannah shook her head. "I do not think so, Anatoly. Past is past. We honor it by remembering—and moving forward."

"We are still tied together, Hannah."

"By memories, Anatoly."

"Not just memories. We have Peter!"

Both their hearts clenched. Another silence ensued, during which their memories and feelings swirled about, almost palpably.

Anatoly didn't play his trump card, but he had more to say:

"I am not proud of my time in prison, Hannah. But not everyone I met there was a thief or degenerate. I met many good persons. Some with special interests and talents. To be honest, there was one, also from Lviv, who was released a few weeks after me. He is a good man and a friend. For a fee, he asked another friend to clean my official record so I could work and travel, even internationally. That is how I came to this country—and how I was able to find you."

Anatoly thought he was advertising his determination and cleverness but all Hannah heard was the same old conniving Anatoly. He recognized the suspicious look in her eyes.

"Hannah, all I ask is that you think about what I have said. Please do not make a quick judgment. I think I deserve that much."

"Okay," said Hannah. "That is fair."

Anatoly wasn't finished.

"Hannah, you didn't ask me how I came to find you. It is something you should know." He told her the story of the two agents who located him in Brighton Beach, New York City. He told her that she was the object of their interest.

"I told them I had no idea where you are, which was the truth. They seemed sure you were in the United States. Day after day they followed me and questioned me. They spoke excellent English but there were a few words that betrayed their Russian tongues. I became very suspicious. What with all the Russian-American politics—and you being a scientist—and Peter being in the army, fighting Russians in Ukraine, I knew they would look for you until they found you. And that worried me.

"One day it occurred to me that they would leave when they had a better idea where you were. That was my moment of inspiration, Hannah. So, you know what I did? I outsmarted them. I followed them all the way here."

"But how?"

"I will explain later. But now I am here, reunited—"

"Anatoly, please—"

"It's okay, you don't need to explain again. I understand your current point of view. But now, please listen to me: I do not know if you have seen these Russian agents but they have been here. If you haven't seen them, they have their reasons. It's a matter of time. So let me help you. I know you have other friends here. I will help them too. I know how these Russians work. They are dangerous. You need my help. Okay?"

Hannah closed her eyes and pressed her hands to her temples. "I need to think. It is all too much."

"I will see you soon, Hannah. We will talk again."

THREE ASSOCIATES

The top floor of The Palace, reconstructed per P.'s specifications, was indeed palatial, but the common understanding that one man lived there alone was just wrong. Two FSB agents (very alike in look and manner) also lived there, each in his own room, on either side of P.'s palatial suite. Katya had her own room within the suite, far enough from P. to respect his privacy, close enough to respond quickly when he yanked her leash. All three spoke some English, but none tried to pass for an American. Nor did they pretend to be lithium experts. They were there to serve and protect P.

KATYA

Katya met P. when she was a young girl and liked him right away. Whenever he patted her head, she recalled her father, whom she did not otherwise remember. She was proud her mother was P.'s Special Assistant.

She saw P. many times over many years, especially during his long trips that required her mother's services. In such circumstances, Katya traveled as part of P.'s entourage, spending her days with her mother and her nights (while her mother worked) with a nice old woman in a gray skirt who smelled of lavender.

When she was barely a teen, the agents in P.'s protective detail began flirting with her. (She was of average height but had bright blonde hair, striking blue eyes, excellent posture and an older woman's impressive bosom.) Katya was very interested in their training, especially their martial arts and concealed weapons. One handsome young agent took her for long walks in a vast forested park where he taught her grappling techniques and how to shoot his Serdyukov pistol (which he fixed with a silencer so as not to draw attention). But Katya proved such an excellent defensive wrestler he began to lose interest in her. One day, during target practice, she spotted a bounding rabbit about thirty yards away and without hesitation put a single bullet behind its fluffy brown ear. The next day the young agent told her his schedule had changed and that he would not be able to see her again.

Katya's mother was called into P.'s private office on the morning of her twentieth anniversary as his Special Assistant. This was not unusual as P. often liked to start his day with some exuberant intimacy. But on this day P. was only solicitous and kind. He thanked Katya's mother for all her services and handed her a velvet giftbox. She knew what was happening. (Months earlier, she'd seen crow's feet marking her mirrored eyes and mouth and knew this day would come.) She only wondered whether the box contained a goodbye watch or necklace. To her surprise, it contained neither. It was a gold keychain with three keys attached.

"Apartment 44. Your favorite building, in your favorite neighborhood. All your expenses shall be paid—as long as you shall live."

Her mother was genuinely surprised. It was much more than she expected.

Remaining behind his desk, P. stretched his hand towards her to suggest that the meeting—and their relationship—were happily concluded. She shook his hand and left, quietly dutiful, as always.

Before she reached her flat, she knew who would be P.'s next Special Assistant. At some level, she'd known for years but had kept her thoughts to herself. When Katya arrived home in the early afternoon, she sat down with her mother in their main room to have tea. As always, her mother poured a small amount of tea concentrate from the small teapot that sat above the nickel-plated samovar and then filled each cup with hot water from the samovar's ornate tap. For mother and daughter, this brief wordless ceremony was their most effusive pretension to respectability, which is why they both clung to it so devotedly.

After the dishes were cleared, Katya's mother opened her purse and withdrew her St. Vitaly medallion. On the back of this tribute to Russia's patron saint of prostitutes were these words engraved in Russian: *Judge not, lest ye be judged.* Her mother pressed the medallion into her daughter's hand without speaking a word of its significance.

"You know where I work. You will go there tomorrow morning and take my place."

Like mother, like daughter, Katya understood many things without needing them to be spelled out.

P. MAKES AN APPOINTMENT

P. knew the growing tumor in his lung must be treated very soon or he would die. Too many weeks had intervened since his last treatment and the tumor had grown.

Before he sat down to breakfast, he ordered Katya to go to Covenant House to speak to Hannah before she went to work. He made it very clear: Katya was to set up an appointment for him later that evening (tomorrow at the absolute latest) to receive treatment—from Hannah—in her makeshift facility in the back of the Civic Center.

P. hoped his first-thing-in-the-morning strategy would unnerve Hannah. He hoped sending his mistress as messenger would humiliate her. He loved Hannah, but she had to be taught a lesson. She would be no good to him as a wife if he didn't set her straight. That was the mistake he'd made with Maria.

KATYA AND HANNAH

As she walked towards Covenant House, Katya worried that P. no longer desired her. He hadn't touched her since they'd arrived at The Palace two days earlier. (Indeed, P. was preoccupied by Hannah's proximity and the notion that he would soon need all his strength for his upcoming laser treatments.)

Katya figured she'd know Hannah when she saw her, and she was certainly right. When she saw Hannah coming down the stairs (looking so much like her own mother—or how she herself would look in twenty years) she intuited that this double twin meant more to P. than her mother ever had, and more than she ever would. This revelation, this stinging bitch-slap, this existential kick in the ass would change her life. But for now, she had her assignment. She stood when Hannah reached the landing.

"I have message," she said, speaking with a clipped, authoritarian tone. "Your patient needs examination and treatment. He comes to your office this evening at six o'clock."

"I'm afraid that's—"

"Then tomorrow. Same time."

WHO IS ANATOLY?

As there was now little need to communicate through backchannels and go-betweens, Yevgeny sent Hannah a text message as soon as he was ready.

"I'm here. I want to see you as soon as possible."

That's all he wrote. Not too much, not too little.

As he hoped, Hannah rushed to greet him as soon as she saw him (not romantically, as he took it, but as a dear friend whom she truly had missed). Without kissing (even though they were alone), they grasped each other tightly, their tear-covered faces side-by-side in a joyous embrace.

When they uncoupled, Yevgeny felt emotionally confident of Hannah's love. Assuming there would be many more opportunities to advance their personal feelings, he thought it best to focus now on their pressing professional issues. He'd just begun discussing Hannah's new salt samples and how they might be tested when Hannah interrupted.

"I had a message from P. this morning," she said.

"You spoke to him? You saw him?"

"No, he sent his whore secretary."

"What did she say?"

"He needs treatment. He insists that I treat him. He is coming tomorrow evening at six."

"Okay, okay," said Yevgeny, as if the development had been expected. "Just be professional. We will be ready for him."

"I know."

"And don't you worry. I will not be far away."

"Good. Dimitri, Jason and Anatoly said same thing. We make strong team."

Pause.

"Who is Anatoly?"

Pause.

"I thought I told you."

"You didn't."

"Oh. He's my husband."

"Your husband?"

Pause.

"My fourth. I divorced him. I sent him papers while he was in prison—but he does not like the divorce."

Hannah saw distress in Yevgeny's wide eyes.

"But the papers were signed?"

"I signed them, but he never did. I am told him we are legally divorced."

Pause.

"Then why is he here?"

"He thinks he can take me back."

Yevgeny wavered, as if on the edge of a cliff.

"Can he?"

"I say no."

Yevgeny spoke softly.

"What does he think?"

Hannah drew a deep breath. She must finally tell Yevgeny what Jason, Dimitri and even Bethany already knew.

"He is the father of my son. He wants us to be a family, like before."

Yevgeny's world tilted.

"Please, Yevgeny. Sit here. I will get some cold water and we will talk."

A LITTLE FAMILY HISTORY

Hannah told him of her four husbands.

"You didn't love them, Hannah?"

"No, not really. I sought safety and security."

"You hoped love would come along?"

"I think so."

"But love is not like watering a plant."

"I know that now."

"And what of Anatoly?"

"Husband number four. Big disappointment."

"But you bore his child."

"I got pregnant."

"An accident, or your choice?"

Pause.

"I was desperate to try something that would make me happy."

"Did it?"

"Yes. My son made me greatly happy. He is my greatest treasure."

Yevgeny felt excluded.

"How old is he, Hannah? Where is he now?"

She burst into tears.

Yevgeny did not offer a tissue or a shoulder to cry on. He just sat there, as if paralyzed. Eventually, Hannah dried her tears with her hands.

"Nineteen. Almost twenty. He is in the army—fighting the Russians. I haven't heard from him in many weeks."

TWO'S COMPANY

Next morning, as was their habit, Jason met Hannah outside Covenant House for their drive to the Civic Center.

"I'm going to miss sailing the sea in our Argo," she said.

Jason turned to her.

"Why? What's changed?"

"Yevgeny has arrived. Now it will be him, Dimitri and myself in our little office by the sea."

"We'll need a bigger golf cart."

Hannah laughed. "You're so sweet." She pressed his hand. "But Yevgeny leased a car when he arrived in San Diego and has brought it here. He will now drive me to and from work each day."

Pause. "You and I, we are still—"

"Yes, of course. Only, Yevgeny is my boss—and also very special to me. If he says he will drive me to and from work, I do not say no." Pause. "But I wanted this last trip with you."

Pause. "I'm sad. I loved sailing with you in our little ship."

"Me too. It like a dream. I digging in the sands and you singing and playing your guitar."

"But that's not over, right? We can still see each other?"

"Yes, but more complicated now. Yevgeny is here. And Anatoly too. And that man—the Russian who moved into The Palace—you understand?"

"I know who he is and how he treated you. That will not happen again."

"Maybe you right. But he is very powerful and dangerous, even here in America."

"I will help protect you."

"I know, but you are not cowboy hero. His men are very strong and they do whatever P. wants."

"But this isn't the Wild West. He doesn't run this place like he does Russia. We're all watching one another."

"I hope you are right. Maybe he come here just for treatments. Maybe that is all he wants."

Pause.

"I have favor to ask you," continued Hannah. "You and I have special relationship. I do not think we know what it is, but it seems special, yes?"

Jason took her hand, even though they were in public. "Yes. You are my Muse."

"What means *muse*?"

"It means you are special to me. You inspire me. Because of you, I will finish my opera."

"I am honored. But I want to say this: Yevgeny has feelings and hopes of me and him. To be honest, I do not think I know my own mind. Yevgeny, you, Anatoly—it is a lot for me to think. And, tell you truth, my mind is often with Peter. Sometimes, I just want to be alone and not be bothered with thinking."

"You want me to slow down? You want something else from me?"

Hannah started to cry. Never before had a man talked so sweetly and selflessly to her. Jason was a wise, beautiful man.

"You be who you are," said Hannah. "You are special. I just wanting to say, I have craziness in my life. I do not want to make more bad choices."

"Thank you for telling me. I will do all I can to help you. Whatever you want."

Hannah squeezed his hand.

"Okay, now please take me to office. I have work with Dimitri and Yevgeny."

CONSPIRACY AND CONFESSION

Next morning, Tova sat by her upstairs window, wondering why the silly golf cart (with the fringed roof and giant eye) had not come for Hannah. Just then, a gray sedan pulled up and parked below her window. Two men (the driver and his front-seat companion) exited the car and moved towards Covenant's front door. Belying her nearly eighty years, Tova hurried down the steps, arriving just as the men knocked for the second time.

"Good morning," she said, opening the door just wide enough for conversation. "What can I do for you?"

Yevgeny stood before her; Dimitri behind him, slightly to his right.

"We are here to see Hannah Belaya."

"Is she in some kind of trouble?"

"No, we work together."

"I see. What kind of work, if you don't mind my asking."

Yevgeny paused.

"Scientific research. We are a team."

Tova felt her anger rising. They didn't look like scientists to her. They looked and sounded like Russian mobsters.

Just then, Sister Carmel entered the front parlor from the chapel.

"*Sister* Carmel, please tell Hannah that two men are here to see her."

Not a minute later, Hannah appeared at the top of the stairs. With that, Tova opened the door wider so Hannah might see her callers.

"Hello!" Hannah cried happily. "Nice to see you both!"

"Like old times," called Dimitri.

"Come," said Yevgeny, as Hannah hurried down the stairs. "We have much to do."

Away they went.

Tova watched the gray sedan until it was out of sight and then closed the door. She was deciphering what she'd just seen when the black drug dealer came downstairs, muttered "Good morning," and then walked out the door, making straightway for her pimp-mobile parked across the street.

Oh my god! Russian mafia—black drug dealer—a conspiracy under my own roof!

Not ten minutes later, Officer Marge Schenk arrived. Tova dragged her upstairs to her private apartment, where she could bring her up to date without being overheard.

"Really, I can't trust anyone but you!"

Marge readied her pen and notebook.

"Tell me everything you saw and everything you heard. Just keep talking while it's fresh in your mind."

Tova began:

"The two men are foreign, like her—no, I can't place the accent—but they seem to know her well."

"Go on," said Marge, scribbling notes

"The second man, not the boss, said, 'Like old times.'"

"Sounds like they've been partners for a while."

"Good point. They could be part of an international ring. I made a copy of her passport. Wait a minute, I'll get it—in fact, here it is."

"Ukraine, Lviv," said Marge, flipping through the pages.

"I don't know where the other two are from and I don't know their names."

"Do you sense a chain of command?" Marge asked.

"Hell, I can't prioritize. That's your job, honey. They all seem like lead suspects to me. But as far as I can tell, it started with that so-called American professor. It was her group of so-called scientists who discovered that huge lithium site on the north shore—the whole northeast corner, I heard."

"Got it," said Marge, taking notes like a real detective. "Now, back to Fred Heinz. Wasn't he instrumental in getting the scientists the necessary permits to explore?"

"Yes, Fred was how she got to our mayors. But I don't think he was involved. I mean, he was involved, but I think he was just an unwitting pawn. You going to investigate him too?"

"Of course. I have to investigate everyone."

"I understand. You have to track down every lead. But listen, I've got to tell you something. I assure you, it's irrelevant to your investigation, but it's very important to me. First, I need you to swear you won't reveal what I'm going to say."

"I can't promise that. What if it involves national security?"

"Well, I suppose. But I assure you it's nothing like that." With that, Tova drew a series of deep breaths. "Just give me a minute. It's not the kind of thing I can just blurt out."

In spite of her tears and labored breathing, Tova told Marge of her relationship with Fred, more or less sticking to the facts of the story.

PECKING ORDER

Hannah assumed Yevgeny would take control of the Saltin office. After all, he was team leader and financier of the entire operation. To his credit, Yevgeny acknowledged Hannah's great contributions in setting up their desert outpost and continued to regard her as second in command. For his part, Dimitri seemed not to mind his bottom position in the pecking order. Now that they were only three, he would have plenty time alone with Yevgeny.

GROUND RULES

It was disconcerting for the three scientists to have their friends visit them at the Civic Center. To clear the air and to set some friendly ground rules, Yevgeny spoke to Bethany; Hannah spoke to Jason; and Dimitri spoke to Fred, asking them not to knock on their door or contact them electronically during work hours, unless the situation demanded it.

Fred didn't mind the rule at all. For him, it was excitement enough to know that there were scientists working in the office across from his.

Bethany and Jason were disappointed until they realized they could spend more time together. They also understood that they should remain at the ready, in case they were needed.

DIAGNOSTICS

All three doctors were inside the Saltin office together for the first time. As soon as Hannah closed the door against intrusion, Yevgeny proclaimed, "He needs new tests before we can proceed."

"I agree," said Hannah. "He needs a complete physical examination, but we are not set up."

"He knows he has wasted critical time," said Yevgeny. "He will order us to proceed with our treatment plan as soon as possible, and he's not entirely wrong."

"But we need data to guide the continuing course of our treatment," added Dimitri.

Yevgeny raised his hand to indicate he had the answer. "Here is how I see it. When P. arrives this evening, we will take blood samples and tell him that one of his men must immediately take them in an air-conditioned car to a laboratory in San Diego. The laboratory will email me the results."

"What about all the other tests he needs?"

"I do not expect P. to remain continually in Saltin. I assume he will make regular trips back to Moscow, where he can receive X-rays, CT scans, biopsies, and further blood tests. He will have the data sent to us, and we can then adjust our salts, laser intensity and schedule of treatment accordingly."

Hannah and Dimitri were silent.

"I know what you are thinking. We are using extraordinary means to keep the bastard alive. But that is our sworn oath."

"We acted otherwise in the past," said Dimitri.

"We did so under duress, when we felt threatened."

"I still feel threatened," said Hannah.

"My dear, we all feel your pain. We are a true team. We are one."

"But what if it happens again?" asked Dimitri.

"Then we will do what we must."

"But what does that mean, Yevgeny? He has thugs here. What can we do?"

"This is not Moscow," said Yevgeny. "This is America. And we have more friends and resources here than he has agents. We will be prepared."

POLICE AT THE DOOR

Later than same afternoon, about two hours before P.'s arrival, a California State Police car pulled off Route 86 and parked in the gravel yard in front of the Civic Center. The officer, who knew of the Center but had never visited, was surprised by the fanciful scallop roof and the slightly unhinged door, studded with faux starfish.

Entering the dimly lighted Center (her hand close to her holster), she called out: "Anyone here?"

Fred was inside, dusting the model of Saltin City.

"Good afternoon," he called from the dim interior. "Welcome to the Saltin Civic Center? First time here?"

"I'm Officer Schenk of the California State Police."

As Marge stepped closer, Fred made out her gray uniform—her banded hat, golden badge, and polished holster glinting in the dim light.

"Nice to meet you, officer. What can I do for you?"

"I'm sure you know, we have a lot of new folks in town."

"I know, it's wonderful. We're all doing our part to make Saltin great again."

"That's great, but right now I'm doing some routine checks. You work alone here?"

"I work alone, but there are several scientists here studying our famous salts."

"I'd like to meet them."

"I'm sure they'd like to meet you too, but I know they're busy right now."

"I'd like to meet them *now,* if you don't mind."

Before Fred could answer, Marge added: "You're Fred Heinz, right?"

"Yes."

Feeling vaguely guilty, Fred led Marge to the back of the Civic Center. "This way, please. Watch your step."

The rear of the Center was better lighted, the screen door facing the desert sea, admitting a wide wash of sunlight.

"What was your name again?" asked Fred.

"The police."

Fred dry swallowed, then knuckle-rapped the door three times. Without waiting for a reply, he called out: "Dr. Yeshevsky? It's me, Fred. There's a police officer here. She has some questions."

The door opened about halfway.

"Hello, I am Dr. Yevgeny Yeshevsky. What can I do for you?" He stood there stolidly, blocking most of the view inside.

"I'm officer Marge Schenk of the California State Police. May I come in?"

Yevgeny drilled his eyes into hers. "No, you may not. This is a medical office and you are not scrubbed clean. Still, I am happy to answer a few brief questions."

Marge was put off by his authoritative tone but quickly recovered.

"How long have you worked here, Dr. Yeshevsky?"

"I am recently arrived."

"From where?"

"The Middle East."

"Specifically, please."

"Next question. I will answer only a few more. We are very busy."

"Who else is here?"

"Dr. Hannah Belaya and Dr. Dimitri Grushina."

"These two people are actual doctors?"

"Of course."

"What is the nature of your work?"

"We are conducting medical research."

"What you are studying?"

"We are researching how salt crystals can be used to fight cancer."

"Interesting. I'd like to know more."

"Impossible. Our research is confidential and privately funded. Now, as we are all here on legal visas and breaking no law, I must ask you to go."

"One last question: How do you know Bethany Church."

"She is a friend."

P. AND FRED SHAKE HANDS

Although P. arrived on time and was anxious to begin his treatment, he wanted to meet the man who managed the Civic Center, who'd been so helpful in initiating the lithium project. And so, ignoring his agents' advice to enter the medical office by way of the Civic Center's rear door, he followed his agents through the fanciful front door and into the Civic Center's main room, where he met Fred Heinz, who was busy straightening the exhibit posters of yesteryear.

Despite never having seen P., Fred knew he was shaking hands with the lithium magnate from Russia, for whom the top floor of The Palace had been built. (Fred was a sucker for power and all that glitters. He knew Saltin's rebirth lay in the hands of powerbrokers like this Russian and was proud to shake his hand. For sure, he'd heard a few people question the ethics of a man who lived alone in a palace, but he didn't care. As the city's historian, he knew Saltin had been built by Bible thumpers and ruthless Capitalists, men who did whatever was necessary to save souls and squeeze profits. He'd be honored to assist P. any way he could. And he was very happy that his new friends—Hannah, Dimitri and Yevgeny—were also doing what they could to help him.)

COSMOENERGY WEST

P. moved as if he were strolling into the office on Stoleshnikov Lane. As if nothing were amiss, he smiled at all three doctors in turn before addressing Dr. Yeshevsky:

"It's been a long time between treatments, doctor. I hope you've made great strides in advancing your methods."

"Indeed, that is always our aim."

"Excellent. And what have you learned?"

"We have learned that even among the many salt samples we have collected here, there is an impressive variability in the level of lithium. In a perfect world, we would test each sample on a variety of diseased cells to learn which affected pH levels optimally."

"But this is not a perfect world."

"It surely is not."

"And yet you have sworn to provide the best possible care to every patient."

Yeshevsky looked him in the eye. "The care of our patients—along with the well-being of our doctors—is our goal."

"Excellent."

"I would add that everyone—in every sphere, at every level—is bound by law and God to do their ethical best."

P. smiled. "Well, Doctor, we have all traveled great distances and at great expense to be here. Shall we get started?"

IMMEDIATE DANGER

Having followed the Russian agents from Brighton to Saltin, Anatoly Bychkov mostly kept out of sight until he learned what was going on with them. When two weeks passed without learning anything more, he decided to visit Hannah again, not to press his case, but to see if she could enlighten him. Unfortunately, he discovered she was now working with colleagues who drove her to and from her office every day but Sunday. Knowing her as he did, he decided his best chance of seeing her alone would be on a Sunday morning, when she was likely to go on a solitary walk after going to church, as was her past habit.

The next Sunday, he watched from a distance as Hannah left Covenant House, then followed her discreetly. When she entered a church, whose façade reminded him of Chartres' Notre Dame, he knew she would stay awhile. He followed her inside, remaining in the rear while she sat up front, hunched in prayer, her clasped hands resting on the back of the pew in front of her.

A long hour later she unclasped her hands and left the pew, returning to the church vestibule, where she saw Anatoly waiting for her.

He knew she would not speak until she was outside. Once outside, he allowed her to set the pace and direction.

She led him in a circuitous walk toward the outer precincts of East Saltin, which were even more dilapidated and forlorn than the area closer to the boardwalk. Finally, they found a broken bench in the shade of a lone tree and there they sat.

Hannah's reserve encouraged him to speak first, which he did, conversing generally about his ten years away, jumping from one topic to another, finally ending with his description of how he met a pair of Russian agents in Brighton Beach (near Coney Island) and cleverly followed them all the way to Saltin. At this point Hannah gasped, realizing the danger he was in.

"Oh no. Oh my god!"

Anatoly reached for her hand and she let him take it.

"What's wrong?"

"Toly, the men you followed here are pretending to be Americans. They have made a big business deal to buy much of the desert sea to mine lithium. If they see you, they will know you can reveal who they really are. They will kill you!"

"But here they are businessmen. They can't just kill people."

"They aren't real businessmen. It must be fake. They are very dangerous."

"We can tell the police."

"Toly, you don't understand. You don't know."

"Then tell me."

Hannah drew a deep breath. "It is almost too much to believe. The two Russians who pretend to be American, they brought a big partner to help with the mining—"

"I heard about that."

"Well, that is fake too. Or somewhat fake. I don't understand it all. But the big partner from Russia, he is really here for other reasons."

"How do you know?"

"I know him."

"How do you know him?"

Hannah told Anatoly how a disguised P. came to the Cosmoenergy office in Moscow and what ensued.

Anatoly was stunned.

"He's here? In Saltin? In this broken little place?"

"Yes."

"Impossible. Where is he staying?"

"The Palace."

"Where they are building?"

"Yes. The new Dacha P."

Anatoly dropped Hannah's hand and sat up straight.

"Help me understand: The agents I followed are posing as Americans, who are posing as mining experts, who are posing as business associates of P.'s, who is here because he has lung cancer and you know a cure and he loves you."

"Yes."

"Hannah, are you sure? It is incredible!"

"It is crazy true."

Anatoly put a hand on her shoulder.

"But you are safe now. They won't harm you if they need you."

"Both my doctor friends can do what I do—and P. knows that."

"So, you are not safe?"

"I am safe as long as he wants me—as his lover, maybe his wife."

"He said such things?"

"Yes. In different words."

Bychkov was disturbed, but even more impressed with Hannah than before.

"How do you feel about it?"

"I would kill him before I married him."

Bychkov recoiled, then felt pleased.

"Does he know that?"

"No. I do not think so."

"Then I would keep that a secret as long as you can."

Hannah smiled. "But, Toly, *you* are in immediate danger. They will recognize you—and kill you."

Bychkov shrugged. "Maybe, maybe not. With so many complications, I do not think they will kill me. This is a small place. They have a business here. P. is getting secret medical treatment. I'm thinking: Maybe they don't want to make a mess. Maybe they want to buy my silence."

Hannah sat back down.

"You have always been clever, but I am very I'm worried. Maybe you should leave."

"Leave? How can I leave you?"

"You are in more danger than I am."

"More reason that I should stay. If I leave here, alone—they certainly will kill me."

Hannah shivered. She was starting to lose control.

"I don't know. I just don't know. Maybe you disappear, like ghost."

Bychkov shook his head. "Hannah, you can't disappear from the FSB. You know that."

She started to cry.

"I am no crybaby, but lately I cry all the time. I worry about Peter and my friends—and you. It is too much!"

Bychkov spoke softly but firmly. "Hannah, in Brooklyn, those men said they were looking for you. I thought they wanted to harm you. I had to follow them. I had to find you."

"I understand. But if you stay here, they will see you for sure, if they haven't already."

"Yes, we both understand that. But what can I do?"

Hannah considered the situation. "For now, don't do anything. I'll introduce you to my friends. Dr. Yeshevsky is very smart. I'll explain the situation."

"Does he already know about me?"

"Yes. I told him you were my fourth husband. And that I divorced you."

"I never signed those papers."

"We are divorced."

"I disagree, but let's not argue now. Anyway, what does Dr. Yeshevsky think about me?"

"He is not happy that you are here. I think he wants to marry me too."

"Then he will not welcome me with open arms."

"Like I said, he is very smart. When we discuss our problems with P., he says a lot about alliances. Maybe he will see some value in having you join our group."

"And if he doesn't see it that way?"

"I don't know. Maybe he shoot you—just kidding. He is gentle man."

LYING LOW

While awaiting word from Hannah, Bychkov busied himself by taking long walks to the Wildlife Refuge (the former marsh, south of Saltin, now dried and withered). For hours he sat on a tree-shaded, stony ledge, drawing sandwiches, cookies and a thermos from his shoulder bag. Except for the drone of insects and the flyby birds that flapped and cawed, it was exceedingly quiet, a good place to sojourn, alone with his thoughts.

He usually began by thinking of his happy days with Hannah. It had been good to be thirty years old, married, a father and living in Lviv. But then he lost his job and could not find another. As he remembered, there seemed to be many more people sitting in cafés than working. (In fact, Ukraine's then slowing economy soon plummeted into a prolonged period of economic depression.)

There he was (as he pictured himself): a jobless man, a jobless husband, a jobless father. Clearly, a job would have done much to raise his self-esteem. Unfortunately, for all his insights and cleverness, Anatoly did not play by the rules and was not a persistent, long-term strategist. Not surprising, he took the easy way out and became a gambler. Not surprising, within three months he'd gambled away his family's nest egg and the additional funds he'd borrowed from cronies. As he recalled, Hannah would not ask her brother to help pay his steep debt—which led him to attempt a stupid theft—which led the police to wrench him from his wife and son and lock him in a prison cell—which, ironically, ended his job search.

Anatoly might not have survived his excruciating prison term had it not been for his imagined reunions with Hannah and Peter. During one such happy reverie, a prison guard tossed into his cell a fresh, formal-looking envelope. Anatoly thought the envelope might be a response to his recent parole review. Instead, he found inside a stapled statement of divorce, which required his signature in three places. With surprising savagery, he shredded the papers, rattled his cage, and pounded the wall to make sure everyone knew how he felt.

Other times in the Wildlife Refuge he dwelled on his early days in Brighton Beach, where he'd gone to start a new life after his release from prison. He often thought of the day the two agents had approached him outside the Starbucks next to his apartment building and what they had said about Hannah. He recalled the business card they gave him and how the shiny whiteness of its reverse side matched the *belaya* of his wife and convinced him to follow them.

CHANCE AND CHOICE

Jason and Bethany were romantic realists. Privately, each understood that Saltin was their current situation, not likely their destiny.

Either could have left at any time. Bethany could have driven away in her luxury sedan to any one of a hundred ports of call. Jason could have boarded a bus back to Fantasy Springs and continued his wandering.

But both were inclined to stay. By turns self-serving and altruistic, they stayed in Saltin to see what they would see, for better or worse.

KATYA IN TOW

On his next visit to the Civic Center, P. left behind his pair of bodyguards, arriving instead with able-bodied Katya in tow. (Though she trailed, she was hardly an afterthought. P. wanted her to see Hannah again, and he wanted Hannah to see her, although he wasn't exactly sure why.)

Katya was instructed to knock and announce his arrival. When the door opened, Katya glimpsed the three doctors inside, her eyes catching Hannah's for a memorable split-second, as P. had hoped. She was then instructed to wait outside, P. pointing to the two vacant chairs and table, set in the shade of the Civic Center's back wall.

JASON AND BETHANY

While P. was being examined for the second time, Katya stared at the desert sea, thinking of the Arabian sands and

Scheherazade stories her mother had read to her when she was a child. (In later years, when her mother worked evenings with P., Katya read the stories herself to fill her motherless hours.)

While staring, Katya espied an approaching sandstorm in the distance, accompanied by an increasingly loud whirring of wheels and motor. The image was enchanting, not threatening, and not once did she think of drawing her loaded pistol. She looked forward to the company.

From a distance, Jason and Bethany thought it was Hannah sitting in the shade, awaiting them. (With so few opportunities for social connection, Jason and Bethany sought out each other's company, especially when the others were professionally engaged. It was Jason who had offered to show Bethany around the desert sea in his weirdly outfitted golf cart.) As they drew close, both were disconcerted to see that it wasn't Hannah, but a Hannah lookalike. *What happened to Hannah?* their expressions said. Katya understood their wondering looks and resented them. *I am me. Not Hannah. Not my mother. Me!*

Captaining the Argo, Jason pulled the fringed, one-eyed vessel within a dozen feet of the Civic Center and cut the engine.

Katya would not speak first.

"Hello," said Jason.

"Hi," said Bethany.

"Hello," Katya said tonelessly, without rising from her seat.

They looked like people she might like to know, but she was acutely aware of her accent and limited English—and they were American. Her loyalty lay inside on an examination table. (She despised P. in many ways, but she loved Russia and would protect its interests with her life.)

"Are you waiting to see Fred or the doctors?" asked Jason.

"For man inside."

Her accent gave her away. She was waiting for P. That, and her uncanny resemblance to Hannah, made them very nervous.

BLOOD WORKS

Dr. Yeshevsky was completing his examination (Drs. Belaya and Grushina assisting, somewhat clumsily, as four was a crowd in the small office. When the laser was in use, one of the doctors would have to remain outside).

"As I explained," Yeshevsky said, handing P. a padded envelope containing two blood-filled vials, "these must be kept cool and delivered to the laboratory in San Diego as soon as possible."

P. buttoned his shirt and took the envelope from Yeshevsky. "My next visit will include a laser treatment."

Yeshevsky ignored the command. (Much had changed since their very first meeting on Stoleshnikov Lane in Moscow. At that time, P. had the advantage of surprise, along with everything else at his imperious command. Meeting again, months later, in a largely desolate town in the American Southwest, their respective positions, especially vis-à-vis each other, had changed considerably.)

"We should have the results in less than a week. We cannot proceed without the new data. You have been away too long."

"Hardly my fault alone, doctor."

"Fault aside, science is science. We must have the results before proceeding."

"But you will prescribe more frequent treatments than last time, yes?"

"I will not make promises. We will proceed based on the status of your cancer and your ability to tolerate treatment."

"Don't you worry about me, doctor. I am judo strong, inside and out."

The doctors stepped aside as P. made for the exit. With the doorknob in his hand, P. turned to face Hannah.

"Next time I'm here, I want you to guide the laser. I want my life in your hands."

EDWINA AND FRED

Early in their relationship, Fred had explained to Edwina that he had no access to a car and that the cost and rigor of traveling by bus to San Diego (where she lived) would be an acute hardship. Edwina completely understood.

"I'll meet you more than halfway, my adorable desert rat" (a moniker Fred had earned by charging, Rommel-like, across the desert sea in a golf cart to join Edwina's end-of-exploration lunch party).

Since that time, the two silvered lovebirds communicated by cellphone and occasionally met for lunch at Fantasy Springs, Edwina sharing stories about her life and deceased husband, Fred opening up about his life and his lost Tova.

Though they'd become quite close, both were insecure about next steps. Neither had been naked with another person in many years. They were even more insecure about revealing their financial woes. (Ironically, both hoped Saltin's lithium concentration might be their financial salvation: Fred was under the mistaken impression that Edwina had benefitted from her academic team's discovery of the lithium site; Edwina was under the misguided notion that Fred had received a tidy sum from Saltin's mayors for his helpful facilitations.) Both imagined that their twilight years would be more easily managed if they spent them together, sharing their resources.

THREE YEARS!

P. had ordered Akhmerov and Zubilin to consult with a certain Russian-born, American-based mining and ore-processing expert to assess what site preparations and infrastructure would be required to support a large-scale, dry-mining lithium operation in the northeast corner of the Saltin Sea.

P. wanted a comprehensive report and, in a sense, got more than he bargained for. According to the consultant's assessment, the following utilities would be essential for day-to-day mining and distribution: electric and solar power, water supply, sewage disposal; offices, employee housing, workshops, warehouses; firefighting and support facilities; security and fencing; and expanded communications facilities. (These were the main items. There were many smaller considerations.)

Given the complexity of the proposed project, the remoteness of the site and the entire lack of existing infrastructure, the report concluded that up to three years would be necessary to construct and install everything needed for the commencement of mining operations. (All this, on top of the understanding that the extracted lithium would have to be shipped seven thousand miles, by land and sea, to Lithotech, P.'s new lithium-ion battery plant in Novosibirsk.)

"Three years!" P. yelled, glowering at his agents. "Too long, too expensive. I want a new plan!"

"STRONG PRESIDENT, STRONG RUSSIA!"

P.'s long, arduous, election campaign had resulted in a pyrrhic victory: an extension of his political career at the cost of his health.

At sixty-six, and with a spreading lung cancer, it was increasingly difficult for him to project a hale and hearty persona. For the first time since acquiring unchecked power, P. began seriously to consider life out of office, which, for him, meant projecting his financial strength in political retirement. (According to the Organized Crime and Corruption Reporting Project, P. had for many years employed a secret cadre of accountants and financial planners to plunder funds from public institutions and state-run businesses in order to fatten his personal accounts and shell companies around the world. With so many billions secreted in so many places, he was reasonably assured of living regally, no matter what corner of the world he was forced to live—if it ever came to that.)

He had counted heavily on the election of the American Idiot to help extend his own political shelf life. But there were strong signs that the American president might not survive his full term, much less be reelected for another four years. If the American Idiot fell from grace, he would be a liability. P. began thinking how best to destroy his promising duumvirate before it damaged his own power.

BLOOD TESTS

Dr. Yeshevsky had directed P. to have his blood samples brought to a specific lab in San Diego because he knew it was one of only three laboratories in California that used a newly FDA-approved blood test for pulmonary cancer. (The test evaluated two indicative proteins—LG3BP and C163A—to assess type and level of the disease.) The results were starkly definitive: the patient had a virulent malignancy in both lungs.

At this point, confirming biopsies might be dangerously invasive. Surgical eradication posed untenable risks. Yeshevsky knew only one possible way of saving P.'s life.

CANCER KILLERS

Based on all the experimentation they had done in Moscow, the Cosmoenergy team knew that the unique Saltin salts (with their highly concentrated, naturally occurring lithium) worked better than all other salts they had previously tested. Even so, it was reasonable to suppose that among the many new samples collected by Hannah (with Jason's help), there would be at least a few that were even more effective in raising the pH level of cancerous cells. In fact, during her weeks of solitary research (in which she'd employed various analytic tools and a special computer modeling program), Hannah had identified four new Saltin salt samples she thought might prove to be their most effective cancer-killers. It only remained to infuse the new salts into P.'s diseased cells and experiment with the power and duration of the laser treatment.

A VISIONARY

It's not everyone who sees a three hundred forty-square mile desert basin and wonders, "What is the best way to fill it with water?" But P. (an imperious, mean-spirited bastard) was also a visionary of sorts. Having had his staff research the geological history of the Saltin Sea, he knew it was a natural basin that had filled with rainwater eons ago and had remained self-sustaining until selfish human politicians in the late-twentieth century sought to improve its natural balance by building dams and canals to ensure its existence in perpetuity.

P. well understood that the best-laid plans of mice and men often go awry. He also understood that almost anything broken can be fixed—and vice versa.

IF ONLY

P. reviewed several cost analyses that compared hard rock lithium mining with lithium brine extraction. In most cases, hard rock mining was a costlier investment and presented a greater chance of landscape damage and pollution. Given the circumstances of the Saltin Sea, brine exploration would certainly be the more financially expeditious process—if the Saltin Sea were a body of water and not a formidable desert.

PROFESSIONAL OPINION

During a meeting with Akhmerov and Zubilin, P. was told that Edwina Lazar Orosco (recently retired professor at University of California-San Diego, who had led Saltin's "lithium expedition") was planning a birthday picnic for her "special friend," Fred Heinz, at the site where they'd had their excavation luncheon a couple months earlier.

"Bring a birthday gift for them both—something cute," said P. to his agents. "When the time is right, ask her if she would one day be so kind as to give you a geological tour of the Saltin Sea, especially those areas we now own. Tell her how helpful it would be to our eventual mining operations."

"What specifically do you want to learn?"

"I want to know why she thinks the sea dried up. Also, ask her what rivers or dams communicate with the Saltin Sea. Don't push her too hard. Just let her talk. I want to know what she has to say."

DIVERSIONS

Anderson and Zimmer presented Fred with a birthday gift, a pair of his and hers *California Dreamin'* t-shirts (which secretly thrilled them both, as it seemed to publicly sanction their couple status).

While the four chatted happily, Anderson turned to Edwina and said, "When you have the time, we'd be honored if you would guide us through the area we purchased."

"Of course, we've seen it before," said Zimmer, "but we'd love to see it through your eyes."

"We know mining," said Anderson, "but we're not quite geologists or chemists. We'd be very grateful for your opinions and insights."

Edwina turned to Fred. "Honey, it's your birthday, but we happen to be in the area."

Fred was thrilled to be a cog in the process. "No time like the present. Lead on, my dear!"

Edwina considered the surrounding area before deciding on a docent's route. Once decided, she had the good habit of never talking while she walked. When she had something to say, she stopped, pointed, and then spoke, always engaging each member of her audience in turn.

"We know from geological history that this region experiences long cycles of drought. Had Saltin's Founding Fathers studied the region's sedimentary layering and stratification, they would have known that. But, to be fair, science has come a long way in the past thirty or forty years."

"So, do you think building a local dam caused the Saltin drought, or was it an inevitable effect of cyclical nature?"

"Actually, very large dams can increase rainfall. They provide lots of water to evaporate, which leads to more precipitation."

"Then why the drought?"

Edwina explained that about ninety percent of the volume of the south-flowing Colorado River is diverted by several canals, all meant to bring irrigation and drinking water to various parts of the Southwest. "The last canal to be built leads to the Jordan-Enterprise dam, which was created to regulate the level of the Saltin Sea. But it's not a very large dam, and it's never been filled to its max capacity. Its stored waters would not have had any appreciable effect on climate and rainfall."

Anderson raised his hand like a shy schoolboy. "I feel a little embarrassed to ask, but why hasn't the dam been used to refill the Saltin Sea?"

Edwina and Fred smiled. They both knew the answer to that one.

"It's a good question that's been asked a million times," said Edwina. "Here's the answer: The waterflow to the dam is modest compared to the diverted flow through the other canals. The Jordan-Enterprise dam was intended to regulate the Saltin Sea, not fill it. When the current drought cycle began in earnest, the Saltin Sea began drying up faster than it could be responsibly refilled."

"What does that mean, *responsibly refilled*?"

"It means the engineers eventually halted the regulating river flow into the Sea, regarding it as a lost cause."

"Couldn't they redirect more water from other canals?"

"Not without affecting the health of all the other communities in the region."

Both agents nodded. "That makes sense."

"Without the long-term cooperation of nature, the only way to refill the Saltin Sea would be an end-of-days biblical flood—or a major rupture of the dam."

"And neither is likely."

"Correct. There's nothing in the planetary forecast to suggest a drastic climate change in this region, much less a worldwide flood."

"What about damage to the dam? An accident? Terrorism?"

Edwina shook her head. "Unlikely. I have friends on the science faculty at the Air Force Academy in Colorado Springs. Suffice to say, there are strong precautions in place against a direct attack on any part of the Colorado River system."

"Thank God for that," said Zimmer.

Anderson nodded in agreement, then added, "So, no event could cause the Saltin Sea to be refilled?"

"Well, there is one other factor."

A MAJOR FAULT

"This property of yours has a major fault."

"Don't tell us it's not valuable."

"No, no, no," said Edwina, shaking her head. "As reported, it is the largest site of highly concentrated lithium in the world."

"Then what's wrong?"

"Hold on a bit, we're almost there."

Edwina led the silent group another hundred yards.

"See this crack?" she said, pointing to a modest fissure in the seabed. "Doesn't look all that impressive, right? But it's part of one of the most famous fault lines in the world—certainly the most famous in the continental United States."

"Is this the San Andreas Fault?" Anderson asked.

Edwina smiled. "Being a mining expert, you would know that."

Both Akhmerov and Zubilin were agitated. They didn't yet know if the news would be good or bad.

"Well, how do you like that," said Zimmer, not liking it at all.

"This is where the fault starts—or ends, depending on your point of view," said Edwina.

"Right here?"

"Right at your feet, and it runs smack through your part of the Saltin Sea before heading northwest."

"Doesn't look like much here."

"Don't be fooled. I've seen stretches as wide as an eight-lane highway."

The men paused to take that in.

"How far does it go?"

Edwina addressed them both.

"Let's see, from here it heads north, passing just northwest of L.A., then continues northwest, passing just east of San Jose and San Francisco, and then it travels under the ocean for about twenty miles and comes up in King Range National Park, right up the coast, about forty miles north of Fort Bragg. That's where it ends, or begins."

"Is that a big fault line, as fault lines go?"

"Certainly not the biggest—but it's more than eight hundred miles and goes through—or very close—to every major population center in California. So, you do the math."

Zimmer seemed to be toting up the possibilities. "Bottom line: what's the likelihood of a major quake?"

"Well, California is earthquake country and there seems to be particular stress on the southern end."

"Where we're standing."

"Exactly."

"Why here?"

"Recently—and I mean very recently—like less than a year ago, more than one hundred temblors were recorded under the Saltin Sea."

"What's a temblor, like a small quake?"

"Not exactly. More like a trembling."

"First sign of a quake?"

"Definitely not the first sign. This region has been trembling for thousands of years."

"So, there might be a quake tomorrow—or a thousand years from tomorrow."

"Yes, that's inexactly correct. But seismic activity has been on the uptick in this area, so I'd bet on a quake sooner than later."

"But you can't say when?"

"Wouldn't hazard a guess."

"Does anyone know?"

Edwina paused.

"I have a friend who might know," she said, and then looked away.

Akhmerov didn't want to push, but he sensed she felt a hook in her mouth. He let a few seconds pass before reeling in her thoughts. "You know someone who can predict an earthquake?"

"In a sense."

Akhmerov waited about five seconds before asking, "Can you explain?"

Edwina did not respond, but Akhmerov sensed her crumbling resistance.

"You can tell us. We share your professional curiosity. Besides," he said, nodding at the cutesy t-shirts Fred was proudly carrying, "we're all friends here."

EXPLOITING FAULTS

Edwina hemmed and hawed before she was finally ready to share.

"I had a friend—well, actually, we were never friends, just professional colleagues—who was very smart but very socially awkward. Think Hollywood mad scientist and you wouldn't be far wrong. Anyway, as I was willing to sit with him occasionally in the Faculty Lounge, he regarded me as his friend."

Fred found all this fascinating, but the agents wished she'd get to the point, which she soon did, explaining that her friend was an expert on the subject of the San Andreas Fault but that his brilliance alone was not enough to carry him and his clumsy social baggage to the forefront of his field. Over the years her friend grew increasingly resentful but seethed quietly, rather than voice his complaint.

"When I last saw him he looked happier than I'd ever seen him. He told me he was going on sabbatical and when I asked how he planned to spend his time, he said, 'I'll be writing the concluding chapters to my most important book. I plan to submit it to our university press as soon as I return. You've been a great friend, but I won't be able to see you until I see you again. I know you understand.'

"Actually, I wasn't sure what he meant, so I just said, 'I wish you great success!' He smiled and said, somewhat sadly I thought, 'Thank you for being my friend.'"

Edwina paused just long enough for the agents to think the story was over and they had missed the point. But Edwina filled her sails with a deep breath and continued, aware that she was expected to wrap up her tale quickly.

"A year to the day later, I saw him in the Faculty Lounge. We hadn't communicated during his sabbatical and I knew not to bother with pleasantries, so I cut to the chase and asked, 'How did your work go?' He told me he was submitting the manuscript in person at the end of that very day. He seemed preoccupied, so I asked nothing more and he offered nothing more—but I never saw him again."

This time Edwina's pause was so lengthy, Zimmer felt dutybound to interrupt: "What happened?"

Shaken, Edwina answered bluntly:

"His manuscript was rejected. No explanation. Next morning, FBI agents took him away. I tried to contact him but there was no response. We never spoke again."

It wasn't certain that she was done talking. But the agents were past polite.

"What happened?"

"What was in his manuscript?"

Edwina heard their imploring voices and rallied. "I don't know details. I heard rumors and scuttlebutt. Apparently, his book was brilliant, precise, but—"

"But what?"

"Dangerous. Extremely dangerous."

"How? Please explain. It's very interesting."

Edwina nodded, finally ready to dish.

"You know how ski patrollers defuse potentially catastrophic avalanches by using explosives to set off small, controlled ones? Well, my friend proposed a process—and postulated the results—of using a similar technique to relieve pent-up stress on fault lines. He focused on the one he knew best—the one we are all standing on."

"Wait, are you saying he described exactly where and how to insert explosives to incite earthquakes?"

"Yes. But not only traditional explosives. Apparently, he described how sonar and laser might also be used."

"He didn't field test any of this, right?"

"Not to my knowledge. But from what I heard and what I personally know about him, he's very exact in his research. I assume he used predictive, computer-generated algorithms to show how various levels of inciting agents, placed in various locations and at various depths, would result in the safe release of tectonic pressure."

"What a wonderful tool for humanity!" said Anderson.

"Could save millions of lives!" said Zimmer.

The agents heaped praise on her friend until her eyes grew watery sad, and then they changed their tune:

"Of course, a tiny miscalculation could have horrific results."

"His research could fall into the hands of extortionists—or terrorists."

Edwina shook her head sadly. "How could he not have known that? How could he have been so naïve?"

"But what else could he have done?" asked Zimmer.

"I agree," said Anderson. "He brought the manuscript to a responsible university press. How can anyone fault him?"

Edwina turned to shed a few tears on behalf of her unfortunate friend. While she was turned, Akhmerov and Zubilin whispered confidentially. Anderson then said to Edwina, "It's important we speak with him."

"Why?" she asked, turning to face them.

"Why?" asked Zimmer. "We are planning mining operations in a region filled with high-stress fault lines."

"Your friend knows so much that might help us," said Anderson.

"But his ideas are dangerous!" she said.

"That's why we need to know more about them."

"We need to know what mistakes not to make."

"I don't know," she said.

"Edwina, we want to make Saltin great again, but we must operate as professionally and safely as we can."

Edwina saw Fred's pleading eyes.

"What should I do?"

"Put us in touch with your friend," said Anderson.

"We will be perfectly tactful," said Zimmer.

"I don't know," she repeated. "I don't think he will respond. I tried, remember? I think he's locked himself away from the world."

"Completely understandable."

"Still, we should try to reach him."

Edwina was vacillating.

"You know," said Anderson, "if his work someday leads to important advances, he will be famous."

"His academic work will be validated," said Zimmer. "It will be his triumph!"

Edwina looked at Fred. "What do you think, birthday boy?"

"I say call him. What do we have to lose?"

THE ART OF THE HACK

The job was easy pickings. Compared to hacking the server of America's Democratic National Committee, this was like taking candy from a sleeping baby.

The agents monitored Edwina's phone. They listened to her carefully spoken message. That's all they needed. They shared her friend's phone number with P., who shared it with his cyber experts in Moscow. Two days later they had electronic copies of all the relevant documents, even those that were password protected—even those that had been hid in the Cloud (in misleadingly titled folders)—even those in a vault-like server of a topflight (and expensive) data-backup and protection service company. They had everything they needed.

They waited a week before contacting Edwina.

"Did you ever hear from your friend?"

"No, I tried. I left several messages, but he never responded. I'm so sorry. I should have called you earlier, but I was embarrassed. I knew you'd be disappointed."

"Don't you worry. We're fine, really."

"We're grateful you tried—and for all the information you shared."

"Now that we know about the fault, we will exercise special caution if we need to do any deep drilling."

"Oh good. I'm glad there are no hard feelings. Fred was worried. Actually, we both were."

"No problem. It's all good. We are moving ahead with our plans."

MAKE SALTIN WET AGAIN

P.'s revised plan was in development but several basic aspects were already fixed: a detonation (of some sort, at some location) would compromise the Jordan-Enterprise dam, whose unleashed waters would flow (or flood, depending on the scope of the rupture) into the ancient basin of the Saltin Sea and pool there, resulting in an environment that would allow P. to extract the vast, concentrated lithium via a more cost-effective, brine-mining process.

Before greenlighting the new plan, P. asked Akhmerov and Zubilin to obtain an updated report based on brine extraction. He asked that the information be sent to him as it became available.

Within days so much information flowed P.'s way, he felt as if he were swimming through a sea of jargon: *hydrological conditions, highly saline environment, microgravity, resistivity, porosity, permeability,* and so on.

The report's conclusions and recommendations made clear that only half of the estimated lithium was projected as recoverable. P. was still dealing with this apparent disappointment when he finally understood the key fact of the report's conclusion: the Saltin Sea would not have to be filled with water to mine its lithium by brine extraction. It was only necessary to have enough water flow into the basin to create a stable underground reservoir. To extract the lithium, the salt-rich waters would be pumped to the surface.

It was then P. enjoyed the report's sweetest revelation of all: Even if only half the projected lithium were recoverable, the record high ratio of lithium to water would be like mining liquid gold.

CHAPTER 10

STAKEOUT

Marge was parked outside The Palace, waiting for *something* to get her stalled investigation rolling. (She'd spent the previous ten days at nine other stakeout locations around the sun-cracked, salt-encrusted town and though she'd sighted Hannah, the tall black drug dealer, the two sketchy Russian scientists, the two purported mining experts from Detroit and the guitar-carrying vagrant who drove about in a hippie golf cart, she never laid eyes on Mr. Big, his pair of black-suited thugs or his blonde secretary, though that did not deter her from making them all prime suspects in her book.) At long last her patience was rewarded: she saw two men in black suits and sunglasses exit the glass lobby door, accompanied by a shorter, thick-set man with a full head of hair and a reddish, chestnut beard. With her smartphone at the ready, she started snapping pictures, making effective use of the app's zoom feature. She then watched as the men approached a black Buick Regal (parked twenty yards in front of her) and took photos of its license plate as the two suited men held open the rear door for the shorter man, whom, she realized, must be Mr. Big. When they drove away, she followed at a safe distance, lest they realize they were being tailed.

BLAST HIS BEATING HEART

P. arrived at the Civic Center (in his mind, the *Treatment Center*) with his two, black-suited bodyguards. (Marge parked about thirty yards away, as discreet as a large fly stuck to a gessoed canvas.) As before, P. had one of the guards knock to announce his arrival. When the door opened and all three doctors stood before him (Yeshevsky, front and center), P. said, "My associates will wait outside for me," a message meant to convey: *I am putting my life in your hands; your lives are in mine.*

Yeshevsky appeared unfazed. "Thank you for coming on time. This way, please."

As soon as P. entered the office, Hannah approached him, holding a paper skirt in a prophylactic wrapper. "Please step behind the dressing screen and remove all your clothes, except for your socks and underwear. Then please put on this skirt."

P. winced, not for the curt treatment, or for having been asked to wear a skirt (he'd deal with those slights another time), but for having neglected to order his agents to sweep the room for video-recording devices. He winced again when he suddenly remembered the secret videos he'd made of the American president when the latter was a fifty-year-old playboy carousing in Moscow. (He recalled, in particular, a sixty-minute extravaganza that featured a dozen naked young girls—all small-breasted, with smooth virgin groins.)

P. stepped behind the screen, stripped down to his calf-high socks and boxer briefs and then reappeared (in his paper skirt), handing his clothes to Hannah without comment.

"Please sit here," said Dr. Yeshevsky, indicating the side of the examination table. "We have received the results of your blood tests and they are concerning. Your cancer has spread and now aggressively inhabits both lungs. We will immediately begin a weekly treatment, employing a slightly different salt compound and a raised intensity and duration of laser." He stepped to the side of the room where an array of instruments had been laid out. "We will give you an injection to relax you and to alleviate the discomfort of the laser burn."

"No anesthesia."

Everyone looked shocked, which is what he wanted. He knew they would not allow him to face the fierce laser, protected only by the sheer force of his will, but (as usual) he felt compelled to project his invincibility.

"That is not permissible," said Dr. Yeshevsky. "We cannot risk you moving even an iota while the intensified laser is focused on a small clot of cancerous cells."

Before P. could utter a word of false protest, Dr. Yeshevsky readied the IV stanchion while Hannah approached with a hypodermic needle.

P. thought he detected a smile. "Ahh, I willingly place myself in your tender care, Dr. Belaya."

While P. lay on the table (awaiting the dulling effects of the anesthesia), Dr. Yeshevsky wheeled in the sizable laser from the closet. This was Dr. Grushina's cue to leave the crowded room, which he did, first taking off his smock and surgical gloves, then carrying away a heated kettle, cookies and a single teacup on a pretty plastic tray.

Outside, in the shade behind the Civic Center's rear wall, he placed the heavy tray on the small round table, surrounded by three chairs.

The two black-suited agents were off to the right, standing by the broken pier. Dr. Grushina didn't wave; he knew they saw him and might eventually join him. Out of strained politeness he resisted pouring his own cup of tea.

Five minutes passed. By now he thought they must be laughing at him and his cooling kettle and pretty tray. They were heartless bastards (he thought), probably the worst of the worst: the ones who beat gay suspects—breaking their arms, kicking their heads.

Finally, he saw them approach—an insultingly slow and measured walk. When they drew near, he greeted them in Russian: "Hello, gentlemen. How are you liking America?" The men never broke stride. They never even looked in his direction. "Moscow better," said the shorter one in Russian. "Easier to visit your mother," said the other. They continued walking without so much as a backwards glance. Dr. Grushina shook so violently, he could not pour his tea.

Inside, while Dr. Belaya prepared the laser, Dr. Yeshevsky administered ultrasound-guided injections of the new salt solution into three locations in P.'s right lung and into two locations in his left lung. When he was finished, he turned to Hannah and said, "He's all yours."

Hannah hadn't been smiling when she approached P. with the needle; her purse-lipped expression merely reflected her struggle to control her wildly agitated feelings. But now, with P. quietly prone on the examination table, helpless as one of his drunk whores, she wore the smile of the malevolent executioner.

P. saw the smile and it excited him, which caused his penis to stir visibly, which fired Hannah's murderous rage.

She panned the red guide beam across his chest, sighting her target: the left lung … the pulmonary trunk … the left ventricle …

I could fry the bastard's beating heart.

She had the shot.

KATYA TAKES REFUGE

Had Marge waited another minute before tailing P.'s black Buick Regal, she would have seen Katya leave The Palace through the same glass door. Of course, she would not have known that Katya had a free afternoon and had decided to take a long walk, away from the boardwalk, far in the opposite direction.

Beyond the town's southern reach, Katya saw a canted and corroded sign that was barely legible: *Saltin Wildlife Refuge.*

The place seemed quiet and lifeless: no chirruping insects, no jumping hares or scratching rodents. If there had once been paths, they were now overgrown with salt cedar weeds and wild rye grass, or been erased by sand-blasting winds.

Choosing byways of least resistance, she walked deep into the Refuge, meandering this way and that. She carried only her muted phone, water bottle, utility knife, pistol and elongated lipstick case (which, when uncapped, was also her silencer).

After fifteen minutes or so, she detected a sound that in almost any other context would have been unmistakable, but there, in that wasteland, was strangely out of place.

She continued walking (though more slowly and with a lighter tread) and soon came upon a stony ledge in the thin shade of a barely breathing desert ironwood tree. Sitting atop the ledge was a man sobbing so heavily he did not hear her approach.

She stopped to watch and listen. As the sobbing continued, she inched forward until she heard Russian endearments and expletives slobbered together. It was the most pitiable image of a man she had ever seen. Still, it touched her deeply. Why was he so bereft? Who had broken his heart?

She thought of the man who had broken her mother's heart—and who would eventually break hers—and realized he would never shed a tear for either of them. With that painful and unnerving recognition, she let down her guard and moved towards the bereft man and when she was nearly close enough that she might have embraced him, he whirled suddenly and pointed a pistol at her unguarded heart.

STRUCK

Katya identified herself, even showing him her pistol in her own carryall. She'd only been out for a walk, she said.

Struck by her resemblance to a younger Hannah, Anatoly put away his own pistol and offered her his hand. Taking his hand, Katya clambered atop the stony ledge, joining him in the shade of the haggard ironwood.

Beginning tentatively and then picking up speed and candor, they talked and talked about their lives, their past mistakes, their belief in God and their hopes for second chances.

Katya was struck by the story of his estranged marriage to Hannah, how he'd been sent to prison for a stupid theft and how he had survived, connived and arrived in America. She listened raptly while he told how he'd been contacted in New York by P.'s agents and how he had cleverly followed them to Saltin in order to reconnect with his wife. Because his story was matter-of-factly told, Katya believed it was true. She also believed that her beloved St. Vitaly had brought her to this blasted garden to meet Anatoly, whom, she thought, was very attractive and not too old for her, certainly younger than P.

Anatoly was struck by Katya's uncanny resemblance to a younger Hannah and the fact that she'd also been drawn to the Refuge and the fact that she carried her own pistol and worked for P., who was at that very moment being treated at the Civic Center by several doctors, one of whom happened to be his estranged wife.

Sitting side by side in that forsaken garden, where everything once fresh and colorful was now withered and browned, Anatoly and Katya saw themselves as a pair of destinies divinely entwined. Before separating (they agreed they should not return to Saltin together), they made a pact to share information until their respective situations were better understood. It was an honest pledge and a leap of faith for them both.

NO SHOT

For whatever reason (moral squeamishness, medical ethics), Hannah did not take the shot. Her mind steady and her aim true, she blasted only the diseased cells in P.'s lungs, harming not a single healthy cell unnecessarily. And when the treatment was over (when she shut down the machine and removed her protective eyewear), she knew two things: she had fulfilled her ethical responsibility; there would be consequences for her inability to eradicate P.

For all that, she knew she could not have acted otherwise. Perhaps in another time, in another universe, the situation might have played out differently. But there and then, by the shore of the blighted Saltin Sea, in the company of Dr. Yeshevsky, it was what it must be.

DUMB AND DUUMVIRATE

"We will take America without firing a shot. We do not have to invade the U.S. We will destroy you from within."

The quote was a favorite of P.'s and appeared below a photograph of his favorite old-time Soviet ruler, a man who knew his own mind and those of his enemies. P. kept the framed photograph on his night table, along with a few other precious keepsakes.

The night following his first laser treatment in America, he lay in bed smiling at his mirrored image on the ceiling. He was thinking how *perestroika* and *glasnost,* which had destroyed the Soviet Union, had been a personal godsend for him, creating as it did a series of spineless predecessors, one of whom, President Y., had promoted him from head of the FSB to prime minister, Russia's second-highest-ranking official.

Lying in bed, he recalled President Y.'s challenges and pitfalls and how he had offered P. several I-scratch-your back, you-scratch-mine deals, which resulted in power being shared between them: a system of co-rulers, or duumvirate. Thinking how he'd always known he could never be completely satisfied with any power-sharing arrangement, he smiled devilishly, remembering how he had eventually ascended the president's throne, assuming complete, autocratic power.

He'd been thinking *duumvirate* on a march larger scale when he first had the self-serving idea to help the America Idiot become president. Having already video recorded the Idiot's perverted frolics, his idea was off to a good start. He thought he might further indebt the Idiot by getting him to borrow huge sums from Russia-owned banks; if that succeeded, he'd have considerable leverage over the Idiot's foreign trade policies, should the Idiot get elected. The rest of his idea (infiltrating American social media platforms, tampering with American electronic polling centers) he left to General G., who headed a special legion of cyber-hacking experts.

The idea had legs (the Idiot was elected), but then the legs got wobbly. P. had understood (even expected) that the new American president would spout over-the-top nationalist tropes and flout basic human values. But when it came to light that the Idiot was brazenly cashing in on his presidency, leaving behind a trail of forensic breadcrumbs as large as boulders, P. privately derided the Idiot as politically amateurish.

P. knew it was only a matter of time before the American Idiot was indicted and found guilty of his crimes, which would eventually malign his own legacy. Before that happened, he thought it might be better if he began distancing himself from his Frankenstein to focus on his precarious health, to preside over the world's most productive lithium mining and manufacturing operation, and to bask in the world's gratitude for having developed the first proven cure for lung cancer.

POTEMKIN HALL

No one but his closest staff knew that P. was spending weeks at a time in Saltin, California. The Russian people, along with the rest of the world (including MI6, the CIA, Mossad, and other intelligence agencies), were fooled into believing that P. was actually in Russia during those periods, executing his usual responsibilities. This deception was achieved by an ingenious, Potemkin-like illusion, in which a large conference room in P.'s Saltin palace—outfitted with interchangeable lecterns, curtains, flags, insignia—was used to simulate the actual venues, mostly in Moscow, from which P. commonly issued press statements. Occasionally, P.'s black-suited agents sent recorded video to a Moscow videographer, who, using the latest green-screen technology, could create almost any scenic context and sell the package to a believing public.

FETISHIST DRAMA

On balance, Yevgeny thought things were going quite smoothly. His team seemed to have settled well into their Saltin routine. Their treatment of P.'s cancer was yielding positive results. P. had not misbehaved with Hannah or acted aggressively toward Dimitri or himself. All in all, it seemed like an auspicious time to meet with Hannah to propose they join hands in marriage. (In fact, Yevgeny had been ready since day one of his arrival, playing out a fetishist drama every night in his hotel room, waltzing about with the salt-sequined wedding gown in his arms, as if holding his beloved bride to be.)

"Hannah, you have been working so hard," he said one late afternoon when they were alone. "Let us have dinner together tomorrow evening and then take a walk."

Hannah was no fool. She'd been expecting the invitation ever since Yevgeny had arrived—and still had not decided what she would say to him.

She cared deeply for him—admired him greatly—but did want to be his wife. But what could she do? She did not think she could say *no* and continue to work with him. (The tiny office would be unremittingly intense and unpleasant.) But where could she possibly go? She hadn't the means to travel back to Ukraine. She hadn't the means to travel anywhere without being apprehended by P.'s agents. *Besides,* she thought, *how could I leave now when we are so close to finding a cure for cancer? And what about Jason?*

SOMETHING MISSING

For a guy who liked to think of himself as spiritual, Jason was a solid realist who recognized that he and Hannah had been closer when they'd been correspondents, separated by continents and many times zones. In those days it had been easier to express their most soulful secrets because they never actually expected to meet. When they finally did meet, they both sensed that something was missing, despite their initial frisson.

Jason knew Hannah had a lot on her mind. And while he appreciated her vulnerable situation with P., the stress of her cancer research, her complicated relationship with Yevgeny and the reappearance of her former felon husband, he believed some other factor was responsible for her emotional aloofness.

He recalled the day she'd led him into the desert to see the mosaic shrine she'd built. At the time, he'd been sure the experience would mark a deepening of their relationship, but it hadn't. In fact, she never spoke or referred to her son again.

Two months later, standing on the boardwalk, Jason realized that Hannah's silent preoccupation with Peter was the obstacle—or void—between them. This led him to consider his own idiosyncrasies, which were many. But he had enough self-awareness to see that his wanderer's life was chief among them and that at the heart of his wanderer's life was his passivity—perhaps his cowardice. He finally understood that for many years he'd been more likely than not to hit the bricks rather than stay and face an intractable problem. He also recognized that the open road was losing its allure.

Standing on the boardwalk, considering his meager options, Jason decided to remain in Saltin to see how real-life events might inspire the last act of his opera. He also wanted to give his relationship with Hannah a little more time.

MAKING AMENDS

Having become increasingly familiar with Hannah's dedicated, professional deportment, P. was more certain than ever that she would make a wonderful wife, personal nurse and First Lady of the Russian Federation, a highly ceremonial position he hoped she would fully embrace in time. (The position had driven his wife Maria to fits of fury, which had led to their divorce and the subsequent cold distancing of his two daughters, Lyudmila and Katya, who'd sided with their mother. Had he not arranged with his friend Artur Volkonsky, Moscow's most successful realtor, to woo and marry Maria, he would not have been able to keep such close tabs on his former wife and daughters.)

P. knew he had caused Hannah much trouble and wanted to make amends. Unlike most suitors (who woo with a standard strategy of dinners, flowers and calculated conversation), P. planned to cut to the chase and address the two things he knew mattered most to her: recognition for her medical and scientific achievement—and the safe return of her son, Peter.

SUITABILITY

For weeks, Anatoly had weighed the relative merits of P., Jason and Yevgeny in terms of their suitability for Hannah, all the while believing he was much better suited than any of them. Ironically, he soon came to see that Hannah was not the woman for him, despite the fact of her being his former wife and mother of their son. He now believed that Katya (who looked so much like Hannah) was his true destined love.

This insight marked a new beginning for Anatoly. He now understood that God had sent him the blessing of a prison penance and the means to travel across the world, so that he and Katya might enter the Refuge to find one another, save one another, marry, and have children.

THEY'RE HERE!

"So, catch me up. What have you learned?"

Marge stretched her legs as if tired from a long day's walking, even though she'd spent her morning at Calpurnia Prison doing paper work and gone straight to Covenant House to meet Tova for lunch.

"Lots of suspicious details—circumstantial at the moment—but I think they point to international conspiracy and fraud."

"Like puzzle pieces," said Tova.

"Exactly. I just need more pieces to fit together so I have a better picture of the operation and who's running it."

"I knew it! My gut is almost always right. Now, please share details. Only what you can, of course. I don't want to jeopardize the investigation."

Marge put down her teacup and leaned closer.

"You know the two agents from Detroit, who call themselves Anderson and Zimmer?"

"Not personally, but I know who you mean. Never trusted them."

"Well, I ran their license plate."

"And—?"

"And, you know those two goons in black suits who live in The Palace, who appear to work for Mr. Big?"

"I know who you mean. Never trusted them either."

"Well, I ran their license plate too."

"Their related, right?"

"Bingo! Both cars are rented through a company in Detroit called American Lithium."

"Not surprising. You check it out?"

"Of course! I'm bucking for detective!"

Both women laughed.

"So, what did you learn?"

Marge looked about as if to confirm they were alone. "I learned that the company seems to be legit."

"Well, that doesn't sound good."

Marge sat back and smiled smugly. "I said *seems* to be legit."

Tova's hand flew to her mouth. "I knew it! Tell tell!"

"Well, I did some digging and everything seemed to be legit, but—"

"But?"

"But when I looked up the street address of the company on Google Maps—"

"Let me guess. You saw a church, a school, something like that!"

"Actually, I saw a small, two-story brick building. Could be an office building."

"Does it show American Lithium?"

"No. But an office building on Google Maps doesn't list individual tenants."

"Then why are you smiling?"

"Because—may I have some more tea?"

Knowing she was being played (and enjoying every minute of it), Tova poured the tea with extravagant precision. "Can I get you anything else?" she asked, solicitous as a geisha.

"No, thank you," Marge said, resettling herself on the divan. "Sorry, where was I?"

"You were about to expose the Russian mafia."

"Well," Marge said, daintily patting her lips with a floral napkin, "here's the scoop."

Tova scooted her chair closer so she wouldn't miss a word.

"I have an old college friend who married and moved to Detroit. I emailed her the address of American Lithium and asked her to stop by and confirm the company's existence at that address, which we know must be current, since it was used to lease the two cars."

"What'd she say?"

"It wasn't so much what she said as what she sent me. Here, look at this. A picture is worth a thousand words."

Marge handed Tova a large color photo of a vacant lot, surrounded by chain-link fencing.

"It's an empty lot."

"Exactly. Not a building in sight."

"Where'd the building go?"

"I don't think it went anywhere. I don't think it was ever there."

"But didn't you find it on the internet?"

"I found the company's website, which shows the same office building as found on Google Maps. I'd already checked out the company's registration papers and tax forms, and they seemed legit."

"But they're not?"

"You see a building in the picture?"

Tova looked again, just to be sure. "No, there's nothing there."

"I think it exists only on paper. A dummy company."

Tova sat up very straight. "I don't understand. You said there's an office building on Google Maps that matches the address."

"I did, but it's wrong."

"Google made a mistake?"

"I don't think so. I think someone hacked Google Maps to upload a photo that shows an office building at the address in question."

"The building doesn't exist?"

"Oh, I'm sure it exists somewhere—just not at the address claimed by the agents of American Lithium."

Tova was quiet, the gravity of the situation slowly dawning on her.

"Now, let me ask you this," said Marge. "When was the last time you heard about a large group of world-class hackers?"

"It's in the news every day. Looks like our national election was hacked."

"Uh-huh. And who are the alleged hackers?"

Tova's hand flew to her mouth. "Oh my God," she said. "They're here!"

DOING HER PART

Wanting very much to do her own part to stop the Russian onslaught on American democracy, Tova left Saltin for the first time in more than thirty years. Her mission: to confront Edwina Orosco, former professor at University of California-San Diego and current custodian of Fred's heart.

Tova assumed it would be easy to find Edwina. In her experience, unscrupulous modern women leave a large digital footprint in their wide and disreputable wake. Just as she thought, she easily located Edwina's home on a quaint side street of University Heights, her nefarious life camouflaged in a neat package of apparent normalcy—another villain living in plain sight. She wasn't surprised, recalling that Hannah (the meth cooker) and Bethany (the drug dealer) lived shamelessly under her own roof.

Tova hadn't planned exactly what she would do or say. She knew Edwina was in bed with the Russians and didn't want the traitorous bitch to turn Fred, whom she knew to be good and kind, but none too bright. She just wanted to give Edwina a piece of her mind. She had no idea what might come of it—perhaps nothing—but she needed to do something to save Fred—and her country.

SECOND THOUGHTS

Edwina called Fred to tell him what had happened.

"A nice-looking woman, somewhat older, stopped me on the street. She was holding an open map. I assumed she wanted help with directions."

"Did she?"

"Well, she started out by pointing to the map but then stopped suddenly, looked me right in the eye and said, 'Are you Edwina Orosco, the professor who did that study about lithium in the Saltin Sea?'"

"You're famous!" cried Fred.

"Well, for a moment I did feel a little bit famous. I thought she might have attended one of my lectures or audited a class. But that wasn't it. Not even close!"

"What did she want?"

"Well, two things. First, she asked me if I loved my country. Just like that. I was completely surprised and said, 'That's none of your business.'"

"What did she say?"

"She said her name was Mary. I expected her to launch into some kind of charity sales pitch, but all of a sudden she gets in my face and starts screaming: 'I know who you are, you Judas bitch! You're in bed with the Russians. You're selling out your country for pieces of gold!"

"Oh my God. What does that even mean? Were you frightened?"

"Yes! And embarrassed! It was the middle of the day. Right outside my home, and she's screaming like an insane witch!"

"Jeez Louise, what'd you do?"

"I was frightened as hell, but I knew not to turn my back and run. I thought she might stab me!"

"Good lord!"

"So, I started slowly backing away, keeping my eyes on hers and saying, 'I'm sorry, you must have the wrong person."

"That was smart."

"I'm not so sure. She seemed to know who I was."

"How? What'd she say?"

"She accused me of introducing the Russian agents of American Lithium to the mayors of Saltin—and how it led to a Russian big wig coming to Saltin to oversee the lithium project—and how the Russians are on our soil and cooking up something terrible."

"What? She's clearly insane. I don't know what she's talking about."

"Fred, that was my first instinct. But the more I think about it, the more I think she's onto something."

"What? She's a nut! Because of you, Saltin has a chance to be great again."

Edwina felt herself slipping into a deep quandary. Recalling how Anderson and Zimmer had coaxed her into contacting Fred in order to get to the mayors—and how they had exhorted her to contact her faculty friend (an expert in explosives and fault lines)—she thought there might be some truth to Mary's street rant and wondered if she should share this with Fred.

"You said she wanted two things," Fred said, interrupting her reverie. "What was the second?"

"Yes, what was it—oh, now I remember. She said I should leave you alone. She said you were good and kind and shouldn't be involved in this Russian business. She didn't want to see you get hurt."

Fred's knees buckled. There were only two women who'd ever cared about him. He was speaking with one of them. The other was his wife, Tova.

JUST A FAÇADE

On the northeast shore of the Saltin Sea (well-guarded from close public view), constructions crews were assembling buildings to serve as future housing for mining workers and staff. But it was all an illusion. The buildings were plywood structures with impermanent supports and trompe l'oeil façades—built not to last. Everything P. did—whether feint or decisive act—was carefully calculated.

BANG FOR THEIR BUCK

P. reviewed the report from Moscow (based on data stolen from Edwina's former faculty friend). The concise report identified three possible sites along the San Andreas Fault. Each site was well-situated for a controlled charge that would be strong enough to damage the Jordan-Enterprise Dam but not nearly strong enough to jeopardize any of the nearby major population centers. The report did not prioritize the three sites. It would be up to Akhmerov and Zubilin to decide which would produce the best bang for their buck.

TO AMERICANS!

Inasmuch as the geography was dangerously rugged, the agents gave no thought to using the cover of darkness for their reconnaissance. They would have to examine each site in the bright light of day, which made the plan particularly challenging.

They were in their room in The Palace, drinking Russian Standard and thinking about their mission. Akhmerov was exploring websites on his laptop.

"What you are you looking at?" asked Zubilin.

"You will not believe our good fortune. There are guided jeep tours of the San Andreas Fault."

"Really?"

"A dozen to choose from."

"Can we suggest places to stop and explore?"

"I'm sure. Americans are exceedingly helpful."

"I love Americans."

"We could not succeed without them."

They clinked glasses. "To Americans!"

LOCATION, LOCATION, LOCATION

Following another of P.'s orders, Anderson and Zimmer drove south on Route 111, passing the Wildlife Refuge and continuing twenty minutes further until they reached the Mexican border. After presenting American passports, they drove south another ten minutes to the busy city of Mexicali, then headed directly to 1221 Todos los Santos, the last and most beautiful home on the boulevard. They arrived just as the attorney, realtor, bank agent and translator had parked their cars and gathered on the spacious front lawn.

The realtor led the way inside, directing the group to an impressive dining room, where elegant place settings awaited. As soon as all the men were seated, a young woman (wearing a caterer's black dress, stockings, and full white apron) appeared through an archway that communicated with the kitchen. In charmingly accented English she took orders for beverages and brunch. (All the men were fluent in English and Spanish, except Anderson and Zimmer, whose Spanish barely sufficed.) As soon as she left the room, the attorney clicked opened his briefcase, withdrew and opened a thick folder and began handing copies of each of its documents to the assembled guests. After all the documents were signed and the certified checks exchanged, the realtor handed Anderson and Zimmer the keys to their new safehouse. Everyone toasted the new owners and brunch was served.

HE REMEMBERED

Yevgeny knew this day would come. From the beginning, he'd recognized that he and Hannah shared a special connection, as if her aura and his glowed with the same intense electrostatic charge.

He recalled how (nearly a year ago) he'd posted ideas on his Cosmoenergy blog and how her comments had stood out among hundreds of others for their sparkling intelligence.

He recalled how he (the mighty Yeshevsky, leader of the Cosmoenergy Federation) had trembled the day he composed a private message for her—and how he'd waited with torturing anxiety for her response.

He recalled her early days of employment, how she was so eager to learn and assume new responsibilities.

He recalled how she walked with him along the moon-lighted riverfront, their hearts nervously fluttering.

He recalled how with each drink at the tavern, each meal at the hotel, their bonds deepened.

He recalled how his secular parents, having discovered their Jewish roots, became anxious for him to become a Jewish husband and father.

He recalled visiting the tombs of the holy Jewish Fathers and Mothers in Hebron and how his shoulders felt heavy with the weight of tradition.

He recalled hiring an artist's assistants to produce a salt-crystallized wedding gown for his dear Hannah.

He recalled thinking it would be a very special day when he finally asked Hannah to marry him.

THE DAY BEFORE THE SPECIAL DAY

On Saturday morning (the day before the special day), Yevgeny visited the manager of the lagoon's plant-curtained bath and rented the establishment for the next morning. He then visited the man who managed The Mount's one functioning restaurant and reserved for the next day's dinner the far corner banquette (whose leather was well worn but not torn, and whose westward-facing window looked out on the lagoon and the dry sea beyond, making it a passably romantic spot). He then walked circuitously to East Saltin's synagogue, considering which streets would make the least depressing route. Unfortunately, the synagogue itself was in much worse shape than he remembered. All the windows were broken or missing entirely. Sand, salt, bits of feather and fecal pellets lay everywhere. He did what he could to sweep the place clear. On the plus side, the mezuzahs had all miraculously survived, as had the ark; although, as expected, it was empty, its holy scrolls having been removed long ago. He had not planned to give Hannah an engagement ring. Her joyful acceptance of the diamond-like wedding gown would suffice.

A VERY SPECIAL DAY

Because the meal was unremarkable and so many topics taboo (Hannah could not bring herself to ask about his parents; Yevgeny could not find the courage to inquire about her son; neither wanted to discuss P.), easy table-talk was almost impossible. Both knew the occasion was meant to be momentous and each assumed the other was tongue-tied with nerves.

Following the unsatisfying meal, Yevgeny suggested they take a walk. Little was said during the ten-minute excursion, which pleased them both. When they stopped in front of the old, derelict synagogue, Hannah had an idea what was in store for her. She took a deep breath; she didn't want to hurt him.

"Please, allow me two minutes. I will be right back," he said, touching her hand reassuringly. Then he entered alone, closing the door behind him.

Hannah looked up and down the derelict street but saw nothing or no one that might forestall her entrance. Her eyes welled up with good-hearted tears, for she felt the crush of Yevgeny's imminent disappointment. She wanted to give him *something*—not hope, for that would be cruel—but something to salve his soon-to-be broken heart.

Inside, Yevgeny match-lighted two, long-tapered candles. He'd brought them earlier that day, along with the salt-bejeweled wedding gown, which he had placed reverently inside the holy ark.

A MODEST PROPOSAL

Hannah had entered and was moving about, examining the room (the canted and splintered pews; the dissonant breezes blowing through the broken windows; the tiny mounds of freshly swept detritus) when Yevgeny suddenly asked, "Hannah, will you marry me?"

Before she could respond, before she could even fully register what he'd asked, Yevgeny threw open the ark's doors, revealing a salt-crystalized wedding gown, glittering in the candlelight like an offering from God Himself.

"Oh, Yevgeny!"

He went to her side (but not too close, even then).

"I love you, Hannah Belaya. Your spirit, your mind, your beauty—"

"Yevgeny!"

"Will you be my life partner, my wife?"

Hannah was silent, considering how to respond.

Yevgeny added, "I know what you are thinking: Our circumstances are dangerously uncertain—and I agree—but all the more reason we should face life's dangers together."

Hannah's heart smiled. Yevgeny had provided her with a graceful exit.

"My dear Yevgeny. I have very strong feelings for you. And what you say is certainly true. But as long as our circumstances are dangerously uncertain, I cannot think about future plans. Besides—"

Unable to continue, she wept into her open hands.

Still, Yevgeny could not bring himself to embrace her.

"Please don't cry. I will protect you. I swear it."

She cried a while longer. Finally, after a gasping spasm, she calmed.

"I believe you," she said, wiping her eyes. "But that is not why I cry. I am not afraid for myself—I have a son."

"Peter."

"Yes. Thank you for remembering."

Again the tears flowed.

Yevgeny checked his pockets for a tissue he knew he didn't have. If he'd had one, he might have offered it while touching her shoulder—an act both intimate and consoling. As it was, he stood like a tin soldier, waiting for her tears to abate, which they eventually did.

"Have you heard from him recently?" he managed to ask.

"No," she said, drying her eyes. "Not for quite a while."

Yevgeny tried to reason: "Well, you haven't been home, where a letter or phone call might have reached you."

"He needs me and cannot find me!"

Her heart-rending words found their mark. Yevgeny felt responsible for Hannah's situation. He thought: *If I hadn't lured Hannah away from Lviv, Peter might have avoided the war—or, at the very least, stayed in contact with his mother—assuming he is alive.*

But it was Hannah who spoke first.

"Yevgeny, please forgive me. I cannot think of my own happiness while Peter's life is uncertain."

Yevgeny offered a pained smile.

"Hannah, in my eyes you are more wonderful than ever. Please forgive me for thinking only of myself. I will do everything I can to help you—and your son."

Hannah nodded weepily.

"I ask one favor," he said. "Please accept the gown. I want you to have it. It belongs to you. It can belong to no one else. It is my token, my gift, my gratitude to you for being such a beautiful and special woman!"

EVER VIGILANT

That evening, Tova was at her upstairs window when she saw Hannah and another person approaching on foot.

Why isn't she in a car? Maybe the slut snuck out for a quickie or a cheap drug deal. What time is it? I better write it down and tell Marge what I saw. You never know what might be incriminating evidence—the gotcha!

When the couple was nearly at the door, Tova could tell that Hannah was crying and that the man was carrying something quite heavy. She couldn't tell what they were saying, but she knew it wasn't English—in fact, she'd bet the house it was Russian. She saw Hannah lean over and give the man a quick kiss on his cheek and take from him the heavy package. The man waved goodbye and walked away.

Tova left her seat by the window and opened her apartment door so she could listen while Hannah struggled up the stairs, groaning under the package's cumbersome weight.

BLOOD DIAMONDS

Next morning (Monday), Tova sat by the window to see whether the man who'd accompanied Hannah home last night was the same man who picked her up every weekday morning at exactly 7:30 and drove her to the meth lab in the Civic Center.

Just as she suspected, at exactly 7:30, Hannah left the house and got into the front seat of the waiting car, whose driver appeared to be the same guy as the night before. Tova smiled; all her suspicions confirmed. (She knew she had a talent for these things—like a sixth sense—and Marge agreed.)

She waited five minutes, until she finished her tea-and-toast breakfast. Then she stood up creakily, retrieved her master key from her desk's top drawer, and walked downstairs to Hannah's room, moving as stealthily as she could.

After making sure the coast was clear, she deftly inserted the key and turned the doorknob gently, stepping lightly into the room and quietly closing the door behind her. The room looked pretty and neat, except for the box beside her bed.

No attempt to hide it! What hubris! Like she's above the law! We'll see about that!

She approached the closed box, wishing she'd put on latex gloves so as not to taint the evidence. (Having seen her share of TV movies, she knew what to expect: meth bags, heroin bricks, all neatly wrapped for the black market.) Gingerly, she lifted the box's horizontal flap—and was shocked by a sparkling whiteness.

She stared awhile, probed the contents with a tentative finger, then slowly (and with difficulty) lifted the heavy evidence from its carton and spread it lengthwise on Hannah's bed.

Oh lord! she thought, staring at the very gown she'd seen in a recent magazine: the one Alexandra wore when she became tsarina. But then, on closer inspection: *No, these are not fine-cut stones. They are raw. Fresh from the mine. Oh my god, they're blood diamonds! Stolen, smuggled, sewn into a gown—and hidden in plain sight, where no one would suspect. Oh, Marge is going to love this!*

Tova took out her smartphone and started taking pictures. *Each stone is huge. Must be worth billions. Drugs and blood diamonds! This conspiracy is wider than I thought. This is a case for Interpol!*

Tova decided not to mail the photos or call Marge on the phone. It was too dangerous. All manner of electronic communication might be tapped and surveilled. She'd wait until Marge came to see her again.

IMMODEST PROPOSALS

P.'s improving health … his explosive plan to mine the world's largest known deposit of concentrated lithium … his desire to capitalize on the cure for lung cancer … and his need to distance himself from the American Idiot had pushed his plan to marry Hannah to the back burner of his priorities. But now, having successfully addressed those other initiatives, he felt ready to renew his efforts to make Hannah his next wife.

For her part, Hannah wasn't as keen on killing him as she had been. For many weeks he'd lain on her examination table, essentially naked and vulnerable. He no longer complained and no longer appeared to be humiliated. In fact, he seemed to have earnestly accommodated himself to this necessary arrangement, which included, she thought, a positive change in his attitude toward her.

He considered inviting her to dine in his resplendent quarters in The Palace, but rejected his own thought as an unnecessary security risk. He then mulled the idea of inviting her to dinner in his newly acquired residence in Mexicali, but thought she might feel threatened if she were alone with him and so far from help. He decided it might be best if they met for dinner at The Mount's only functioning restaurant and then took a walk, perhaps to either of the two still-standing churches in East Saltin, the one with the stained-glass window or the one with the inscribed wooden door. Hannah rejected both ideas, suggesting instead that they meet at the foot of Salvation Mountain.

SALVATION MOUNTAIN

Some say it was inspired by Masada, others say Calvary. Either way, the flat-topped hill (just southwest of the Refuge) was the only vertically impressive vantage in Saltin. The summit was a spare, fence-encircled outlook with four outward-facing benches. It was surprisingly well preserved and an excellent place for self-reflection. As to looking outward, a strong naked eye could see almost to the north end of the Saltin Sea. With a pair of binoculars, one could make out the Jordan-Enterprise Dam and (in the opposite direction) Mexicali.

P. met Hannah at the foot of the mountain. (He had ordered his black-suited agents to stay behind but they'd balked, citing their duty to protect his life at all costs. As a compromise, P. carried a security alarm; in effect, a portable panic button. If he needed assistance, the heavily armed agents could arrive in less than two minutes.)

There were two ways to reach the top of Salvation: a direct path (a stone staircase of some two hundred steps) and a longer path that circled round and round.

"If I weren't weakened by the treatments, I could easily bound to the top."

Hannah chanced a small smile. "Of course," she said. "But it's the hard journey that makes the happy arrival. Let us take the long way around. More time to know each other."

P. felt outplayed but didn't mind. Hannah was an exceptional woman.

The path was relatively narrow. One person might pass another, but two could not walk comfortably side by side. Hannah took the lead, P. angled behind her.

As they approached the summit, both were keenly aware of their transactional expectations. P. was hoping to convince her to marry him for a great many practical reasons; Hannah was wondering what she might be willing to do for his promise to secure Peter's safety.

PERSPECTIVE

Time is well-known for its ability to alter perspective, but altitude and distance can also work their magic. From the top of Salvation, all the structures of Saltin City could be seen in panorama, without the obvious signs of their deterioration. The hotels, the boardwalk, the remnant pier, and the Civic Center all looked hospitable in the distance. The whole of the empty sea (the eddies of wind-blown sand, the beachheads of pulverized fish bones, the shoals of more recently dead and decomposed fish, the silvery patches of lithium and the omnipresent salt) looked—from a distance of miles—like a wintry, desert watercolor.

Having reached the summit, P. followed Hannah as she walked about its fenced perimeter. When she finished, she chose the bench that faced the south shore of the sea most directly. They sat together, but not very close. Both stared into the distance with their hands in their laps. They were alone.

P. spoke first. "Do you have a special place in Lviv where you go to think or pray?"

Hannah was nearly dumbstruck. The question seemed so honestly and simply asked, nothing like the imperious P. she thought she knew.

"I'm just wondering. I know you are a spiritual woman, but is there a special place—a park, a church, a cemetery—where you feel most spiritually connected?"

Hannah was reluctant to reveal her special sanctuary. (She'd revealed it only once before, to Jason, when he'd known her as Astral Star.) On the other hand, she needed to connect with P. if she were to get his firm promise to find Peter. (She did not know that the previous day Russia had captured three Ukrainian ships in the Black Sea, obliterating any chance of a near-term peace accord and, more likely, setting the stage for a full-scale invasion of her homeland.)

"Yes, I have such a place," she said.

"Lovely. I thought you might. Can you describe it?"

She momentarily closed her eyes. When she reopened them, she continued staring into the distance.

"St. Nicholas Orthodox Church. The oldest in my city. Thirteenth century."

"I know the church. It is a holy place."

"Then you know it is very strong, built of large white blocks. My favorite is a beautiful dome whose lights I watched from my bed when I was little girl. I had my confirmation there. I sang 'The Prayer of St. Michael the Archangel.'"

P. turned away. (Her words were unbearable. His own darling daughters, with whom he hadn't spoken in months, had sung the same prayer at their confirmations. Further, the prayer was his personal favorite: *St. Michael the Archangel, defend us in battle. Be our defense against the wickedness and snares of the Devil.)* He wiped his eyes and turned back to Hannah, who hadn't spoken while he'd been turned away.

"The church has a special holy quiet," she said, continuing. "I think the big white stones keep out the noise of the world and the dome amplifies my prayers. I think St. Michael hears them, and the rest of the Cosmos too."

P. looked at her strong profile. "You are a very special woman, Dr. Hannah Belaya. I am very sorry I began our relations with such inappropriate behavior. I truly apologize. What can I do to make it up to you?"

THE BLACK-SUITED AGENTS

While P. and Hannah were atop Salvation, P.'s agents continued working on their surveillance reports. The subject of one of their continuing reports was Anatoly Bychkov. Having recorded him twice at the Civic Center, they'd ran his image through several facial recognition databases, eventually discovering that he was Hannah's fourth husband and had traveled to the United States on what appeared to be a forged passport. Their report suggested that he had likely contacted Dr. Hannah Belaya to reconnect, extort, or (possibly) to reestablish relations with their son, now a member of the Ukrainian army, stationed in Crimea.

Because the car he'd bought in Brooklyn had been properly registered and because Bychkov had used a tracking device linked to his not-so-bright smartphone, they'd been able to hack its GPS system and trace his journey west. It was then they discovered that he had effectively tailed Akhmerov and

Zubilin from Coney Island to the Saltin Sea. Of course, the black-suited agents realized immediately that Bychkov must now know that their teammates were not lithium agents, as advertised, and could thus blow the whistle on P.'s zillion-dollar plan to dominate the lithium market. They were surprised (and a little disappointed) that P. did not order them to eliminate Bychkov immediately. Normally, they would never question P., but the unusual close quartering of the Saltin assignment afforded them special license and so they hazarded a question as to his reasoning. P. explained (though in a curt manner that forestalled further discussion) that Bychkov's untimely death, however expertly handled, would be reported and thus could interfere with his business plans. That was that. The agents had to content themselves with keeping a casual eye on Bychkov, which was an easy task, as he spent almost all his time alone in the Refuge.

THE IMPORTANCE OF INSIGNIFICANCE

For all their experience and professionalism, the black-suited agents never bothered to account for the comings and goings of Katya. Why would they? Having seamlessly replaced her mother, Katya was a commonplace fixture, cloaked with a common fixture's invisibility. When she wasn't on call, she roamed unnoticed, like a house cat. When she grew bored (as she did during the long hours P. spent in the Civic Center), she left The Palace for the Refuge, where she found Anatoly—and love.

She visited Anatoly often. To avoid notice, she practiced what tradecraft she had acquired through her observations of agents over the years. Among other strategies, she entered the Refuge at different times and by different routes, avoiding patterned behavior.

The black-suited agents never knew about her affair with Bychkov. As far as they knew (and as far as they cared), Bychkov spent his days alone in the woods, like a village idiot crying over what might have been. The agents knew P. would order his elimination when the time was right.

TOVA AND MARGE

The following day, when Tova knew that Hannah would be at her meth lab, she called Marge and invited her to brunch.

"I want to show you something. That's all I'm going to say."

As soon as Marge arrived, Tova got down to business.

"Later for tea and biscuits. I need to show you something. Follow me."

Marge followed Tova upstairs to the first floor, observing her cues of silence and stealth.

"Before I open the door, I just want to say that I suspected a leak, that's why I entered in the first place. So that's probable cause, right?"

Rather than explain, Marge acknowledged her question with a nod.

Tova opened the door. "That's it," she said, pointing to the large box beside the bed.

As soon as Marge moved forward, Tova added, "I think you'll want to put on a pair of examining gloves. You have them, right?"

Marge smiled, snapped on a pair of latex gloves, and approached the box.

"Wait!"

Marge froze. "What's wrong?"

"Marge, I tampered with the evidence."

"What!"

"Well, I didn't actually tamper. I just took it out of the box and looked at it. I had to see what we had. So, one set of prints will be mine. I'm so sorry."

Marge loosed an audible sigh of relief.

"Okay. You did right by telling me. Don't you worry."

"You sure?"

"Look, you're an informant and innocent third party. As soon as you suspected foul play, you contacted me. Don't worry. I've got your back."

"Oh, God. Thank you. I was so worried."

Marge patted her shoulder. She then lifted the heavy gown from its box and carefully spread it on Hannah's bed, just as Tova had done.

"What do you think?" asked Tova. "You think they're blood diamonds?"

"Wow. This is rare."

"It's the real deal, right?"

"It might be. Look," she said, turning to Tova, "we have to do this right. Let's pack it up, just like it was, and get the hell out of here. I'll take a raincheck on brunch. I need to haul ass to the nearest judge to get a warrant."

The two women rearranged the gown and box so no one would suspect they'd been there. And no one would have, if Bethany hadn't noticed them and contacted Hannah.

A FAVOR

Hannah assumed the police had entered her room because of the gown. She thought the salt-jeweled gown might be illegal in America or maybe there was some other problem with it. She did not want to tell Yevgeny. He already had so much on his mind. Besides, this wasn't his country. He did not know all the rules.

She wondered who else could help her. Bethany had a car, but she also lived in Covenant House and her every movement drew attention. She thought of Jason. She hadn't told him about Yevgeny's marriage proposal and the wedding gown. She thought it might make him sad, but she had no better option.

"Jason, I need your help. Bethany saw Mother Mary and police coming from my room. I am frightened. Can you do me favor?"

THE WEIGHT

As soon as Hannah saw Mother Mary gathering the new half-way parolees for a lesson of general life instruction in the library, she called Jason and he immediately came to Covenant House, meeting her out front. Without speaking, he lifted the heavy box at her feet and carried it to the back platform of Argo, where they used to keep their desert digging tools.

"Please take me to see my son."

Jason knew of Hannah's Haj-like journeys into the desert but didn't quite know what to make of them. Until that day she'd never seemed willing to discuss the subject.

As they rode together in Argo, she asked, "You wanted a child, yes?"

He had mentioned it before. "Yes. My wife and I wanted children. I think I wanted it more than she did."

"Why it not happen?"

"I think I told you. For many years we were too busy with our music. We made a lot of money and had a good life. When the business became slow, I thought it was a good time to have a baby."

"She not agree?"

"No, she had other ideas."

"They not include you?"

Jason paused. "She betrayed me. You understand *betrayed*?"

Hannah nodded. "She lied. She hurt you."

"She went away with another man. I know you understand, because I know you've been betrayed. You told me."

"Yes. I had four husbands. They all betrayed me. Only one man not betray me."

Jason smiled, but he'd misunderstood.

"My son Peter. Before he was born, even while I carried him, I knew he would not betray me. He would always be my strength. My rock."

Jason swallowed his pride. "That's why you named him Peter."

"Yes."

"And that's why you visit him here."

"Yes—but more. I come here to send him strength. When I pray for him, he is stronger, and then I feel his strength. In this way we are both stronger and closer."

They rode a while in silence.

"I'm not sure what I can give you, Hannah, but I'll give you whatever I can."

Hannah smiled sadly.

"When I was younger, I had four husbands, none of them good. That was my fault as much theirs. Now, I am not so young, and I have four men who want to be my husband."

"Me and Dr. Yeshevsky."

"And P. And Anatoly, for the second time."

"Four men, again."

"Yes. I'm not sure what it means, but it feels important."

Another pause.

"Hannah, what are your thoughts about the four men, myself included?"

She smiled and touched his shoulder.

"You are special. I think you suit me best of the four. Maybe we could be happy."

"You don't sound happy."

Hannah winced but didn't cry.

"My heart—past and future—lies in the desert, where only God knows what will happen. Until I know about Peter, I can do nothing."

"And that's why we are here," he said, slowing the cart as he approached the Civic Center.

"Yes, to visit Peter."

A brief silence, then: "What's in the box?"

"I will show you. First, let's make sure no one is here. If we are alone, I want you to drive me to Peter."

"You don't want to walk?"

"I do. But I do not think I can. The box is very heavy."

"I'll carry it. It's heavy, but I can do it."

"Are you sure?"

"Yes, of course."

DRESS REHEARSAL

Jason parked Argo behind the Center, where it could not be seen from the highway. It was Sunday and they had the place to themselves. He walked to the back of the golf cart and lifted the box to check its heft.

"Uh, I changed my mind. It's very heavy and it's a long way. We better take the cart."

Hannah readily agreed, realizing that the empty cart might provoke visitors to wonder where they were.

Jason eased the cart down the ramp (twenty feet to the right of the stone stairs), then drove across the empty sea. After several minutes, they saw the glinting shrine in the distance, a colorful oasis between the two shorelines, invisible from both.

Jason stopped about twenty yards away (closer would have felt like a sacrilege) and turned off the motor, its hum hanging in the air like an afterimage. When it finally faded, the silence felt profound. They both sat perfectly still.

"Come. I will show you," said Hannah.

Both got out and moved to the back of the cart, where they stood side by side, staring at the simple carton.

"Carry it to Peter, please. Then I show you."

Jason hefted the carton in his strong arms and carried it to within a yard of the shrine.

"Here?"

Hannah nodded.

Jason placed the heavy load on the desert sea floor and then walked slowly around the mosaic. (Had he not already known that it represented Peter's visage, the arrangement of glass stones would have seemed inscrutable, even haphazard.)

Meanwhile, Hannah had moved towards the box and stood silently beside it. She looked about to make sure they were alone. They were.

"Okay. You close your eyes and I show you."

With his eyes closed, Jason heard a soft wind blowing north from Mexico . . . a single bird's cawing . . . then a rustling and clicking, like the parting of a beaded curtain.

Using both her hands (and all her strength), Hannah lifted the impossibly heavy gown by its shoulders, holding it up against her standing body.

"Okay, look."

Jason looked at Hannah and saw a desert bride.

He went to her, embraced her. Pressing his body against hers (keeping the gown vised between them), they danced a few steps in the desert as bride and groom.

DRY FORECAST

They did not speak much on the way back. What had happened, and what each felt or thought they felt, required no explanation. For the moment, both were content.

"You okay leaving the gown there?" he asked.

"It belongs there. It is safe in the box."

"Well, no one can see it. And it's unlikely to rain."

"Unless God wills it."

Hannah was aware that her recent speech included more references to God than was usual for her. But she did not examine her frame of mind or her heart, for she felt there was too much going on. It was all she could do to place one foot in front of the other.

P.'S PROMISE

Based on his experience on Salvation Mountain, P. believed Hannah was warming to him. Still, he knew her willingness to consider his proposal was based largely on his promise to deliver news of her son Peter.

He thought her position was fair, if problematical. In normal circumstances, he would have ordered his staff to contact their embedded spies in Ukraine to discover the required information. But the recent increase in tensions had blacked out that possibility, at least temporarily. With other large matters pressing, P. decided to invent a story that would satisfy Hannah.

EDWINA AND FRED

"Sorry, I know it's late. Were you sleeping?"

"No," he lied, looking at the time on his phone. "Just reading a magazine."

"Oh, okay."

"You having trouble sleeping?" he asked.

"Yes."

"What's wrong?"

"I think something bad is going to happen."

Fred paused to indicate his displeasure. They'd had this discussion before and he didn't want to have it again. "What could possibly happen? Things look great."

"I'm not sure," she lied. In fact, she had an unnervingly clear vision of impending disaster. Worse, she felt largely responsible. "I've been thinking about what that woman said to me."

"You mean the crazy witch who accosted you right outside your home?"

"I know it sounds crazy, but I'm not crazy. Do you think I'm crazy?"

Fred forced himself to back down. "No. I think you're brilliant and beautiful."

"Then why aren't you taking me more seriously?"

"Because I don't see what I can do that would change anything."

"You live in Saltin. You know the mayors. You could talk to them."

Fred heard the stridency in her voice. He heard honest-to-goodness fear.

"Okay. I'm sorry. I do take you seriously. I'll talk to the mayors the first chance I get. I promise."

Another man's promise carelessly made and never kept.

THE REPORT

P. was very happy with the report he received from his scientists. While it noted that a nuclear explosion in the San Andreas Fault would be highly unlikely to trigger even a small earthquake, it pointed out that a "traditional" explosive could do the trick if (and only if) it resulted in the movement of enough mass to shift the pattern of local stresses in the Earth's crust. The report also made it clear that a traditional explosion, however large, was unlikely to have the desired effect by itself but would require a subsequent shift of seismic proportion to create an earthquake. To that end, the scientists suggested (citing their gratitude to the U.S. Geological Survey) a specific target near the San Andreas Fault and the Saltin Sea: a four-mile-wide underground cavern, whose five-foot-thick, surface-level roof was supported by relatively slender, natural columns. Specifically-placed explosives (lowered through holes bored into the surface roof) could break enough of the columns to cause the entire four-mile-wide roof to collapse, resulting in a sudden shift of mass substantial enough to incite a small earthquake. Such an earthquake could reach and rupture the Jordan-Enterprise Dam.

PACT WITH THE DEVIL

P.'s overall plan had many variables but only three essential objectives: the flooding of the Saltin Sea; his timely removal to Mexicali; Hannah's safe survival. The fate of everyone and everything else was beyond his caring.

To move along his marriage proposal to its hoped-for conclusion, he explained to Hannah how he could reward her cancer-cure discovery with an array of scientific awards and citations, and though he could not guarantee a nomination for the Nobel Prize, he promised her a handsomely compensated directorship in a new Moscow research facility.

He also promised the safe return of her son. Using Peter's letters and birthday cards (discovered in her Lviv apartment after her hurried departure), his Moscow staff had created an audio message (purportedly from Peter to his mother) containing words and phrases that Hannah would recognize as her son's. Using these personal details as passwords into Hannah's heart, the message explained (in a voice disguised by authentic-sounding static) that he'd been seriously hurt by an explosion but was recovering nicely in a Russian army hospital outside Donetsk. He was well treated and hoped to be released as soon as the war ended. He did not think it would happen very soon, so he wished her much love for her birthday, the following month.

"You see, Hannah, I can give you many things, including Peter. And what do I ask in return? So little. Just that you might care for me. Be my wife. Help keep me strong, so I can keep Russia strong, which, believe me, is the best thing for the world."

Hannah had been shaken by the audio, even though she wasn't completely certain it was authentic.

"I thank you for all your offers, but I need to consider everything you said."

"I will be leaving soon for a business trip. It's important—for us both—that you make your decision soon. I care for you very deeply, Hannah. I can give you a wonderful life—and Peter too."

NIGHT SHIFT

Four days after P. had received the report from his scientists, a special agent arrived at The Palace from San Diego, driving an unmarked black van, which he parked in a particularly secure location by the back of the hotel, accessible only by P. and his staff.

For the next two days, P.'s two black-suited agents took turns guarding the van while Akhmerov and Zubilin worked upstairs with the new agent, reviewing drilling techniques and the process of hard-wiring dynamite charges for a remote detonation. On the third night after the new agent's arrival, the three men drove to a GPS-directed location to put their plan into action.

It was a moonless night, but Akhmerov and Zubilin felt reasonably familiar with the terrain, having taken two jeep tours of the southern fault line. By then they were also familiar with the process of boring holes and inserting wired, cylindrical charges, which they hoped would destroy enough of the subterranean columns to allow gravity to bring down the four-mile-wide, five-foot-thick, rocky dome. It took the three-man team eleven nights to prepare the site for destruction.

LAST VISIT

Nearly two weeks passed and Hannah hadn't yet responded to P 's proposal. Though she knew she could never love him, not even for a minute, she could not bring herself to forsake a possible lifeline to Peter that might be his only hope.

At the conclusion of what would be their final laser treatment, P. told her that he planned to leave the next afternoon for a two-week trip and needed her decision as soon as possible.

"Can you meet me tomorrow in the lobby of The Palace before noon?" he asked her.

"I will be there," she said, appearing as calm as could be.

"Thank you, Hannah. And I thank you and your team for destroying most of my cancer. I hope tomorrow you will make me a very happy man."

The next morning (a Saturday), less than two hours before her scheduled meeting with P., Hannah asked Jason to give her a ride to the Civic Center. When they arrived there, she told him she needed time alone with Peter.

"I need to talk to him about important things. Please wait half hour, and then I return with you. I need to be back before noon. Okay?"

"Of course, Hannah. Whatever you like."

ROADLESS FUTURE

Sitting in the shade of the Civic Center's rear wall, Jason watched as Hannah walked away into the desert sea. When she was gone from his sight, he felt strangely alone and disoriented. Every which way he turned was empty. Nothing beckoned. During all his wandering, there had always been a destination. Always another road to follow. Staring at a roadless world unnerved him. He had no answer for it. Of course, there was the highway behind him, but that seemed not to matter. Behind him felt like the past—as in, been there, done that. For the moment, he saw no enticing pathway, other than the unseeable one that led to Hannah.

WHAT WILL BE, WILL BE

Hannah had always been a woman of powerful intuitions. Perhaps this explains her attraction to alternative sciences and cosmological speculations. P.'s deadline was something very different. It was formidably definitive and repercussive: she had to make a choice—or a choice would be made for her. But how could she choose? The choices were impossibly difficult and unattractive, and she hadn't the benefit of knowing what she needed to know in order to choose with a clear head and open heart. Still, she did not consider her situation dire. There was a part of her that was accepting. For all her strength, education and empowerment, she believed what will be, will be. All she could do was love and hope for the best.

SEISMIC WAVES

The special agent and his assistants, Akhmerov and Zubilin, had finished their work.

"We are ready," said the special agent. "Let's move the car to the road. We should be at least a thousand feet from the blast."

When the men had moved the prescribed distance, Zubilin asked, "How long will it take the quake to reach the dam?"

The special agent reviewed the variables. "Let's see. The dam is only thirty-six kilometers away, and the ground is stiff bedrock. The waves will move quickly."

"How quickly?"

"Well, after the mound collapses, the quake will strike the dam in about ten seconds."

"Ten seconds!"

"Don't worry. We're in no danger. When the dam breaks, the water will flow southeast to Saltin."

"And we're headed west to sunny San Diego?"

"Precisely."

"Okay then, let's do it."

"You both ready?

"Ready."

"Ready."

"On my count: one, two, three!"

NATURE'S DOWNWARD COURSE

Because most dams are built sturdily enough to withstand an over-the-design-limit earthquake, it takes an especially strong jolt to produce a catastrophic failure. The Jordan-Enterprise Dam had a grout curtain (to minimize leakage) and a spillway (for the safe release of floods) but even those failsafes were not enough.

As predicted, the quake shook the dam's façade, which begat widening fissures, which foretold doom.

THE SIREN'S CALL

Six hundred feet above sea level, the dam's escaping waters made a fast and sinuous descent toward a giant desert sink, two hundred twenty feet below sea level. Along the way the frothy waters picked up speed and the deadly heft of rocks and trees.

The dam's Emergency Manager was alerted as soon as the threat was detected. Unfortunately, within scant minutes the situation had reached a Level IV alarm: *Dam breached; Flood in progress.* With no forewarning, no time for preparation, he did what little he could. He initiated emergency warnings by phone, e-text and radio. He personally notified designated contacts in the three areas of concentrated population: Fantasy Springs, Calpurnia State Prison, and Saltin City. As a courtesy, he contacted the Mexican government, though he did not expect the flood to reach as far as Mexicali.

PREPAREDNESS

As soon as the detonation was confirmed, the special agent sent P. a prepared phone text: *Work done. Headed to the beach.*

P. smiled at his success but was disappointed that Hannah had not come in person to tell him her decision. *So much to admire—but a weak character. She would not have made a good wife. I will miss her, a little, but I do not need her. My cancer has been halted. My team has learned all they need to know about the salt-laser treatment. Yeshevsky and his team are unnecessary.*

That's as far as P. would allow himself to feel at the moment. As to his preparedness, he'd been thorough, as always. His own car had been loaded with everything essential. Sensitive materials that could not be taken along had already been destroyed.

"Let's go," he called to his black-suited agents. "We should hurry. Where is Katya?"

HIGHER GROUND

Radio, cellphone and PA warnings instructed the public: *Only take pets and valuables within close reach. Do not waste time! If caught in flood waters, grab hold of a permanent structure.* But the overriding message, the one repeated more than all the others was: *Seek higher ground!*

MARGE'S MESSAGE

The warden of Calpurnia State Prison announced over its PA system: *"Flood Warning! Not a drill! Evacuate first and second floor. All prisoners, staff and visitors proceed to floors three and four. Remove all patients from the infirmary."*

Marge regarded herself as an exception. During the tumult, no one saw her leave the compound and get into her car. She drove to Saltin as fast as she dared, never glancing at her rearview mirror, afraid the flood waters would swallow her. As she drove, she called Tova and left a message: *There's a flood coming! Get everyone in the house into your apartment—pronto!*

Having received Marge's message, Mother Mary moved as fast as she could to save her daughters. Luckily, she quickly found Sister Sharon and Sister Carmel in the library, and the six news girls (whose names she could not remember) playing cards in the community room. She explained about the flood.

"I'll find the others. All of you go to my apartment. Close the windows and stay there. I'll be there soon."

She spent no time looking for Hannah. She'd seen her leave two hours earlier with that good-looking man in the silly golf cart. *She'll get what she deserves,* she thought.

That left Caitlin Connor and Bethany, the skinny black woman.

"Caitlin? Caitlin? Where are you!"

She checked the laundry room and chapel but didn't find her.

"Caitlin! Where are you!"

She checked the exercise room. There, on the floor, twisted in some infernal yoga position, lay Caitlin, a black arc of headphones clamped hard on her ears.

Mother Mary shook her shoulder to get her attention.

"Caitlin, a flood is coming. Go upstairs to my apartment and wait with the others. Go now! Hurry!"

Caitlin ran to her room for a few essential belongings, then scampered upstairs to safety.

Mother Mary then peeked into the kitchen and foyer. Not seeing Bethany, she hobbled upstairs as quickly as she could, entered her apartment and shut her door behind her. *Another one I could live without.*

Bethany had been walking on the street when her phone buzzed with an incoming call from Yevgeny.

"Where are you?" he asked.

"I went for a walk. I'm nearly back to my apartment. What's wrong?"

"There's an emergency. I will meet you outside the house in two minutes. Hurry!"

Two minutes later, Yevgeny pulled up in his car. A door flew open, courtesy of Dimitri, who waved her inside.

"Come. Get in. We must hurry."

Away they went, watched by Mother Mary from her upstairs window.

"Well, well, there she goes," she muttered under her breath. "They all stick together—and they'll all burn in hell—or drown, whichever comes first."

SALVATION MOUNTAIN

Of the roughly two dozen permanent residents of Saltin, most lived in its two surviving hotels (The Palace and The Mount) or in Covenant House, or in the few dilapidated and abandoned buildings that provided a squatter with little comfort and less security.

There was also the Civic Center, where Fred lived, but on this day, he was in the lobby of The Palace, chatting happily with the two mayors when the flood warnings came.

Because both The Palace and The Mount had only two accessible floors, all present Saltin residents not associated with Covenant House decided to take refuge atop Salvation Mountain. Moving quickly from their respective hotels to the nearby garage where the golf carts were kept, they formed a makeshift caravan and sped away.

JASON AND HANNAH

Jason had heard a rumble, like a garbage truck driving down a rocky stream. With each second it sounded louder but he saw nothing threatening or even amiss. He remained at his table, sipping tea, knowing Hannah was out there in the invisible distance, likely walking about the shrine of glass stones, communing with her son Peter.

Then he saw a lip of frothy water, like a tiny tide, coming from his left. (Had he remembered to bring his cellphone, he would have known what was happening; Hannah had her phone, but she'd turned it off before beginning her pilgrimage, as she always did.) It was an odd tide Jason saw: no ebb, just ceaseless flow. Sensing disaster, he jumped to his feet, knocking the pretty teacup to the ground and shattering it. Within seconds he was in the golf cart, driving down the ramp.

As there was only an inch or so of water on the ground, he was able to control the cart. But in the several minutes it took to reach sight of Hannah, the water rose several inches and the cart was swerving like crazy. When Hannah was twenty yards away, he barely recognized her. Having fallen and risen several times, she was completely soaked and muddied, her hair plastered to her face.

Jason shut the motor and leaped from the cart, but the fast-moving water was now six inches deep, making it difficult to stand and even harder to walk. He saw glass stones floating away and Hannah clutching something glittering to her chest. He struggled mightily to reach her.

"Hannah, come. Get in the cart."

Whether unhearing or insensible, she remained silent, crouched in the rising water, her salt-jeweled gown clutched to her chest like her own child.

Jason tried to lift her to her feet, but she was staunchly heavy and the swift waters unbalanced him. Finally, he had no choice but to yank the heavy gown out of her arms and toss it into the flood, where it was quickly swept from view.

By this time the water was nearly a foot high. With all his considerable strength he pulled Hannah into their usual seats on Argo. There they sat in stunned silence, the sorriest human island in history. A minute later they were adrift, carried away by swift waters nearly two feet deep. (Argo never had a chance. Its fringe top was a fraud of a sail, and the forward-looking eye of Athena was blind in this godless crisis.)

The water was now rising very quickly, carrying them across the sea. Within two terrifying minutes they saw the boardwalk and shorefront buildings looming ahead. They still had hope of a safe landing, but then the raging waters rose suddenly like a tsunami, carrying Argo at its crest. Before their fatal impact, they had time to intertwine their fingers and kiss, their last romantic gesture in this sad world.

JASON'S LAST WORDS

What the hell is happening? Must be a dam breach. I shouldn't be here. I should have left this place. But then Hannah would be alone. Oh, God, just let me reach her.

It's getting deeper, faster. There she is, I see her! Hannah, come. Get in the cart. What are you holding? Let it go!

(The water continues rising; Peter's stones sail away.)

Get up! Put your arms around my neck. Hurry! Good. Sit here, next to me. Good. We'll be okay.

(The water suddenly rises to a great height; they sit at its crest, as in a crow's-nest.)

Hannah, we're going to hit the shore. Give me your hand. (He entwines his fingers with hers and kisses her mouth.) *Darling, close your eyes.*

HANNAH'S LAST WORDS

What is happening? Where water coming from? This my punishment? Four times married. Four times I think maybe again.

(The rising waters knock her off her feet. She rises and falls, again and again.)

I will not see P. again. Good. I wish I had never seen him. I just pray: let Peter be well and live long.

(Crouched against the furious flow, she sees Peter's stones sail away and feels something pushed into her lap.)

What is this? My gown! Most beautiful thing I ever have. Oh Yevgeny, I am so sorry to leave you. You such a good, dear man. I hope you live—Dimitri too.

Jason, I see Jason! My captain. He come to save me! I feel his strong hands. Goodbye, gown until I see you again!

(The gown sails away, its empty sleeves flailing.)

We are sailing fast, very fast. I do not think we find our Golden Fleece. So high we are!

(She entwines her fingers with Jason's, tastes his mouth on hers, relishes its sweetness.)

I close my eyes and see beautiful place. You are with me.

A DESERT FLOOD

The suddenly released waters kept coming, gathering speed, headed for the Saltin Sea. When the flood hit the hard-baked, desert sink, it flashed forward, a raging torrent carrying along rocks, trees and the remnant pier. As it approached the lagoons and broken boardwalk, it rose to a height of more than twenty feet before slamming with tremendous force into the shorefront hotels, derelict casinos, broken churches and synagogue. Some of its force diverted left and right, but most of the flood raged down the canyon of Commonwealth Avenue, bypassing Salvation Mountain and flooding the Wildlife Refuge. About a mile later, it petered out.

FROM HER UPSTAIRS WINDOW

Tova watched as a diverted part of the flood lifted Marge's car as it pulled in front of Covenant House and lodged it sideways in an empty storefront across the street. Tova saw Marge's face contort with panic as high waters rushed by, submerging the car entirely. Horror-struck, Tova collapsed onto a divan and lay there, attended by her daughters.

A tree or some other flotsam missile must have struck Marge's side window, shattering it, instantly filling the car with water. Later, when Tova found the strength and courage, she looked again out her window and saw Marge's car was still there, most of the water having drained out, Marge's lifeless body slumped behind the wheel.

SHOCK AND HORROR

The small crowd atop Salvation Mountain stared at the flood waters and while they could not see the actual devastation, it was easily imagined by all.

"Our city!" cried Fred, thinking of Edwina and his washed-away dreams. "It's gone!"

And it mostly was, though from the top-floor window of Covenant House someone was waving a towel or sheet.

"What will we do?" said the mayor of West Saltin.

"Where will we go?" said the mayor of East Saltin.

After the initial shock, the lucky survivors looked at each other with mixed expressions of guilt and gratitude.

Dimitri, Yevgeny and Bethany huddled in a tight circle, away from the others.

FINAL ACCOUNTING

It took some time to sift through the devastation and detritus. When Yevgeny learned the news of Jason and Hannah, he dropped to his knees, his heart flooded with grief. Despite the condoling wails of Bethany and Dimitri, he felt tragically alone.

Later that same day, someone brought him the bridal gown, but he would not look at it; not because it was filthy and ruined, but because it now symbolized to him his ill-considered scheming that had led to the deaths of Jason and Hannah.

I will never forgive myself, he thought. *Not if I live a thousand years.*

~

As powerful and voracious as was his guilt, Yeshevsky soon felt the call of his responsibilities as doctor and scientist. Though he knew he would never receive credit for the salt-laser cure he had developed with Hannah, he knew he must carry on. Unwilling to tempt fate by returning to Russia, he decided to permanently relocate the Cosmoenergy Federation in Jerusalem. Dimitri and Bethany followed him there, assisting him with every aspect of the operation.

The three became inseparable, in and out of the office, often visiting Yevgeny's parents in Hebron. The elderly parents still hoped Yevgeny would find a wife and have a family, but they were grateful that the beautiful Bethany and the oddly devoted Dimitri were such loving friends. Yevgeny's mother wondered about the dress she had given him, but never asked.

~

After the flood, most of the water eventually receded, filling the low-lying basin of the Saltin Sea to a height of nearly three feet. According to P.'s scientists, the water would seep below the surface within a year, filling the sea's underground reservoir.

Though anxious to begin planning his new lithium business, P. stayed three days in Mexicali with his two black-suited agents for some much-needed rest and relaxation.

He never let on, but the sudden subtraction of both Hannah and Katya had left a large hole in his heart. For the rest of his life, he would be a fitful sleeper.

Back in Russia, he contacted his lovely daughters and asked if they would have dinner with him.

His cancer was in remission.

~

Tova never looked out her upstairs window again. Covenant House's first floor was ruined and the building was declared unsafe. Less than a week later, Tova moved into a nice two-family house in San Diego, joined by Sister Carmel and Sister Sharon, who would live out their days in the first-floor apartment. Caitlin had gone her separate way and, despite heartfelt oaths to keep in touch, she and Tova drifted apart.

The house was in a quaint neighborhood called University Heights, just the other side of Park Boulevard, where Edwina Lazar Orosco lived. Less than a week after the flood, Edwina invited Fred to live with her. They never married but lived together happily enough.

On several occasions Fate tempted Fred and Tova by arranging for them to be in the same store or crossing the same street at the same time. In each instance they thought they recognized each other, but as neither took any initiative, they never engaged.

~

At the time of their death, Anatoly and Katya were in the Wildlife Refuge, enjoying a pistol-shooting contest and planning where they would live after they married. Because they had both stoppered their ears against their pistols' sharp reports, neither heard the flood waters until it was too late.

Their bodies were found outside the Refuge, about a mile away, Katya clutching her St. Vitaly medallion and Anatoly holding fast to his white sack.

~

Akhmerov and Zubilin spent two weeks in their San Diego safe house, awaiting their next order, which came by way of an official letter from P. that awarded each of them the gift of retirement and an officer-level pension. They spent the next two days drinking themselves silly. On the plane to Moscow, both wondered nervously what they would do with the rest of their lives, at home with their wife and kids.

PETER

Two months after resettling in Israel, Yevgeny used his impressive networking skills to discover that Peter had survived the war and had returned to Lviv, to the same apartment he had shared with his mother. He also learned that Peter had joined the medical clinic where Hannah had worked before joining him in Moscow.

Yevgeny wrote to Peter, beginning a correspondence in which both shared their memories of Hannah and their medical and scientific aspirations. The correspondence was warm and professional but moved each of them to tears. Two months later, Yevgeny offered Peter a job at the relocated Cosmoenergy Federation in Jerusalem. When Peter learned that his mother's friends Bethany and Dimitri also worked there, he quickly accepted Dr. Yeshevsky's generous terms.

For Yevgeny and Peter, it was (as the American saying goes) a win-win. When Yevgeny looked at Peter, he saw Hannah's aura and immediately felt a fatherly affection for him. For Peter, Yevgeny was the loving father he had all but forgotten.

THE END

www.ingramcontent.com/pod-product-compliance
Lightning Source LLC
LaVergne TN
LVHW090549110826
845146LV00001B/79

* 9 7 9 8 9 8 8 0 2 3 4 9 4 *